MEMORY'S SHADOW

Joseph McRae Palmer

MEMORY'S SHADOW

www.josephmcraepalmer.com

ISBN (paperback) 978-1-961782-26-6

Cover design: Donna Cunningham@BeauxArts.design

Prologue

Welcome back, folks, to another thrilling volume of my memoir. In our last episode, you heard about the crew of *Thunder* kicking up dust in Arizona and pulling off a daring rescue at Lindblad Crater on the Moon, all while stopping the Astral Maul. You'll also remember how I, in my infinite wisdom, managed to cap things off with a colossal blunder. That's right—yours truly thought it was a great idea to use my half-baked sydereal powers to take a swing at Ban'ach. Spoiler alert: it didn't go over well, and I ended up in the Collective Dominion's version of legal hot water.

Now, I need to level with you before we go any further. This story is going to be a bit different. If you're hoping for more high-octane adventures aboard *Thunder,* you might be a little disappointed because, well, *Thunder* doesn't feature much in this chapter of my life. But don't let that stop you. What happened in Astrithon may not have involved many starship battles or daring rescue missions, but it was just as crucial to shaping who I became as a captain and an officer.

My time in Astrithon was a crucible, one where I had the chance to learn from some of the best minds in the Dominion. I spent months pouring over the principles of space warfare, mastering the intricacies of the sydereal arts, and trying—keyword, trying—to grasp what it means to be a professional military officer. I had mentors who pushed me, challenged me, and made me see the galaxy in ways I never could have imagined. Sure, it wasn't as glamorous as leading a crew into battle, but it was the foundation I needed to do just that later on.

And those pesky criminal charges? Let's just say you're not going to guess how those ended. Even if you did, I wouldn't believe you because, frankly, I barely believe it myself. The universe has a strange sense of humor.

So, grab a seat, buckle up, and prepare for what I like to call *Kory Drake vs. the Universe: The Astrithon Chronicles*.

1

In the observation lounge of the Dominion starship *Nira,* I stood in front of an ellipsoid window that spanned from one wall to the other, its sheer size making the rest of the room feel almost incidental. The curvature of the glass distorted my reflection just enough to give me an unflattering view of myself—a tall, muscular human with a perpetually messy mop of hair and eyes that currently screamed, "I should have stayed in bed."

Earth receded in the distance, a glowing jewel of blue and white steadily shrinking against the endless backdrop of space. The night side of my home planet faced us now, and city lights from the dense population centers of China and India hinted at the outline of Asia's coastlines. It was beautiful, and it made my chest ache. A bittersweet pang of nostalgia mixed with the overwhelming knowledge that I was leaving it all behind—possibly for good.

I'd left Earth before—trips to Luna and even the Sun-Earth L1 point—but I'd always been close enough to feel tethered to home. This time, the tether was snapping. I was on a starship bound for the Dominion capital world, Astrithon, thousands of light years away. My destination wasn't a diplomatic mission or a galactic sightseeing tour. No, I was headed there to stand trial. Alone.

Well, mostly alone. Zeta was also on the ship, though she didn't provide much in the way of comfort. Zeta, an alien igna and crown princess of the Collective Dominion, was somewhere on a deck far above me in luxury quarters befitting royalty.

The lounge was eerily quiet except for the soft hum of the ship's engines. It was the kind of silence that made you hyper-aware of your own breathing. My reflection in the window stared back at me, and for a moment, I considered what I'd gotten myself into. If I'd known that trying to recover my stolen memories from Ban'ach, a Soul Ravager, would result in interdimensional criminal charges, maybe I'd have thought twice. Or maybe not. Self-preservation isn't exactly my strong suit.

A door behind me hissed open. I turned to see a floating white sphere about two feet in diameter hovering in the doorway. Captain Lorian, an igna housed within that unassuming capsule, greeted me with her polite, measured voice. "Kory Drake, allow me to show you to your quarters."

Her tone was neutral, perfectly calibrated, as if she couldn't decide whether I was an honored guest, a slimy criminal, or an annoying fly buzzing around her ship. I took one last glance at Earth, letting its faint glow sear itself into my memory. Then I nodded. "Lead the way."

The corridors of *Nira* were sleek and immaculate, a far cry from the tight hamster's maze of *Thunder*, my old ship. The walls here gleamed with a silvery sheen, and soft, recessed lighting gave the impression that I was walking through a futuristic luxury hotel instead of a Dominion military transport. I might have appreciated it more if not for the persistent sense of impending doom.

Captain Lorian led me to my quarters—a modest stateroom tucked into an unassuming section of the ship. The room's musty smell hit me the moment the door opened, like it hadn't seen an occupant in years. The decor was purely functional: a bunk bed bolted to the wall, a foldout desk and chair that looked like they might fold out of existence if I leaned on them too hard, and a tiny bathroom that managed to make "claustrophobic" feel like an understatement. No windows, no frills, no comforts. The perfect room for someone on trial for crimes they didn't understand.

"Thank you," I said to Captain Lorian, trying to sound gracious. She nodded (well, her floating sphere nodded, which was mildly unsettling) and left without a word. I shut the door behind her, kicked off my boots, and collapsed onto the bottom bunk. The mattress was thin enough that I briefly wondered if I was being punished for something already.

Staring at the ceiling, I tried not to let my thoughts spiral. Spoiler alert: I failed.

Zeta. My former friend. My estranged consort. My accuser.

She'd been the one to train me in using the Syderealium, the interdimensional realm where consciousnesses resided. She'd warned me not to try recovering my stolen memories of my dead parents from Ban'ach, warned me about the consequences of tampering with the balance of the Syderealium. And I'd ignored her. To be fair, she hadn't explained that the consequences involved being labeled a Soul Ravager and hauled across the galaxy to stand trial, but details, right?

Zeta had become a stranger. She'd nullified our consortship, severed the link between us, and turned me in to the Dominion authorities. In her eyes, I was a criminal, plain and simple. The fact that I'd acted in self-defense? Irrelevant. The fact that Ban'ach had been actively trying to consume me? Details.

"Principles," I muttered to the empty room. "Great for her, not so great for me."

The room's silence pressed in again, broken only by the faint hum of the engines. I pulled the thin blanket over myself, half-expecting it to disintegrate in my hands. Closing my eyes, I tried to imagine what the trial would be like. Would it be swift and merciful? Long and torturous? Would I even make it out alive? Probably not, if my track record was anything to go by.

At least I'd provided Zeta with a cautionary tale.

"How Not to Use Interdimensional Power 101," starring me.

I sighed. If I survived this, I would definitely be writing a memoir.

Assuming anyone would want to read it.

2

The next day, I found myself in *Nira*'s library, combing through anything I could find about the Collective Dominion's legal system. What I really needed was a book titled *Dominion Law for Dummy Humans*. You know the type—something that breaks things down in simple, digestible terms. Because let's face it: when you ask an expert to explain something and they come back with a wall of jargon, it's about as helpful as a screen door on a spaceship. I needed something I could actually understand. And considering I never even finished high school, that "something" had to be pretty basic.

Fortunately, *Nira*'s library had an electronic encyclopedia—kind of like Dominion Wikipedia—complete with a surprisingly decent translator that converted Dominion Standard into English. I navigated to the legal section and skimmed through headings, trying to piece together the big picture.

The problem was this: I'd been charged with a Dominion crime. But what did that actually mean in their society?

When we reached Astrithon, would I be arrested on the spot? Thrown in jail? Would I even have a lawyer, or was that too much to hope for? Did they have anything remotely resembling constitutional rights? And more importantly, as a human, would any of it apply to me?

The journey to Astrithon would take nearly a week, so I had plenty of time to park myself in the library and dig in. Bit by bit, I started to get a clearer picture of how the Dominion legal system worked—or at least the parts that might directly impact me. It wasn't comforting, but at least I was starting to understand the rules of the game I'd stumbled into.

Most of my readers are probably from the UHC and are therefore familiar with its legal system. It's based on British Common Law and the Bill of Rights from the old USA's constitution. In the UHC, an accused criminal is assumed innocent until proven guilty, has a right to question evidence, a right to a speedy trial, and is guaranteed legal representation. The accused is protected from self-incrimination, meaning that he or she cannot be forced to testify regarding the facts of the alleged crime.

The Dominion had some similarities but also some important differences. First of all, the concept of lawyers didn't seem to exist. There were judges, but they were drawn from government officials. There were prosecutors, but again, this seemed to be some kind of government position appointed by the Nova Throne.

The accused was not allowed legal representation, at least not in the strict sense of having a defense lawyer specifically assigned to one's case who had to maintain strict lawyer-client confidence. No, that's not how it worked in the Dominion. It was the *judge* who was responsible for protecting the accused's rights and providing legal advice.

Another difference: During hearings, certain citizens of

high rank were allowed to intercede on behalf of the prosecution or the accused. They could express their opinions on whatever matter was before the court, and the judge had to listen to them and give consideration to their statements.

Regarding arrest and jails, the Dominion had detention centers for holding dangerous persons awaiting trial. But there were no prisons for holding those who were punished. Why? Because prison time wasn't an accepted punishment. If an accused were found guilty, the possible outcomes were paying a fine, suffering corporal punishment, exile, or death.

Another difference from the UHC was that the judge did not determine the punishment. The Nova Throne did, and this privilege was customarily exercised through the sovereign's appointed representative, the prosecutor. The judge was responsible for deciding the facts of the case and judging innocence or guilt but had no say in the punishment if the accused were found guilty.

The system sounded chaotic and downright terrifying. I could be exiled or even executed because of what I'd done. And I wondered: to where would I be exiled if that were the punishment? I couldn't find an answer to this in the library. In some ways, that sounded worse than death.

The library door swished open. I glanced up from my terminal and saw Zeta float into the room.

It was my first time seeing her since we boarded the ship. I rose to my feet and faced her.

Zeta acted as if she hadn't seen me, which was impossible. The library was small, and we were the only two people in the room.

"Zeta..." I said tentatively.

She moved toward a terminal at the other end of the room.

Relations had been strained between us ever since she'd accused me of sydereal assault. I understood why she felt betrayed, but I thought she could have given me a greater benefit of the doubt. We'd been close friends, after all. "Zeta," I said, "don't be like this."

She paused in her movement. "Kory Drake, Zeta is content that you look well." She sounded like anything but content. Like she was making a polite comment to a stranger. After she said this, she continued floating across the room to an unoccupied terminal.

I stood there indecisively. What was I supposed to do to repair our friendship?

"Zeta, how can I make this better? How can I fix our friendship?"

"The consortship is terminated, and there is nothing left to say."

I took a step toward her. "So, just like that, you've forgotten everything we passed through together? I don't mean a thing to you?"

"Zeta is too occupied with her duties to concern herself with a resident of Earth."

I felt my face flush, and my heartbeat quicken. I took a deep breath. "Listen, you gas box, you might be able to dismiss me because you're mad, but I don't give up on my friends that easily. Loving someone means never giving up on them, even when they've done something you don't like. You're mad at me for what I did. I *get* it. I understand if that makes it difficult for you to talk to me. In fact, as soon as I've had my say, I'll disappear so you don't have to look at me. But, Zeta, if you have ever felt any affection for me, if you ever trusted me, if you ever liked being around me, then promise me you won't abandon what we had."

Have you ever had a falling-out with an alien? Not the

romantic kind—more like the platonic equivalent of a lovers' quarrel. Let me tell you, "awkward" doesn't even scratch the surface. The room practically vibrated with unspoken tension, broken only by the faint hiss of the ventilation system and the steady hum of *Nira*'s tractor drives pushing us through veilspace.

Zeta floated silently above the library terminal, her octahedral capsule as inscrutable as ever. I caught myself wishing—yet again—that she had a face or at least something that could give me a clue about what was going on in that brilliant mind of hers. But no, her featureless, polished form betrayed nothing. Talking to her was like trying to reason with a particularly stoic brick wall. Expressive, she was not.

Her capsule rotated slowly on her vertical axis. "Kory Drake, you have broken your covenant with Zeta. You promised not to try to steal back your energlyphs from Ban'ach; then you did it anyways. How can—"

"Zeta, it was a moment of weakness." I leaned toward her, pointing with my finger to emphasize my words. "I was alone, captive, with Ban'ach talking about how she would turn me over to the Kergan Empress as her plaything. I *had* to do something. Or did you expect me just to give up?"

"Sydereal battery is never an acceptable reaction. Better that you had died than tainted yourself with the stink of this crime!"

I couldn't believe she would say that. I took a step back and folded my arms. "Do you really believe that? You'd rather I was dead?"

"Zeta does not...in an ideal..." I'd never once seen Zeta lost for words. "Kory should have waited for Zeta's help. Zeta and Busto were coming for you."

"I didn't know that," I said. "I had to act on my own. I'd been stripped and restrained, and Ban'ach was whipping me. The only weapon I had was my sydereal strength. And I used it."

"Kory Drake, it does not matter what Zeta thinks or feels. The fact is that you have violated one of the Dominion's most important laws. You have emptied two maracs glyphshades and injured Ban'ach's. Zeta may be the crown princess and heir to the Nova Throne, but even she cannot ignore the law. And she *will* not."

I rested my hands on top of my head and stared above her capsule. "So, you're just gonna turn me over to the police and forget about me. You sure have an easy time abandoning your friends. Maybe it would have been better had we never met!"

I spun on my heel and stomped out of the library. If the hatch had been on hinges, I would've slammed it shut just for the satisfaction of the noise. Instead, it slid shut silently behind me, robbing me of even that tiny release.

Tears stung my eyes as I marched down the exterior corridor toward my quarters. My chest felt tight with a mixture of frustration, sadness, and anger. Passing one of the ship's crew—a tall, ape-like alien with bat-like ears—I felt a pang of isolation. Up until about an hour ago, I hadn't even known what species they were. That was the kind of thing Zeta should've told me. She should've been that friend I could count on right now.

Instead, she'd given up on me so quickly. And now, she wasn't there when I needed someone to help shoulder the weight of my legal problems, reassure me, and tell me things would somehow be okay.

At least the library had given me something valuable. I'd learned that the crew member I'd just passed was one of a kavreni, a client race of the igna. They were bipedal humanoids, taller and slimmer than humans, with bat-like ears and a fine coat of auburn hair covering their entire bodies. Most of *Nira*'s crew were kavrenis, with a few ignas scattered among them.

The thought distracted me briefly, but couldn't hold back the storm of emotions for long. I was light-years away from Destiny, my closest friend, my street sister. And now, my one supposed ally on this alien ship had abandoned me to my fate.

I was headed to a world I didn't understand, to stand trial for defending myself with the only weapon I had at the time: my sydereal talents. And what waited for me there? Disgrace? Imprisonment? Execution? The possibilities churned in my mind, heavy and relentless, each worse than the last.

I wasn't a pacifist. How could I be? I'd survived five brutal years on the streets of San Jose. Homeless. Alone except for Destiny. I'd fought for every scrap, every inch of safety, using whatever resources I had.

When Zeta came into my life and handed us *Thunder*, I'd taken that same scrappy survival instinct and poured it into our missions. I'd fought the Kergans with everything I had—tools, weapons, sydereal talents—and I'd done it to protect my fellow humans.

I had no regrets. Not about the choices I'd made, not about the battles I'd fought. Not even about the enemies I'd made.

Outside my cabin, I punched the entry pad. The hatch slid open with its usual quiet efficiency, and I stepped inside. Tossing off my ship slippers, I flopped onto the small bed, staring at the ceiling. My thoughts were a tangled mess, looping endlessly back to the same questions and the same frustrations. What was I going to do when we reached Astrithon?

Why was Zeta so distant, so cold? Why now, when I needed her more than ever, was she turning her back on me? I tried to put myself in her shoes—she was the crown princess, the heir to the Nova Throne. That kind of responsibility must weigh on her like a mountain. Maybe, in her eyes, I was no more than a gnat—an annoyance she wished would just disappear.

Still, that didn't make it sting any less.

I felt powerless. Stripped of agency, without influence or resources. Maybe agreeing to face these criminal charges had been the worst decision of my life. Sure, refusing to respond would've made me an outlaw. I'd be cut off from the crew of *Thunder,* but at least I'd still be on Earth. Free. Destiny would've stuck by me. We'd have found another way, another community to call home.

Instead, I'd trusted Zeta. Trusted her people, her promises of justice and fairness.

What a mistake.

3

Five days after departing from Earth, *Nira* exited veilspace at the L2 point outside the orbit of the Dominion homeworld of Virelia. I stood in the observation lounge, watching as we approached the planet.

Coming from L2, the dark side of Virelia faced us. Dozens of splotches of bright lights shined from the illumination of large cities. Thousands of flashes of light circled around the planet in orbit, indicating orbiting habitats. Some of those were tens of kilometers in diameter and formed a mist-like ring around the world.

The star around which Virelia orbited was called Ignisara. A K-type main-sequence star, Ignisara was slightly smaller and dimmer than Sol. Virelia was the capital world of the Collective Dominion, but the true homeworld of the ignas was Ignisara itself. Ignas, like Zeta and Captain Lorian, lived inside capsules when on terrestrial planets and their kind were a rare sight. 99.9% of the population of the ignas resided on Ignisara or other stars of the Dominion's colonized systems. Their bodies were composed of stellar plasma held together in complex magnetic fields that were somehow organized into sentient bodies.

Virelia itself was the homeworld of the kavrenis, who had evolved there. It was a terrestrial planet much like Earth, composed primarily of salt-water oceans, with about one-third of the surface covered by continents.

These trivia I had learned from the library as I tried to fill the gaps in my knowledge during our journey. The ignas were the senior race and had elevated the kavrenis to sentience using genetic manipulation and bioengineering.

Over the course of a few hours, we drew closer to Virelia. As *Nira* crossed the terminator, the shadowy edge dividing night from day, I got my first real look at the planet's sunlit side.

Virelia could have been Earth's long-lost twin. The continents had unfamiliar shapes, but the colors were familiar: deep greens, expansive blues, and snowy whites at the poles. Massive clouds and weather systems sprawled across the surface like delicate strands of stretched cotton, forming gaps that revealed the land and sea beneath.

We descended toward the planet, heading for the eastern edge of a rectangular continent. From high above, I could see lush greenery abruptly meeting white sand beaches, which bordered an ocean so vast it made the Pacific look like a puddle. Even at 50 miles up, the shallow cyan waters shimmered, and the shorelines gleamed like veins of polished silver.

The vibrant greens and blues gave way to a sprawling gray mass that looked like the body of an enormous spider. Long, spindly limbs stretched outward for miles, forming the colossal metropolis of Astrithon—the capital of the Collective Dominion and home to the Nova Throne.

As *Nira* approached the city's northern edge, I noticed

something extraordinary. Hundreds of gigantic globes floated above Astrithon like shimmering soap bubbles, each one a thousand feet or more in diameter. Inside these vast terrariums, I could see distinct landscapes—miniature worlds with unique vegetation, topography, and even weather systems. The sight was mesmerizing, a surreal display of Dominion engineering and artistry.

Captain Lorian navigated the ship with practiced ease, expertly steering us away from the floating spheres. The ship's smooth trajectory gave me time to marvel at the breathtaking view, though the enormity of the city below made my stomach twist. This was Astrithon—a place of power, beauty, and now, my uncertain future.

At the heart of Astrithon rose a ring of nine skyscrapers, each stretching miles into the sky like impossibly slender needles piercing an embroidery board. A delicate-looking circular bridge connected their tops. From my vantage point, it seemed like the whole structure could collapse with the slightest breeze. But the scale was deceiving—each building stood five miles tall, and the ring itself spanned ten miles in diameter, a feat of engineering that defied comprehension.

We flew past the ring, heading toward the city's northern edge. We passed a sprawling park among the dense labyrinth of towers and spires. At its center glimmered a golden structure, a tetrahedron that radiated brilliance as if it housed a furnace of sunlight. It stood half a mile tall, its shimmering walls surrounded by leafy forests and green fields that formed a natural barrier between it and the rest of the city.

Elsewhere, broad avenues sliced through the urban expanse like rivers carving through canyon walls. Few small buildings were in sight; everything was massive, with towering structures lining the streets like cliff faces.

The roads carried a trickle of ground traffic while the skies above teemed with thousands of air vehicles, darting along restricted routes in an intricate, crisscrossing web of movement.

As we flew over the city center toward its northern outskirts, the towering skyline began to soften. The buildings became shorter, spaced farther apart, and gaps appeared between them. Soon, I spotted smaller apartment buildings and what looked like single-family homes—if the residents of Astrithon favored that kind of suburban living. The scene grew so familiar I could almost believe we were flying over a distant suburb of San Jose. Parks dotted the landscape, neatly arranged neighborhoods surrounded public buildings and parking lots sprawled in clusters. The roads and airways still flowed with an unrelenting current of vehicles, a testament to the sheer scale of the city's population.

Through the broad window, I caught sight of the Astrithon spaceport coming into view. Vast concrete pads, each the size of a football field, were spread out around a central terminal. Spacecraft ascended and descended in a dance of controlled chaos. On the ground, a swarm of vehicles and figures buzzed around the landed ships, their movements resembling an anthill in full operation.

Nira slowed and hovered above an empty pad, momentarily holding position as if contemplating its descent. Then, as gracefully as a feather falling, we began to lower. The ship made several soft thumps—likely the landing gear extending—as the pad grew larger and the figures below became distinguishable. Finally, with a faint bump, we touched down, the engines humming as they powered down.

I was in Astrithon.

4

I returned to my quarters and began packing my meager belongings into my worn backpack. It didn't take long—just a few changes of clothing, toiletries, a notebook with a pen and pencil, and the tablet computer I'd been issued at the base. Thirty seconds, tops. That was the extent of my worldly possessions.

When I opened the hatch to leave, I nearly collided with a kavreni male standing rigidly in the corridor, his jumpsuit spotless, his posture unnervingly formal.

"Captain Lorian has requested that you remain in your quarters until Her Highness Z374 has disembarked," he said. The words, cool and precise, were rendered into English by the magical little translation box hanging from a lanyard around my neck.

I nodded, swallowing my frustration, and stepped back inside. There was no arguing with protocol, apparently. I dropped onto the edge of my narrow bed, staring at the bulkhead across from me. Clearly, I wasn't much of a priority for the crew right now. My escort to wherever I was supposed to go would happen when it happened.

What stung most wasn't the delay. It was knowing I wouldn't get to see Zeta before she left. A bitter ache twisted in my chest, sharp and unrelenting, like a knife being driven deeper with each breath.

I had tried to mend things between us, to bridge the chasm that had formed since the fight with Ban'ach and all that followed. I'd come to terms with the fact that we could never be consorts again, but this? This cold, deliberate distance she maintained—it was like a slap to the face every time I reached out and got nothing in return.

Why couldn't she see how much I needed her help? Why did she have to be so indifferent? This icy version of Zeta was nothing like the fiery, affable friend I'd come to rely on. I thought I knew her better than this. Maybe I didn't know her at all.

I sat in my quarters waiting for fifteen or twenty minutes. Occasionally, I would hear a *thumb* or a *bang* as the crew unloaded baggage and did whatever tasks they had when visiting a spaceport.

Finally, the kavreni returned to my hatch. "Follow me, Mister Drake."

I nodded and stepped behind him.

The crewman led me down two decks and toward the stern airlock. Several more kavrenis joined us, though the new guys carried bags and looked like they were leaving.

The parts of *Nira* we passed through were less refined in appearance, more utilitarian. We crossed a voluminous cargo hold in which a machine like a forklift was moving crates toward where a large hatch had opened up to the outside. From it, I got my first whiff of Astrithon air. Warm and humid and smelling of rotting vegetation.

We arrived at the stern airlock, passed through it, and

descended a gangway leading to the tarmac. At the bottom of the gangway stood a group of armed kavrenis accompanied by one igna floating in a tetrahedral capsule. Their gazes fixed on me as soon as I came into view.

I pulled on the straps of my backpack, tightening them down. Butterflies played in my stomach. My shoulders tensed. The exterior temperature was hot, and the air humid. Sweat immediately broke out on my brow, and I could feel it clinging to my coveralls.

As soon as I stepped onto the tarmac, one of the kavrenis held up a hand, and the igna spoke. "Kory Drake, you shall follow us."

The armed kavrenis didn't point their weapons at me, but neither were their weapons being held at rest. Their eyes swept up and down my body. Two of them stepped around me until I was surrounded, while the crew members of *Nira* who had debarked with me continued walking across the tarmac unescorted toward the distant terminal.

"So, you're my welcoming committee?" I said, trying to come across as not worried. I'm pretty sure I failed at that.

The igna responded by flying away, following the crew members. One of the armed kavrenis gestured with his or her (I hadn't learned to distinguish their genders) rifle in a way that made it obvious I was supposed to follow the igna.

I started walking at a fast pace to catch up to the igna. I was taller and had a longer stride than my escort, but they had no trouble keeping up. Each of them wore a heavy vest covered with devices. They looked like police officers would on Earth, and maybe that's what they were.

We crossed the tarmac. It must have been a half-mile march. Occasionally, the *thrum* of a starship tractor drive would knead my insides as a ship departed or arrived.

By the time we reached the terminal, sweat pooled in

my armpits, and wet spots appeared on my chest and arms. Ropes of sweat streamed down the side of my face. The kavrenis didn't seem to be affected. They had large eyes and ears that had unfurled, giving them the appearance of bats. Those must have provided some kind of thermal control.

We entered the terminal through a heavy steel door and into cool air. At least the Dominion believed in air conditioning.

After a short walk, we arrived at some kind of checkpoint. Two kavrenis stood behind a kiosk and signaled for us to stop. The kavrenis spoke to each other in their native tongue, which sounded a little like Arabic, though their voices were pitched higher, like they were all sucking on helium.

"Would somebody please explain to me what is going on? Am I under arrest?" I asked.

The igna turned to me and said, "Kory Drake, you are an unregistered foreigner and must first pass through Migration Control. From here, we will escort you to officials of the Dominion Judiciary."

"Please step forward and identify yourself," one of the kavrenis behind the kiosk told me.

I shrugged and came closer. "My name is Kory Drake. I am a citizen of the United States of America, a nation of Earth."

The kavreni wagged their head from side to side. "Another human. Do you declare yourself as a refugee?"

I didn't know what to say. I looked at the igna and said in a soft voice. "I don't know what my status is. I was an insurgent on Earth fighting the Kergans. I was told that I was fighting under the authority of the Dominion Ministry of War."

"Do you have any money?" the igna asked. "Do you

have somewhere to stay in the city?"

For all I knew, I wouldn't need any of that because I was about to go to jail while awaiting trial. "No, I don't have anything like that. Not that it will matter."

"You should declare yourself as a refugee," the igna said. "A royal decree gives each human arriving on Astrithon who declares themselves a refugee a monetary grant to help you get established until you can find employment and permanent shelter."

There were more humans here? "How many humans are on Astrithon?" I asked.

"As of today, there are 203,732 humans within the city limits who have been registered."

My jaw dropped open. That many? Here? How had so many made it off Earth? I know, it was only a tiny percentage of the total population of my planet, but still, that was a lot of people. And that was just in this one city. "I'll take the grant."

The igna and the kavreni official exchanged several sentences while the official tapped on a computer display screen. Their assistant behind the kiosk took out a small card about the size of a business card and inserted it into a slot next to the computer.

"Press your hand here," the official said, pointing to a bare metal plate on the kiosk.

I pressed my palm against the cool metal. "Like this?"

"Aye. Hold still."

I felt a tingling in my hand like it had gone numb.

"Done. You may remove your hand," the official said.

I pulled my appendage back and looked at my palm, expecting to see wounds. But it looked fine. "What was that?" I asked.

"It is for your BioCred," the official said without looking

at me, focusing on the display before him.

"My what?" I asked the igna. "And what is your name?"

"You may call this person Ajue. The kavora is preparing your BioCred. It—"

I held up my hand. "Hold on, this is all new to me. What's a kavora?"

I worried about Ajue and the kavrenis growing impatient with me, but Ajue responded with a gentle voice. "Kavora is the term used for a female kavreni. Kavor is the term for a male kavreni."

"Okay, so she's a female kavreni."

"Aye."

"What is the BioCred?"

"It is a device biometrically linked to you that carries your identifying information and your Civex balance."

"Civex?"

"It is the monetary denomination used throughout the Dominion. Your refugee grant will be deposited into your BioCred."

"What if I lose it?"

"That is highly unlikely because it will be attached to your forearm."

I drew in a sharp breath. "Like...surgically attached?"

"Nay, it will fuse with your skin." She must have noted my nervous response. "It is less intrusive than it sounds. You will feel nothing when it is attached."

The kavora held up the small card. "It is ready," she said. "Hold out your arm and bare your forearm."

"Which one?" I asked.

"Either."

I pulled the sleeve of my left arm and held it out. The kavora reached out with the card, pressed it down onto the inside of my forearm, and applied pressure like she was treating a wound. I felt that tingling again, and the card grew uncomfortably hot.

The computer beeped, and the kavora drew her hand back.

I looked at my forearm. Embedded in it was the card, but it was flush with my skin. I pressed it with my finger, and the texture felt just like my normal skin. The only difference was the outline of the card on my skin, with some alien symbols written inside the border. It looked just like a very precise tattoo.

"What do I do with it?" I asked Ajue.

"When presenting ID or transferring payment, hold your BioCred up to designated terminals."

I nodded.

"How do I check what's on it?"

"Do you have a Dominion hand terminal?"

"I think so." I unslung my backpack and pulled my tablet out. The one that Zeta had given me at the base. "Like this?"

"Indeed." She scrolled through it and opened an app I'd never used before. "Press your BioCred to the screen."

I did so, and immediately, a window opened showing my identifying information and a balance of 550 Cevix. Hopefully, that was enough money to get me a few meals and somewhere to sleep. Assuming I didn't become a guest of the local jail.

The igna and the kavora jabbered to each other, and one of my guards gestured at me. "Come this way. Follow Ajue," they said.

We turned down a long corridor that stretched for hundreds of yards into the distance.

"Next, you will meet representatives of the Dominion Judiciary," Ajue said.

5

By the time we reached the end of the terminal, I was utterly drained—tired and overstimulated by the onslaught of unfamiliar sights, aliens of every shape and size, foreign languages buzzing in my ears, and strange mechanisms whirring and flashing in ways I couldn't begin to understand. All I wanted was to find a quiet room where I could sit alone for a while and let my brain reboot.

Unfortunately, fate had other plans.

My escort led me out of the corridor, up a flight of stairs, and through a heavy door. On the other side, I was greeted by a group of five waiting figures: three ignas, their ethereal forms shimmering within their plasma capsules, and two kavrenis, their tall, slender frames, and sharp bat-like ears making them unmistakable. They stood clustered together, their gazes locked on me the moment I stepped in.

So much for quiet.

"Ajue, Kory Drake has been designated?" one of the new ignas asked.

"Aye, sir."

The new igna who'd spoken was in a spherical capsule adorned with intricate golden scrollwork. I'd never seen anything like it before on an igna.

"Kory Drake, Ajue presents the igna known as Qut. He is an assistant prosecutor of the Dominion Ministry of Justice or the judiciary."

I nodded but said nothing.

"Kory Drake," Qut said, "You stand accused of sydereal battery and are hereby arrested until a magistrate presides over your indictal. How do you respond?"

I didn't understand some of what they were saying. "What is an indictal?"

"It is a judicial hearing at which you will be officially notified of the criminal charges against you. The judge will also decide whether you will be detained until trial or released."

It sounded just like an arraignment. What would they do if I refused to respond or if I said no? But I'd made a promise to Zeta to respond to the charges and not become an outlaw. "I will go with you."

One of the kavrenis pulled out a chain link with loops on both ends and stepped toward me. "Hands behind your back."

"You don't have to cuff me," I said.

"Yes, we do. You have been detained and must be secured when being transported."

Two of the kavrenis stepped forward, grabbing my upper arms and attempting to force them behind my back. Instinctively, I resisted, pulling against their grip. I was much larger than them and could've made things difficult if I wanted to. But what was I going to do? I was standing in the middle of a spaceport, surrounded by armed aliens, on a planet thousands of light-years from Earth. If I fought back, they'd probably find a way to make my life infinitely worse.

With a frustrated sigh, I relented, pushing my arms back until my hands hung awkwardly behind me. One of the kavrenis quickly snapped cuffs onto my wrists. Then came leg irons, secured tightly around my ankles, and finally, a chain looped around my waist. Additional lengths of chain locked my cuffs and leg irons to the belt, leaving me bound like some kind of interstellar prisoner on display.

As the kavrenis worked, I became acutely aware of the crowds moving through the spaceport. Aliens of every shape and size bustled past, some pausing to gawk at the spectacle. Not a single human face stood out in the sea of unfamiliar beings. About ninety percent of the crowd were kavrenis, their bat-like ears and lithe frames dominating the flow of traffic. Floating capsules containing ignas glided among them like glowing specters. I even spotted a few maracs and a dozen other species I couldn't begin to identify.

It was a sobering moment, standing there shackled and surrounded by beings who didn't look or think anything like me. If anyone had doubts about me being an outsider here, the chains certainly made it clear.

A minute later, one of the kavrenis left and returned, driving a small electric cart with seven passenger seats. Somebody grabbed my chains and yanked me forward, pushing me down into a seat in the center. Two large kavrenis sat on either side of me. One of them held my backpack, which they'd removed when they put the cuffs on me.

The cart started moving slowly down a long corridor in the terminal, dodging pedestrians. Sitting there restrained and surrounded by hostile, alien strangers, I'd never felt so isolated and alone.

I thought about my friends who I'd left behind. Destiny

Austin, my street sister, and my closest friend, with her sharp wit and practical attitude. Now she was captain of *Thunder*. By now, she should have accepted an igna Heliacal consort of her own. I hoped she was happy but felt a twinge of jealousy that some stranger was now enjoying her company.

I immediately felt guilty for feeling that way. I wanted her to be happy. My situation sucked, but I'd gotten myself into it. It wasn't Destiny's fault.

Clemen Busto, with his gruff personality and Marine ideals, would be keeping Destiny in line and ensuring the crew of *Thunder* were well-trained and disciplined. The older man had become a stabilizing influence in my life, one that I would miss.

I remembered Phoebe Brooks. The endearing crush she had on me and her patient friendship that would have turned into a romance instantly if I'd reciprocated similar feelings for her. I never had, and yet Phoebe never once held it against me. The young woman would likely have been promoted to Destiny's executive officer after I was gone.

My friends were back on Earth fighting the Kergans, surviving, and protecting humanity. And what was I doing? I was an arrested criminal awaiting trial for mysterious crimes that, a few months ago, I didn't even know were possible. Sydereal battery? Come on, it sounded like a rare illness rather than a crime.

The cart exited the corridor and rolled into a vast atrium that seemed more like a jungle than the inside of a building. Trees and lush gardens filled the space, their greenery spilling into the pathways. Hundreds of kavrenis moved about, their numbers giving the air a faint, sharp scent of ammonia that tickled my nose. Their chatter—high-pitched chirps and squeaks—barely registered within my hearing range, creating a background noise that was almost musical in its rhythm.

Curious glances followed me everywhere. I was clearly an oddity, and my human frame stuck out like a sore thumb among the crowd. Nearly all the kavrenis were naked from the waist down. What clothing they did wear appeared functional rather than modest, with pouches and pockets to carry objects rather than to cover themselves.

With the sheer variety of kavrenis in view, I found myself studying their body types more closely. The typical kavreni resembled a large monkey with the head of a bat, but with a significant difference—their knees bent backward, making their legs fold opposite to a human's. Their bodies were covered in light fur, with a dense mane crowning their heads. The ears were enormous, supple, and constantly swiveling like miniature radar dishes, pointing in all directions. Their noses were small and flat, blending seamlessly into their faces.

The most striking feature was their long, whip-like tails, almost as long as their entire bodies. These tails moved with precision and agility, often holding objects or gesturing like an extra hand. Despite their height, kavrenis were less massive than humans. Their spindly arms and legs comprised most of their length, while their torsos were small, slightly larger than their heads. Their lower legs were significantly longer than their thighs, giving them the appearance of walking on stilts.

There were no visible external genitalia, and their smooth, muscular groins were typically uncovered. It was probably to keep their highly agile tails unimpeded, I guessed.

At first, I couldn't tell the difference between kavors (males) and kavoras (females), but after observing several hundred of them, I began to notice subtle distinctions. Roughly half of the kavrenis had a swelling in their lower abdomen, and in many cases, their clothing left this area exposed. It was clear that these were mammary glands—two small, low-set breasts located just above the pelvis. These were the kavoras.

Kavors, on the other hand, had narrower hips and broader shoulders and necks compared to the kavoras. Their manes were also thicker and lighter in color. Though kavors appeared to be more heavily built, kavoras were generally taller and more elongated and graceful.

It was fascinating, in a slightly surreal way, to see this alien species moving about so naturally, their movements fluid and efficient. It made me feel every bit like an outsider in this bustling world.

The cart passed through the atrium and through an exit to the outside, where a large vehicle rested on a concrete pad. By the presence of tractor pads and lack of wheels, I knew it to be an air vehicle of some kind.

The two guards sitting next to me unbuckled my belt and prodded me toward a windowless compartment at the rear. I walked with an awkward gate because of the leg irons, which had barely enough slack in them to allow me to climb the three steps up the ramp.

A guard strapped me in the back, and he and two kavoras took seats in the rear with me. They watched me closely but didn't respond when I asked questions during the flight. Unlike the partially clothed civilians I'd seen in the terminal, these guards wore full-bodied coveralls, the bulkiness of which suggested some kind of body armor. The easiest way to tell the one kavor from the two kavoras was because of his thick, blond mane, which he kept tied back in a practical ponytail.

I felt the aircar lift off but could see nothing outside. We accelerated forward to what must have been a very high velocity, given how long and strongly I was pressed back into the cushions of my seat. At least 200 knots, I estimated.

After a flight of about ten minutes, we decelerated and descended. The driver landed with little finesse, throwing me forward into my seat straps. With my hands restrained and chained to my waist, I was unable to reach out and grip the armrests.

I was escorted out of the van and into what looked like an underground garage. The kavor walked by my side with his hands holding the chain around my waist from behind and efficiently directing me. None of my guards said a word. They communicated with shoves and hand gestures. Occasionally, I heard high-frequency chirps, especially when approaching doorways and passing moving objects.

We entered a cold, concrete building. The floors and walls were undecorated, and the building fixtures were plain and utilitarian. All the staff appeared to be kavreni and wore brown uniforms covering their upper bodies. I had been detained enough during my adolescence to recognize a jail, even if I was among aliens.

"Do I get a phone call?" I asked my escort half-jokingly. Who was I going to call? "When do I get to talk to my lawyer?" I wasn't holding out much hope for that. Everything I'd read about the Dominion legal system suggested that I would be entirely subject to the mercy of the judges. There was no right to legal representation.

My guards continued to ignore me. They led me through several twisting hallways until we came to a large and noisy room filled with officers dressed like my guards and other people restrained like me. Most were kavrenis, but I saw one other human across the room. I tried to get her attention, but she looked like she was wasted on a drug of some kind, staring into the distance while sitting cuffed next to a kavora officer.

My guards spoke to a kavora worker behind a counter

in their song-like language while gesturing to me repeatedly.

The worker pointed at me and spoke heavily accented English. "Mister Drake, place your BioCred on the panel, please." She pointed to an aluminum disk on the tap of the counter.

The kavor guard released my hand restraints and I extended my left wrist and placed the surface of my BioCred on the disk.

Something made a beep sound, and the worker told me to step back. Then she had me stand inside a metal cage that looked a lot like an airport metal detector. A minute later, I was told to exit, and my guards led me out of the room, down the hall, and into another room.

A kavor worker stood in the middle of the room, and two armed guards stood against the walls. He said something I couldn't understand. My guard, who was carrying my backpack, passed it to the worker. He opened it and started taking objects out while tapping on a terminal. He was probably taking an inventory. After recording each object, he placed it into a clear crate.

My guards unlocked my restraints and removed them. "Strip," one of them said.

It was a strip search.

I knew the dance. It was a typical jail. I removed my shoes, unzipped my coveralls, and slipped them off. Then I removed my undershirt, boxers, and socks.

The worker took my clothing and logged them.

I stood there in the nude. My guards stared at me, spending an uncomfortable amount of time studying the hardware that they lacked.

I glared back at them.

When the worker finished logging my clothes, he put on

gloves, snapping them with a flourish. He said something, and my guards seized me by the arms and legs.

I was then subjected to a highly invasive cavity search. They would have made a proctologist proud.

I expected to be given a jail-issued jumpsuit, underwear, and slippers. I was surprised when my guards cuffed me while still naked and led me out of the room. They marched me deeper into the building, through a mantrap, and into a cell block.

Was this how they were going to leave me? Unclothed? Unprotected?

We stopped halfway down a dimly lit hallway at a cell door. A guard opened it, my cuffs were removed, and I was shoved through the door.

The cell was dim, the only light coming from a small window in the door as it was shut. But I immediately saw dozens of kavrenis standing and sitting. The cell was so crowded there was barely space to walk.

Everybody was naked, like me. Apparently, they didn't believe in clothing for prisoners. I tried not to be embarrassed, but it was impossible to do so with all of them staring at me.

After seeing all the people, I next noted the pungent stench of ammonia, so powerful that my eyes watered. I was beginning to recognize it as the smell of unwashed kavreni bodies.

A flurry of high-pitched chirps were fired at me from all directions. Many of the kavrenis held their tails pointed at me. I wondered what that could mean.

I held my hands up. "I'm sorry, I don't understand." The guards had confiscated my translation box. I backed away until I bumped up against a wall. I felt a harry arm pressing against my side.

Somebody shoved me away. I stepped forward, then tripped on a figure sitting on the floor who I couldn't see in the darkness. Falling, I landed on more furred bodies.

The cell erupted into commotion. Screaming and chirping. It sounded like a chimpanzee war in an African forest.

A fist struck me on the side of the head. Lights flared in my skull.

I pushed away, feeling my hands strike somebody. I ducked and crouched, covering my head with my arms as feet kicked me and fists punched me.

Then something sharp poked me in the right leg, and I felt an excruciating pain like fire had been injected into it.

Then I felt a second sting, this time in my right butt.

I bellowed from the pain. Fire danced in my veins. I spasmed on the floor as my body was tortured by the two points of magma burning on my body. Over the next minute, the pain gradually subsided, but then my right leg and butt went completely numb. Had somebody injected me with something?

"What is your problem, you assholes?!" I screamed.

I flailed around, and though it was almost completely dark, I could tell the kavrenis were keeping away from me.

A hand patted me on the head. "Easy there, *pata*," somebody said in accented English. A woman's voice. A *human* voice. A second hand came to rest on my back.

6

I reached out and felt my hand contact smooth, cool skin. "Are you human?"

"Yes, we're the only two in the cell, *pata*," she said in a whisper with her mouth right up against my ear. I could feel her naked breasts pressing against my shoulder. I'm sure I was blushing purple. "You need to be careful not to annoy the batties, *pata*." Her accent sounded Spanish.

"*Batties*?"

"Yeah, *pata*, the kavrenis. Batty is slang for an individual kavreni. Did they get you?"

"Get me?"

"Yeah, did they sting you? You were screaming somebody was pulling your fingernails." She released me and sat next to me with her shoulder touching mine. In the darkness, I could just barely make out her outline.

"Is that what that was?" I rubbed my thigh and my butt where they'd gone numb. I could feel a hard nodule at the center of each area of numbness, like a huge mosquito bite, though they didn't itch. "How'd they do that?"

"The batties have a stinger in their tails."

When I entered the cell, I remembered that some of the kavrenis were pointing their tails at me. "Geez! That would have been nice to know! Blast it! Nobody is telling me anything!" I'd annoyed the gangly bastards, and they'd stung me! "How bad is it? Do I need a hospital?"

She patted me on the back and chuckled. "No, *pata*, nothing like that. It's only deadly to small animals. It's a mild neurotoxin that'll leave you numb for a couple hours. You'll be fine. By the way, I'm Berta."

I sensed a hand being held out, so I grasped it and said, "Hi, Berta, I'm Kory Drake."

I heard a gasp of indrawn breath. "Funny coincidence. Your name's the same as that of Kory Drake, who's been in the Earth news."

"Who'd that be?"

"Seriously?" Her head tilted to the side. "Did you just get here?"

"Yeah, I just got transported here to respond to some bullshit charges."

"From Earth?"

"Yeah, from..." I stopped myself in time before revealing our secret base's location in Wolf Jaw. I didn't know who I could trust. "From the US. And where're you originally from?"

"Bolivia. I've been here about nine months in Astrithon." Her voice dropped into a hiss, and her face came closer. "You're not the real Kory Drake, are you?"

I chuckled. "Of course I am. That's my name. Who do you think I am?"

"The guy who's been in the news. Commander of the *Thunder*. Who rescued those human slaves from the Moon and sabotaged some Kergan doomsday weapon."

"Yeah, that would be me. Though, I didn't know I was in the news."

"*Mierda!*" She reached out and grasped my shoulder. "*En serio?!* You're a hero. What the hell are you doing in jail?!"

I groaned. "That's a long story."

"*Carajo!* I can't believe it. Who'd you piss off?"

"Royalty."

"*Royalty?*"

"Princess Zeta."

"You know her?"

I supposed it didn't matter anymore if people knew about my relationship with Zeta. "She was my Heliacal consort on *Thunder*. I did some stuff...well, some stuff she didn't like." I wasn't supposed to talk about the Sydereallium. The UHC military tightly controlled knowledge of it. "I'm in trouble. What are you in here for?"

She sat up straight and pushed her chest out. I saw the vague outline of generous breasts jiggling in the shadows. She obviously was not self-conscious of her nakedness. "Disrupting an Official Proceeding," she said with a tone of pride.

"What, like a protest?"

"Yes, I interrupted a joint Dominion-UHC meeting on the status of human refugees. I'm waiting for my indictal."

"Right," I said, "one of the officials who arrested me told me about that. I'm supposed to have one of those...indictals, too. Do you know how long it will be?"

"Usually a couple days."

"Damnation. I'm gonna be stuck in this cell for *two* days?" I looked around in the darkness. I saw nothing like beds. There was an apparatus by the door that, if I wasn't mistaken, was some kind of toilet. Maybe that's where the horrid ammonia smell was coming from.

"Yeah, it sucks pretty bad. The jails on this planet are pretty bad. I'd rather they just got it over with and caned me so I don't have to wait here for the stupid indictal."

"Cane you? Is that gonna be your punishment? They're going to hit you with a stick?"

She nodded. "Probably. This is my fourth time here for disrupting a meeting. The Dominion is totally into corporal punishment, *pata*."

"What were you doing before you came to Astrithon?" I asked.

"I was a law student at *Universidad Mayor de San Andres*, in La Paz. In my second year. Then, the invasion, the school shut down, and I eventually took a refugee ship with my parents when the Dominion evacuated the Bolivian government."

"You speak good English."

"Thank you!"

"So, why do the...batties keep us in conditions like this? And where are all the ignas? I thought they were in charge."

"They are, but the ignas are very hands-off when it comes to running their empire."

"Empire?" That's not the way Zeta had described her nation.

"In everything but name, it is an empire, with Queen Z373 as the empress. She rules over sixteen star systems and twenty-seven inhabited planets and colonies. The ignas don't have time to worry about the little details of governing over their people. On this planet, the batties are in charge of most things. Like this jail."

"You seem to know a lot."

"I was training to become a politician back in my country. I pay attention to these sorts of things."

"And why do they keep us like this? In the dark and

naked?" I gestured at myself with my hands. "It's not what I expected from an enlightened society."

Berta laughed. "Oh, they think they're enlightened. They have their reasons. First of all, kavrenis are nocturnal and can see nearly as good with their ultrasonic echolocation as with eyesight. For them, putting us in a dimly lit room is entirely humane, because it makes the batties more comfortable.

"Regarding having no clothes. The batties don't really have any nudity taboos. When clothing is used, it's for utilitarian purposes, but being naked is the natural state for them when in their private homes. Only us humans are bothered by these conditions, and the jail management doesn't care about us as long as we don't die."

"So, they're just more liberal about social norms," I said.

She shook her head. "No way, *pata*. If you get caught kissing in public, you can be sent to jail."

My mouth dropped open. "Why?"

"Well...you've probably noticed that the batties don't have much equipment in their nether regions. Yeah?"

"Sure. No genitals."

"Oh, they've got them. But their reproductive organs are in their mouths."

"You're kidding!" I hissed.

"One hundred percent serious. Under their tongues. For the batties, public kissing is equivalent to copulating and is therefore considered an unlawful lewd act."

"You talk like a lawyer."

"Comes with the territory. Anyways, that law has caused all kinds of problems for humans."

"You mean they don't make any legal exceptions for us?" I imagined a man and woman out on a date and sharing a chaste kiss, then police yanking them apart, cuffing them, and taking them to jail. Then stripping them and tossing them in a dark jail cell. The image was so bizarre I almost started laughing.

Berta shrugged, her long, curly hair reflecting light. "There're plenty of us trying to get their laws changed. But no luck so far. Just be careful not to kiss anybody where a batty can see you. Even if they don't turn you in, it's extremely offensive to them."

"So, how do two batties show affection then?"

"Their tails."

"Yeah?"

"Oh, yeah. There's a whole industry built around tails and the kinks the batties get off on with them. If you ever see two batties playing with each other's tails, then you're witnessing the equivalent of foreplay. They don't usually do it in public, though. At least not the respectable kavrenis."

"And we humans have nothing to fill in the gap."

She patted me on the shoulder. "Now you know what it's like to be a minority."

We sat there in silence for a couple of minutes. The hard concrete floor was cold under my skin. The numbness in my leg and butt made it feel like I was missing half my body. I wondered when we'd be fed and given water. When I asked Berta, she said it was irregular, and she hadn't been fed in at least twelve hours.

"The batties have weird biological cycles," she said. "They generally only eat once daily, usually in the dark. They don't like the daylight much."

A couple of hours later, the numbness began to wear off, and my leg and butt woke from their prolonged nap. Both throbbed with a deep, aching pain, like I'd pushed my muscles beyond their limits. I stretched my leg out as best I could and tried some tentative stretches within the cramped confines of my floor space.

Condensation dripped steadily from the ceiling, ensuring I remained perpetually damp, chilled, and miserable. The dark cell had become my world, and as my eyes adjusted to the gloom, I could make out more details—the faint lines of Berta's face and the shadowy forms of the kavreni prisoners around us. Berta sat slumped against the wall beside me, her legs pulled up to her chest, her head resting on her knees. She was asleep—or at least trying to be.

Despite everything, I couldn't help but notice how striking she was. Her ivory skin looked impossibly smooth, like polished marble and dark curls tumbled down her shoulders in loose, unruly waves. Even in this wretched place, her naked form—soft curves and graceful lines—stirred something in me I didn't want to feel. I forced my gaze away, ashamed of myself for even noticing. What would she think if she caught me looking at her like that? I felt a simmering anger at the kavreni guards for stripping us of our dignity, for creating a situation where even basic decency felt like a struggle.

Time dragged on, and I drifted in and out of sleep. Occasionally, the door would creak open, and a guard would shove a new prisoner into the cell or call out a name to take someone away. I tried to keep my mind occupied, counting the prisoners in a futile attempt to stave off boredom. At one point, we peaked at thirty-one kavrenis and two humans.

It was a pitiful distraction, but in this damp, oppressive darkness, it was all I had to hold onto.

In the middle of what must have been the night cycle, I was jolted awake by the screech of the cell door opening. A kavreni guard's high-pitched, squeaky voice called out in English, "Roberta Marin!"

Berta stirred beside me, lifting her head groggily. "That's my card, Drake," she murmured, holding out her hand.

I clasped it firmly, giving it a quick shake. "Take care, Berta."

She stood gracefully, her movements careful as she turned her body to shield herself from my view in the light spilling through the open door. Over her shoulder, she tossed me a look that was equal parts smirk and farewell. "If you ever need anything, look me up. Hallows District. Roberta Marin."

"Hurry up!" the guard barked, his tone sharp.

"Thanks!" I called after her, my eyes locking onto hers as I etched her face into my memory. "Same to you. Good luck!"

As she moved across the crowded cell, she tripped over someone's leg and fell to her knees, sparking a wave of grumbles and muttered threats from the kavreni prisoners. She ignored them all, pulling herself up with quiet determination. The door closed behind her, sealing me once again in darkness.

7

Time in the cell wasn't measured in hours or minutes but in the increasingly creative ways my brain came up with to torment me. Without a day-night cycle or any kind of chronometric anchor, I had nothing to calibrate against. My internal clock spun wildly, the result being that I could have been in there for two days, two weeks, or just two hours stretched out like taffy by sheer boredom.

Eventually, I started trying to extract intel from the guards. Every time the door opened, I'd throw out a query: "What's the time?" "What's the news?" "How's the weather out there?" Predictably, the guards ignored me. Once, frustrated by their lack of customer service, I decided to take a direct approach, marching up to one and demanding answers. Big mistake. She responded with the classic tail-sting maneuver—an elegant and brutal piece of evolutionary hardware. The neurotoxin hit fast: an explosion of pain localized to my left shoulder, followed by numbness and an unnerving loss of coordination. If nothing else, I had to admire the efficiency of the design.

Food deliveries became my de facto clock. They fed me twice, and since the batties—pardon me, the kavrenis—eat once a day, I calculated I'd been locked up for about two days. That said, the unrelenting monotony made it feel like I'd aged into a whole new tax bracket. I also started missing the brief companionship of Berta. At least she talked. The kavrenis in my cell didn't seem interested in engaging, either because they didn't speak English or because they'd collectively decided I wasn't worth the effort.

The food itself was decent. Not gourmet by any stretch, but leagues better than the gruel I'd imagined. Apparently, the kavreni dietary plan is biologically incompatible with mine, so I was given a special meal tailored to human digestion. The spread included a robust chicken stew, some cooked vegetables, half a loaf of bread, and a pint of weak beer. Generous portions, but given the approximately 23-hour interval between feedings, I forced it all down. Survival is about energy management, and one does not squander calories when running on a prison schedule.

When a guard opened the door and called "Kory Drake," I almost took it for a dream. I just sat there on the floor, looking at him. It wasn't until he called a second time, along with a comment about "clipping my tail if I didn't get moving," that I woke to the reality that I was finally going to get to talk to somebody.

The pair of guards cuffed me and escorted me to another room, where they gave me the clothes I had arrived in to dress in. As I put them on, I asked for information about where I was going, but they ignored me. They did not return the rest of my belongings, and as soon as I was dressed, they put me in the leg irons and waist manacles again in preparation for transport. I assumed they were taking me to my long overdue indictal.

The guards put me into a ground car and drove me a

short distance to another building. It had a large sign on the outside written in what I recognized as the Dominion common script, which I didn't understand. But the building screamed of being a government facility. You know the type: like somebody built a box out of clay, then poked hundreds of holes in it for windows and doors and slapped glass into them.

The guards escorted me inside, where I saw a heavy flow of kavreni, igna, and human pedestrians. Some moving with purpose, others wandering seemingly at random and without purpose.

As we passed close to a group of three humans, I called out to them. "Hey, friends, what is this place?"

A middle-aged man looked up in surprise and caught my eye. "The Seventh Dominion Judicial Complex."

I nodded a thanks at the man. I was definitely headed to my indictal. Maybe now I would get some answers. I was tired of this uncertainty and scared of becoming lost inside the Dominion legal system.

I wondered about Zeta and what she was doing at the precise moment. Had she moved into the royal palace with her mother? Was she busy with the duties that she had complained were so pressing? Did she think about me at all? Maybe worry? Or had she condemned me in her own mind to oblivion?

The guards took me to a large room with a half dozen holding cells and placed me in one of them. I used the toilet, then sat in the chair—there was no bed—and waited.

About an hour later, a different armed kavor came and got me. He escorted me down a short hall to a small chamber that contained three pews facing a long pair of tables. The guard brought me—still manacled—to a chair behind one of the tables and pushed me into it. He hung a small translation box around my neck.

At the other table sat an igna and a kavora. The igna was in their capsule and mounted on a self-propelled walker that gave it arms and hands for manipulating objects.

Across from our tables was a long bench behind which were three empty computer terminals.

The igna at the other table stood in his walker and trudged over to me. It was Qut, the prosecutor. I recognized him because of his black spherical capsule with the intricate gold scrollwork.

"Kory Drake," Qut said, "in a moment, the judges will hold your indictal."

"Don't I get some legal help?" I asked. "I don't know anything about your laws or courts. This process seems very unfair."

Qut's walker bobbed up and down. The machine was about seven feet tall and looked like it could squash me into a paste with one of its feet. "The Judge Advocate will speak on your behalf."

"Don't I get to talk to them in private before we start this?"

"Don't be absurd. That could inappropriately prejudice the judge."

"I thought that was the point of having an advocate?"

"Qut wouldn't normally explain the obvious, but you are just like the other ignorant humans. Listen: In a moment, three igna judges will enter. There is the Chief Arbiter, the Judge Accuser, and the Judge Advocate. They will hear your indictal and decide what will be done regarding your trial preparations. You will sit here quietly and listen. Say nothing unless a question is directed at you. Do you understand?"

"I suppose so. And what are you doing here?"

"Qut is the royal prosecutor representing Her Highness Queen Z373. Qut is explaining these things to you because he is more liberal-minded than most ignas and believes you weak humans need extra instruction."

I smirked. "How noble-minded of you."

"Indeed," the arrogant igna said without a hint that he'd noticed my sarcasm.

Qut turned his walker and returned to his seat behind the other table.

I glanced behind me. The three pews were beginning to fill with people. About half kavrenis and half humans. Many of them carried tablets and were writing on them. I didn't recognize anybody and wondered why there were so many spectators here.

A kavreni wearing a ceremonial robe of some kind walked to the front of the room and loudly announced, "Subjects! All hail Chief Arbiter Vexa, Judge Accuser Kyrn, and Judge Advocate Zor!"

"Hail!" the rest of the people in the chamber called out, and everybody rose to their feet.

After a moment of processing what I was seeing, I decided the smartest move was to follow the example of the others in the room. I rose to my feet, my manacles clanking noisily in the otherwise silent chamber.

A few seconds later, a door at the back of the courtroom slid open with a faint hiss. Three ignas floated in, their capsules gliding effortlessly through the air as they made their way to the long bench at the front. Each took position behind one of the glowing computer terminals, their movements precise and deliberate.

Chief Arbiter Vexa assumed the central seat, her capsule an imposing purple octahedron adorned with intricate red scrollwork that glimmered faintly under the chamber's artificial light. To her left, Judge Accuser Kyrn positioned herself, her silver cube capsule embellished with striking gold scrollwork, its edges catching the light like polished mirrors. Finally, on the right, Judge Advocate Zor settled into place. Her white dodecahedron capsule, detailed with stark black scrollwork, radiated a quiet authority.

Once the judges were in position, the rest of us followed suit and resumed our seats. The faint scrape of chairs and the rustle of fabric were the only sounds as the kavreni in robes retreated to a back corner, their presence now unobtrusive but ever-watchful.

"This indictal is initiated for the accused, Kory Drake of Earth," Vexa announced to the room, "in the matter of record 7.261.093.487. The tribunal acknowledges the spectators and urges them to exercise proper decorum during this hearing. These judges also recognize, with pleasure, the presence of the Glyphspeakers—"

Loud murmuring started in the spectator pews, and many of those with tablets began scratching away at them with excited expressions on their faces.

A loud electronic *beep* sounded in the room, making me jump. "Silence!" Vexa roared. "Vexa will clear this room if necessary!" She paused momentarily as if waiting for anybody to dare contradict her. "Vexa recognizes the presence of the Glyphspeakers Nyrris, Kaelos, Velkryn, and Arctis."

Four displays appeared on the walls behind the judges with images of what looked like animated avatars in the form of bizarre cartoon characters.

Despite Chief Arbiter Vexa's warning, soft murmuring started up again in the pews. I heard several people saying "Arctis" in surprised tones.

Vexa continued her speech. "The Honorable Glyphspeakers are attending this hearing via syderealdyne and will act as Echelon Advocates. Welcome, Glyphspeakers."

I was getting lost in all the new jargon and titles. I didn't want to cause a splash, but this process felt very unfair. I raised my hand and waived it.

Utter silence fell in the chamber as every face turned to look at me.

I blushed but kept my hand raised, hoping Dominion culture recognized the human signal for requesting a word.

"What is this? The accused is *improperly* seeking an audience," Vexa said.

"He is human and new to this world," Judge Advocate Zor argued. "He does not know Dominion ways. Zor argues for a waiver."

"Waived," Vexa said. "Kory Drake, you have something to say?"

"Yes... uh... your honor... sir... um... madam," I stammered out while lowering my hand.

"Please address Vexa and the other judges as simply Judge. Yes?"

"Okay. Judge, I'm new here. Could you explain what a Glyphspeaker and an Echelon Advocate are?"

The three judges floated backward and huddled for a minute. I could hear whispering from them. Then, they returned to their terminals.

"Judge Advocate Zor," Vexa said, "you may address the accused."

"Kory Drake," Zor said in the soft voice of a human female, "it is not customary for the accused to initiate questions during hearings in Judicial Tribunals. Judge Vexa has waived her right to censor you, but you must not interrupt again.

"Now, to your questions. Glyphspeakers are members of the Dominion Supreme Council, which, as you may know, are igna glyphshades of ignas who have died and been elected to the Council. Echelon Advocates are Glyphspeakers who choose to speak on behalf of the prosecution or the accused during a criminal tribunal.

"Zor would add her opinion that Echelon Advocates are quite rare these days, and to have *four* of them present at your hearing—and a simple indictal, no less—is unprecedented. You should—"

"Dissent," Judge Accuser Kyrn interjected, "unsolicited advice."

"Maintained," Vexa said. "Judge Zor, anything else?"

"No, Judge Vexa," Zor concluded.

The exchange between the judges made my head whip back and forth between them.

"Prosecutor Qut," Vexa said, "are you prepared to present the sovereign's charges to this tribunal?"

"Aye, Judge," Qut responded. "Qut has transferred the charges to your terminals."

Vexa looked at her terminal for a minute. Then she faced the chamber and said, "The sovereign, Her Highness Queen Z373, charges the accused, Kory Drake of Earth, with three instances of sydereal battery and one instance of conspiring with an astral deity."

I had already expected the charges of sydereal battery, but the last charge caught me by surprise. "What?" I blurted out. "That's absurd!"

The loud *beep* sounded again in the room, making half the spectators jump. "The accused will remain *silent*!" Vexa yelled.

But I wasn't the only one disrupting the hearing. People

in the audience were whispering to their neighbors, and many were staring at me, especially the humans. I wondered if they were reporters of some kind. The tablets they typed on seemed to give them away.

The fourth display on the wall, the one displaying the avatar of the Glyphspeaker Arctis, flashed. "May I speak?" came a gravelly voice in an English accent.

"Aye, Honorable Arctis, please grant us your council," Vexa said with grave deference evident in her voice.

"The accused, Kory Drake, is merely vocalizing his objections to these ridiculous charges," Arctis said. "As I have said on many occasions, the balance of power in our criminal proceedings overly favors the Dominion sovereign, putting the accused at a distinct disadvantage. The fact that the prosecution knows of these charges and the accused has not been notified before this hearing merely proves my point!"

I noticed that Arctis, unlike other ignas, used the first person to refer to himself rather than the third.

"But you've all heard me say as much in the past," Arctis continued. "Now, to my specific point. This particular inquiry has gained much attention because we've never encountered a mortal under the rule of Dominion Law who has been charged with sydereal battery. Why? Because we've never encountered one who was capable of it as an untrained novice.

"I propose that the accused did not exhibit the criminal intent expected in such a crime because he simply. Could. Not. Have." Arctis paused theatrically. "Because he is untrained. It is an injustice to charge him with these crimes, just as it would be an injustice to charge a child with the crime of aggravated theft because she stole a dessert from the family icebox.

"Lastly, the evidence I have seen indicates that Kory Drake acted in self-defense. Again, where is the criminal intent? He was acting to protect himself from a terrible fate at the hands of a Kergan Soul Ravager. As I have advocated on many occasions, our laws must be changed to allow for limited use of sydereal power in an offensive capacity when the situation warrants it.

"I object most strenuously to how this young human is being treated, and I assure you many Glyphspeakers share my opinions. Let the sovereign be warned!"

Hearing this influential person speaking on my behalf caused me to relax, and the relief was so profound that I had to fight back tears. I didn't know who this Arctis was, but he was obviously a friend.

"Thank you, Honorable Arctis," Vexa said, "your opinion has been noted. Let me humbly remind you that this is an indictal, not a trial. Our only purpose is to notify the accused of the charges brought against him, to decide on pretrial detention, and to schedule future hearings.

"To that end, Judge Kyrn, please give the court your arguments for or against detention."

"Thank you, Judge Vexa," Kyrn said. "Kory Drake has been accused by witnesses of committing grave injury to the glyphshades of living beings and of conspiring with an Astral Titan. He represents a significant threat to our people. If left uncontained, he could destroy other members of the public. Kyrn argues in favor of pretrial detention in isolation."

Vexa rotated to look at the Judge Advocate. "Judge Zor, your arguments for or against detention, please."

"Kory Drake is a young human who is still at the age when most of them are receiving an education. He is immature. The fact that he has exhibited sydereal talents—

that he is a so-called flairsparked—is not his fault. I agree with Honorable Arctis; I fail to see the criminal intent behind these acts.

"Furthermore, if the accused is detained in isolation, as Judge Kyrn has argued so fervently for, he will never receive the vital training in the sydereal arts that he so desperately needs. He will be isolated from his culture and his people. In effect, he will be punished for crimes that have not been proven. If he is detained and later found innocent, the Dominion will have committed an injustice of the gravest magnitude. Zor argues in favor of supervised release under the stipulation that the accused remain within the boundaries of Astrithon while awaiting further legal proceedings."

Zor turned back to her terminal.

"Vexa now makes her ruling," the Chief Arbiter said. "The accused is granted supervised release with the understanding that he is to remain within Astrithon city limits until this tribunal is concluded. Any questions?"

"Are you asking me?" I asked.

"Yes."

"Does that mean I'm free to go?"

"Aye, but a tracking device will be attached to your body, and you must report regularly to the bailiff's office. Now, this court must schedule your next hearing."

I sighed with relief. I wasn't out of trouble yet, but at least they weren't going to send me back to that horrible jail cell.

The judges and prosecutor exchanged conversation for the next few minutes, discussing my next hearing, called the precedium, in which the prosecution would present evidence indicating I'd likely committed the crimes they accused me of. It wouldn't be a full trial, but it would be a chance for my advocates to argue in favor of dismissing the charges if the prosecution's evidence was weak. The precedium was scheduled for fifteen days in the future.

Concluding the hearing, Judge Vexa said, "Kory Drake, you are free to go as soon as the bailiffs return you to the jail for out-processing and return of your belongings. Chief Bailiff, you may remove the accused's restraints."

The people in the room stood while the judges exited the chamber. The displays of the Glyphspeakers flickered off.

One of the guards approached me and removed my hand and foot restraints. The kavor said in heavily accented English, "Do nots departs. You must comes with usses to the jail, yesses."

I started following him out of the chamber when a crowd of kavrenis and humans squeezed around us.

A woman shoved herself in front of me. "Mister Drake, how do you feel about the charges against you?"

"Who are you?" I asked as I tried to keep up with the guard.

"Lalita Abbas, with BBC Galactic News." Seeing me about to leave the room, she yelled out, "Are you innocent?"

"Yes, I'm innocent!" I yelled out to all the reporters. "This is all a huge misunderstanding."

The reporters trailed me, calling out my name. It was so strange to experience this in an alien world in a foreign courthouse. It seemed that reporters were the same everywhere.

I *did* want to get my story out there. But I didn't want the guard to leave me behind—though I doubted he would let me go anywhere yet—and I was still processing my situation.

I was free.

But not exactly.

And I had to present myself for the precedium in fifteen days.

8

The guards escorted me back to the jail, where my belongings, including my trusty backpack, were returned to me. It contained just about every worldly possession I had, and I couldn't shake the nagging worry that some opportunistic staff member might have swiped something. But after a quick rummage through the contents, everything seemed to be accounted for.

Even the six Gold Eagle coins Destiny had slipped me before I left Earth were still safely tucked in their hidden compartment. Each of those coins was worth a month of living in relative comfort back home. I had no idea how much value they'd hold here, though. With all the ignas' advanced nanotech making rare metals as common as dirt, I figured they might not be worth much at all. Still, it was nice to see them—like carrying a small piece of Earth with me.

Before I left, the jail staff strapped a tracking bracelet to my left wrist. They also gave me written instructions outlining how to make my mandatory daily check-in call with the bailiff's office. Then, without much ceremony, they led me out of the building and onto the street.

I stood there on a busy street of Astrithon with no clue where to go. I knew nobody in the city except for Berta. And all she'd told me was she lived in the Hallows, wherever that was. Humans were living in the city, but I didn't know where.

But I'd survived on the streets of San Jose for five years. I'd slept in doorways and under overpasses on the hard ground. Nothing could be as difficult as that. My most important priority was food because I couldn't eat any of the kavreni diet.

I picked a direction and started walking. The street had a sidewalk, not unlike in a human city, though it was narrower and paved with a marbled surface that looked like stone, not concrete.

Ground vehicles streamed by in both directions, though the traffic was relatively light given that most of the kavrenis were sleeping at this time of day. There were small cars, barely big enough for two kavrenis. Larger cars as big as SUVs. I saw cargo trucks and public transports of some kind. They must have been buses, though they didn't look like any bus I'd ever seen. The passengers sat with their backs pressed to the center and their legs hanging off the side.

I walked for two hours, as measured by my watch. During the first couple miles, I saw no other humans. In my walking direction, I could see a cluster of incredibly high towers rising into the sky. They had a ring on top. I recognized it from the descent over the city when the *Nira* landed. Though I didn't know the names of those buildings, I used them as a landmark to keep me oriented.

I grew more and more hungry as the hours ticked by. At least I had a mostly full water bottle, which I'd filled on *Nira* before disembarking. But in the hot, muggy air of the city, I sweated heavily, and soon, I had damp spots on the chest, back, and armpits of my coveralls.

I looked for cars that were the kavreni equivalent of taxis but saw nothing obvious. Even if I had found one, would I even be able to talk to the driver? And maybe everybody here used rideshare services, like the batty version of Uber.

The local sun, named Ignisara, moved slowly from West to East across the sky. The planet Virelia rotated opposite to Earth, so the sun rose in the west and set in the east. It was more orange-colored than Sol because Ignisara was a cooler star, and Virelia orbited closer to it. The days were 23 hours and 5 minutes long. The planet had a modest 5-degree axial tilt, much smaller than Earth's 24 degrees, so Virelia had mild changes in the seasons.

The sun dipped lower on the horizon, casting long shadows across the city streets. A knot of anxiety tightened in my stomach as I realized I might have to spend the night outside if I didn't find shelter soon. Across a wide avenue, a large structure caught my eye. Buses rolled in and out of its cavernous openings, and a crowd of kavrenis loitered on the sidewalk nearby.

Curiosity tugged at me, especially when I noticed the kavrenis reacting to the occasional human entering or exiting the building. Each time, they seemed to stumble over one another, ears flicking and tails twitching, trying to grab the human's attention. Whatever they were attempting, it didn't appear to be working.

With no better prospects and a faint hope that the humans might have some useful information, I carefully crossed the busy avenue toward the crowd. As I got closer, I could make out eight or ten kavors, all dressed in short tunics that exposed their hips and agile tails.

The moment they noticed me, their ears shot up like radar dishes, and their eyes locked onto mine. Then, all at once, they surged toward me with an almost electric excitement.

I froze, watching their movements carefully, particularly their tails, which could be dangerous if they wanted them to be. But I saw no immediate signs of hostility, just an eager energy that felt overwhelming. They reached me in seconds, jabbering in high-pitched voices, one over the other, vying for my attention. It took me a moment to realize they were speaking accented English.

"Mista! Mista! You needs exchange?"

One kavor, who stank of ammonia, bumped into my shoulder. "I finds you bestest room in city!"

I turned away and found myself face-to-face with another kavor, shorter than the rest but wearing a clean tunic, and his shaggy mane was pulled back into a neat bun. "Friend human! Rynar so happies to sees you!" He was practically yelling, but he had a very good approximation of a human smile on his face, which I'd never seen any batty manage. It showed his sharp incisors off very well.

"You needs room? Foods for yours tummy? Woman, maybes?" He jogged his eyebrows up and down. "No worries, Rynar wills be yours friend, yes he will!"

Something about the kavor named Rynar instantly made me feel at ease with him. I'd passed thousands of kavrenis that day, but none had caught my attention like this short kavor. He was tiny compared to me, making him very small for a kavor. His fur was almost entirely black, which was unusual for his species, but his mane was thick blond, clean, and combed.

He'd also practiced his human body language; maybe that's why I had locked onto him. He kept the tip of his tail out of view and exercised his facial muscles in ways I don't think the kavreni body was supposed to work, but he did a fair job at replicating human expressions.

I blocked the other voices out and turned my attention to Rynar. "I'm new to the city. I don't know anyone or anything. I need food and maybe a room." Rynar was nodding emphatically so hard I was worried he'd give himself whiplash. I rested a hand on his muscled shoulder, and he didn't flinch at the contact. "Is that something you can help me with?"

Rynar raised his arms above his head as if praying to heaven. "Yes sirs, you betchas, Rynar is your kavor, bests guide in the city, he is. Oh, sirs, you are in luck today today today. Comes with mees." He grabbed my upper arm and started pulling me up the sidewalk.

Several of the other kavors started getting pushy, trying to get my attention. Rynar was about to walk away with a potential customer.

Rynar suddenly stopped, turned around, and yelled something out at them in a loud voice that got all their attention. I couldn't understand a word of it, but his hand rested possessively on my shoulder, and I knew he was telling them to back off.

The rest of the kavors turned dejected and went back to crowding the entrance of the bus terminal.

We continued walking for a few paces. Then I stopped him. "How much do you charge?" I asked him.

"Oh, Rynar usually charges 10 Cevix for a day, but I likes you, friend. I charges you only 5 Cevix and gives you the best guide to the city, I does this thing, yes."

I was utterly at this guy's mercy. For all I knew, a single Cevix could be worth a fortune or next to nothing. He could have been charging me an arm and a leg, and I wouldn't have had a clue. But at that moment—desperate, exhausted, and without better options—I decided to trust him.

It turned out to be one of the best decisions of my life, made on a whim when I had nothing else to lean on. Taking a breath, I decided to lay my cards on the table.

"Look, Rynar," I said, leveling with him. "I'm a refugee. I've only got 550 Cevix and some gold coins. I need to get settled in the city, find a job, and do it safely."

"Oh, you humanses are so sad," Rynar said with a good approximation of a frown. "Those nasty Kergans monsters, whats they does to you. Do not worry, my friend! Rynar will takes care of yous! Best guide in the city, he is, he is, he is. You bees needing a room. Rynar can show yous good room, lots of money; okay room, little money; bad room, for almost nothing. What you wants?"

"Well, don't get ahead of yourself," I said. "Where are all the humans staying in the city? I know there are a bunch here, but I've seen very few."

"Ah, yeses, you wants the Human Quarter, you does. Do not worry yourself, friend. Rynar will be takings you there, he will, he will!"

"Yeah, that's what I want. Do you have single-room occupancy hotels here? For long-term stays?"

Rynar nodded. "Yesses, I knows whats yous talking about. Rynar has just the places in his mind. You trusts Rynar, he takes cares of yous."

"Okay, but first, food. Human food."

"Yes, sirs. Does friend haves a names?"

"I do. Kory Drake. Call me Kory." I reached out a hand.

He took it and gave it a firm shake. "Well mets!" He turned and started walking again. "Comes, we gets taxi. You haves a BioCred, yesses?"

"Yup," I raised my left arm. He saw my BioCred. Above

that, on my wrist, was the tracking device.

Rynar's eyes got wide when he saw it. "Yous in somes kinds of troubles, yesses?"

I shrugged. "Yeah, you could say that. To be honest, I just got out of jail." I said it, hoping it wouldn't scare him away.

I didn't have to worry. "Nasties police! They got nothings betters to do than bother hard working kavrenis and humans, no they don't! You need help leaving? Rynar knows kavora who can remove that," he said, pointing at my tracking device.

I shook my head firmly. Becoming a fugitive was the absolute last thing I needed. "No, thanks, Rynar. I appreciate the offer, but I'll handle the authorities on my own."

His ears relaxed, folding back into his mane, and he let out a soft chuff of resignation. For a moment, I thought that was the end of it.

Then, without warning, he glanced over his shoulder and let loose a series of high-frequency chirps so piercing it felt like someone had stuck a whistle directly into my ear canal. Before I could even register what was happening, a ground car screeched to a halt next to us on the street.

Rynar leaned into the window, jabbering rapidly with the driver. They seemed to reach some sort of agreement in record time because Rynar beckoned me into the backseat. Still a bit stunned, I climbed in, and moments later, we were speeding off, the vehicle weaving with purpose through the traffic.

At that moment, I realized I had a friend. Sure, he was technically hired help, but Rynar had been the friendliest face I'd encountered since I met Berta. And more importantly, I trusted him—because he knew that if he treated me well today, I'd likely hire him again tomorrow.

9

Given the advanced technology in the Dominion, I was surprised that the taxi Rynar and I were in required a person to drive it—in this instance, a scruffy-looking kavor with stains on his shirt. Then I remembered that the Dominion was party to a galactic treaty forbidding the use of advanced machine intelligences for automation.

The driver took off like it was the start of a race. He drove so close to other vehicles—tailgating, cutting other cars off, making sudden lane changes—I was sure we'd become the cue ball in a game of billiards.

Despite this frantic pace, the driver was so relaxed I was worried he would fall asleep at the controls. I kept looking at him to ensure his eyes were still open.

After a few minutes, I decided I wasn't about to die and tried to relax in the back seat.

Rynar pulled out a hand-rolled cigarette of some kind, lit it, and inhaled deeply. It smelled of burning wood.

The driver jabbered something in the kavreni language and reached back his hand. Rynar said something in return, took another deep drag of his joint, and gave it to the driver, who then brought it to his thin batty lips and sucked on the paper tube.

The smoke irritated my throat, and I started to cough. Covering my mouth, I looked for controls that would lower the window but couldn't find anything.

With tears streaming down my cheeks, I heard Rynar talking to me. "You no wants, Misters Drakes?" He held out the joint, clearly offering to share.

I shook my head. "God, no! Please put it out! How do I open this window?"

Rynar said something indecipherable, reached across me, and flipped a switch hidden underneath the door handle. The window immediately slid down, and I got a breath of fresh air.

"Misters Drakes not likes velithar?"

I coughed again. "Is that what that is?" I said with a trembling voice.

"Velithar is... good thing, yes. It makes mind... floats? Yes, floats. You hears more than hear, like sound are alive. It calm, very calm, but also... tricky. Some feels happy, some... not so much. Human try, maybe good, maybe bad. It is likes wind: soft or storm. Depend who you are."

"I don't think so, Rynar. Please, put it out." I wasn't about to suck on some potentially poisonous herb and kill myself the first day in Astrithon.

Rynar shrugged, took one more deep drag, then opened his window and tossed the smoking joint out the window.

Rynar and the driver exchanged a few words, and then both released a rapid series of high-pitched, staccato clicks and trills like the playful chatter of birds.

Rynar reached out a hand and patted my shoulder. "Is okays, Misters Drakes. Wees not makes funs of you." He attempted to smile, showing off his needle-like incisors.

After about ten minutes, we drove onto a high suspension bridge that crossed a wide river. It must have been at least a mile across. Below, I saw rushing brown waters dotted with a multitude of watercraft ranging in size from tiny canoe-like vessels to large tugs pushing barges.

Rynar pointed out the window at the waters. "Is the Zyrathis."

"The river?" I asked.

"Yesses, is the arteries of Astrithon. We also calls it the Vein of Life. Now is vyrrhal. Makes river run high and fast. Very, very dangerous."

"Vyrrhal?"

"Yesses, season with muches rain."

"Like a monsoon?"

"Monsoon is English words?"

"Yes, in tropical regions, it's a season when there is a lot of rain, nearly every day."

"Yesses, vyrrhal and monsoon the same. Buts I likes vyrrhal. It is holy season. A time of birth, growth. Gift from the gods, it is."

As we drove over those raging waters, I looked at them and saw nothing that looked like a gift. More like a deathtrap. How many of those little boats sunk each year, sucked into some whirlpool, or smashed to pieces by a drowned tree?

Dark clouds covered the horizon behind us, and I saw flashes of lighting, though too far away to hear the report of thunder.

The taxi came to the other side of the Zyrathis. Traffic became slower, and there were many more pedestrians. Almost all of them were humans. Crossing the river was like entering a different world.

"Nows we ins the Human Quarter," Rynar said.

"On the other side of the river?"

"Yesses."

"All humans?"

"Noes. Many kavreni lives here also." He pointed at his chest. "Rynar live here, in the Hallows."

"Oh! I know somebody who lives there. A human."

Rynar shook his head. "Nots possible. Hallows is kavreni neighborhood."

"Roberta Marin. Do you know her?"

His eyes got wider. "Ah, yesess, Miss Marin. Yesses, hers lives with Kavreni family. Very unusual. I not knows her well, but hers is well liked by kavreni."

The taxi turned down a narrow street and drove for about another hundred yards. Then, the driver pulled over and stopped.

"This our stop," Rynar said. "Pay driver and follows." He got out his door.

Our taxi fare was 0.5 Cevix. I held out my BioCred over a panel nested between the back seats, and it deducted the amount from my account.

While getting out of the car, I noticed another car stopped about 50 feet behind us, out of which a large black man was getting out. His hair was cropped short. He glanced in my direction, then immediately averted his eyes and looked to his side at a nearby shop.

I dismissed him and twisted my head to look for Rynar, who had crossed the street. His stilted legs and thin arms would have made him look like a stick figure if it wasn't for his large, bat-like head with the two huge ears projecting up like sails. He chirped twice in my direction and waved.

I moved through throngs of people toward him—a mix of humans and kavrenis. I saw no ignas.

I followed Rynar into a plaza covered by dozens of market stalls. Mostly humans selling things. I heard English, Spanish, Mandarin, and other languages I couldn't recognize. It almost felt like home.

Thunder crashed, and rain started to fall. Rynar grabbed my arm and pulled me under a nearby awning. Under it, I found a food vendor selling what looked like tacos. My stomach immediately growled.

"Is goods?" Rynar asked, pointing at the stall.

"Yes, perfect!" I moved to the back of the line of people waiting to order food. Rynar stayed at the edge of the awning, watching.

When I reached the front of the line, I ordered five tacos of pulled pork and a large drink of horchata. It cost me just 0.70 Cevix, which pleased me greatly. Between the taxi fare and the food, it looked like my 550 Cevix would go a long way.

I sat on a plastic chair with my food on a paper plate and my drink propped between my thighs.

The tacos were delicious. How were these people getting pork and tortillas? Were they produced here on Astrithon? The refugees from my homeworld had only been on this planet for a year. Could they have made the transition already so quickly?

While chewing on a portion of my third taco, I saw the large black man I'd seen earlier. He stood in another market stall nearby, looking at clothing. I wouldn't have thought anything of it, except I noticed he kept glancing out of the corner of his eye in my direction.

Maybe he was a reporter trying to get my story. But I didn't recognize him, and I was starting to suspect he was following me.

I quickly ate the rest of my food and chugged down my

drink.

"Yous humans eats fast!" Rynar said.

"It's fine. That was good food, Rynar. Thanks!" I held up both thumbs.

"Good! I hears other humans talks about this place."

I poked him in the ribs gently with my elbow and pointed with my jaw in the direction of the black man. "See that black man over there? The really tall one?"

Rynar started to turn his head.

I squeezed his shoulder. "Don't look straight at him. Just get a glimpse."

Rynar nodded, then rotated his large eyeballs to look at the man. He also emitted several high-frequency chirps.

"Do you recognize him?" I asked.

"No, buts sometimes hard to tells you humans apart. I sorry."

I shook my head. "No, it's okay. Maybe it's nothin', but he might be tailing us."

"Tailing?"

"Yeah, following. He was in a car that arrived behind our taxi."

Rynar's lips suddenly pulled back in an expression that exposed his teeth, and his eyes narrowed. His ears waggled to the sides back and forth. "Can do nothing."

"Don't worry about it. I just want to keep an eye on him and lose him before you take me to the hotel."

"Ah, yesses, Rynar understands." His ears relaxed, and he smiled.

I dropped my used plate and cup in a trash bin and followed Rynar out into the rain. We stopped at a small stall selling clothing, and I bought an umbrella. I had a feeling I'd be needing it frequently.

I opened it and offered to share it with Rynar, but he

shook his head. By now, his fur was matted with water, but the rain didn't seem to bother him. Indeed, he seemed to like it, combing his long fingers through his mane and working the water deeper.

We walked down a busy street for several blocks. I occasionally had us pause so I could look behind us. I saw the close-cropped curly hair of the black man poking above the crowd some 20 yards behind us.

I was definitely being followed.

Abruptly, Rynar called out a trill of chirps and started talking in his tongue to somebody on the other side of the street. He turned to me. "Mister Drake, you gives me a minute to talks with friends?"

"Sure. I'll wait here."

Rynar nodded and crossed the street, dodging between moving cars. I watched him approach a group of three kavrenis sitting on stools next to a small table. They had a large umbrella covering dozens of tiny tubes packed into bundles and resting on the table.

Rynar came close and started talking to them with great animation, his arms swinging in wild gestures.

I was curious about the kavrenis. About their language and their culture. Rynar didn't have to leave me behind, and I didn't think he was trying to hide anything from me. I was honestly curious about what he was doing with those other kavrenis.

Impulsively, I took a step forward into the street, determined to listen in on Rynar's conversation.

Suddenly, an arm shot out and wrapped around my chest, yanking me back. "Watch out!" a young woman shouted, her voice sharp with urgency.

I stumbled backward onto the sidewalk just as a massive truck blared its horn and thundered past, right through the space where I'd almost stepped. The blast of air from its wake hit me like a physical slap, and I stood there frozen, trying to process how close I'd come to getting flattened.

When I finally snapped out of it, I turned to look at my savior.

Under a green umbrella stood a vision. A golden siren with the bluest eyes I'd ever seen stared back at me, her expression a mix of concern and faint amusement. Her honey-colored hair pulled into a braid that dropped past her shoulder, simple gold earrings that matched a necklace glimmering around her neck. Her oval face was striking, with a delicate chin, a perfectly balanced nose, and a single bead of water clinging stubbornly to the tip of it.

I'm not easy to move. At 6'4" and weighing over 225 pounds, built like a tank, it usually takes more than a single arm to budge me. Yet she'd pulled me out of harm's way with ease. She was tall, her eyes nearly level with mine, and wore a flowing green saree that concealed most of her body. But her muscular neck and shoulders hinted at strength far beyond what her graceful appearance suggested.

I blinked at her, still trying to make sense of the near-death experience—and the fact that someone so powerful had seemingly come out of nowhere to save my life.

"Geez, thanks for that!" I blurted, feeling the heat of embarrassment crawl up my neck.

Her right hand rested lightly on my left shoulder, and she smiled—a warm, dazzling smile that made me forget how close I'd just come to becoming street pizza. "You must be new here," she said, her words laced with a soft German accent.

I tried to gauge her age, but her face had that timeless quality some beautiful women possess. She could have been anywhere between sixteen and thirty-six.

She was, without a doubt, the prettiest woman I'd ever met. For a moment, I stood there like an idiot, tongue-tied and terrified that if I spoke, she'd just turn and walk away. Finally, I scraped together some courage. "A little," I admitted, internally cringing at the lameness of my answer. Then I added, "You know this place?"

Her grin widened, revealing teeth so white they could have made a dentist weep. "A little," she said, laughing softly. "That truck just about flattened your handsome face."

I blushed harder, rubbing a hand across my forehead like I could erase the mortification. "Yeah, I guess I'm a little tired. I was just trying to cross the street to get to my friend."

She glanced to the other side of the street, her golden hair catching the light as she turned her head. All she saw was Rynar and the small group of kavrenis huddled together. "You mean them?"

"Yeah, the small one in front," I said. "Rynar's his name. He's my guide."

Her hand slipped from my shoulder, and I immediately felt the loss, like a chill had crept in where her warmth had been. But then she smiled again—a smile so radiant it felt like stepping into sunlight. Her voice was light, yet it carried a melody that could charm the stars. "Yeah, I know him. He's good people."

I sighed, realizing we were blocking the sidewalk as people muttered and stepped around us. I ignored them. "I'm Kory Drake," I said, offering a faint smile.

"Ah, yes, I thought I recognized you." She chuckled her laugh light but knowing and placed a hand on her chest. "The war hero."

She extended her hand, and I took it. Her skin was warm and smooth, her grip firm and self-assured. It wasn't the kind of handshake that begged for approval—it demanded respect.

"Hardly," I said with a dry chuckle. "Don't believe everything you've heard. Listen, I owe you one. Can I buy you a coffee?"

Something flickered in her eyes—just for a moment. I might have called it regret if I'd known her better, but I wasn't sure.

"I can't," she said, glancing at a sleek hand terminal. "I'm headed somewhere, and I'm already late."

She raised a hand in a casual goodbye. "But you can usually find me at mealtimes in the Midnight Plate."

"Midnight Plate. Got it," I said, trying not to sound too disappointed.

Without another word, she turned and walked briskly back the way I'd come. Her strides were long and purposeful, her posture upright, her gaze sweeping over everything as if she were cataloging the city in her mind.

I crossed the street—this time carefully checking for oncoming vehicles—and made my way to Rynar's side.

Curiosity tugged at me, and I glanced back, hoping to catch another glimpse of the tall German woman. She was easy to spot, her height making her stand out in the crowd.

Just as my eyes found her, I froze in shock. She deliberately collided with the large black man who'd been following me. The impact sent him sprawling onto the pavement, his arms flailing as he knocked over a shop display with a thunderous crash.

She paused for a moment, her head turning slightly to glance back at the man now buried under a pile of merchandise. Then her gaze lifted, locking onto mine. We stared at each other for a heartbeat, her blue eyes calm and inscrutable. She blinked once—slowly, deliberately—then turned and strode off without offering so much as a hand to the fallen man.

It wasn't an accident. I knew it in my gut. Whatever she'd done, it had been on purpose. And somehow, I couldn't shake the feeling that her intentions had been anything but random.

I grabbed Rynar and yanked him toward an alley. "Rynar, we got to go!"

"Mister Drake!" he bellowed. "Whats is it?"

"Now's our chance to lose that tail. He fell down!" I pulled him into the shadows some 20 feet into the alley. "Now's our chance."

"Okays, I gots it. Oh! But I was abouts to buy the lushest velithar I ever see! The silver leaves so firm! Yous should have seen it!"

"I'm sure it would have made a fine joint, but we need to move!" I hissed.

"Yesses, sir. Follow me!"

Rynar jogged deeper into the alley, and I ran to catch up. On his long legs, he moved quickly, dodging obstacles and leaping over them with little effort.

Soon, I was breathing heavily, and sweat poured down my body despite the cool rain falling around us.

I glanced behind us several times but saw nothing of the black man. I was pretty sure we'd lost him.

I thought about the German woman colliding with the black man. She had saved my life and then helped me with the tail. She'd helped me twice within a matter of minutes. It couldn't have been a coincidence. Especially after seeing that piercing look in her blue eyes she'd given me right before she turned her back. As if she were communicating telepathically, *I took care of him, now get out of here.*

And I didn't even know her name.

I mentally chastised myself for the oversight. I'd been so taken in by her beauty that I'd not even asked her. What a moron!

"Hey, Rynar," I said between gasping breaths. "Did you see that blond-haired woman I was talking to back there? The tall one?"

Rynar looked at me over his narrow shoulders. "Noes, I thinks not."

I frowned. "She said she knew you."

"Whats is her names?"

I growled. "That's the problem. I didn't ask."

Rynar rattled off several chirps. I'd heard him do that several times, including with the taxi driver, and I thought it might be laughter. After a moment, he stopped and said, "Like two echoes lost in the dark."

I shook my head, not knowing what he meant, but it sounded like a kavreni proverb. "Sure," I said.

I hadn't gotten her name, but she'd said she frequented the Midnight Plate. "Hey, Rynar, do you know a place called the Midnight Plate?"

He slowed to a walk, and I dropped into a stroll next to him. "Yesses, is human dinner," he said.

I scrunched up my face. "Dinner?"

"No, how yous says it. Um... *diner.*" He held up a slender finger and smiled.

"Ah, okay, a diner. Like an all-day restaurant."

"Yesses."

"Okay, take me there later."

"Now?"

I was tempted, but it wasn't mealtime, and I really needed a shower after sitting in jail for two straight days.

"No, first, hotel. Second, sleep. Tomorrow, diner."

"Yesses, heres we are." He pointed at a three-story building we were standing in front of.

10

The hotel was called Vista Rooms. It was an SRO—single-room occupancy—hotel for long-term stays. The business was owned and operated by humans and had been built less than a year ago as part of the first incursion of refugees into the Human Quarter.

I rented a room for fifteen days, paid up front, for 52.50 Cevix. I didn't see the point of paying for any time longer than that since that's when I'd have my precedium.

My room was small, but that's what I'd expected. It was just big enough to hold a twin bed, a small side table, and a chair, with room in the middle to walk around the furniture. The bathroom was communal and down the hall, one for men and one for women.

No cooking was allowed in the rooms, so I had to leave the hotel to find my meals. That suited me just fine because I was still trying to get to know the Human Quarter.

After renting my room, I dismissed Rynar for the day, paying him his 5 Cevix and getting his promise to come the next morning.

I showered, washing all the grime off from being in jail for two days.

After I was clean, I felt hungry but decided to skip dinner and go straight to sleep. I hadn't slept hardly at all during my time in jail. Only the brief naps I could manage while leaning against the walls and resting my head on my knees.

I woke to daylight streaming through the window and somebody banging on my door.

I rolled out of bed and slipped on a pair of sweatpants. I didn't even know what time it was because my watch wasn't synchronized with local time, and I hadn't yet bought a hand terminal.

I opened the door and saw Rynar's smiling face.

"Mister Drake!" I opened the door wider to let him in. "So nice to sees yous!" His ears pivoted from side to side as he walked in, and I heard gentle high-frequency chirps coming from his head as he echolocated his surroundings.

"Hey, Rynar. What time is it?"

He told me the local time. If my calculations were correct, I'd slept for 14 hours straight.

After I changed, we went to breakfast at the Midnight Plate, which fortunately was close by, just a quarter mile from the Vista Rooms.

The diner was built in a style similar to that of the hotel. It had been constructed at the same time and using similar Dominion nanoforges to raise it out of the dirt.

I walked through the doors and into a cloud of scents: Bacon, eggs, pancakes, coffee. I salivated, and my stomach growled in response. "I could eat a horse," I said.

I looked around for the German woman but didn't see her. Maybe she would come in while we were eating.

Rynar and I found an empty booth. Rynar was the only

kavreni in the diner, and he got many looks from the human customers, but fortunately, no complaints.

I ordered the diner's Grand Slam Breakfast with fried eggs, bacon, sausage, pancakes, and hash browns. The diner also had a kavreni menu, and Rynar ordered something called chyrrat.

When our food arrived, I saw that the chyrrat consisted of cooked insects in a brown sauce that smelled fruity. Looking at it made my skin crawl, but I did my best to ignore it.

My conversation with Rynar turned to kavreni diets. I learned that kavrenis are insectivores and chyrrat is a popular dish among the working classes. He seemed to eat it with relish.

We finished our meal without seeing the German woman enter the diner. I felt disappointed and hoped she hadn't given me false information with the intent of ghosting me. But then I thought of that last look she'd given me, and I was sure she intended to find me again. I wasn't just some random encounter to her. That made me feel better.

After breakfast, Rynar took me out shopping.

The first thing we procured for me was a hand terminal, or a *dot,* as the humans in Astrithon called it. I bought an inexpensive model for 8 Cevix that was good enough to hold all my data and give me access to the Virelia internet.

If I'd had a dot yesterday, I could have exchanged contact info with the German woman, I thought with regret.

After that, we purchased new clothing for me better suited to the Astrithon climate. The pants and shirts were loose-fitting and made of synthetics that breathed well.

With the shopping finished, we stopped by my room to drop off my purchases and went to lunch again at the

Midnight Plate.

Still no sign of my German siren.

But, during all our errands that morning, I'd also not detected anybody following us. Not even reporters, which I'd expected after the reception I'd received at the courthouse. Maybe they just hadn't yet figured out where I was.

While finishing lunch, Rynar looked me in the eye and said, "Mister Drake, I am your guide," his English sounded better today. "Whats do you want to see."

I nodded and chewed on a bite of burger. I noticed Rynar averted his eyes whenever I took a bite out of the juicy meat. "You know, Rynar, I, of course, want to see Astrithon. But, I'd also like to learn your language."

Rynar chirped, and his ears pointed at me. "Kavreshen? You wants to learns it?" He said excitedly.

"Sure, why not?"

"'Tis very difficult for humans. You not have the pitch control."

"But surely there's a few things I could learn, no?"

"Maybe. I will help you."

We spent the next fifteen minutes practicing Kavreshen greetings. Rynar was right, it was difficult. Much of the meaning in words was communicated by the pitch of a sound. Words were like miniature songs, and I'd never been a good singer. But I managed to recognize "Hello" and "Goodbye" and respond accordingly.

Our plates were empty. "Okay, Rynar," I said. "I want you to give me a tour of the Human Quarter."

"No problem, this we do now!"

We paid for our food and left the diner.

The Zyrathis River roared alongside us, its muddy waters

swollen from weeks of relentless rain. It lapped hungrily at the edges of the Human Quarter like it wanted to swallow the whole place whole and be done with it. Somewhere upriver, I could hear the faint buzz of Dominion skiffs—alien boats, sleek and quiet. Out here, though, the river just stank of sewage and desperation.

"Kory Drake!" Rynar squeaked, throwing his arms wide as if unveiling some grand work of art. "Welcome to... the very Grand Human Quarter!"

The kavreni's long, wiry tail flicked dangerously close to a sludge puddle, but I ignored him and took in the chaos ahead. "Grand" wasn't the word I'd have chosen. A muddy, half-flooded street—jokingly called the "Refugee's Parade"—stretched out before us, packed with people and improvised carts. Rain trickled from tarpaulin roofs, plinking down like music from a broken instrument. A handful of kids splashed barefoot in the filthy water, their shrieks of laughter cutting through the hum of desperate voices bartering for everything under the gray sky.

"Home sweet home," I muttered.

"What is sweet about this?" Rynar chirped, cocking his oversized head. His massive ears twitched, rain streaming off their edges. "It smell more... like damp and cooked meat. No sweet. None at all."

I gave him a side-eye and didn't bother explaining sarcasm. Kavreni biology didn't seem to include a sarcasm detector—or taste buds, for that matter.

We trudged forward through the muck, skirting around a rickety cart stacked with salvaged Dominion batteries. I kept one hand close to my jacket pocket. The Human Quarter was full of people looking for an easy target, and I wasn't about to let someone slip a hand where it didn't belong. Around me, families huddled under sagging awnings, trading scraps of metal, cloth, and food. Real food

—vegetables and rations produced by the UHC hydroponics sheds—not the weird insect-and-spice slurry the kavrenis ate.

We were halfway down a hidden market alley—a mud-choked stretch of stalls where rain dripped through tarps, and the air reeked of spices, burned oil, and fish—when Rynar suddenly froze. His oversized ears flared forward like radar dishes, twitching eagerly as he sniffed the air.

"What?" I asked, already suspicious.

Rynar's squeaky voice rose in excitement. "Kyrrakh Vynnar!" He spun toward a food stall that looked as miserable as everything else in the Quarter. A kavreni vendor loomed behind the counter, coiling something shiny, oily, and pale into little wooden bowls. Steam rose off them in lazy curls, and the smell hit me like a slap in the face—salty, sour, and somehow fishy with a hint of algae left to rot in the sun.

"God, what is that smell?" I groaned, covering my nose with my sleeve.

"Deliciousness!" Rynar chirped, already bouncing up to the stall. "You will love it! It refreshes the spirit. Cleanses the soul."

"It smells like it cleanses sewers," I muttered, but Rynar wasn't listening.

He swiped his BioCred over the metal plate on the counter and grabbed a bowl of the steaming... whatever it was. The vendor handed it over with a proud nod, and Rynar turned back to me, grinning so wide I could see all his little teeth. "Look! Look how beautiful it is!"

I looked. It wasn't.

Inside the bowl, pale, rubbery coils sat glistening in their own oil, sprinkled with crushed green paste. The coils wobbled slightly when Rynar moved the bowl, as if they were alive and considering their options.

"Yeah, no," I said immediately, taking a step back.

Rynar's ears flattened in dramatic disappointment. "But why?"

"Because it looks like someone pulled it out of a clogged drainpipe. And because I like my insides the way they are—working."

"It is good for the insides!" he squeaked, holding the bowl under my nose. I caught another whiff of it—salt, brine, and something alarmingly chemical—and gagged.

"Rynar, I'm not eating whatever eel guts those are."

His ears popped up again. "Eel guts? No! It is entrails. Very different!"

"Oh, well, that changes everything," I deadpanned.

Rynar ignored my sarcasm and picked up one of the oily coils with his fingers. It squelched as he held it up, glistening like something that belonged in a biology lab. "See? See the shine? That is the brine. It means it is fresh!"

I held up both hands. "Hard pass."

"Try just one bite!" Rynar pleaded, shaking the coil for emphasis. "Humans like salty things, yes? This is very salty!"

"That's not salt, Rynar. That's regret."

He huffed in mock indignation, his ears twitching as he dropped the coil back into the bowl with a wet plop. "Yous humans. Always missing out on the best things in life."

"Yeah, well, we also don't keel over from eating your fermented sludge, so I'll take the loss."

Rynar sighed dramatically and cradled the bowl as if it were precious. "Fine. Mores for me. I will eats your share, Kory Drake. I will eats it all for yous."

"Knock yourself out," I said, turning to keep walking. Behind me, I heard him slurp loudly, followed by a contented squeak that I was almost certain was for my benefit.

"You do not knows what you are missing!" he called, his voice muffled through a mouthful of entrails. I felt my stomach lurch.

"Sounds like a great way to die, thanks," I said flatly. Kavreni food was off-limits—something about their biology made their food toxic to humans. And the same went the other way. I saw a kavreni try to drink human coffee and heard he spent two days twitching on a med table.

We moved deeper into the Quarter, past rows of slanting shanties made from scrap metal, plastic tarps, and whatever else could be hammered together into something vaguely house-shaped. Water streamed off every surface, forming grimy little rivers that ran through the streets and into gutters so clogged with debris they might as well not exist.

It smelled. God, it smelled. Wet metal, sweat, burnt oil, sewage—it all mingled into something sour and heavy that settled in the back of my throat.

Rynar inhaled deeply. "The smell is strong, yes?" He chirped happily. "But honest. Like the Quarter says, 'Here, we live! Here, we fight!'"

I shot him a look. "Is that supposed to make me feel better?"

He grinned at me, all sharp little teeth. "It should. You humans are very strange. You grow where nothing should grow." He gestured around us with one long arm. "Like weeds in stone."

We passed a filtration station, where a line of refugees stood hunched under the rain, each clutching a mismatched container—plastic bottles, old nutrient pouches, even rusted metal buckets. A few volunteers passed out clean water, their faces worn and hollow. Nearby, a gaggle of kids played in the flooded street, shrieking as they shoved each other into the mud. I stopped for a second, watching them. They didn't care about the rain, the hunger, the grime. Kids never did.

"Come!" Rynar tugged at my sleeve again, leading me into the River Market.

The market was chaos wrapped in noise and color. Vendors shouted prices from under mismatched plastic tarps that flapped wildly in the wind. Tables overflowed with whatever people could scavenge or barter: bundles of hydroponic greens, Dominion solar cells with wires dangling like severed nerves, boots made from repurposed kavreni material. A few traders had boats moored just off the muddy riverbank, crates stacked high with supplies brought in from god-knows-where.

Rynar danced ahead of me, chittering excitedly. "This is real living, yes? Humans sell. Humans trade. You make this place yours."

I ignored him, my eyes drawn to the far edge of the Quarter where the Earth Government-in-Exile loomed. The massive prefabricated structure sat on higher ground, its walls streaked with rain and rust. A tattered Earth flag hung limply at the entrance, half-forgotten in the downpour. Guards in mismatched uniforms—some Earth military, some barely more than rags—stood watch, rifles slung across their chests.

Beyond the river, the Dominion skyline glowed faintly through the mist. The Aetherian Spires stabbed upward into the clouds, their edges shimmering with bioluminescent light. These were the circle of towers I had used as landmarks the other day. High above, the Voidwalk hung like a halo, its lights dancing like stars brought to earth. From this side of the Zyrathis, it might as well have been another world entirely.

"They look at us from there," I said, almost to myself.

"The kavrenis?" Rynar's ears twitched. "Yes. They wonder what you are."

"What we are?"

He grinned again, a strange expression on his bat-like face. "You are survivors. This place, this Quarter—it is ugly, yes. But it grows. You grow."

I stared at him for a moment, then back at the muddy, crowded streets. The sound of the market carried on—people shouting, children laughing, water dripping. Rynar's words stuck with me, though. Ugly or not, this place was alive.

The Dominion might've given us this land, but we'd made it ours.

After several hours looking around, we ate lunch at a food stall that served both kavreni and human food. I paid for it, we ate, and I said, "Next, let's go visit the city. I'd like to see the Voidwalk."

With Rynar's help, I rented a ground car for the rest of the day. He claimed he was a competent driver licensed to drive on Astrithon's streets.

We headed north across the Zyrathis. I sat in the front passenger seat while Rynar drove. Despite the light rain falling, the friendly alien had his window open.

Occasionally, he would stick his head out and emit a burst of chirps as he echolocated vehicles and obstacles. Kavreni eyesight seemed really good, but obviously their echolocation added something they couldn't get from vision. Perhaps it was ranging information.

Our first stop was at a shop that traded in rare metals, where I hoped to sell my Gold Eagle coins for a decent amount. It was true that the Dominion had easy access to gold, which suppressed its price, but it was still valuable. After haggling with the owner for fifteen minutes and convincing him of the uniqueness of the coins, I was able to sell the six coins for 492 Civex, nearly doubling my bank balance.

Rynar drove us north toward the Aetherian Spires that rose out of the horizon like nine needles punching holes in the heavens.

The sky was overcast with dark monsoon clouds. As we approached the most southern Aetherian Spire, only the bottom 2,000 feet of the 5-mile-tall structure was visible below the clouds.

The Spire was streamlined against the prevailing winds and covered with a translucent glassy surface that seemed to glow from some inner light.

Rynar parked our car in a vast underground garage below the Spire. We entered a high-speed elevator large enough to host a party. On our way up, it stopped several times to take on people. Kavrenis and the occasional human or igna.

We arrived at the top 8 minutes later. Exiting the elevator, we entered a large observation deck. It opened onto a skywalk called the Voidwalk, an elevated walkway connecting the nine Aetherian Spires.

Walking out onto the Voidwalk, I realized it was made of dark glass so that I could see the clouds below us. It felt like I was walking on air.

Up here above the clouds, the sun's warm rays shone down on us. The air should have been cold and thin at this altitude, but it wasn't. I noticed a shimmering field of some kind wrapping around the Voidwalk and surmised that it must have been maintaining a healthy atmosphere for visitors.

The Voidwalk contained small shops, restaurants, and taverns at regular intervals, with open spaces between them to allow pedestrians to approach the railings and look out upon the city.

The scale of the engineering was mind-boggling. Just constructing one of the Spires would have been beyond the capabilities of Earth's best scientists and engineers. But to build nine of them and connect them with something like the Voidwalk was a feat all its own.

After spending a couple of hours touring the Voidwalk, we descended to our car and drove to the southeast of the ring of spires. Rynar parked the car, and we walked a few blocks until we reached a fence enclosing a large green space.

In the center of the fenced-off area was the giant golden tetrahedron I had seen during the approach of *Nira* into Astrithon. Called the Ignarion Palace, it was the personal residence of the Queen, Z373, here on Virelia.

Though her nominal permanent home was on the local sun, Ignisara, she spent most of her time in Astrithon because it was the capital of the Collective Dominion.

I gazed across the hundreds of yards of gardens separating us from the shining palace. I wondered if Zeta was in there right at that moment.

Did she ever think of me?

Would she ever look past my attack on Ban'ach and understand my intent?

Would I ever see her again?

We weren't allowed on the palace grounds, but we walked the palace perimeter for an hour. I observed frequent aircar traffic coming and going from the building.

Zeta's home was so close but might as well have been in

another galaxy. There was no approaching it. And even if I did get inside, who's to say that she would even talk to me? I was under a Dominion indictment.

After the palace, we drove around for several more hours and visited other well-known places in Astrithon. The Celestial Conclave, where most of the Dominion executive offices were located and communicated with the Supreme Council.

The Undercore, a vast network of underground tunnels and caverns hidden below the city where most of its industry was located. Populated almost exclusively by dark-loving kavrenis, it was a dim, confining space nominally ruled by the queen but, in fact, controlled by crime lords and labor unions.

The Skyflow Gardens, which were the floating bubbles of gardens I had observed when arriving at Astrithon. We didn't have an aircar, so we didn't actually visit any of the flying gardens, but we stopped and observed one that was at a particularly low altitude. I tried not to imagine the disaster that would occur if that mass of millions of tons of stone, water, and vegetation suddenly came crashing down onto a city neighborhood.

As the sun was beginning to set, Rynar drove me back to my hotel room. I paid him for the day and agreed to meet him again the next day.

After a quick shower, I was ready for dinner. I left the hotel and walked toward the Midnight Plate.

11

I walked into the diner, the streetlights outside casting their glow across the entrance while the interior illumination tiles threw soft shadows over the checkered floor. The booths looked improvised as if thrown together with whatever materials had been at hand. It was a reflection of the Human Quarter itself—functional, rough-edged, and unpolished. But the air smelled like coffee and grilled meat, rich and inviting. The place exuded a humble charm, as though it carried the weight of countless conversations and satisfied appetites, despite being no older than the eighteen months since humanity had arrived in Astrithon.

I spotted her immediately. The German woman—my siren. She was seated in a corner booth, a steaming cup of coffee in front of her, her back to the wall so she could watch the door. She pretended not to notice me, her gaze fixed on her cup, but I caught the subtle tension in her posture. She'd seen me.

I made my way between the booths, nodding briefly at the server and ignoring the other customers, my focus locked on the enigmatic woman. As I reached her booth, she glanced up. Her honey-colored hair was pulled back into a practical braid that fell over her shoulder, and her piercing blue eyes locked onto mine with an intensity that stole my breath.

"I found you," I said with a smile, stopping beside her table.

She shrugged, glancing at her almost-empty cup. "I didn't lie to you," she replied simply.

"Can I sit?" I asked, gesturing to the seat across from her.

She nodded. "Nobody's using it."

I slid into the booth just as the server approached. I ordered a coffee and gestured for a refill for the woman I hoped would soon be more than a fleeting acquaintance.

When the server left, I folded my hands on the table and studied her. There was something in her expression—a quiet expectation mingled with shadows, as though she carried a burden she wouldn't yet name. "I never did get your name," I said, breaking the silence.

"You never asked," she replied with a slight shrug. Her voice was calm, unhurried. She wore a green saree over a yellow blouse, simple yet elegant. She wasn't wearing any makeup—not that she needed it. Her flawless skin, with a natural flush to her lips and cheeks, carried its own effortless beauty.

I chuckled lightly. "Let's fix that." I extended my hand across the table. "I'm Kory Drake."

She studied my hand for a beat before taking it. Her grip was firm, her skin warm, her long fingers easily enveloping my own.

"And you are?" I prompted, starting to feel I might have to coax the answer out of her.

A glimmer of amusement lit up her eyes. "Sofia Kohl."

I nodded, holding her gaze as she released my hand. "Nice to meet you, Sofia."

The corners of her mouth curled into the faintest smile, but her silence lingered, leaving me to wonder what was going on behind those captivating eyes.

The server returned, interrupting the moment as she set down a fresh mug for me and refilled both of our cups. I thanked her, then turned my attention back to Sofia as the aroma of coffee curled around us like an invitation to keep talking. But still, she said nothing. Whatever Sofia was, she wasn't one to fill silences easily. I didn't mind—there was something intriguing about earning every word she spoke.

I watched as Sofia dropped a sugar cube into her coffee, followed by a dollop of cream. She stirred with a measured rhythm, her spoon clicking softly against the mug. As she glanced up at me, I caught a flicker of curiosity in her blue eyes.

"You find a place to stay?" she asked casually.

"Yeah, a spot just up the street," I replied, keeping it vague. I might have been intrigued by her, but trust was another matter entirely. "Listen, I owe you. First, for saving me from that truck that almost turned me into a street pancake, and second, for dealing with the guy who was tailing me."

Her left eyebrow arched in a perfect curve. "What guy?" she asked, her face the picture of innocence.

I couldn't help but grin, a chuckle slipping out. "Oh, come on. You know exactly who I'm talking about—the guy you so conveniently body-checked into a shop display right after you walked away."

Her expression didn't change, but there was the faintest hint of amusement in her voice as she replied, "How rude of me." She took a slow sip of her coffee, as if the subject was hardly worth her time.

I shook my head, unable to hold back a laugh. "Not rude at all. That guy had been following me for over an hour. I couldn't shake him. No idea who he was or what he wanted, but after your little... tumble with him, I managed to lose him."

Her eyes narrowed ever so slightly. "Don't be crude."

I raised both hands in surrender. "No, no, I didn't mean it like that. Look, it's obvious you know how to handle yourself."

She tilted her head, her gaze sharpening. "And where's that brilliant deduction come from?"

I let out a sigh and gestured broadly. "The way you move, the way you handled that guy. You're not just strong —you're precise. It's like you've done this before. You a soldier?" I asked, the thought solidifying in my mind.

She didn't answer right away. Instead, she set her mug down gently, her fingers lingering on the handle. There was something about her—an edge that spoke of training and experience, a sharpness in how her eyes constantly scanned the room. I was certain I was right, but she wasn't the kind of person to give anything away for free.

She dropped her hands into her lap and looked away, her gaze distant. "What do you want, Mister Drake?"

"It's Kory, Sofia," I said, feeling an awkward knot tightening in my stomach. What did I want? The truth was simple—I wanted to get to know her. But admitting that out loud suddenly felt too raw, too personal. "I want to buy you dinner. How about it? You hungry?"

A small, knowing smile tugged at one corner of her lips as she turned her head back to meet my eyes. Her expression softened, almost as if she saw through me. "Maybe some other time, Kory. I need to be going."

"Another coffee, then?" I tried, grasping for anything to keep her there just a little longer.

She shook her head, her smile lingering but faint.

"Listen, you seem to know your way around this city," I said, shifting tactics.

She tilted her head, her lips curling into something closer to a smirk. "You're quick with these assumptions," she replied, her voice carrying a faint edge of amusement. "Quite the snooper, aren't you?"

I held a hand to my chest as if she'd wounded me. "I only ask with the best intentions, trust me. I'm alone in this city, under criminal indictment, and all my friends are light-years away. You better believe I'm trying to figure things out. Sofia, whether you meant to or not, you've become part of the picture I'm trying to piece together. Forgive me if I'm grasping at straws, but I'm just trying to fill in the gaps. I don't mean any harm."

She gazed at me for a long moment, her eyes searching mine as if measuring my sincerity. Then, almost abruptly, she tilted her head back and downed the last of her coffee in one smooth motion, like she was finishing a dare. "To answer your question, yes, I've seen a lot of the city. And it'll eat you alive if you're not careful, Kory. Watch your steps and be careful of your friends."

She began gathering her things, and I felt panic rising. I was about to lose her, just like that. "Should I be careful with you?" I asked, my voice softer than I intended.

She stood, her tall, lithe frame casting a shadow over the table. Her face, framed by her honey-blonde hair, caught the light like a glow, her features unexpectedly vulnerable for just a second. Her cheeks flushed, and her eyes seemed to glisten. "Hardly," she said in a near whisper, her voice catching just enough to make me wonder what she was thinking.

She reached out and patted my folded hands, her touch brief but electric. A light floral scent wafted from her hair, mingling with the coffee still on her breath. "Take care of yourself, Kory," she said, her face just a few inches from mine, before turning and walking away.

"Maybe I'll catch you again," I called after her. "I still owe you a meal."

She raised a hand in farewell, not looking back. And then she was gone.

The server appeared at my table moments later, snapping me out of my thoughts. "Need anything else?" she asked.

I ordered steak and fries, my appetite suddenly roaring back to life now that the conversation was over.

As I waited for my food, I turned my thoughts over like a puzzle, each piece sharper in the quiet aftermath of her departure. Sofia Kohl. I hadn't gotten much from her—just her name and the barest glimpse of who she might be. But it wasn't distrust that held her back; it was something else entirely. It almost felt like she was trying to protect me. From what, I had no idea.

I glanced at the empty seat across from me, her absence lingering like a shadow. Whatever it was she wasn't saying, I had a feeling it wouldn't be long before I found out.

12

Dinner finished, I stepped out of the diner and onto the street, greeted by the cool embrace of the night. Most of the humans who had filled the streets during the day had retreated indoors, replaced by kavrenis conducting their nocturnal business. The Human Quarter was never quiet—one world waking as the other slept, each threading its own rhythm into the same cityscape.

My hotel was nearby, but the idea of confining myself to my room felt stifling. My stomach full and my thoughts restless, I decided to stretch my legs. Turning at an unfamiliar intersection, I wandered into a part of the neighborhood I hadn't yet explored.

Passing an empty lot, I saw a group of kavreni children playing under the faint glow of streetlights. Their large ears flopped as they chased each other, their high-pitched squeals carrying a purity untouched by the burdens of their surroundings. Nearby, a pair of kavoras sat on a bench, chatting quietly while keeping a watchful eye on the children.

Crossing the street, dodging a slow-moving tram, I caught the fruity, sweet aroma wafting from the entrance of a kavreni bar. The place was packed, the chatter and laughter spilling out onto the sidewalk. The air smelled distinctly of their preferred drink: methanol. Harmless to them, fatally toxic to me. A stark reminder of how different our worlds were, even when they overlapped.

I reached a quieter stretch of sidewalk, empty and dimly lit. The buzz of activity faded, replaced by the low hum of distant vehicles and the occasional chirping of night creatures. I decided I'd walked far enough and started to consider heading back to the hotel.

That's when I heard it—the squeak of tires and the low thrum of an electric motor braking hard behind me.

I glanced over my shoulder, my stomach clenching. A dark van veered off the street, coming to an abrupt stop next to me. Too close.

What the hell?

My instincts screamed at me. Something was wrong. I jumped to the side just as the side door slid open with a metallic clatter.

A pair of long, sinewy kavreni arms shot out, grabbing my jacket and fumbling for my arm. Their grip was strong but clumsy.

Adrenaline surged through me. I swung my arms wide, then brought them down hard onto the kavreni's, breaking their hold.

Inside the van, chaos erupted. High-pitched chirps and guttural barks filled the air. A human male's voice cut through the noise, sharp and furious. "Idiots! Grab him!"

My heart pounded as I turned and bolted back the way I'd come, sprinting down the street as fast as my legs would carry me. My breath came in sharp bursts, the world around me a blur of shadow and light.

The pounding of feet echoed behind me, growing louder. A quick glance over my shoulder revealed three figures—two kavors and a man—closing in. My chest tightened, adrenaline spiking.

I pushed harder, my feet slamming against the pavement, propelling me forward. I scanned the street, desperate for a building, a door, anywhere I could duck into and lose them. But nothing presented itself, and I wasn't about to lead them back to my hotel. That was the only place I could rest, my only sanctuary. I couldn't afford to blow it.

I made a sharp turn at the next alley, hoping it would cut through to another street. The narrow path was lined with dumpsters and dimly lit by a single flickering light above. My breaths came in short, ragged bursts, each one louder than the silence of the alley.

The sound of feet faded behind me—except for one pair. Just one. Had I lost the others?

I was twenty feet from the next street when something heavy slammed into me from behind. The impact drove me to the ground, the pavement scraping my left palm raw. A sharp sting ran up my shin as something sliced through the skin.

Before I could react, a kavor was on me, wrapping his spindly limbs around my torso in a crushing grip. His sinewy arms coiled like steel cables, and his tail arched back, poised to strike. In the dim alley shadows, I could just make out the glint of the stinger aimed right at me.

Instinct kicked in. I shot my arm up, breaking the hold on one side, then twisted hard to my left. The kavor's tail struck down but missed, hitting the ground with a sharp thud. Wasting no time, I balled my free fist and brought it down on the tip of his tail with every ounce of strength I had.

A piercing scream erupted from the kavor, his grip loosening enough for me to shove him away. I scrambled to my feet, ignoring the burning pain in my hand and shin, and delivered a swift kick to his chest. His light, wiry frame flew backward several feet, colliding with a pile of trash bags.

I staggered toward the alley's exit, limping, blood dripping from my hand and leg. Just as I reached the end, two silhouettes appeared, blocking my way—a kavor and the man.

"Got him!" the man barked, his voice sharp and triumphant.

They'd outflanked me. I cursed under my breath, my mind racing for options. Turning back, I tried to run deeper into the alley, but the kavor bounded after me, his powerful legs launching him twenty feet in a single leap.

I swung my elbow in desperation, but he dodged with an unsettling, fluid agility that reminded me just how alien he was. My attack threw me off balance, and when I recovered, I saw the gleam of a blade in the man's hand as he advanced toward me with the deliberate stance of a seasoned fighter.

At least he doesn't have a gun, I thought bitterly.

"What do you want?!" I shouted, my voice echoing in the narrow space.

The man smirked, his expression illuminated briefly by a shaft of light from a nearby window. His pale face was marred by a deep scar running from his temple to his jaw. Bald, stocky, and built like a bull, he carried himself with the confidence of someone who had been in too many fights —and won most of them.

"Just a chat with my boss," he said, his tone almost casual, but his eyes gleamed with menace.

I kept walking backward, careful not to trip on the uneven ground. My mind raced, analyzing the situation: two kavors and one human. The kavrenis were fast, agile, and had tails that could sting, but they weren't particularly strong. The human, though… he was the real threat.

This wasn't going to end well. I had to think fast.

I didn't believe Scarface for a second. If this was just a "chat," why was he waving a knife at me?

The second kavor had recovered from his failed leap and was now circling around behind me. The first one—the one whose tail I'd throttled—lay on the pavement, moaning softly. His condition gave me no comfort; I was still outnumbered, and Scarface's blade gleamed menacingly in the dim light.

Scarface lunged, leading with the knife, while the second kavor leaped again, his tail arcing toward me.

Instinct took over. I dropped to the ground, rolling into a reverse somersault, then sprang to my feet, launching into another sprint down the alley.

The pounding of feet behind me was relentless.

Here we go again.

Scarface shouted something, his voice echoing off the walls, but I couldn't make out the words. A sharp, high-pitched chirp followed—a signal, no doubt. The second kavor was closing in fast.

I glanced over my shoulder just in time to see his tail strike. The stinger punched through my jacket, shirt, and skin, injecting a payload of venom into the muscle just behind my left shoulder.

Fire erupted under my skin, radiating outward like molten metal coursing through my veins. I knew the venom would soon numb the area, but for now, I had a brief window of control—and I intended to use it.

Ignoring the searing pain, I whipped around, grabbing the kavor before he could retract his tail. His stinger was still stuck in me, and I used it to yank him closer.

His wide, bat-like eyes widened in surprise. He clearly hadn't expected resistance.

I pulled him into a crushing bear hug, squeezing with every ounce of strength I had. His wiry frame struggled against mine, but his long limbs were no match for my sheer size and muscle.

His mouth opened in a choking gasp.

I reared back and smashed my forehead into his face. Once. Twice.

Something cracked. His nose, I thought grimly. His body sagged, but he kept thrashing, his claws raking at my jacket.

Scarface was closing in, his blade reflecting faint streaks of light as he advanced. I had seconds—if that.

"Fine," I muttered through clenched teeth. "Let's finish this."

I shifted my weight, pinning the kavor's spindly feet under my own. With a burst of strength, I tightened my arms around him like a vice and twisted my torso with all the force I could muster.

There was a sickening crack, like a branch snapping in half. The kavor's head lolled limply to one side, his body going slack in my arms.

I let go, and he crumpled to the ground, lifeless.

Scarface charged at me, knife leading the way. My left shoulder was already numb, dead weight dragging down my balance. The venom's effects were spreading fast into my back and chest, making me feel like I might collapse at any second. If that happened, I was as good as dead.

He dropped his head like a bull, charging full tilt.

Poor knife-fighting technique. I thanked Clemen Busto for all those hours sparring with him.

Lucky for me, Scarface was left-handed, and I was right. With my good arm, I swatted the knife aside and dipped my useless shoulder to deflect his momentum. He hit me hard—like a battering ram—but I outweighed him by at least fifty pounds. He rebounded off me like a cannonball ricocheting off a wall, stumbling to the ground.

His knife slipped from his grasp and clattered into the shadows.

I knew if he got back up, I'd be done. My upper body was failing fast, and I had no strength left to grapple. So I did the only thing I could—I rushed him and aimed a brutal kick at his face.

That was my mistake.

I overcommitted, putting too much force into it. He twisted to the side, dodging the kick, and wrapped his arm around my leg. With a grunt of effort, he yanked, pulling me off balance. My back hit the pavement hard, the air blasting out of my lungs.

"Okay, big guy," he spat, still gasping from the earlier impact. "Now you've pissed me off!"

He swung a punch straight into my left side. Luckily for me, the entire area was numb—I felt nothing.

Thinking fast, I rolled into him, using my legs to pivot and my larger mass to pin him beneath me. It was a sloppy maneuver, but it worked—briefly.

He grunted and punched me from behind, his fist hammering the side of my head. The first strike blurred my vision; the second sent stars shooting across my field of view.

Desperate, I threw my head backward, aiming for his

face. He saw it coming and shifted, dodging just enough to avoid impact.

"They never said I had to take you alive!" he snarled, his rancid breath hot against my cheek.

He shoved me hard, rolling me onto my side. My good arm got pinned beneath my weight, and my useless left arm dangled, numb and unresponsive. I tried to kick, a desperate scissor motion, but he was ready for it this time, dodging my legs with ease.

Now he was on top of me.

His fist came down, smashing into the side of my skull again and again. He wasn't aiming for my face—maybe he wanted me conscious, or maybe he just liked drawing out the pain. Either way, the hits were taking their toll. My vision wavered, and my thoughts slowed.

"STOP ALREADY!" he screamed, his face contorted, veins bulging.

I knew I was finished. But if this was it, I wasn't going quietly.

I smiled up at him, blood dripping from my lip. Then I spat, the bloody saliva landing square on his face.

Stunned, he froze for a moment before his expression twisted into pure rage. "You little—"

The shadows behind Scarface shifted unnaturally, warping like liquid smoke. One of them coiled and lashed out like a striking cobra, landing a deep, resonant thunk against the back of his neck.

Scarface crumpled instantly, collapsing to the pavement beside me, his knife clattering away into the darkness.

The shadows moved again, reshaping themselves into a figure—a familiar one. Long hair framed the silhouette, and a robe billowed faintly as the figure stepped into the dim light. My foggy vision struggled to focus, but I saw enough to make out the shape of a woman.

"Kory!" The voice was sharp, commanding—and unmistakable.

Sofia.

She knelt beside me, her hands moving quickly over my body, brushing debris and checking for injuries. "Are you hurt?" she asked, her voice low but urgent.

I tried to respond, but my tongue felt thick, and the words came out as a slurred mess. "The batty… got me… with his tail. Can't feel… left side… chest or arm…"

Her hands froze for a split second before she cursed under her breath. "*Shysuh!* Let's get you out of here before more of them show up."

She hooked her arms under my shoulders and heaved, grunting with effort as she levered me into a sitting position.

"I… don't know if I can walk," I muttered. "He hit my head."

"*Verdammt,*" she hissed, her voice tight with frustration. "Your hotel is close. Let's go. Up to your feet!"

"How do you—" I stopped myself mid-question, realizing that she somehow knew exactly where I was staying. But before I could press her, she cut me off.

"Shut up. *Gott helfe mir,* you're bloody heavy!" Despite her complaints, she managed to hoist me up.

I slung my good arm across her shoulders, leaning heavily on her as we stumbled out of the alley. My legs felt like they belonged to someone else—uncooperative and leaden. Sofia's smaller frame bore most of my weight, her strength far greater than her slender build suggested.

We passed a few kavrenis on the street, their oversized ears swiveling toward us, their eyes glinting with curiosity. To them, I probably looked like a drunk being escorted home by a very patient girlfriend. If only it were that simple.

Sofia's presence, however, was impossible to ignore. Her firm, steady body against mine was warm, her scent a mix of soap and something faintly musky. Her loose hair tickled my nose whenever I turned my head toward her.

I shook the thought away, jarring my already battered brain. Seriously? A gang of armed thugs had just jumped me, and this was what my mind chose to focus on. Maybe Scarface had knocked a screw loose.

Sofia guided me back to my hotel without needing directions, confirming that she did, in fact, know where I lived. When we reached the door to my room, she grabbed my limp left wrist, held my BioCred to the scanner, and waited for the panel to flash green with a satisfying clack.

Inside, she helped me onto the narrow bed. Her hands were firm but gentle as she eased me down.

Her icy blue eyes locked onto mine, sharp with concern, as she retrieved a small penlight from her pocket. She shone it into my pupils, muttering something in rapid-fire German. "*Shysuh, doo hahst eyenuh gehheemerschootehroong*... Don't go to sleep."

But sleep was already dragging me under. Her voice, her presence—it all faded into a soft blur, the last thing I remembered being the worried intensity in her gaze.

13

I woke to somebody knocking on my door.

"Misters Drakes, ares you awakes?" came Rynar's goofy high-pitched voice through the door. He knocked again.

"Just a second. I'm coming."

I glanced around the room, searching for Sofia, but it was clear—I was alone.

For a moment, I wondered if everything that had happened was just a bad dream. That comforting thought was obliterated the second I tried to stand. A bolt of pain shot through my head like a lightning strike, leaving me reeling.

Groaning, I sank back down to the edge of the bed, gripping the mattress as nausea churned in my stomach. Every nerve felt frayed, and the room tilted slightly as I tried to steady myself. This was no dream—unfortunately, it was all too real.

"*Yoo* hoo!" Rynar again called. "Rynar gots something for yous!"

I forced myself to my feet, every step feeling like my

skull was caught in a vice. Trudging to the door, I leaned heavily against the frame before pulling it open.

Standing there was Rynar, a wide, triumphant grin plastered across his face as he held up a sack like he'd just hit the jackpot.

I sighed and stepped aside, waving him in. "Come on, Rynar. What's got you so excited?"

"Misters Drakes, you no look good," Rynar said, shaking his head.

"Rynar, I told you to call me Kory."

"Yesses. Misses Kohl tells me what happens to yous last night."

I turned my head to him. "You talked to Sofia?"

"She calls me an hour ago and tells me to come to you and brings breakfast." He held up his hand and shook the sack. "I gots your favorite! Bacon and egg breakfast burrito with coffee!"

I groaned and pointed to the side table. "Just set it there. I'll eat it later."

I sat on my bed and waved Rynar over to the chair.

He shook his head. "Nopes. Misses Kohl tells me not to stay long. She say you have... uh, what the word... *concussion*. She stay up all night with you."

"Really?"

"Indeedy, yesses."

"And how do you know her, Rynar? Sofia?"

He smiled. "I know her long time."

"*What* do you know about her?" I probed, looking for more info.

"She my friend, but I not knows muches about her. She very... uh... private."

I wished she hadn't left my room before I could grill her. That's twice now that she'd saved my life and three times she'd helped me. Something with her wasn't adding up. She knew where my hotel room was. She'd laid Scarface out on the ground with one strike last night—and how had she even known that I was in trouble?

Sofia was an enigma. Maybe she was my *lucky* German siren.

"Yous not look well," Rynar said. "I goes now, but comes back later with somes lunch."

"Thanks Rynar. Sorry, I'm not up to going out today, but I'll still pay you for the day."

He shook his head. "Noes, not necessary. Today, I not guide. Today, I friend. Tomorrow, I bees guide again."

His words touched me deeply, and I had to fight back tears for a moment. I'd felt so alone coming to this planet. I'd only been here for a few days, but I'd already met three great people, and one of them was a kavor.

"Thanks, Rynar," and I meant it. "You're a pal."

He let himself out, and I lay on my bed, thinking.

What I needed right now was a way to escape the pounding in my head. The left side of my body had finally stopped being numb, but it didn't feel like much of an improvement. A massive welt had formed where the kavor's stinger had jabbed me, the bruising a sickly mix of black and yellow. My body ached, and my mind felt scrambled, yet I couldn't let myself sit idle. Not when an obvious threat loomed out there, and here I was—stationary, vulnerable, practically inviting them to come back and finish the job. I had to think.

But thinking clearly wasn't happening in this state.

I needed to find clarity, to shake free of the pain and confusion. There was only one place I knew where I could escape my broken body for a while. I closed my eyes, slowed my breathing, and focused inward. Gradually, I allowed myself to slip into a meditative state, feeling my consciousness untether from the aches and bruises of the material world.

I reached out and projected my mind into the Syderealium—a place where the limitations of my physical self could no longer hold me back. Here, I could breathe without pain, think without fog, and maybe even find the answers I needed.

In what felt like the blink of an eye, my consciousness shifted out of the physical plane and into the local Syderealium. The transition was seamless, like stepping through a doorway into another world.

My glyphshade floated above a vast, shimmering globe teeming with millions of smaller glyphshades, their movements chaotic and mesmerizing. They flickered like fireflies, smaller and dimmer than my own, a reminder of the multitudes who shared this realm.

I instinctively moved across dimensions, gliding to a quieter, more serene part of the Syderealium, far from the noisy vibrations of the material plane. I didn't consciously decide to go there; it just happened. Zeta had once explained that this was a hallmark of being flairsparked—the innate ability to navigate the Syderealium without needing to think about it.

The pain that had wracked my head and body vanished, slipping away like a distant memory. My physical senses became external—acknowledged as distant facts, no longer shackling my mind. For the first time in hours, clarity surged through me, untainted by the fuzziness of a concussion. My thoughts sharpened, and I began to analyze my situation with precision.

I listed the facts:

1. Someone was actively searching for me.

2. That someone clearly intended harm.

3. I had been followed—likely every time I left my hotel room.

4. Sofia Kohl had been among those watching me.

5. Sofia, however, had intervened to protect me, indicating friendly intentions.

6. I was under indictment for sydereal crimes, awaiting my precedium hearing.

7. The tracking device on my wrist allowed the authorities to monitor my location at all times.

I paused on that last point. Was the wrist tracker being used to leak my location? Was there a breach in the judiciary? The idea chilled me, but it couldn't be discounted.

I continued my assessment:

8. I had no job, no real resources, and little understanding of how the Human Quarter functioned.

9. My current hotel room was far too obvious a residence—an easy target for anyone with bad intentions.

If the judiciary's tracker wasn't the source of the leak, my enemies must have some other way of locating me. Either way, staying here wasn't an option. I needed to relocate—find somewhere less predictable, less exposed. The question was where and who I could trust to help me make the move.

My thoughts were interrupted by a disruption in my sydereal space. A bulge appeared in the walls of my bubble, pushing inward.

A vertical line appeared in the middle of the bulge in my bubble, then widened into a doorway.

I prepared to end my projection, feeling a surge of unease.

A large and strikingly intricate glyphshade entered my bubble. Its movements were slow and deliberate, pausing as if to take my measure. The glyphshade radiated a beautiful and deeply unsettling presence, its energlyphs swirling with a hypnotic complexity.

"May I approach?" the voice said, rich and resonant. There was something hauntingly familiar about it, though I couldn't place it.

"Who are you?" I asked, bracing myself.

"We've already met, in a manner of speaking, though we've not been formally introduced," the glyphshade replied. "I am Arctis."

I gasped, unable to mask my shock. "The Glyphspeaker?"

He dismissed my reaction with a subtle shrug of his energlyphs. "At your indictal, yes. I've been waiting for you to make an appearance here in the Sydereallium."

Arctis. His name alone carried weight. He was a dead igna who had achieved a form of immortality by maintaining the coherence of his glyphshade within the Sydereallium. While my glyphshade reflected my consciousness tethered to a living body, his represented a mind unmoored by the constraints of flesh.

As a member of the Dominion Supreme Council—a Glyphspeaker—Arctis wielded extraordinary authority, counterbalancing the powers of the sovereign. The Dominion's constitutional monarchy was unique, with its upper legislative house composed of glyphshades of deceased igna. Imagine an Earth government where the spirits of the dead participated in public life. Fascinating in theory, though I wasn't sure it was entirely wise.

Yet here he was—a figure of immense age and influence—drawn to me for reasons I couldn't begin to fathom.

"What do you want with me?" I asked, doing my best to keep my voice steady.

Arctis's glyphshade shifted, his energlyphs swirling with a subtle but unnerving grace. "You, Kory Drake, are more interesting than you know."

"I appreciate your defense of me at the hearing," I said. "But, again, what do you want?"

Glyphshades did not express body language, at least none that I'd been able to detect. But it was easy to read emotions because they were emitted from the energlyphs like vapor. Right now I sensed curiosity and intrigue from Arctis.

"In all honesty, I am fascinated by you. A human flairsparked with unequaled sydereal talents. As I said at your hearing, I believe you have been unfairly treated by my government and singled out for punishment. I don't want the life of a young human like yourself be destroyed when you are still maturing and hold so much promise."

"Thank you." I was suspicious of Arctis's motives. Why this interest in me? Surely, he was a busy person with better things to do than obsess over my life. He was a politician, and an uncorrupt politician was an oxymoron. But he was also powerful, and I needed help. Maybe he could give me that.

"The judicial has me in a bind," I admitted. "I never intended to destabilize the Sydereal ium. All I was trying to do was defend myself from Ban'ach, a Soul Ravager. And the contact I had with Pyrakos was not my doing. A chance encounter. I barely escaped with my life."

Arctis's energlyphs pulsed with light. "I believe you. Somebody with your talents should not be punished for their good intentions, even if you did something dangerous. The queen should be nurturing you. She is a good igna. But she has advisers and elements of the government constantly talking in her ears, and many of them are opposed to you."

"Why? I've done nothing to them. I've fought the Kergans for them. I am a loyal friend to the princess, Zeta."

"Some do not see that. Qut, the prosecutor on your case, is highly placed in the judiciary and has made it clear he intends to make an example of you. He has painted you as a potentially corrupting influence on Zeta. In the queen's eyes, prosecuting you is necessary to protect her daughter, both physically and her reputation."

"What am I going to do?"

A floor began forming below our glyphshades, then walls and a ceiling. They appeared to be made of finely hewn pink granite. A fountain appeared in the middle, shooting blue-tinted water out of flowers. The construction was not done by me, so it must have been Arctis's doing.

"How are you doing this?" I asked, distracted.

"Ah? You have not learned to manipulate the Syderealium?"

"No, I didn't even know this was possible."

"Who trained you?"

"Zeta, though we had little time to do it. And that was all focused on teaching me how to defend myself from sydereal assaults."

"Well, I understand, then. Zeta is just like you, a novice to the Syderealium."

Arctis drew closer to me. "Kory, I have a proposal to make you."

"I'm listening."

"I will tutor you in the Syderealium and some of its secrets. In return, I would appreciate your support for my cause."

"Your cause?"

"Yes," Arctis said, drawing out the word. "I lead a faction in the Supreme Council who are opposed to Qut and others of his ilk and the undue influence they have on the queen. He is a corrupt igna who will do anything if it means more power in his hands."

"Like what?"

"Just take my word for it. His pursuit of your prosecution is not based in seeing that justice is applied to your case, but as a means to demonstrate he is willing to harshly punish alien criminals."

"Why does he want to do that?"

"There are segments of Dominion society who do not like the influence that new alien species have on the government. You humans are of special note. These people disagree with our support of your war with the Kergan Empire, seeing it as a distraction. Obviously, they'd like to exploit your trial as a way to prove that humans are dangerous and our relationship with you all is unhealthy for the Dominion."

"He's pandering to them? Is that it?"

"Indeed, for the sake of maintaining his appointment as Chief Prosecutor."

"You want me to oppose him."

"Aye."

"That's easy. I'm already doing it as part of my defense."

"You are correct, but I want you to be more vocal about it."

"What do you mean?"

"I want you to speak out in the news outlets. Let the Dominion public know about how you've been treated. Give them the true story behind what happened."

I thought about the risk of doing something like that. "But, Arctis, that could incriminate me in the trial. They could use my statements against me."

"It is a risk, but you will be forced to testify, regardless.

Why not get your words out in front of everybody now, while it can do some good? Put pressure on Qut and the queen?"

"The judge is going to force me to be a witness?"

"Yes. Does that surprise you?"

"It does. In my nation, a citizen has a right to silence to protect themselves from self-incrimination."

"Truly?" I tried to nod my non-existent head, but my affirmation still came across in my emotions. "How interesting. Well, that's not how we do things. So, why not get your story in front of the public so it can do some good for you and for me?"

"I see."

"And I will tutor you in the Syderealium and, of course, will continue to aid your defense in whatever way I can."

"This seems very generous of you."

"Thank you." He emitted triumphant pride. I wondered what he was really after. But he was also powerful, and I needed his help, even if I didn't trust him.

"I accept," I said.

"Excellent! Shall we discuss the Syderealium?"

"Yes, please!"

We spent the next couple of hours discussing the fundamental principles of using consciousness to manipulate the fabric of the Syderealium.

By the end, Arctis had taught me how to fabricate geometric shapes and suspend them in my little pocket of the Syderealium—a personal space I had unknowingly constructed from a sliver of dimensions. It was, in essence, my own miniature universe.

As a flairsparked, I had the ability to use my willpower to maintain these objects even when I wasn't present. The realization was both empowering and daunting; the responsibility to manage a fragment of reality was no small thing.

I thanked Arctis for his guidance and agreed to pursue opportunities to be interviewed by news reporters, ensuring that my story—and the truth—reached the right ears. We strategized how best to frame my narrative within the larger political challenges he faced. Being involved in such high-stakes maneuvering was strange, but if it helped, I was willing to play my part.

When I exited the projection, I felt a noticeable improvement. My headache had faded, and my body felt like it had finally been given the chance to rest and recuperate.

Glancing at my dot, I noticed a message waiting for me. It was from a Colonel Mariyam Patil of the UHC Armada. The subject? An official summons to "performance counseling."

That didn't sound promising.

Although Colonel Patil wasn't in my chain of command—at least as far as I knew—I wasn't about to ignore her message. I noted the appointment time: three hours away. I sent a quick confirmation, then headed down the hall of the hotel to use the communal shower.

After that, I planned to grab lunch and figure out how to navigate my way to the UHC Armada offices. Whatever this "performance counseling" was, I had a feeling it wouldn't be a casual chat.

14

I dressed in my best clothes—which weren't much. I had never been issued a dress uniform, only a ship working uniform. It would have to do.

At the Midnight Plate, I looked for Sofia but didn't spot her, and I didn't have time to wait around to find her. But I wanted to talk to the woman. I needed to know who she was and why she was interested in me. And when I learned the reason why, I was certain it was going to be anything but personal. She had an agenda of some kind. Normal people didn't risk their lives like she had for complete strangers.

From the diner, I hired a taxi to drive me to the center of the Human Quarter, where the UHC government-in-exile buildings were located, including the office of Colonel Patil.

I was an hour early but didn't know the way and wanted to ensure I arrived on time. The location was only a few miles away, and I could have walked, but I didn't want to arrive sweaty with the monsoon humidity and heat.

The office building was a small one-story structure with

a wooden sign on the outside reading: "UHC Armada Training Command Astrithon."

Interesting.

While waiting for my appointment, I found a shaded spot outside and browsed my dot. Using the Dominion's internet—remarkably similar to Earth's, but with some alien quirks—I searched for reporters in the Human Quarter. Thankfully, my dot's translation feature converted most pages into readable English.

I focused on news sites covering humanity and, unsurprisingly, got plenty of results. Despite Earth's status as a backwater single-planet species under Kergan occupation, the Dominion's media seemed fascinated by our war with the Kergans.

I narrowed my search to news organizations with offices in Astrithon, the Dominion capital. That left me with a couple of dozen options, including some familiar names from Earth. Apparently, several well-known Earth-based outlets had followed their governments into exile. BBC, ABC, Fox, NPR, CGTN, and RT all had a presence here.

I drafted emails to BBC, ABC, and Fox. I introduced myself, explaining who I was and offering to share my story. I kept it concise but included my contact information before signing off.

Maybe they wouldn't bite. Just because Arctis wanted me to speak to the media didn't mean the media would be interested. Still, I'd fulfilled the Glyphspeaker's request, and that was all I could do for now.

At the time of my appointment, I entered the office building, followed the hallway signs, and found myself outside an office with a sign reading: "Commanding Officer of Officer Training Command Astrithon (OTCA)."

An enlisted spacer sat behind a desk, and I introduced

myself to him. I told him I was there to meet with the colonel.

He looked me up and down, noting my lack of an appropriate uniform, and told me to take a seat.

A few minutes later, he called me back, and I followed him to a large office in the rear.

Behind a brown metal desk sat a woman in a service uniform with the shoulder boards of a colonel. She had shoulder-length steel hair pulled back into a bun and wore reading glasses. She glanced up at me with brown eyes.

I came to attention and said, "Lieutenant Commander Kory Drake reporting as ordered, ma'am."

Looking at the spacer, she said, "Thank you, Henry, that will be all."

He shut the door.

The woman looked at me without smiling. "I'm Colonel Mariyam Patil." She spoke with an Indian accent. "Formerly of the Indian Air Force, now I'm head of UHC Officer Training Command. Have a seat, Commander."

I took the offered chair and sat stiffly, looking at her, not knowing what to expect. Why was I here?

She watched me and shook her head. "We're promoting babies to be lieutenant commanders. Unbelievable. But you're not the first I've seen. That's what happens in war."

She seemed to be talking to herself, so I didn't reply.

"Commander Drake, you've made quite the name for yourself on Earth. That action at Lindblad Crater was especially remarkable and well executed."

"Thank you, ma'am."

She held up a hand as if to stop me. "That being said, you've thoroughly pissed off the Dominion royals."

"I assure you—" I started to say.

"*I* am talking, Commander." She sighed. "It's

unbelievable. You're under criminal indictment, and we can do little about it. Now, you were going to say something?"

"Ma'am, it's a huge misunderstanding. During combat at Lindblad, I faced a Kergan Soul Ravager and had to use unconventional means to defend myself and my crew. The ignas aren't happy with how I did it, but I've never been one to pull my punches in a fight."

She shook her head. "Commander, we have these things called the Rules of War. Right now, with the Dominion's help and influence over us, they say what those are. My understanding is that you knowingly disregarded instructions given to you by your Heliacal consort—Princess Zeta, unbelievable—" she brought a hand to her forehead and blew out a breath "—you disobeyed her and used *proscribed* sydereal techniques."

She held up a finger and looked at me over her glasses. "Now, I won't pretend to know what those are. You have some unique talents, Mister. You got yourself into this, and now you're going to have to get back out of it. Do you understand what I'm saying?"

I nodded. "I think so. You're saying that the UHC government can't intervene." That's what I had been assuming.

"Correct."

"Ma'am, I've accepted that and am prepared to answer the charges against me. But, with no disrespect intended, why am I talking to you? You're not in my chain of command."

She folded her hands and leaned back in her chair. "I'm getting to that, Mister Drake. Perhaps we can't do anything about your current charges. But we can do something about your future.

"With that being said, I am formally notifying you of

your transfer to the UHC Officer Training Command. You are to be enrolled in OTS—Officer Training School—which we have established to train all our new officers who have been pushed into command of UHC Armada starships. You and others like you."

"It would have been nice to get that training *before* I had to take command of *Thunder*."

"We understand. The realities of war prevented that. The war with the Kergans is currently in a stalemate, and we have started rotating commanding officers like you here to Astrithon for an intense three months of remedial training."

"You're enrolling me."

"Yes. It wasn't the plan, but since you are detained on Astrithon until this silly trial is concluded. We might as well take advantage of your free time."

"Ma'am, I appreciate the opportunity, but I've heard my trial could take *years*." In the jail, Berta told me the Dominion legal system was slow, especially for trials, and it could be over a year until I went to trial. "What happens when I complete OTS?"

"We'll cross that bridge when we get there. But, despite your lack of formal training, you are still a limited duty officer of the UHC Armada, and we're not about to let you sit on your derriere."

"Understood."

"Your vacation is over."

I blushed at her assumption. I'd just survived an attack by gangsters yesterday and was standing trial for charges that could lead to my execution. But I needed to look at this as the opportunity it was. "Yes, ma'am. When and where do I report?"

"Henry has your contact information. You have a dot?"

"Yes, ma'am."

"He'll forward instructions and official orders to you. We have a new class starting in two days so that the wait won't be long." She leaned forward. "Now, do you have any questions?"

"Yes, ma'am. I've had some security issues. People have been following me, and last night, I was attacked—possibly a kidnapping attempt."

Colonel Patil nodded, her expression unreadable. "Yes, we are aware."

My eyebrows shot up. "You are?"

She met my surprise with a calm, measured response. "The UHC government has assigned you a protective detail."

"You could've fooled me," I said, unable to keep the incredulity from my voice.

She softened slightly, her face losing some of its sharp edges. "Commander, you may have created a bit of a mess, but it is in the UHC's interest that you be exonerated of these charges. We can't achieve that if you're dead or captured, right?"

"Fair point," I admitted. "Still, a heads-up would've been appreciated."

"Your protection detail is instructed to remain unobtrusive. There are political reasons for this."

A thought struck me like lightning. *Sofia Kohl*. She must have been part of my protection detail. Her behavior made sense now—she hadn't just been following me for her own amusement. Knowing this didn't erase all my questions but was a relief. I'd definitely have to corner her about it later.

"Anything else, Commander?" Patil asked, her tone turning brisk again.

"Yes, ma'am." I gestured to my wrinkled shirt. "This is

the best uniform I've got. I assume I'll need something more appropriate for OTS?"

She waved a dismissive hand. "Don't bother me with details like that. When OTS begins, you'll be provided everything you need, including a stipend and an allowance for uniforms. Housing will also be arranged at our training facility, which should help address your recent security concerns."

"Yes, ma'am."

"Oh, and one more thing. You'd have found out eventually, but I'll let you know now," Colonel Patil said, leaning slightly forward. Her tone was calm but carried a weight that demanded attention. "Your rank of Lieutenant Commander has always been temporary. You were appointed during a time of war to lead an insurgent cell, but you were not officially commissioned. At the start of OTS, you will lose your rank and revert to an O-0 or Officer Candidate. If you successfully complete OTS, you'll likely be commissioned back to your former rank. Is that understood?"

"Yes, ma'am." The news didn't sting as much as I thought it might. If anything, it felt like the right move. I'd never felt entirely deserving of such an elevated rank, to begin with. At least now, I was on a path to earn it legitimately, which brought clarity and purpose. "I'm surprised."

"At what?"

"That you would commission me as a Lieutenant Commander again."

She pursed her lips, her hands playing with a pen. "Commander, there are few enough of you who know how to command a Dominion warship. Even fewer have successful battle experiences, like yourself. Don't undersell your value to our military."

"Aye, aye, ma'am."

"If that's all, I have a full schedule and need to move on."

I stood and snapped to attention. "Thank you, ma'am."

"You're welcome, Commander. You're dismissed."

I turned sharply, opened the door, and left the building.

Walking outside, I couldn't help reflecting on how much my life had just shifted. I'd been fretting over how I was going to fill my time while awaiting trial, but now that problem was solved—at least for the next three months. A new chapter was beginning, and I felt like I had some direction for the first time in a while.

15

I decided to walk back to my hotel instead of hailing a taxi. It would save me money, and honestly, I needed the time to think.

Where was this protection detail? They had to be close if they were going to protect me, but I hadn't noticed anyone shadowing me for days. Other than the encounter with Scarface and those kavors last night, I hadn't had any overt problems. Could these people really be that good at staying hidden?

As I walked, my eyes flicked around, scanning my surroundings. I studied faces, clothes, postures—anything that might indicate someone tailing me. Maybe it wasn't a person; perhaps it was a vehicle following me at a distance.

The more I thought about it, the more I realized the answer might not be on the ground at all.

I shifted my focus to the air traffic above. It didn't take long—maybe ten minutes—before I spotted them. Or at least one of them, because who knew how many there might be? An aircar, the color of a starless night, shaped like a smooth lozenge with four tractor pods jutting from its edges. It hung back, maintaining an altitude of about 250 feet, just far enough to blend into the crowded skyline unless you were looking for it.

How did Sofia fit into this? If the team was primarily in the air, how had she managed to be on the ground every time I ran into her? Was she part of this group, or was she operating separately?

I felt conflicted about the whole setup. On one hand, I was relieved someone was looking out for me. On the other, I couldn't ignore the twinge of embarrassment. I'd always prided myself on being able to handle my own messes. Having a secret team of babysitters felt... uncomfortably humbling.

As I trudged toward my hotel, I occasionally glanced back at the aircar. It never wavered, trailing me like a shadow. Just before I reached the front entrance, I changed course and headed toward the Midnight Plate instead.

When I reached the diner, I stopped outside, turned on my heel, and faced the aircar directly. Squinting into the faint glow of its running lights, I made a pointed gesture: first at myself, then at the car, and finally at the inside of the diner.

The message was clear enough. *If you're watching me, at least join me for a cup of coffee.*

I entered the diner, found a booth in the back, sat facing the door, and waited. When the server approached, I ordered two coffees.

Five minutes later, Sofia appeared at the door, giving me final confirmation of my suspicions. There was more to her than her appearance revealed. Her eyes were in constant motion, measuring, recording—a pretty mouth set in a firm expression with full lips the color of strawberries.

She saw me immediately and walked straight toward my table. Noting the second coffee cup, she blushed.

I motioned for her to sit.

She sighed and took the seat, picking up the cup in her hands and blowing on it.

"You ran off this morning before I could thank you," I said.

"Sorry, I had to be somewhere," she said.

I shook my head. "'S okay. You don't owe me anything, and I certainly don't have a say in your schedule."

One side of her mouth curled up, and her eyes squinted slightly.

"Or am I mistaken?" I responded.

Her cheeks puffed out from a deep sigh, and she rolled her eyes. "Who gave us away? Colonel Patil?"

"Us?"

"Who was it?"

"Just a hint I was given. Something that Colonel Patil said at my meeting with her. She mentioned there was a protection detail assigned to me." I shrugged. "It didn't take a lot of arithmetic to calculate that you must be part of it."

Her lips pressed together in a straight line. "Guilty."

"So, who are you? Are you really named Sofia Kohl?"

"Yes, that was true. And I've told you no lies," she said, her German accent giving a rhythm to her speech, the *z*-sound slipping into a substitute for some of her consonants. It was endearing, and I repeatedly caught myself mesmerized by the movement of her soft, red lips as words spilled from her mouth. "Just avoided some truths. And we're not trying to hide from you, but rather from the Dominion authorities. We don't want them to know that we don't trust their ability to protect you."

I chuckled. "Oh, I'm certain you've already proved your

worth. You keep saying 'we'. Who is 'we?'"

She glanced out of the corner of her eye and seemed to avoid my gaze.

I waited a moment for an answer, then said, "Look, I'm not mad. I just want to see all the pieces on the board, is all."

She took a sip from her coffee and set it down. "I'm WO-2 Sofia Kohl with the UHC Military Police. My partner is out in the aircar. His name is Charlie."

"You're a warrant officer? A policewoman?"

"*Chief* warrant officer. I'm with a tactical team. We specialize in close protection and hostage rescue. They put me on your detail because they thought I would be less obvious."

"Well, that you are. I didn't start suspecting until this morning after I woke up—too many coincidences," I said, my voice quieter than intended. A twinge of disappointment gnawed at me. I'd had a crush on Sofia from the moment I first met her. But now, I'd learned the truth. The reason I kept running into her wasn't fate or even the possibility of mutual interest—it was because I was her assignment. Our connection wasn't personal; it was *professional*. And I didn't like that one bit.

"Just ignore us. Please," she said, her tone softer, almost pleading. "Let us do our job."

I half-smiled, the gesture more bitter than amused. "And here I'd begun to think you wanted to be friends." I looked down at my cup, stirring it slowly, the movement giving me something to focus on other than the awkward weight in the air between us.

She blushed again and folded her hands. "We can't. It gets in the way of the job."

"Yeah, I understand. It's just that I'd been counting the number of friends I have in this city and thought I'd reached a third finger." I held up my hand to illustrate.

She looked embarrassed, and I suddenly felt bad for complaining. She was risking her life for me. The least I could do was to cooperate.

"Ah, forget it." I continued. "I'm just missing my crew back on *Thunder*. It's amazing how one can live in such a huge place like Astrithon and yet feel so alone."

She cleared her throat. "Who knows, maybe sometime after I complete this assignment, we could meet up and chat. Don't count me out already. It's just that I can't allow any personal feelings to get entangled with my job. We're talking about *your* safety, Kory. That's what this is all about."

"Sure, I understand."

I played with a paper napkin. "About that... You guys, being police and all, do you have any clue who those goons were that jumped me last night?"

She shook her head. "It's out of our hands. Astrithon gendarmes picked them up. One was a fatality."

"Yeah, I thought so. The kavor who's back I broke?"

She snorted. "Broke? *Mein Gott,* you shattered his ribcage and crushed his heart. He died instantly."

"I'm not gonna be in any trouble for that?"

"No, it was a clear case of self-defense, and regardless, Charlie cleaned up the scene. The gendarmes think it was a case of random gang violence."

I raised my eyebrows. "They have that kind of thing here?"

She tilted her head. "It's a large city with 50 million kavrenis, lots of money, and concentrated political power. You *better* believe they have organized crime here."

Just another risk to worry about. "Care to make any guesses as to who hired them?"

"I'm gonna have to answer with 'no comment.' An

ongoing investigation and blah blah blah. We've got some clues, but nothing definitive. Anyways, it's not my domain. I'm not an inspector. My job is to kill bad guys before they kill you."

We sat there in strained silence for a few more minutes, the discomfort palpable. I couldn't shake the unease of having the police shadowing me everywhere, and Sofia's subtle glances made it clear she was worried about how I might disrupt her job—or complicate it.

"I'll see you again soon," she said at last, giving me a curt nod as she stood. Without waiting for a reply, she turned and glided out of the diner, her posture as composed as ever.

After settling the bill for our coffees, I stepped outside and started the walk back to my room. Sure enough, the dark blue aircar resumed its distant shadowing, keeping just far enough away to not feel overtly intrusive.

How had I not noticed them before? It hit me as I walked: humans aren't wired to look up for threats. Our monkey brains evolved for life in trees, scanning the forest floor for predators like snakes, big cats, or bears. That's why kids are so drawn to climbing trees, building treehouses, and playing on swings and jungle gyms. It's instinct—get to higher ground, and you're safe. Up there, you're king of the castle, untouchable by the dangers lurking below.

As I was walking, my dot chimed. I picked it up and checked the message—my orders from Colonel Patil's office, along with a map and directions to the training facility.

I opened them and studied the documents. They ordered me to report for in-processing and indoctrination in two days.

How would my status as an accused criminal affect my time as a trainee at the OTS? Obviously, I would have to be excused on the days when I had a hearing at the judiciary.

What would my fellow students think of that?

My instructors?

Would it be held against me?

I thought about Destiny. According to my dot, it would be morning at Wolf Jaw base. Destiny would have just finished breakfast in the mess and probably was doing ground tactical drills with Busto and the other crew members of *Thunder*. I hoped, as captain, she wasn't giving Busto too hard of a time. Thinking of their constant banter made me smile. My chest ached for them.

Would I ever see them again? There was a very real possibility I might not. The Dominion could find me guilty and execute me or banish me. And even if I was found innocent, there was no guarantee the UHC leadership would send me back to my former unit.

At that moment, it hit me that with this assignment to OTS, I was officially no longer a member of *Thunder*'s crew. Something about that seemed wrong. Families shouldn't be separated like that.

I felt anger at Zeta for taking the Dominion's side against me. For informing them of my fight with Ban'ach and her two guards. It was true. I had emptied her two bodyguards and injured Ban'ach using my sydereal talents. But at the time, it seemed the only way to defend myself.

And it had worked. If I could go back in time and repeat the experience, I would make the same decisions. The alternative would have been death or capture, turned over to the Kergan Empress as her new toy. No, thank you!

But even after all the pain and suffering I'd gone through since my assault on them, I still had not managed to recover the memories of my parents. With each passing day, the hole in my personality that represented their absence continued to grow. Ever since Ban'ach stole my memories of them, it had become more and more challenging to stay motivated. Depression was a constant threat.

Even worse, trapped her on Astrithon, I had no obvious way of tracking down Ban'ach and attempting to recover my memories again. She was thousands of light-years distant, safe from me.

16

The next day, Rynar insisted on taking me on a "proper tour" of the Human Quarter's main attractions so I wouldn't get lost when I moved into the OTS training facility. As if I hadn't already seen enough of the Quarter to last me a lifetime. But Rynar was practically bouncing on his toes, his enormous ears flapping slightly with every enthusiastic movement, and I didn't have the heart to tell him no.

"Today, Kory Drake," Rynar announced proudly, "you will see all the wonders of your people!"

"Wonders," I repeated flatly. "That's a big word for a muddy refugee camp."

Rynar didn't miss a beat. "Everything is wondrous if you look at it with the right ears!"

I didn't bother correcting him. I just sighed and followed along.

The Government-in-Exile Headquarters loomed on a patch of slightly higher ground—though "higher" just meant it didn't have ankle-deep mud. The building was one of those massive prefabricated command hubs, an ugly metal box that looked like someone had dropped it from orbit and forgotten to clean it off.

The faded insignia of old Earth nations decorated the walls—flags, crests, all of them stained from eighteen months of rain. A battered Earth flag hung limp at the entrance, the stars and diamonds barely recognizable.

"Behold!" Rynar chirped, sweeping his long arms wide. "The leaders of your mighty species! I assumes they ares inside doing... important things?"

"Arguing over the last coffee ration, probably," I muttered.

The guards at the door—a couple of tired-looking men in mismatched uniforms—shot us dirty looks as we walked by. One of them had a rifle slung across his chest, though judging by the way he held it, I wasn't sure it even worked.

"You haves a government," Rynar continued, oblivious to the glares. "That is very respectable! Many displaced peoples would simply gives up. But you humans are persistent. Like hive insects. Or fungi!"

"Thanks, Rynar," I said, staring at the door. "That's inspiring."

Rynar tilted his head. "I mean this in the best way."

Rynar practically skipped as we made our way upriver to the UHC Armada Headquarters, which had been carved into an old Dominion warehouse. Unlike the Government-in-Exile, the Armada's base had some teeth—scrap metal walls fortified the perimeter, and a massive Earth-made turret sat on a swiveling mount near the entrance, its muzzle pointed skyward like it was daring someone to try something stupid.

"Kory Drake, is this where they keep your warships?" Rynar asked, his ears perking up like he expected a fleet of starships parked outside the gate.

"They're not my warships, but yeah. This is where they coordinate everything." I jerked my chin at the gates, where a trio of grim-faced officers in patched-together uniforms barked orders at a handful of recruits doing push-ups in the rain.

Rynar stared, wide-eyed. "They shout so much. Are they angry?"

"They're always angry," I replied. "That's how you know they're doing their jobs."

"Ah," Rynar squeaked thoughtfully. "Kavrenis do not shout so much. Perhaps that is why we lose wars."

One of the officers shot me a withering glare, probably for lingering too long outside the gate. I shrugged and turned to leave, nudging Rynar to move along. "Come on, before they recruit you."

"Me? I would be an excellent soldier!" Rynar puffed out his chest, though his high-pitched voice betrayed any seriousness he was aiming for. "I can carry things, and I am very hard to hit! I am fast!"

"Sure you are, Rynar," I said. "Come on, next stop."

The Monsoon Clinic sat at the edge of the Quarter in what looked like a collection of oversized tents held up with duct tape and sheer willpower. The largest tent flapped noisily in the wind, its surface stained with mud, rust, and the occasional suspicious streak of something darker.

Inside, the air was hot, humid, and thick with antiseptic. Dominion medics worked alongside human volunteers, their movements quick and sharp as they triaged the never-ending line of patients waiting for help.

"You humans build very strange hospitals," Rynar said, wrinkling his nose. "Where are the floating healers? The light machines?"

"We don't have Dominion tech lying around for free," I

grumbled. "This is what we've got."

A doctor passed by, snapping at a nurse to get more clean bandages. He looked like he hadn't slept in days. Across the room, a kid was crying while someone wrapped his swollen foot—probably infected from stepping in the floodwater.

Rynar's ears drooped a little as he watched. "It is very sad," he said softly.

"It's life," I replied. "You do what you can with what you've got."

He nodded solemnly. "Your people are tough, Kory Drake. Like… river stones."

I raised an eyebrow. "That's poetic."

"I am very poetic," he squeaked, perking up immediately.

By the time we reached the Lantern District, the drizzle had let up a little, and the evening was starting to set in. Strings of mismatched lanterns—old Earth bulbs, Dominion bioluminescent coils, even salvaged kavreni glow-globes—hung between buildings like makeshift stars. They cast warm light onto the muddy streets, where people gathered outside canteens and taverns, talking and laughing over weak beer and slightly burned food.

Music—an old Earth guitar, maybe, with a raspy voice singing something half-remembered—drifted through the air, almost masking the hiss of water dripping off tarps.

"Isn't this nice?" Rynar squeaked, spinning in a little circle to take it all in. "It is very cheerful! So much color!"

I gave a half-smile. "Yeah, this part's not so bad."

A group of kids ran past, their hands full of glowing sticks they'd probably swiped from a vendor's stall. A woman under a lantern-lit awning was selling roasted meat skewers, the smoke curling into the air like incense.

Rynar sighed contentedly. "Humans. You finds joy even here. It is strange, but I likes it."

"Yeah, well," I said, leaning against the wall. "We don't give up easy."

"Noes." Rynar grinned up at me. "You are likes weeds in the cracks of stone, Kory Drake."

"You really need to work on your compliments, Rynar," I said, shaking my head.

He ignored me, staring up at the lanterns with that childlike wonder only a kavreni could pull off. For a moment, the Human Quarter didn't look quite so bleak. It wasn't much, but it was something—warm lights in the dark.

At the end of the day, I paid Rynar and let him know I wouldn't be needing him for a while since I'd be entering OTS. He looked disappointed—and honestly, I felt a twinge of the same despite my excitement about starting the program. The scrawny, furry alien had truly become my friend, and I'd miss seeing his eager face each morning.

Not long after he left, my dot chimed with a new message. I opened it.

Dear Kory Drake, I am Rusty Aiken, a reporter with ABC News here in Astrithon. I was forwarded your offer to make yourself available for an interview regarding your trial and war record. I would like to meet with you and do a recorded interview. If this interests you, please respond with your agreement and a time and place for the meeting. -Sincerely, Rusty Aiken

They'd gotten back to me surprisingly fast. I'd sent that offer out just yesterday. But with OTS starting tomorrow, I doubted Colonel Patil would approve of me doing a news interview while enrolled as an officer candidate. In fact, I was probably supposed to notify the UHC Public Relations office about the offer.

Still, this was personal. The UHC could've stepped in to help with my legal mess, but instead, they left me twisting in the wind after I made a mistake during a sanctioned military operation. If they weren't going to lift a finger, I'd solve my problems my way.

I quickly typed out a response.

Dear Mr. Aiken, Thank you for your interest. I'd indeed like to meet with you, but it will need to be tonight. Tomorrow, I'm scheduled to enter training and will likely be unavailable for at least three months. Apologies for the short notice, but if you're available, you can meet me in my hotel room.

I added my hotel and room number, then hit send.

Barely a minute later, a reply came back.

Perfect! I'm leaving now and should be at your hotel within fifteen minutes. - Rusty

That was fast. Too fast. I glanced at my reflection in the dusty mirror. After trudging around the Human Quarter all day, I was sweaty, grimy, and absolutely not camera-ready. I bolted out of the room and sprinted down the hall to the communal showers to clean up and make myself at least somewhat presentable.

17

The overhead light panel buzzed faintly, casting a harsh, uneven light over the room. The table between us was bare except for Rusty Aiken's sleek recording device and microphone, which seemed out of place in the otherwise spartan setting. I shifted in my chair, feeling the edge of the seat dig into my back, but Rusty appeared perfectly at ease.

He perched on his chair with a wiry frame that looked like it had been molded for sitting in cramped spaces. His rumpled gray suit hung loosely on his thin frame, and the faint scent of stale coffee clung to him. His green eyes gleamed as they darted around the room, taking in every detail—the peeling paint, my battered boots near the corner, and the unmade bed against the wall. His half-smirk grew wider, as if he were cataloging my entire existence for later dissection.

"So," he said, leaning forward as he adjusted the microphone, "Kory Drake. War hero to some, criminal to others." His voice carried a note of amusement that set my teeth on edge. "Let's cut straight to it—how does a homeless street kid from Earth end up captaining a guerrilla starship?"

I took a slow breath, keeping my expression neutral. "It wasn't exactly by choice," I said carefully. "Earth was under occupation. I was living on the streets, and Zeta—Princess Z374—offered me and my street sister, Destiny, a chance to fight back. The *Thunder* was given to us by the Collective Dominion to support Earth's insurgency efforts."

Rusty tilted his head, his smirk deepening. "Given to you? So, they just handed over an armed alien warship to a couple of kids? Sounds like a sound military strategy."

I kept my jaw tight. "We weren't just kids. We proved ourselves capable. And it wasn't about strategy; it was about desperation. The Kergan Empire had enslaved humanity. We had no choice but to fight."

He sat back, tapping a finger on the table. "And you thought a stolen—excuse me, 'gifted'—warship was your birthright to lead the charge?" His tone dripped with mockery.

I felt a flicker of anger but suppressed it. "It wasn't about birthright. It was about doing what had to be done when no one else could."

Rusty leaned forward, resting his elbows on the table. "From stealing food to commanding starships—quite the leap, wouldn't you say? What made you qualified to lead?"

I frowned. "When you grow up on the streets, you learn quickly how to survive, how to lead, and how to protect the people you care about. My bond with Destiny taught me the importance of trust and responsibility. That's what I carried into my command."

He raised an eyebrow, feigning curiosity. "Trust and responsibility, huh? Interesting choice of words for someone who led an insurgency. Resourcefulness or recklessness?

You killed Kergan soldiers on Earth and then expected no consequences."

I leaned forward now, my voice firm. "The Kergans killed billions of humans and enslaved even more. If fighting back against that is reckless, then so be it."

Rusty's smirk didn't falter. "But let's be honest, Commander. Your rise wasn't exactly conventional, was it? You were thrown into a role you weren't prepared for and made decisions that some might call... shortsighted."

I clenched my fists under the table, refusing to give him the satisfaction of seeing me react. "I made the best decisions I could with the resources I had. And I stand by the choices I made to save lives."

Rusty tapped his pen against his chair, as if considering his next move. The air in the room felt heavier, the tension coiling tighter. I could see the gleam in his eye—he was enjoying this, the push and pull of the conversation, the way he tried to paint me into a corner. This interview was turning out much more hostile than I had expected. But what did I know? This was the first time I'd ever talked to a reporter. Maybe they were all like this.

Rusty's green eyes gleamed with curiosity. "Let's pivot to your military career, Commander. Specifically, the operation at Lindblad Crater. The official record says it was a success—Kergan forces neutralized, hundreds of enslaved humans freed. But what about the cost? What can you tell us about your decision to use sydereal weapons during that mission?"

My stomach tightened. I'd known this question was coming, but it still hit like a punch. I leaned back in my chair, keeping my expression neutral. "The mission was high-risk from the start. We were outnumbered and outgunned. I used every tool at my disposal to save lives and ensure the success of the operation."

Rusty's smirk deepened as if he'd just caught a fish on the line. "Every tool, huh? Including sydereal weapons, which, as I understand it, are forbidden under Dominion law."

I took a slow breath, my fingers curling into fists under the table. "I made the best decision I could with the tools I had to protect my crew and the innocent people enslaved by the Kergans. That's all I can say."

Rusty pounced on my vagueness. "All you can say? Come on, Kory. The Collective Dominion thought your actions were worth charging you with a crime. Doesn't that suggest they didn't see it as a heroic rescue? Some might call it reckless."

I bit back my frustration. "Some might. But they weren't there. They didn't see what we were up against."

Rusty leaned forward, his pen poised like a dagger. "Let's talk about these so-called 'sydereal powers.' Most of us don't even know what they are. Some say it's magic; others say it's just a hoax. Which is it, Kory? What did you really do at Lindblad Crater?"

I could feel my pulse quicken, but I kept my face calm. "I can't discuss that subject. It's not for me to say." Information about the Syderealium was considered classified by the UHC.

Rusty raised an eyebrow, his smirk never faltering. "So you're pleading ignorance? Or is it guilt?"

I leaned forward, narrowing my eyes. "It's neither. It's information I can't talk about. And even if I could, the Syderealium is not something that can be easily explained or dismissed with words like 'magic' or 'hoax.'"

He chuckled, shaking his head. "*Sensitive Information,*" he said with air quotes. "Convenient. But the people deserve to know, don't you think? Don't they have a right to understand what kind of weapons their leaders are using—or forbidding—on their behalf?"

I folded my arms, feeling the tension rising in my chest. "The people deserve to know a lot of things, Rusty. But this isn't about what they deserve. It's about keeping them safe. And sometimes that means not putting everything on public display."

Rusty's smirk faded, replaced by a calculating expression. "So you're saying the public should just trust you, trust the Dominion, trust the same system that's putting you on trial?"

I met his gaze, my voice steady. "I'm saying that there are things bigger than me, bigger than this trial, that I can't speak about. But if I had to do it all over again, I would. Because what I did saved lives. That's what matters."

For a moment, there was silence between us, the air in the room heavy with unspoken accusations and unresolved tension. Rusty tapped his pen against the chair again, his eyes studying me like a specimen under glass. Then he leaned back in his chair, a faint smirk returning to his lips. "What does it feel like, Kory, to be painted as both a hero and a criminal? Do you think this trial is fair?"

I hesitated. How could I answer that without digging my own grave? "It's a strange thing," I began carefully, "to fight for justice only to have it turn against you. I stand by what I did at Lindblad Crater. Lives were saved because of those decisions. But this trial… it feels more political than just."

Rusty tilted his head, the smirk tugging at his lips, sharpening like a blade. "Political? Are you suggesting the monarchy has it out for you?"

My pulse quickened. I glanced at the recording device between us, painfully aware of how my words could be twisted. "I'm saying that justice should be impartial. When it isn't, people start asking questions."

Rusty leaned back in his chair, feigning a relaxed posture as he twisted the proverbial knife. "Many believe the Dominion monarchy is more interested in preserving its power than in delivering justice. Are you saying you're a victim of this system?"

I clenched my fists beneath the table. He wasn't just fishing for controversy; he was trying to bait me into outright rebellion. "I think... it's more complicated than that," I said slowly. "Let's just say there are bigger forces at play than I realized when I took command of *Thunder*."

Rusty's smirk widened. "So, Kory Drake believes he was set up to fail? That this trial is less about justice and more about politics?"

I leaned forward, meeting his gaze with all the intensity I could muster. "I'm saying that the lives I saved matter more to me than the politics of this trial. People can paint me however they like, but at the end of the day, I did what I thought was right."

Rusty's pen hovered over his notepad. He tapped it twice and gave me a knowing look. "You heard it here first, folks: Kory Drake believes the Dominion monarchy is playing politics with justice."

I stared at him, my chest tight with frustration. He had twisted my words just enough to fit his narrative, and I could already see the headlines forming in his mind. *Hero or Scapegoat? Kory Drake Calls Out the Monarchy.*

Rusty adjusted his recording device one final time, a glance at his dot suggesting he was preparing his last words. He leaned back in his chair, fixing me with his sharp, calculating gaze. "Before we wrap up, Kory, any final words for those watching—especially the people back on Earth?"

I sat straighter, the weight of the moment pressing down on me. This was my chance to say something meaningful, something that might cut through the controversy and doubt. "Earth is my home," I said, my voice steady. "I fought for it because it's where I come from, and I'll fight for what's right no matter where I am. That's who I am, and that's what I'll always stand for."

Rusty raised an eyebrow, his smirk softening just a fraction. "Bold words, Commander Drake. Let's see if the Dominion agrees."

The room felt heavier as Rusty packed up his equipment, his movements deliberate and methodical. I watched him, an uneasy mix of anger and regret simmering beneath my skin. His questions had been relentless, calculated to back me into a corner, and I had let him. I had handed him the soundbites he wanted—the ones that would fan the flames of dissent and controversy.

Arctis would be happy, of that I was confident.

Rusty finished zipping up his bag and straightened. "Thanks for your time, Kory. I think this is going to make for one hell of a story."

I didn't respond. My jaw tightened as I walked him to the door and watched him disappear down the dimly lit hallway. When I closed the door behind him, the sound of the latch clicking felt louder than it should have.

Alone in the silence, I slumped into the chair, my mind replaying the interview in an endless loop. Every word I'd spoken felt like a misstep, every answer a crack that could be exploited. Rusty's final smirk lingered in my memory, a reminder of how deftly he had manipulated the conversation.

I rubbed my temples, the weight of the impending fallout pressing down like a storm cloud. Would my words be enough to sway public opinion? Or had I just handed my enemies the ammunition they needed to bury me deeper in the muck of this trial?

18

The next morning, after packing my meager belongings and checking out of my hotel room, I reported to the OTS commandant's office.

"Lieutenant Commander Kory Drake reporting as ordered," I said, standing at attention in front of the CPO behind the desk.

The grizzled veteran barely spared me a glance, his sharp eyes cutting through me like I was something unpleasant stuck to his boot. He snatched the orders from my outstretched hand, scanning them with a practiced, disinterested air.

"As of right now, your temporary rank of Lieutenant Commander is terminated," he barked. "You're an Officer Candidate—E-0. That's Mister Drake to me and everybody else. If you make it through OTS, you might get your rank back. Until then, you're nothing but a student. Got it?"

"Yes, Chief," I said, standing straighter.

"I'll still call you 'sir,' but don't let it go to your head. You're not an officer here. You're here to learn, not lead." He pulled a clipboard from under the desk and slapped it into my hands. "This is your in-processing checklist. Read it. Follow it. No excuses. Every step, exactly as written."

"Yes, Chief."

"Good. Move, Candidate. Don't make me repeat myself."

"Yes, Chief!" I snapped, spinning on my heels and heading for the door as his glare bore into my back like a heat ray.

I won't dwell too much on my time at Officer Training School. Not because it wasn't critical—it absolutely was—but because it was a school, and I've never thrived in academic environments. Let's just say it wasn't my idea of a good time.

The program was divided into three grueling phases: Indoctrination, Intermediate, and Capstone.

Mornings were dominated by physical conditioning—early, brutal, and relentless. Afternoons were consumed by academics, where we were force-fed doctrine, strategy, and principles of leadership. Evenings were reserved for personal study, though exhaustion often made it feel like a test of endurance more than intellect.

The enlisted drill instructors, or DIs, were responsible for our physical training. And they didn't just limit themselves to barking orders during calisthenics. They put us through the wringer: zero-gravity drills that left us spinning like amateurs, hand-to-hand combat sessions where we were systematically dismantled, and obstacle courses designed to crush even the fittest among us. They didn't teach; they broke us down to rebuild us from scratch. And they enjoyed every second of it.

There was one drill instructor who seemed to have it out for me: Senior Chief Petty Officer Sinclair. She was a towering woman with a gravelly voice that could probably cut steel. Whether it was something about me personally or just her general distaste for all officer candidates, I'll never know, but she had a knack for finding me at my worst moments.

It happened during a grueling five-mile run—one of those muggy mornings where the air felt like soup and every breath burned your lungs. I was leading the pack, my legs pounding the pavement with a steady rhythm. The other candidates were following my pace, struggling to keep up, but still hanging in there. I thought I was doing fine, even well, by DI standards.

Apparently, Sinclair disagreed.

Out of nowhere, she pulled up beside me, her voice booming over the sound of our pounding feet. "Pick it up, *sir!* Is this all you've got? Or are you saving your energy for your next court appearance?" The other candidates, already struggling, faltered slightly at the jab.

I kept my eyes forward, my jaw clenched, willing my legs to pump harder. I wasn't about to let her get under my skin. But Sinclair wasn't done.

"Look at this fine example, candidates!" she barked, her voice dripping with sarcasm. "A war hero leading the pack like he's jogging through a park! You call this leadership? You call this effort?"

Her insults came rapid-fire, each one prefaced with the mocking "Sir" that regulations demanded. She leaned in close, her words and spit flying into my face as I tried to focus on the horizon ahead. My hands itched to wipe my face, but I didn't dare break stride. Not when everyone else was watching.

I pushed myself harder, forcing my legs to extend just a little farther, my arms to swing with a bit more force. But no matter what I did, it wasn't enough for Sinclair.

"Faster, *sir!* You're setting the pace for this pack of sorry excuses! Or are you just trying to prove you're the best at being mediocre?"

Her words weren't just for me—they were aimed at the entire group, using me as a cudgel to whip everyone into shape. I could see it working; the candidates behind me were red-faced, sweat pouring off them as they tried to keep up. My frustration grew. Sinclair wasn't just attacking me; she was dragging everyone else down by association.

The tension boiled over when, about a mile from the finish, one of the candidates—a wiry kid named Choi—stumbled and went sprawling to the ground. He let out a groan, clutching his knee, and the pack broke formation as others hesitated to help him.

Before I could stop myself, I turned to Sinclair. "Permission to assist, Senior Chief!" I called, my voice firm but clipped.

Sinclair's eyes narrowed. "Negative, Candidate Drake. He falls, he gets up on his own. Keep moving! Or are you quitting, too?"

The injustice of it burned in my chest, but I had no choice. I nodded stiffly and kept running, the group reforming behind me. But I couldn't let it go. As we approached the final stretch, I slowed just enough to let the pack overtake me.

Sinclair was on me immediately. "What's this, Candidate? You giving up your big lead? Or is this some kind of noble gesture to inspire the weak?"

I didn't answer, conserving my breath for the final push. With the pack ahead, I matched their pace, shouting encouragement. "Let's go, Choi! You've got this! Don't quit now!" The others picked up the call, and even Sinclair went quiet for a moment as the candidates surged forward together, their collective energy renewing.

At the finish line, we collapsed in a heap, gasping for air. Choi limped in last, but he made it, his face pale but determined. Sinclair stood over us, her expression inscrutable.

"Well," she said finally, "it's about damn time you all showed some backbone."

It wasn't praise, but it wasn't the scathing critique I expected either. And as I looked around at the exhausted but unified faces of my fellow candidates, I felt a flicker of pride. Maybe Sinclair had been right to target me. Maybe she saw something I hadn't realized yet.

Later, as we rehydrated and stretched sore muscles, Choi clapped me on the shoulder. "Thanks for not leaving me behind, Drake," he said quietly.

Sinclair walked by, her eyes meeting mine for a brief moment. She didn't say a word, but the faintest nod of acknowledgment passed between us. It wasn't forgiveness, but it was a start.

The academic classes were taught by commissioned officers of the UHC and covered a broad array of subjects: military history, planetary operations, military law, shipboard operations, and spacemanship. Each course was demanding, and the instructors had no tolerance for mediocrity.

Military history was especially chaotic. The Armada had been cobbled together from the former naval and air force organizations of Earth's largest, now-defunct nations. Officers from the United States, China, the UK, Russia, and India had all influenced the curriculum, resulting in an overwhelming amount of material. Each nation seemed determined to highlight its own heritage, turning the course into a sprawling, global patchwork. Keeping the timeline of events straight felt like navigating a maze in zero gravity.

Some of the material was thankfully familiar to me thanks to Zeta's tutelage and the time I'd spent training to captain *Thunder*. Subjects like spacemanship and shipboard operations were second nature by now, which gave me an advantage. But military law and history? Those were beasts I hadn't yet tamed.

Evenings were devoted to homework and study, with assignments that seemed designed to test our endurance as much as our intellect. Sleep was a luxury, and exhaustion became a constant companion.

I was assigned shared quarters with another cadet, Kuro Miyagawa. He was Japanese and spoke very little English, which initially made me wonder how he could manage in an English-language curriculum. I also worried about how we'd communicate—it wasn't like I could lean on my non-existent Japanese skills.

Those doubts evaporated within the first week. Miyagawa wasn't just managing the coursework; he was excelling. It quickly became clear he was the best student in our class. He had a quiet, meticulous way of tackling problems, and when I struggled with military law or history, he would patiently sit down with me and explain the concepts in simple, precise terms. His English might have been broken, but his understanding was flawless.

Over late-night study sessions, we formed an unlikely friendship. He didn't say much about his life back on Earth, but I learned that he came from a family of engineers and had an encyclopedic knowledge of naval strategy. His calm, disciplined presence was a steadying force for me during the chaos of OTS.

Miyagawa wasn't just my roommate; he became my greatest ally in surviving the mental gauntlet of officer training.

I continued to see Sofia every couple of days. Even with my relocation to a more secure training facility, she maintained her role in my protection detail, her vigilance never wavering. I wasn't sure if the UHC believed my pursuers couldn't penetrate the school's defenses or if they simply trusted Sofia and her team to stay one step ahead of any threat. Either way, her presence had become a steady, if mysterious, part of my life.

We would often meet in a quiet corner of the school cafeteria. Over cups of coffee, we'd chat. Well, I'd chat—usually about the endless grind of OTS. I'd give her the gory details of drill instructors yelling, the torturous calisthenics, or my struggles with military law. Sofia, ever the stoic listener, would smirk or nod, offering the occasional quip that kept me grounded.

When the conversation turned to her role, I'd ask if she'd uncovered anything new about the people hunting me. Her answer was always the same—a simple, unsatisfying shake of her head. "Not yet," she'd say, her tone clipped, her expression unreadable.

But over time, our conversations began to drift beyond duty. Despite her repeated insistence that we weren't friends, personal details slipped out. I learned she had served as a Feldjäger—military police—in the German Bundeswehr. Born in Munich to a single mother, Sofia grew up in a city of art and culture, surrounded by centuries of history. Her mother, she confided, was a pianist who played in local cafes to make ends meet.

Sofia's voice tightened when she spoke of her mother. She had been killed during the Kergan invasion, leaving Sofia orphaned and alone. When the German government fled to Astrithon, Sofia had been among the evacuees. She had joined the UHC's nascent military not long after arriving, quickly rising through the ranks due to her sharp instincts and discipline.

Yet, there was something in her eyes when she spoke about her evacuation from Earth—something haunted. I sensed that there were pieces of her story she wasn't telling me, fragments too painful to share. I tried, gently, to draw out those hidden details, but she always deflected, her walls as sturdy as the steel hulls of the Dominion's warships.

Still, those glimpses into her past forged a deeper connection between us. She wasn't just a protector assigned to shadow me; she was a survivor like me, carrying her scars in silence. The more I learned about her, the more I admired her resilience—and the more I wanted to earn her trust.

I was trying to focus on the lesson when the door creaked open. The instructor stopped midsentence, and every head turned to see who had disrupted our study of orbital combat formations. A messenger stood there, holding a sealed envelope.

"Candidate Drake," the messenger said, scanning the room until his eyes landed on me.

I stiffened, already sensing this wasn't good. "Yes?"

"You're ordered to report immediately to the commandant's office."

A murmur rippled through the room. My stomach tightened as I grabbed my tablet and rose from my seat. The instructor gave me a sharp nod, and I murmured an apology before stepping out into the hallway, acutely aware of the stares on my back.

The walk to the commandant's office felt like trudging through a battlefield. What had I done now? My brain cycled through possibilities. Had something happened back on Earth? Had my trial been moved up? Or—my gut churned at the thought—was this about the interview?

When I reached the office, the aide outside didn't even ask for my orders. He just nodded toward the door. "Go on in. She's expecting you."

That wasn't reassuring.

I stepped through, closing the door softly behind me, and froze. Colonel Patil stood behind her desk, leaning forward with her hands braced against the surface. Her face was the color of a boiled lobster, and her eyes were practically glowing with fury.

"Get in here, Drake!" she barked, her voice so loud I felt it in my chest.

I snapped to attention. "Candidate Drake reporting as ordered, ma'am."

"Shut the door!" she snapped.

I did, and the click of the latch felt like the sound of a cell locking behind me.

Her glare drilled into me as she straightened, and then the storm hit. "Do you have any idea what kind of shitstorm you've unleashed?"

I blinked. "No, ma'am."

Her fist slammed down on the desk, rattling everything on it. "That's because you don't think! You don't think about the consequences of your actions! You went and gave an unauthorized interview to a reporter about your trial, about your military operations, about classified material! And now the UHC PR office is tearing its hair out trying to spin this disaster!"

I swallowed hard, but my mouth was dry. My fingers itched to explain, to defend myself, but I knew better. I stood there like a statue as she continued her tirade.

"You've embarrassed this organization, Drake! Do you know how many fires I've had to put out because of you? How many angry comms I've taken from Dominion officials? You didn't just take a shit in the queen's throne room—you lit it on fire and danced in the flames!"

Her voice was so loud I was sure anybody walking out on the grounds could follow the one-sided conversation. Her words stabbed, but I forced myself to nod. "Yes, ma'am. I understand."

She paced now, her boots striking the floor like a metronome of doom. "I don't think you do, Candidate. You've got no idea how close this came to derailing your entire career. You're already under a microscope because of your trial, and now you've handed them a magnifying glass and said, 'Here, make it worse!'"

I swallowed the frustration bubbling in my chest. Sure, it was easy to yell at me now, but where had the UHC been when I'd needed help? When nobody lifted a finger, I'd done what I thought was necessary. But I wasn't going to voice that here. Instead, I kept my face blank. "You're right, ma'am. It was poor judgment."

"POOR JUDGMENT?!" she thundered, whipping around to glare at me. "That's the understatement of the year! This little stunt of yours has earned you a written reprimand. Effective immediately, it's going into your record. And you'd better believe it'll sit there like a loaded torpedo, waiting to explode at the worst possible moment."

I nodded, my jaw tight. "Understood, ma'am."

She stared at me for a long moment, her chest heaving as she fought to rein in her anger. Finally, she pointed at the door. "Get out of my sight, Drake. And for God's sake, use your head before you decide to play hero again!"

"Yes, ma'am," I said, saluting sharply.

I turned and left, her words echoing in my head like cannon fire. As I walked back to my class, I tried to swallow the knot of regret in my throat. The interview had felt like the right move at the time—my only move—but now? Now, it felt like I'd painted a target on my back.

And yet, some small part of me still believed it had been worth it. For justice. For the truth.

I just hoped I could survive the fallout.

Ten days after I entered OTS, I received a reminder from the Dominion judiciary about my upcoming precedium hearing. The message came with a cold efficiency that only added to my growing anxiety. The hearing was scheduled for the following day.

I immediately notified the class officer, who, thankfully, was already aware of my special circumstances. After some paperwork and a lot of questions, I was granted a one-day pass to take care of my "business." As I left the office, I caught sight of Sofia across the courtyard, her sharp blue eyes scanning the grounds.

For reasons I couldn't quite explain, knowing she would be with me during the hearing made the whole ordeal feel just a little less daunting.

19

The three igna judges floated at the front of the courtroom, their faint, otherworldly glow illuminating the polished obsidian table before them. Their energy seemed calm and controlled, a stark contrast to the storm of emotions roiling inside me. I sat stiffly behind my table, willing myself to maintain a veneer of calm as Prosecutor Qut delivered his argument.

Qut's capsule, mounted on his intimidating walker, loomed over the room like a predatory beast. The jagged angles of the metal seemed to reach for me, begging to slice away my composure until I spilled some damning truth. It was absurdly over-the-top, bordering on theatrical. If it wasn't so terrifying, I might have laughed.

Behind me, a wall of reporters tapped away on their dots, capturing every syllable of this circus. Their eyes darted between Qut, the judges, and the displays mounted above us. The irony wasn't lost on me: at my own hearing, the only voice they wouldn't hear would be mine. Judge Advocate Zor, supposedly my representative, sat silent as a shadow. She hadn't spoken once.

Above the judges, five large displays showcased the avatars of Glyphspeakers attending remotely. Each screen glowed faintly with the geometric shapes and pulsating energlyphs that marked their presence in the Sydereалium. My eyes darted to the familiar glyphshade of Arctis. He was here again. I didn't know whether to feel relieved or uneasy.

My jaw tightened as Qut's voice droned on, sharp and accusatory, dissecting every decision I'd ever made. The faint hum of the judges' capsules and the rhythmic clatter of the reporters' typing filled the room like an oppressive heartbeat.

Focus, Kory, I told myself, stealing a glance at Zor. She was inscrutable, her capsule still and featureless. If she planned to defend me, she was playing a game of patience I wasn't sure I could afford.

The judges' energy brightened slightly, their attention narrowing on the prosecutor as he reached the crescendo of his argument. I clenched my fists beneath the table, my mind racing. The stakes of this hearing were more than my reputation—they were my survival.

"Kory Drake did at that moment knowingly and with criminal intent attack Z'rath and V'lokk, two citizens of the Kergan Empire, and did empty them of their energlyphs. He robbed—"

"Prosecutor Qut," Arctis interrupted. "With all due respect, what you claim *may* be true, but where are these witnesses? Where are *any* witnesses?"

"The two citizens in question, Z'rath and V'lokk, are deceased as a result of the attack. As to other witnesses, Qut will attend to that business in a moment."

Zor finally spoke up. "Zor objects. The worthy Prosecutor is making claims without foundation. He is testifying!"

"Maintained," Chief Arbiter Vexa said. "Prosecutor Qut, you shall avoid proposing evidence to this court that is based on speculation and rumor."

"Yes, Judge Vexa," Qut replied politely. "Qut was preparing to call a witness who will testify of these facts. Qut was merely smoothing out the road."

"Then move along," Vexa replied. "Your opening remarks have been noted. This hearing is for us, the judges, not the media sitting in the pews."

Light laughter sounded from behind me.

"The sovereign calls forward Her Highness Z374, also known as Princess Zeta, to testify," Qut said.

I turned in response to movement at a side door. Through it floated the familiar white octahedral capsule of Zeta. My friend. My former consort.

She was about to testify on behalf of the prosecution.

My hands shook and sweated. This was the ultimate betrayal. I knew this hearing was not the actual trial. The precedium was merely a meeting for the prosecution to demonstrate to the judges that they had sufficient evidence against me to justify going forward with a trial. But I also knew this was a preview of what awaited me in my trial.

Zeta floated across the room and came to rest in front of the judges facing the prosecution and defense tables.

"Princess Zeta, we are honored by the presence of your Royal Highness," Qut said obsequiously. "Thank you for giving us some of your valuable time."

"Zeta is obeying a court order," she said. "She will give you the truth."

"Very well. Qut will turn the time over to the judges to question you."

Zeta rotated on her vertical axis to face the judges.

"Princess Zeta," Chief Arbiter Vexa said, "you are present at the precedium of Kory Drake, who stands charged with crimes of sydereal battery and conspiring with an Astral Titan. Is the accused in this courtroom?"

She bobbed once. "Aye, Judge, he is sitting at the table there."

"Describe to us the events leading up to and during the sydereal assault to the best of your memory."

The courtroom fell completely silent. I clenched my hands and looked down at my table.

"Zeta and Kory Drake were part of a military operation to free human slaves from a mining facility on Luna, Earth's moon, and to sabotage a Primordian artifact the Kergan Empire was attempting to activate. Kory was the commander of the operation, and Zeta his Heliacal Consort.

"Toward the end of the operation, some of us, including Zeta and Kory, entered the artifact to seek a way to disable or destroy it. This journey required Kory to navigate using the Syderealium."

"Why him?" Judge Accuser Kyrn asked.

"Kory Drake is a highly talented flairsparked human," Zeta said.

"So he is capable of consciously operating in the Syderealium, correct?" Kyrn asked.

"Aye, it is so. He is more capable than even most ignas Zeta knows of."

"Very well, please continue your testimony."

"The team had penetrated deep into the artifact using Kory to guide us. He led us to the core, where members of the Kergan Empire had established a control mechanism.

"Upon entering, Kory was immediately seized by a trap and carried away from the rest of our party. We tried to follow him, but the way was closed.

"Zeta used her Heliacal link to track Kory's location. The remaining team members, including Zeta, pursued Kory along an alternate path, descending an atrium stairway, where we encountered and eliminated multiple armed guards of the Kergan Empire.

"After about an hour of searching, we located Kory Drake. He had been taken captive by the Kergan Soul Ravager Ban'ach and was being held in an interrogation room by her and her two bodyguards."

"Is it true that the two bodyguards were Z'rath and V'lock?" Zor asked.

"Zeta does not know their names."

"Objection, Judge Vexa!" Arctis yelled.

"Silence, Glyphspeaker," Vexa replied. "The witness is still testifying." He gestured with a pointer to Zeta. "Please continue, Princess."

"Zeta and the team opened the door of the interrogation room. Zeta saw the two bodyguards slumped on the floor. Kory and Ban'ach were locked in a sydereal projection.

"Zeta immediately projected into the Syderealium and witnessed Kory Drake locked in a sydereal assault on Ban'ach. The glyphshades of the two bodyguards were also present but had been emptied. Stripped of all their energlyphs and Kory Drake's glyphshade showed evidence of having recently consumed energlyphs."

There were audible gasps from the audience and from several of the Glyphspeakers.

"Zeta witnessed Kory Drake striking at Ban'ach with a sydereal probe, wounding her slightly. Zeta immediately intervened, ejecting both Ban'ach and Kory Drake from the projection.

"When Zeta exited the projection, Ban'ach had already escaped the interrogation room, temporarily incapacitating the human members of our team with a stun weapon."

Zeta stopped speaking.

"Did anything else happen regarding the sydereal battery?" Kyrn asked.

"Nay, Zeta has shared all relevant information."

"Judge Vexa," Zor said, "the witness has failed to identify the two victims, Z'rath and V'lock."

"Aye," Vexa said, "but she *did* confirm the attack on Ban'ach."

"It is important that we understand the intent behind this act," Zor said.

"Nay, Judge Zor, that is a question for the criminal trial. We must only establish the facts justifying the charges. The witness has testified that Mister Drake did knowingly attack and injure Ban'ach. However, Vexa agrees to dismiss the charges related to Z'rath and V'lock unless the prosecution has other evidence. Prosecutor Qut?"

Qut's walker stood. "Not at this time, Chief Arbiter."

I sighed with relief. I supposed that was good news. But I still stood accused of attacking Ban'ach.

"May I speak, Judge Vexa?" Arctis said.

"Yes, you may."

"There is a special context within which these events took place. They happened during the execution of a military operation against the Kergan Empire. Rules of Engagement should have allowed humans to use lethal force against the Kergans. Given this *very* important fact, I do not understand why Kory Drake has been charged."

"Judge Kyrn shall respond," Kyrn said. "Glyphspeaker, there is one fundamental reason. Lethal force was not used in this particular attack. Rather, *sydereal* force was used by Mister Drake, a completely different matter, one that violates our laws regarding conduct during war. This young human could have destabilized the entire Sydereallium and called down an Astral Titan on Earth! But most important of all, it is the law. You know this!"

"Do not patronize me, Kyrn!" Arctis responded. "By the Nexus, I am a Glyphspeaker! And I tell you that this law is wrong!"

"It is not our place to judge whether a law is good or bad," Vaxa said. "Only what the law *is*. And Judge Accuser Kyrn has spoken correctly. Kory Drake has violated the law, regardless of whether he did so or not, as part of a military operation. Whether he had criminal intent to do so will be a question we will answer at the end of the trial.

"Now, we are not done here. We have one more charge to address. Princess Zeta. Tell us of the events surrounding and related to the charge of conspiring with an Astral Titan."

They weren't going to let me have any say unless I spoke up. I raised my hand.

"Mister Drake, you have a question?" Judge Vexa said.

"Yes, Judge, I would like to share my version of the facts."

"Nay, this is a precedium, not a trial. We are present to hear the prosecution's evidence to ensure they have proper cause for moving forward with the trial. Your presence here is a courtesy, no more."

I glowered and leaned back in my chair.

"Now, Princess Zeta, the Astral Titan, if you would."

Zeta's capsule tilted back and forth several times. "Zeta knows little. As she said, we were in the artifact and escaping after we recovered Kory Drake. During the journey, Kory Drake stopped for a moment to project into the Sydrealium to obtain a fix on our location. Something important happened during that moment. When he ended the projection, he looked shaken. Our team asked him what happened, but he would not speak of it.

"A few days later, Zeta learned from Kory Drake that he had encountered an Astral Titan named Pyrakos. The Titan tried to consume Kory, but he used his sydereal skills to avoid it and escaped after delivering an oath to the Titan."

"And what was this oath?" Judge Kyrn asked.

"According to Kory, he promised Pyrakos to destroy the Primordian artifact once he exited the artifact. He did so as a solemn oath."

"Judge Vexa," Zor said, "I object. Princess Zeta is testifying for the accused. This is a rumor. Hearsay."

"Maintained," Vexa said. "Judges, disregard Princess Zeta's testimony regarding her statements about Pyrakos. That is unless the witness knows firsthand about this encounter with the Titan?"

"No, Judge," Zeta said.

"Ah," Judge Kyrn said, "but she did confirm that something troubling did happen when Kory Drake entered the Sydereal ium that second time. Did she not?"

"Aye, Judge Kyrn," Vexa said. "But Vexa does not see how this is relevant."

"If Qut may," Qut said, rising to his feet. "The sovereign has an authority to call next who will show relevance."

"Very well. Princess Zeta, do you have anything further to say to this court regarding these events?"

Zeta was silent for a moment. Then she said, "On a personal note, Zeta would just like to say that Kory Drake has always acted honorably and with great—"

"Objection!" Kryn cried out. "The witness is delivering unsolicited testimony."

"Maintained," Vexa said. "Princess Zeta, you are excused."

Zeta floated away. I wished she had a head with eyes so I could try and catch her gaze. Was she looking at me? I used to be able to tell what she was feeling because of our Heliacal link, but that was long gone.

"Prosecutor Qut, your next witness," Vexa said.

Qut stood. "Judge Vexa, the sovereign calls forth Seeker Vorran."

An igna floated through the door. He possessed a cube capsule colored gray and emitting purple light. He flew across the room and took a position in front of the judges.

"State your name and the organization you represent," Judge Vexa said.

"This igna is called Seeker Vorran. Vorran is a scientist at the Royal Sydereal Observatory at the Zenith Citadel."

I heard whispered mutters in the audience behind me.

"Prosecutor Qut, relevance?"

"Aye, Judge, Seeker Vorran has information regarding a sydereal event coinciding with the exact time that Princess Zeta testified of Kory Drake entering the Syderealium the second time and experiencing a disturbing encounter."

"Very well. Seeker Vorran, if you please, tell us of this event."

"Aye, Judge. Vorran was working at the Royal Observatory on the date and time in question. At precisely 20377.148328 on Ignisara date 14024-203, my team observed a significant fluctuation in the quasiplanar flux density across the Syderealium's axial vectors. This disturbance was characterized by a pronounced destabilization of the astral gravitic lattice—a phenomenon consistent only with the transient passage or activity of an Astral Titan.

"Specifically, the astral harmonics registered a Class-VI oscillation, a rarity indicative of an entity with immense sydereal mass interacting directly with the local sydereal plane. The disturbance was further corroborated by a 17-microquark shift in the phase coherence of adjacent sydereal loci, which rules out naturally occurring stellar phenomena as the source.

"In simpler terms, the Syderealium itself exhibited patterns of disruption that are uniquely attributable to the active interference of an Astral Titan, precisely on the aforementioned date and time, and were localized using ToA data to the Syderealium location projecting onto the Earth's Moon."

My eyes glazed over during Seeker Vorran's explanation. But he spoke with great confidence, and the courtroom was dead silent during his testimony.

"Very good, Seeker Vorran," Judge Vexa said. "Any objections to this witness's testimony, Judges?"

"Nay," Judge Kyrn responded.

"Zor questions it," Judge Zor said. "This evidence is circumstantial and does not prove that Kory Drake met with an Astral Titan, let alone conspired with one. Nor has he proved that the Titan was this Pyrakos."

"Hear, hear!" Arctis yelled from his display.

"Seeker Vorran, do you have any further evidence that supports the presence of the accused being in the company of said Astral Titan?"

"Nay, Judge. This is an inexact science. We may localize an energetic Titan in position and time but not identify them or observe their activities. It is quite dangerous to approach one, as Vorran is sure you understand."

"Yes, understood. The witness is excused."

Seeker Vorran flew out of the courtroom.

"Judge Vexa, a word, please," Arctis spoke.

"Yes, Glyphspeaker Arctis."

"The sovereign has failed to prove that Kory Drake was

in the presence of Pyrakos or that they conspired against the Dominion. Perhaps Mister Drake *did* encounter a Titan. If he did, given the fact that he survived it, that is extraordinary, and his act should be celebrated, not condemned! I object to the sovereign's evidence."

"Vexa understands," the Chief Arbiter said, "and she hears your words. But, again, this is a precedium, not a trial. Vexa urges the prosecution to obtain further evidence by the time of the trial, but for the purposes of proving just cause for the charge, Vexa is going to accept this evidence. But it is circumstantial, Prosecutor Qut, and that is an issue that must be addressed at the trial. Do you understand?"

"Indeed, Chief Arbiter Vexa. The sovereign will present further evidence at the trial."

"Very well. Do you have any further evidence to present?"

"Nay, the sovereign rests."

"Then Vexa is ready to make a ruling."

She turned his attention to me. "Kory Drake, the charges of sydereal battery against Z'rath and V'lock are dismissed, though the sovereign is entitled to resubmit those charges at a future date if further evidence supporting them is found.

"The charges of sydereal battery against Ban'ach and conspiring with the Astral Titan Pyrakos are approved, and you must stand trial for them. Your status in supervised release is continued until that time.

"We will schedule an evidentiary hearing in... let me check Vexa's schedule... one moment." She studied the terminal on her table. "The evidentiary hearing will be held on the 15th of Clymeron 245. That's in 203 days."

My jaw fell open. That was almost seven months in the future. And it wasn't even my trial. It was only a hearing at which the prosecution and the accused would submit all their evidence in preparation for the trial.

What was I going to do until then?

I would be long out of OTS but still confined to Astrithon. All I wanted was to return home to my crew. Furthermore, as long as I was on this planet, I couldn't pursue Ban'ach.

20

After the hearing, I stepped out of the courtroom and made my way toward a nearby park. The streets of Astrithon bustled with their usual mix of Dominion citizens—ignas floating serenely in their capsules, kavrenis striding with their strange, backward-jointed legs, and the occasional human weaving through the crowd. It was a sensory overload I barely noticed anymore.

As I walked, I glanced over my shoulder. Sure enough, the dark blue aircar trailed me at a discreet distance, its tinted windows giving no hint of the two people inside. Sofia and Charlie. Ever vigilant, ever present.

I wanted to be alone, just for a moment. But I didn't have the energy—or the will—to try and lose them. They were only doing their job, after all. Protecting me from threats I wasn't even sure were still out there.

The real question was: why?

Why was the UHC investing so much in me? Assigning a full-time protection detail, going to all this effort? It wasn't exactly subtle, either. It felt like they were sending a message—to who, I wasn't sure—but it wasn't just about my safety.

Something else was going on, something I couldn't quite put my finger on. What was it about me that warranted this level of expense and attention? Sure, I was flairsparked and had some training as a starship captain, but there were others like me. I wasn't that special. Not enough to justify all of this.

There was a bigger picture here, one I couldn't see yet. And that made me uneasy.

I passed an open gate into the park. Purple alien vegetation spread around me. The center of the park was taken up by a decorative rock garden filled with geometric patterns formed by different colored stones. It was beautiful and oddly relaxing there. I sat on a bench on one side where there were few pedestrians.

On the other side of the garden, an igna approached—a spherical capsule, black, covered with gold script.

I ignored them and went back to studying the patterns swirling in the rocks.

The igna paused in their movement, then started floating in my direction and stopped about 5 feet away.

"Ah, young human, you wonder about this rock grove, don't you?" the igna said with a female voice. "It is called the Sar'jenan Array, and it is far more than a garden. Each stone here is a fragment of our history, carefully placed to whisper to those who will listen."

She spoke with the voice of a mature woman. She gestured with a pointer toward a spiral pattern of black and white stones.

"This path," she continued, "marks the Cycle of First Ascension. It recounts when our kind first reached beyond our world to touch the Sycerealium. The black stones tell of our struggles—our failures—and the white, our triumphs. Together, they remind us that neither darkness nor light can exist alone."

The igna floated lower, her movements deliberate, as she pointed to a cluster of pale blue stones arranged in a hexagonal grid.

"This here," she said, "is the Array of Kevalis, our greatest scientist. He charted the first sydereal pathways, allowing our minds to bridge stars. These stones are placed to reflect his discovery—a harmony of geometry and vibration."

She rose slowly, her attention steady on Kory.

"Every step here is a lesson, young Kory. Each pattern is a story of resilience, a warning, or a call to action. This garden does not exist simply to be admired. It is here to remind us—of where we came from and where we are destined to go."

I noticed she used my name. She paused, her voice lowering.

"Perhaps one day, Kory Drake, your story will be placed here as well. But that depends on what you choose to do with the path before you."

“Who are you?” I asked, tired of being spied on.

“This humble igna is called Seraphis. I was at your hearing. Seraphis hopes you do not take offense at her interest in your affairs.”

I shrugged. “I'm used to it now.” I studied her capsule more closely, noting the intricate details of the golden symbols inscribed all over. I'd noticed that ignas of high rank had scrollwork written on their capsules, though curiously, Zeta did not. “You must be somebody important. Why would you follow me?”

She floated closer until she came to a stop adjacent to

me. "Full disclosure, then. You are Kory Drake, the flairsparked captain of the starship *Thunder*. And Seraphis is a celestarch of the Dominion Armada."

"Celestarch? What's that?"

"Just a rank. Seraphis is an armada officer. Roughly the equivalent of a vice admiral in your American navy."

My body went stiff. "Oh... my apologies, ma'am, for my disrespect."

She chuckled. "Nay, human, it is Seraphis who has pursued you. You are currently a student in the UHC Armada OTS. This is good. I am the premier of the Dominion Space Warfare School."

"What is that?"

"It is a school of advanced studies to train our armada officers like yourself. Seraphis is keenly interested in you as a potential student."

What did this igna want with me? Had she maybe been sent by Arctis?

"In case you hadn't noticed, I'm an accused criminal. You saw what they've charged me with. If I were you, I wouldn't waste any time on me."

"Seraphis is familiar with your case. It is unprecedented. The ignas have so few who are even capable of sydereal assault that it is not a crime we often see. Indeed, Seraphis does not know of any historical cases. The law is obsolete, broken, and you, young human, stumbled upon it."

I looked away. "It seems like there are good reasons for having it. When I attacked those bodyguards, I did feel how it affected the Syderealium."

"Remarkable. What you did is something we ignas only hear of in legend. These are the acts of Soul Ravagers or gods. And you did it for the right reasons. Not for vengeance or to make them suffer, but to defend yourself and recover your stolen memories."

I nodded.

"The reason Seraphis is interested in you," she continued, "is that we teach a class at the SWS on sydereal theory and how it relates to combat tactics. There are things a powerful flairsparked could do during ship-to-ship combat that could give an overwhelming advantage."

I gazed at her. "I know you have flairsparked ignas. Zeta is one."

"Oh, we do, but they are not very powerful."

I grunted. "Zeta sure seems powerful to me."

"Ah, you mistake skill for power," she said, her tone smooth and calculated. "Zeta has been trained her entire life to manipulate the Syderealium, yes, but her power is no greater than the average flairsparked. Minuscule, really, compared to what you're capable of. Any normal flairsparked would have been consumed by the mere presence of Pyrakos. Yet, you survived."

I flinched, the memory of Pyrakos washing over me like a cold tide. That encounter had been anything but ordinary. The oppressive presence of the Astral Titan had felt like my very consciousness was unraveling, pieces of me being pulled into him. Only sheer willpower had kept me from dissolving completely.

"It wasn't exactly comfortable," I muttered, my voice tight.

"Seraphis recognizes your potential, Kory. We are offering you an opening at our school. There, you'll be taught advanced tactics, strategies, and methods far beyond what most flairsparked could hope to learn."

Ah, there it was—the offer. I had been expecting it, and I liked the sound of it—except I knew there would be a catch. There always was. "And what do you want in return? Let me guess: I'll be your guinea pig."

She tilted her capsule and shook slightly. "Guinea pig?"

"Sorry, I mean test subject."

"Ah, Seraphis sees. Well, not quite," she said. "We want to determine if some of our proposed sydereal tactics are practical. Your unique talents and power make you an ideal candidate to attempt them. Seraphis would like you to work closely with Professor Kelarn on these experiments. If you agree, we will facilitate your admission into the Space Warfare School."

I leaned back, processing her words. The temptation was undeniable. Training at SWS would open doors for me that I couldn't pry open on my own. But the thought of being some sort of test subject, trial-and-erroring experimental tactics? That was another thing entirely.

"And if I don't agree?" I asked, keeping my tone neutral.

Her capsule didn't falter. "Then you'll remain as you are, struggling to navigate a battlefield far more complex than anything you've faced before. The choice is yours."

I stared at her, my mind churning. This wasn't just about training—it was about control. Yet, deep down, I knew I couldn't pass up the opportunity.

"I'm still in OTS. I just started and have another eleven weeks to go."

"That is perfect. That coincides with the start of a new term at the SWS. If you agree, Seraphis will approach the UHC Armada staff for their approval of your assignment. What do you think? Do you accept?"

I couldn't think of a better way to spend the seemingly endless wait for my trial. Plus, this could be a chance to sharpen my skills as a ship captain. Sure, it sounded like the kind of place where I'd stick out like a sore thumb—no college degree, no formal pedigree—but that wasn't my problem. If they wanted me, they'd have to figure out how to accommodate me.

"Yes, ma'am," I said, forcing a tone of confidence. "I'd like that very much."

"Excellent," she replied, her tone crisp and satisfied. "Then we are agreed."

We hashed out a few more details about dates and logistics before she finally rose to leave. As Seraphis floated away, I couldn't help but feel a mix of apprehension and determination. Whatever this place had in store for me, I'd make sure I left stronger than when I arrived.

21

"Alright, listen up!" Lieutenant Abioye's voice cut through the room like a laser beam. "Command and control, or C2, is the backbone of space warfare."

It was the fourth week of OTS, and she wasn't here to hold our hands. Her ebony skin gleamed under the overhead lights as she paced the front of the classroom with the deliberate intensity of a prowling predator. She didn't suffer fools—or hesitation.

"Who here can tell me why it's important? And no," she added, her sharp gaze scanning the room, "'so people know what to do' isn't the answer I'm looking for."

The room stayed quiet, everyone suddenly engrossed in their notes—or pretending to be. Hesitantly, Zhou, the brave or foolish soul seated a row ahead of me, took the bait. "Uh... it's about giving orders and making sure they're followed?"

Abioye snapped, "Orders and obedience? What are we, robots? That answer's pathetic. Let me put this in terms even you can understand: without C2, your fleet is a headless chicken. Ever seen a headless chicken win a battle? I haven't."

Zhou stammered, "Well, I—"

Abioye cut him off, "No, you haven't. And do you know why? Because the moment you lose C2, the enemy will chew you up and spit you out. Picture this: your carrier is taking a beating, your escorts are out of position, and your spectrals? Oh, they're too busy chasing shadows. Meanwhile, you're standing there, clueless, because you didn't establish proper control."

Arline Tatum, sitting behind me, spoke up. "But isn't that why we train? To act independently if things go wrong?"

"Oh, so now you're a genius?" Abioye asked sarcastically. "Sure, independent action sounds great until your frigate captain decides to play hero and abandons the convoy. Or better yet, your spectral commander thinks it's a good day for target practice and hits friendly ships. Independence without alignment is chaos. And chaos gets fleets destroyed."

I gritted my teeth and asked the question I knew Abioye was waiting for one of us to ask. "So what's the solution, then?"

Lieutenant Abioye leaned forward, her voice sharp. "The solution is understanding that C2 isn't just about issuing orders—it's about ensuring every damn unit knows your intent. It's about redundancy. It's about communication that doesn't fail when the enemy jams your systems or blows your relay into the local star. You plan for chaos, but you don't let it win."

Her eyes locked on me. "Drake, what do you do if you can't get your orders?"

My neck tensed up. I'd read the assigned chapters from

the reading but I didn't remember anything that addressed this question. "Uh… fall back onto your most recent orders and your training. That's why we have things like Rules of Engagement and Standard Operating Procedures."

Abioye grinned coldly. "Excellent. Your crew should already know what to do. That's why you drill them until they hate you, why you rehearse every scenario until they can act without hesitation. But don't get it twisted—decentralized command isn't a free-for-all. Every decision must align with the mission, the ROE, and the SOP, or you're just another fool with ships getting blown. C2 isn't just about tech and radios. It's also about policies, procedures, and training. It's about setting expectations and ensuring your ship commanders and their crews meet them.

"C2 is what separates leaders from amateurs. If you can't master it, you're not leading a fleet—you're sending it to die. Let's hope you've got what it takes to be the former, not the latter."

Abioye turned around and started writing on the whiteboard. "Now, let's talk about how you implement C2 in the real world. Like I said, it's not just about fancy technology or pretty diagrams on a holoscreen. It's about clarity. Every order you give must be understood, without hesitation, by the most junior sailor in your fleet. If they don't get it, it's your failure, not theirs."

Lieutenant Abioye paced aggressively, glaring at us. The creases of her pressed trousers and shirt were so sharp she could have sliced cheese with them.

"Your systems are going to fail. Your comms will be jammed, your relays knocked out, and your command ship might take a hit that leaves you spitting blood. What then? If your fleet falls apart without you holding its hand, you've already lost. That's why intent is king. No matter the situation, every officer under your command needs to know the mission, the goal, and how to execute it.

"Miyagawa," she pointed at my roommate. "How do we plan for something like that?"

Like always, my roommate was instantly ready with a response. "Ma'am, through preparation and contingency planning."

Abioye smiled. "Very good. Remember, you can't predict everything, but you *can* prepare for anything. You rehearse contingencies until they're muscle memory. You drill your people so hard they curse your name in their sleep. You write standing orders so clear that even a deckhand on their first deployment knows what to do if the flagship goes dark."

The instructor slammed a hand on the podium for emphasis. "And you plan redundancies: redundant comms, redundant sensors, redundant chain of command. If you're relying on one system, one person, or one brilliant plan, you're already screwed. War doesn't care how clever you think you are—it cares how adaptable you are when everything goes to hell.

"These are the basic principles of C2. You must learn to apply them. Because when the shooting starts, no one's going to care about your theories. The only thing that matters is whether your fleet executes, survives, and wins. Anything less, and you'll be remembered as a footnote in someone else's victory."

Despite her abrasive personality, I liked Lieutenant Abioye. She was tough but fair and incredibly smart. Originally from somewhere in West Africa, she spoke with a lilting accent that seemed to emphasize every word.

"Now, let's get more technical. C2 isn't just about giving orders and pushing buttons. It's the integration of every asset at your disposal into a cohesive operational force. It's the neural network of your fleet, the difference between precision execution and catastrophic failure. Who can tell me the foundational principles of effective C2?"

Tatum responded, "Effective communication and coordination."

Abioye narrowed her eyes. "Effective communication? Coordination? That's a surface-level answer. I'm looking for details. What are the mechanisms that make communication effective in a high-stress, contested environment? If I lose a relay, if the enemy floods the spectrum with noise, how do I coordinate anything? Tell me. I've already given you the answer earlier. Have you been listening, Mister Tatum?"

Tatum blushed and blew out a breath. "Um... redundant systems? Pre-established protocols?"

Abioye nodded sharply. "Better. Yes, redundancy and protocols. But how do you make redundancy meaningful? Let's say you have three comms systems, all jammed. What's your next move?"

I raised my hand, and the lieutenant pointed at me. "Fallback to pre-planned orders, ma'am."

She stepped closer. "Fallback to pre-planned orders. Good. Now, here's the real question: how do you design those pre-planned orders so that they're actionable without context? What happens if my fleet commanders are cut off from real-time updates, but the tactical situation changes?"

We all looked at each other with uncertainty.

Abioye smirked. "This is why C2 is an art as much as a science. Your pre-planned orders must include your intent —clear, unambiguous guidance that allows every unit to make decisions aligned with the overall mission, even in isolation. And here's the kicker: you have to trust them to do it. If you micromanage, you create bottlenecks. If you're too vague, you create chaos."

She strode to the holoboard, pulling up a map of a naval engagement.

"Let's break this down. Here's a hypothetical fleet: one carrier strike group with two frigates and a spectral acting as a forward scout. You're the fleet commander. You issue an intent: deny the enemy access to this sector. Now, I hit your comms with a directed CEMP. Boom—you're dark. What should your carrier group commander prioritize? Speak up."

Miyagawa replied, "They'd launch CAPs—Combat Air Patrols—to maintain space superiority while holding a defensive posture."

Abioye nodded. "Good start. But what if I launch a decoy missile strike, pulling your strike craft out of position? What's the frigate commander's role?"

Heidi Gustavsson, a Swedish candidate, replied, "They'd screen for the carrier and intercept incoming threats?"

Abioye raised an eyebrow. "And what if my real attack sneaks by—an enemy spectral targeting your logistics ships? Are your frigates equipped to detect and engage? Did your own spectrals identify stealth threats before your comms went out? How does your fleet adapt when it's operating blind? Think deeper."

The room fell silent as we scrambled to piece the scenario together.

Abioye snapped a finger. "This is what I mean by alignment. Your frigate commanders, your carrier air group, even that lone spectral—they need to know your intent so thoroughly that they can adapt without waiting for orders. But here's where it gets tricky: alignment without centralization requires training, discipline, and trust. How do you train a fleet for decentralized C2? Anyone?"

I responded, having already hinted at this answer earlier. "Through rigorous drills that simulate these scenarios, ma'am."

"Good answer, Mister Drake. Yes, drills. But not just any drills—iterative, escalating drills. You start with simple scenarios. Then, you introduce fog-of-war elements: comms blackouts, false intel, and time pressures. You drill until every commander and crew can act in sync without a direct line to you. Because guess what? In real warfare, your perfect plans will unravel in minutes."

She paused and pointed at a highlighted zone on the map. "One more question. You're back online after 15 minutes of blackout. You find out that one of your frigate commanders broke formation to engage a decoy target, leaving a gap in your defensive perimeter. What do you do? Do you reprimand them for deviating from the plan or commend them for taking initiative?"

Feeling more confident, I took the bate. "It depends on the outcome, sir."

Abioye glared at me. "Come, now, Mister Drake. I expect better of you. Outcome-based thinking will get you court-martialed. You judge based on intent and execution, not hindsight. Did their actions align with your stated intent? Did they mitigate a threat in a way that preserved the mission's integrity? If the answer is yes, you commend. If no, you correct—but only to reinforce alignment, not to crush initiative."

Feeling chastised, I folded my arms and looked at my notebook.

Abioye stepped back, scanning the room. "Command and control isn't just about moving pieces on a board. It's about clarity, redundancy, adaptability, and trust. Fail at any of those, and you don't just lose ships—you lose wars.

"Now, review your intent statements for the capstone exercise tomorrow. And if I see one vague or contradictory order in your plans, you'll wish I'd blown your ship myself."

22

The cafeteria felt like the inside of a broken clock—too much noise, too many moving parts, all grinding together in a rhythm that didn't quite fit. Officer candidates packed the tables, their chatter bouncing off the walls, trays clattering as if no one had been taught the concept of quiet. The food smelled vaguely like chicken, though it could've just as easily been rubber dipped in gravy. I weaved through the chaos with my tray and spotted her at a table by the window: Sofia Kohl, as rigid and unshakable as a marble statue.

Her back was straight, her plain clothes immaculate, and her tray arranged like she'd measured the angles with a protractor. She was carefully slicing into what passed for a meal, every movement deliberate, as if she were defusing a bomb instead of cutting overcooked vegetables.

"Mind if I join you?" I asked, trying to sound casual, but my voice cracked like a kid's on the first day of school.

She glanced up, her sharp blue eyes locking onto mine. For a second, I thought she'd dismiss me with a single word, but instead, her mouth curled into the faintest hint of a smile. "Please do," she said in that crisp, German accent of hers, the tone as flat as the cafeteria's mashed potatoes.

I slid into the seat across from her, feeling like I'd just survived an interrogation. "Big day of lectures," I said, arranging my tray like I cared about its placement. "Nothing gets the adrenaline pumping like a PowerPoint on armada procurement procedures."

Her knife paused mid-slice. She looked at me with a flicker of amusement, one eyebrow arching. "You sound disappointed, Kory. Did you expect something more exciting?"

"Exciting? No. Soul-crushing? Absolutely."

She exhaled, soft and sharp, the closest thing to a laugh I'd ever gotten from her. "You would not last one day in procurement."

"I don't know, Sofia. I think I'd make spreadsheets look good," I said, leaning forward slightly, trying to gauge her reaction.

Her lips twitched, but she didn't take the bait. Instead, she went back to cutting her food into precise, symmetrical pieces. "Tell me, Kory," she said without looking up, "why do you talk so much?"

"It's a gift," I said with a grin. "Keeps people on their toes."

"Or it is a curse," she muttered, shaking her head.

I took a bite of something that was supposed to be a vegetable and decided to change tactics. "So," I said after swallowing the unholy mush, "what's a Feldjäger do when she's not keeping me out of trouble?"

Her eyes flicked up again, sharp and assessing. "We enforce discipline, protect convoys, secure VIPs. Very boring, usually."

"Boring?" I repeated, leaning back in mock disbelief. "You? I don't buy it. You've got action-hero written all over you."

Her knife stopped mid-cut. She tilted her head, her expression unreadable. "Action-hero? Do you think I ran through explosions with pistols in both hands, shouting clever one-liners?"

"I mean," I said, spreading my hands, "you're not denying it."

For a moment, she stared at me, and I could've sworn I saw a flicker of something—amusement, maybe—but then her expression shifted. The walls went up, and her hands folded neatly in front of her plate.

"Berlin," she said quietly. "I was there when it fell."

The words hit like a punch, unexpected and heavy. She'd been right in the middle of one of the worst battles of the Kergan invasion.

"When the Kergans arrived," she continued, her voice measured but distant, "my unit was tasked with evacuating civilians. Families. Children. We held the route for as long as we could, but the invasion was... chaos. No one knew where the front lines were because the Kergans were the front lines. They came from everywhere."

Her words came slowly, like she was dragging them out of some locked corner of her mind. I didn't interrupt.

"They broke through faster than anyone expected," she went on. "By the time we got the last convoy moving, my team... we were cut down. Forty of us. By the end, only three were left."

She stopped, her fingers tightening against the edge of her tray.

I swallowed hard, unsure of what to say. "You got those people out, though," I offered, my voice softer now.

"Not all of them," she said bitterly. "Some were too afraid to move. We had to drag them into the trucks while they screamed that it was already too late. That the sky was falling."

Her eyes locked on mine then, and I saw it—an ocean of pain, rage, and guilt, all barely held together behind the fortress she'd built around herself.

"I hear their voices sometimes," she admitted, her tone almost a whisper. "In my dreams. The ones who didn't make it. The ones we couldn't save."

The cafeteria noise seemed to fade, the world narrowing to the two of us at that table. "Sofia," I said, leaning forward, "you did what you could. More than anyone else would've done. Those people got a chance because of you."

For a moment, I thought she might snap at me or shut down entirely. But instead, she exhaled slowly and gave me a faint, rueful smile.

"You have a way of making complicated things sound simple," she said.

"It's a talent," I replied, grinning despite the lump in my throat. "I call it 'charming nonsense.'"

She shook her head, but this time, her smile was genuine, however fleeting. "You are trouble, Kory Drake."

"Only the good kind," I said, leaning back with a wink.

She let out a soft snort, then went back to her meal, the faint smile lingering. For the first time, I felt like I'd seen the real Sofia Kohl—hidden behind the polished uniform and unshakable professionalism. It was only a glimpse, but it was enough to keep me coming back.

The rain had stopped, leaving the air damp and heavy as Sofia and I walked back toward my quarters. The lamps lining the walkways cast golden pools of light on the slick pavement, and the buzz of the day had finally started to fade. Sofia walked beside me, her hands tucked neatly behind her back, her stride precise and measured as always.

"So," she said, her voice breaking the quiet, "you were a captain, yes? Of this... *Thunder*?"

I smirked. "*Starship Thunder.* You know, it's more impressive when you say it like that."

"Ah, my apologies." She gave a small shrug, her tone teasing. "Captain Kory Drake of the *Starship Thunder.* Is that better?"

"Much better," I said, grinning. "You're learning."

She raised an eyebrow. "And what was it like, this 'command'? Did you shout orders from a grand chair while dramatic music played in the background?"

"Pretty much nailed it," I said, laughing. "Except replace 'grand chair' with a tight couch squeezed in the back of the flight deck. And the dramatic music? That was mostly just the ship's alarms telling us we were seconds from dying."

Sofia chuckled softly, the sound light and warm. "So, not quite as glamorous as the stories suggest."

"Not even close," I admitted. "But it was ours, you know? *Thunder* wasn't much, but we made it work. My crew trusted me, even when I didn't always have a plan. Especially when I didn't have a plan."

She tilted her head, studying me with that sharp, unrelenting gaze of hers. "And now?"

"Now?" I shrugged. "Now I'm stuck playing officer candidate while trying to prove to the Dominion I'm not some kind of intergalactic criminal mastermind."

"Ah, yes," she said, her voice turning mock-serious. "The infamous charges of sydereal battery and conspiring with an Astral Titan. Truly diabolical."

"You forgot jaywalking in the Sydereallium," I added,

smirking. "That one's a real doozy."

Her laugh caught me off guard—short, genuine, and almost musical. She shook her head. "You make jokes, but you are... how do you say... walking on thin ice?"

"Thin ice is where I do my best work," I said, flashing her a grin.

By the time we reached my quarters, I realized the room was dark, which was unusual. Miyagawa, my rigidly studious roommate, was usually glued to his desk, rambling about ship systems or Dominion tech.

"Looks like we've got the place to ourselves," I said, flipping on the light. The room lit up with the sterile glow of the overhead fixtures, revealing the standard-issue twin bunks, steel desks, and a pile of Miyagawa's datapads that looked ready to topple at any moment.

"Convenient," Sofia said, her tone unreadable. She stepped inside, her gaze flicking briefly over the space before settling back on me.

"Home sweet home," I said, dropping onto the edge of my bunk. "Not exactly the *Thunder*, but at least the walls don't rattle every time someone sneezes."

Sofia leaned against the desk, crossing her arms. "And yet you still miss it, don't you?"

I nodded, my smile fading a little. "Yeah. I do. Not just the ship—everything. The crew, the chaos, even the bad coffee. Being captain was... I don't know. It felt like I was actually doing something, you know? Making a difference."

"You still are," she said softly. "Even if you do not see it."

Her words hung in the air for a moment, heavier than I expected. I glanced up, and for the first time, her usually impenetrable expression seemed to crack just a little.

"Thanks," I said, my voice quieter. "Coming from you, that means a lot."

She looked at me for a moment longer, then straightened, brushing a strand of blond hair back into her tight bun. "You are welcome, Kory," she said, her voice shifting back to its usual composed tone.

I was about to crack another joke, something to lighten the mood when she moved.

It happened so fast I barely had time to register it. One second, she was standing by the desk; the next, she was closing the distance between us in a rush of motion, her blue eyes blazing. Her hands grabbed the front of my uniform, and before I could process what was happening, her lips crashed into mine.

The kiss was fierce, unyielding—like everything about Sofia. It wasn't tentative or hesitant. It was a storm, pulling me in and drowning out every other thought in my head.

For a moment, I just froze, my brain struggling to catch up. But then I responded, my hands finding her waist, pulling her closer as the world narrowed to just the two of us.

When she finally pulled back, her breath was quick, her cheeks flushed. She didn't let go of my uniform, her hands still gripping the fabric like she wasn't entirely ready to step away.

"That," she said, her voice slightly unsteady, "did not happen."

I blinked, still dazed. "Uh... pretty sure it just did."

Her eyes narrowed, but there was a flicker of something behind them—something warm and vulnerable. "Then it stays between us," she said firmly.

"Your secret's safe with me," I said, grinning despite the thunder still pounding in my chest.

She hesitated, her grip loosening slightly, then stood up and stepped back, smoothing her jacket like nothing had happened. "Good. Now, get some rest, Kory Drake. You have another thrilling day of lectures tomorrow."

And with that, she turned and marched out, leaving me sitting there, my mind spinning and my heart still racing.

"Well," I muttered to the empty room, "that was unexpected."

23

Lieutenant Commander Santiago Rodriguez, our instructor for Starship Navigation and Spacemanship, stood at the front of the classroom, his hands clasped behind his back, gazing out at us. Behind him, a holographic display projected a spinning, three-dimensional map of the local star cluster. Brightly colored nodes marked potential entry points for dimensional bubble initiation: Lagrange points, the heliopause, and the calm zones outside stellar magnetic interference.

"Good afternoon, candidates," he began, his tone warm but firm. "Today, we're going to discuss the delicate art of faster-than-light navigation—specifically, the use of dimensional bubbles within the Syderealium. As candidate officers, understanding this technology isn't optional; it's your lifeline. So let's get to it."

Rodriguez tapped a control on the podium, and the hologram zoomed in on a Lagrange point between Earth and the Moon. The display annotated gravitational vectors and neutral-force zones.

"Let's start with the basics," he said. "Candidate Drake, define a dimensional bubble."

I hesitated, leaning forward slightly. Why did all the instructors seem to always call on me first? "Uh, it's a... localized pocket of space-time that isolates a ship from the material plane. It lets us use the Syderealium to cut travel distances."

"Partly correct," Rodriguez said, nodding. "But oversimplified. A dimensional bubble is a controlled environment where a ship's sublight propulsion interacts with manifold pathways in the Syderealium. Without that control, the bubble would destabilize instantly. Now, why can we only initiate a DB in specific locations?"

I scratched my head. "Because... the forces outside those zones... disrupt the bubble?"

"That's imprecise," Rodriguez said. He turned to the hologram and pointed at the annotated vectors. "Miss Tatum, help him out."

Arline Tatum adjusted her glasses. "Dimensional bubbles require a stable entry environment. Gravitational and magnetic forces must be neutral, or below a critical threshold, to avoid distortion during formation. That's why we use Lagrange points or move outside the heliosphere."

"Better," Rodriguez said, smiling. "Neutral environments allow Phase Oscillators to establish a coherent bubble without interference. What happens if you attempt to create a DB near a strong gravitational well or magnetic flux?"

"The bubble collapses," Tatum said confidently.

"Not just collapses," Rodriguez corrected. "You also risk dimensional shear. Mister Zhou, what's the consequence of dimensional shear?"

Zheng Zhou leaned back slightly. "It destabilizes the

ship's systems and might... tear it apart?"

"Correct," Rodriguez said, though his tone sharpened. "Specifically, shear causes severe phase misalignment, scattering ship components—and crew—across untraceable dimensions. Ships lost to shear aren't just destroyed; they're obliterated. Moving on."

The hologram shifted, showing a multi-colored map of manifold pathways within the Sydereailum. Arcing lines represented compressed spatial corridors ships used to traverse the galaxy.

"This," Rodriguez said, "is a manifold network. Mister Miyagawa, describe its purpose."

Miyagawa studied the display. "The manifolds are folded paths that shorten the distance between two points. Ships travel through them using harmonic alignment."

"That's the theory," Rodriguez said. "But what governs the stability of these paths?"

Miyagawa hesitated. "Gravitational... and energy fluxes?"

"Correct, but too vague. Manifold pathways are dynamic, influenced by nearby stellar activity, gravitational echoes, and interstellar events. That's why Manifold Mapping Arrays—MMAs—are critical. Miss Gustavsson, explain how MMAs function."

Heidi Gustavsson leaned forward. "MMAs use gravimetric sensors, quantum wave detectors, and harmonic resonance scanners to chart manifold topography in real time. They identify stable corridors and flag areas of turbulence."

"Close," Rodriguez said, raising a finger. "But MMAs don't just map turbulence; they predict its onset, giving navigators time to adjust. What happens if you navigate a turbulent manifold?"

"Dimensional drift," she replied immediately. "The bubble loses alignment and veers off-course."

"And what does that mean for your ship?"

Gustavsson faltered. "You… might end up off-target?"

"Off-target is an understatement," Rodriguez said. "Drift can pull your ship into a dead zone or a high-energy manifold. Either scenario is lethal. That's why Drift Compensation Matrices are onboard. Mister Zhou, how do they work?"

"They monitor the bubble's alignment and… apply corrections automatically?" Zhou ventured.

"Automatic corrections, yes," Rodriguez confirmed. "But they're not infallible. Severe drift requires manual recalibration. Candidate Drake, what happens if recalibration fails?"

I swallowed. "Emergency collapse of the bubble and re-emerge into real space?"

"Only as a last resort," Rodriguez said. "Emergency collapse is dangerous and should only occur in a safe zone. Miss Tatum, describe a safe zone for reintegration."

Tatum nodded. "Neutral-force locations, like Lagrange points or calm areas beyond the heliosphere."

"Correct. But reintegration protocols are precise. Mister Miyagawa, what ensures spatial accuracy during reintegration?"

"Gravitic Anchors," Miyagawa said. "They synchronize the ship with the target's gravitational signature."

"And what's the acceptable drift margin?" Rodriguez asked.

Gustavsson jumped in. "Point-oh-two AU."

"Right," Rodriguez said. "Exceed that margin, and you risk emerging into a hazardous zone. Or worse, not emerging at all."

The hologram shifted again, displaying a malfunctioning ship struggling in turbulent Syderealium currents. Sensor alerts flashed on the display.

"Final question," Rodriguez said. "Mister Zhou, if your Sydereal Projectors fail mid-traversal, what's your last resort?"

Zhou's face tightened. "Manual bubble collapse and re-entry into real space, sir. Target the nearest neutral-force zone."

"Correct," Rodriguez said, his gaze softening. "But remember, candidates, that situation is as much about composure as skill. If you panic, you've already lost. That's why we drill these scenarios until they're second nature."

He stepped back to the podium and deactivated the hologram. "Now, let's move on to something equally critical: integrating FTL into military operations. Candidate Drake, how would you use FTL to gain an advantage over an enemy fleet in open combat?"

I cleared my throat, scrambling for a response. "Uh, you could use it to strike from an unexpected angle, sir? Maybe jump behind their formation to hit vulnerable support ships?"

"Not bad," Rodriguez said, tilting his head. "But oversimplified. Surprise is only an advantage if it's paired with timing and precision. Imagine this scenario: You jump behind an enemy fleet, but your maneuver places you too far from your intended target. What happens then?"

I hesitated. "I guess the enemy has time to react, sir?"

"Exactly," Rodriguez replied. "And in that time, your fleet might be caught between their main line and their reinforcements. Surprise turns into a disadvantage." He turned to the rest of the class. "Mister Zhou, how do you ensure an FTL strike is both unexpected and effective?"

Zhou sat up straighter. "You'd have to coordinate your re-entry point with precise targeting data, sir. And… time it so their fleet is already committed to another engagement?"

"Better," Rodriguez said with a nod. "Timing is everything. A successful FTL strike disrupts an enemy's command and control structure. You don't just hit their ships; you collapse their ability to respond. And that brings us to the next question: Miss Gustavsson, what risks must you mitigate when using FTL offensively?"

Gustavsson furrowed her brow in thought. "Drift during reintegration could scatter your fleet. And if the enemy predicts your maneuver, they might set a trap at your re-entry point."

"Precisely," Rodriguez said. "FTL offensives are as much about deception as execution. You must mask your intent—false course projections, decoy signals, even simulated DB initiations can confuse your opponent. But if they know where you'll re-emerge, you're handing them an easy kill."

The hologram shifted again, displaying a simulated fleet engagement. One group of ships, marked in red, maintained a defensive line while a blue fleet split into two groups. The second group disappeared into the Syderealium, leaving the first to engage.

"This simulation demonstrates a coordinated FTL pincer maneuver," Rodriguez said. "The blue fleet divides, drawing the red force's attention to their main group. Meanwhile, the second group initiates a DB and re-emerges behind the red formation. Mister Miyagawa, what factors determine whether this maneuver succeeds or fails?"

Miyagawa leaned forward, studying the display. "The timing of the re-entry, sir, and the accuracy of the second group's positioning. If they're off by even a few degrees, they might miss the optimal engagement angle."

"Correct," Rodriguez said, tapping the hologram to highlight the re-emerging blue group. "Additionally, the second group must maintain communication with the main fleet. FTL maneuvers create a delay in traditional signals, so you'll rely on pre-established coordination protocols. Candidate Drake, how do you ensure your second group isn't detected during their approach?"

"Uh, by minimizing emissions while in the Syderealium, sir." I offered.

"Partly correct," Rodriguez said. "Emission control is vital, but so is choosing your entry node. If you initiate a DB too close to the enemy, their sensors might pick up the distortion. Always use neutral-force zones outside their effective scanning range."

He paced back to the podium and folded his arms. "Now, let's address defensive applications. Miss Tatum, how could FTL technology be used to defend a vulnerable station or colony?"

Tatum adjusted her glasses again. "You could position a rapid response fleet at a nearby Lagrange point, sir. If an attack occurs, they could jump directly to the target's location."

"Good," Rodriguez said. "But what if the attackers use their own FTL capabilities to evade your response?"

"You'd have to predict their exit point and position interdiction forces there," she replied.

Rodriguez nodded. "Exactly. Defensive FTL operations require not only reaction but anticipation. The Collective Dominion is developing Syderealium suppression fields—experimental devices that disrupt DB stability in a localized area. Mister Zhou, what's the strategic value of such a device?"

Zhou's eyes lit up. "It could block an enemy's escape or

force them to re-emerge prematurely, sir."

"Correct," Rodriguez said. "It turns their greatest advantage into a liability. But remember, candidates, these technologies are still in their infancy. The burden of effective FTL use falls on you. Master it, or our enemies will."

The room fell silent as he let that statement hang in the air. Rodriguez stepped back toward the podium and tapped a command, causing the display to shift again. This time, it highlighted several Lagrange points in a simulated star system. Around one of them, a dense field of glowing red dots appeared.

"Let's talk about a particularly controversial tactic: using minefields to deny access to neutral-force zones such as Lagrange points," Rodriguez said, his tone measured but firm. "Miss Tatum, as a defender, why might you deploy mines around a Lagrange point?"

Tatum adjusted her glasses, leaning forward slightly. "To prevent the enemy from initiating a dimensional bubble near the point, sir. Without access to a neutral-force zone, their FTL options are severely limited."

"Correct," Rodriguez said, nodding. "By mining these zones, you create a deterrent. The enemy must either clear the mines—wasting time and resources—or risk severe damage attempting to bypass them. Now, Mister Zhou, what's the downside of this approach for the defender?"

Zhou furrowed his brow, clearly thinking it through. "If the enemy captures the system, they could use the mines against you, sir. And... it might also block your own fleet's access to the Lagrange point?"

"Precisely," Rodriguez said. "Mines don't discriminate. If your fleet needs to retreat or re-enter the system, those same defenses could become an obstacle. There's also the matter of maintenance. Minefields degrade over time, and deploying or replenishing them requires significant resources. Candidate Drake, what about the strategic risks? How could a defender's reliance on mining backfire?"

I hesitated, then ventured, "It could make you predictable, sir? If the enemy knows you always mine Lagrange points, they might plan around it."

"Good," Rodriguez said, his tone approving. "Predictability is a weakness in war. An intelligent enemy will exploit it. For instance, they might lure you into defending a heavily mined zone, only to strike elsewhere. Or, they could deploy specialized countermeasures, like remote mine-clearing drones, rendering your defenses useless."

He paced to the other side of the room, gesturing to the hologram. "Now, let's switch perspectives. Mister Miyagawa, why might an aggressor mine a Lagrange point?"

"To deny the defender access to FTL entry and exit points, sir," Miyagawa answered quickly. "If they can't reach the point, their ability to maneuver strategically is crippled."

"Exactly," Rodriguez said. "For an aggressor, mining neutral-force zones can isolate a target system. But Miss Gustavsson, what are the downsides of this tactic for the attacker?"

Gustavsson tilted her head, thinking carefully. "If the defender has strong local forces, they could clear the mines before you finish your main operation, sir. And... deploying mines could reveal your strategy or position."

"Correct," Rodriguez said. "Mines are powerful tools, but their deployment isn't subtle. The act of laying a minefield can give away your intentions, particularly if you're targeting a specific neutral-force zone. Additionally, overly relying on mines can spread your resources thin. If your fleet is busy mining, they're not fighting."

He stepped back toward the podium, folding his arms. "Let's consider a hypothetical scenario. The UHC Armada is defending a critical colony orbiting a gas giant. The Lagrange points are mined to deny enemy access. The aggressor's fleet enters the system and begins systematically clearing the mines. Mister Drake, as the defending fleet commander, what's your move?"

I thought hard, trying to picture the scenario. "Uh... I'd deploy ships to harass the enemy while they're clearing the mines, sir. Force them to divide their attention."

"Good instinct," Rodriguez said. "A minefield is most effective when combined with active defense. If you allow the enemy to clear it unopposed, it's nothing more than a speed bump. However, harassing them comes with its own risks. Mister Zhou, what's the danger of engaging the enemy during their mine-clearing operation?"

Zhou answered quickly, "You might overextend your forces, sir, leaving other parts of the system vulnerable."

"Exactly," Rodriguez said, nodding sharply. "Overextension is a common mistake. Mines should augment your defense, not replace sound strategy. If you overcommit to protecting a mined zone, you risk losing control elsewhere."

The hologram shifted again, this time showing an enemy fleet laying mines around a neutral-force zone while a blue fleet—representing the defenders—attempted to counter.

"Now, let's look at it from the attacker's perspective. Miss Tatum, as the aggressor, you're mining a Lagrange point to deny the defender access. What are your immediate priorities?"

Tatum sat up straighter. "To complete the minefield quickly and secure the area with a holding force, sir."

"Good," Rodriguez said. "But let's add complexity. Mister Miyagawa, what happens if the defender launches a surprise attack on your mining operation?"

Miyagawa frowned, studying the display. "Then you'd need to divert your main fleet to protect the operation, sir. That could leave your other assets exposed."

"Correct," Rodriguez said. "Mining is not a quick process. It ties up your resources and makes you vulnerable. That's why timing and deception are critical. Miss Gustavsson, how might an attacker use FTL to make their mining operation more effective?"

"They could deploy decoy fleets to draw the defender away, sir," Gustavsson said. "Or use staggered FTL maneuvers to keep their movements unpredictable."

"Exactly," Rodriguez said. "An effective mining operation is as much about misdirection as execution. If the defender doesn't realize you're mining until it's too late, you've already won half the battle."

He paused, letting the simulation run for a moment before turning back to us. "Candidates, the decision to mine a neutral-force zone isn't one to take lightly. It's a double-edged sword. Whether you're defending or attacking, you must weigh the costs and benefits carefully. Mines can deny access, disrupt operations, and buy you time—but only if used intelligently. Misuse them, and they can just as easily become a liability."

Rodriguez deactivated the hologram and faced us directly. "For your next assignment, I want each of you to draft a tactical analysis of a hypothetical battle scenario. Choose one role: defender or aggressor. Detail how you would use minefields in combination with FTL maneuvers to achieve your objectives. Identify the risks, countermeasures, and potential pitfalls. We'll review your strategies in the next session."

My head buzzed with the possibilities and challenges as I considered the scenario Rodriguez had laid out. As we filed out, I couldn't help but think about how every decision—every mine placed or maneuver planned—could be the difference between victory and defeat.

24

The morning was already unbearable—hot, muggy, and thick with humidity that clung to my skin like a second layer of clothing. Every breath felt like inhaling warm soup, and the alien vegetation lining the trail only made it worse. Massive, waxy-leafed plants towered overhead, their deep purple fronds drooping under their own weight, dripping condensation onto the trail. Vines as thick as my forearm curled around the trunks of strange, bulbous trees, their bark glowing faintly with bioluminescence, even in the daylight.

Somewhere in the underbrush, an alien creature let out a low, vibrating call—a sound halfway between a cricket's chirp and the hum of an electric motor. It was joined by others, their overlapping cries creating an eerie, rhythmic background that buzzed in my ears as I ran. I couldn't help but notice the flashes of movement out of the corner of my eye—small, scaled creatures with limbs that didn't seem to agree on whether they should be climbing or flying.

This was Astrithon in the monsoon: alive, oppressive,

and completely unlike Earth.

My boots crunched against the gravel trail as I pushed myself forward, sweat rolling down my back. The OTS instructors called these long-distance runs "character-building." In this heat, I was pretty sure it was just character-melting.

The trail ahead narrowed, flanked by dense undergrowth and strange, flower-like growths the size of dinner plates. They gave off a sickly-sweet smell that mingled with the sour tang of sweat in the air. The other candidates ran in formation, their expressions glazed, focusing only on keeping pace. My mind drifted, lulled by the monotony of the run and the suffocating heat.

That's when I noticed it.

The forest had gone quiet. The rhythmic hum of the alien wildlife was gone, replaced by an uneasy stillness. Even the air felt heavier, like the world was holding its breath.

I glanced over my shoulder, scanning the line of candidates. They all looked the same—tired, sweaty, miserable—but the quiet gnawed at me. Something wasn't right.

I turned back just as a faint glint of light caught my eye—something metallic, reflecting the weak sunlight filtering through the canopy. My gut twisted, the sense of unease sharpening into alarm. A split second later, I heard it: the telltale whip of something cutting through the air.

Instinct took over. I threw myself sideways, hitting the dirt just as a small, weaponized drone zipped past, its blades whirring with an eerie, high-pitched hum. The air it displaced felt unnaturally cold against the sticky heat of the forest. It turned sharply, recalibrating, its insect-like frame glinting as it hovered, its blades shifting with a metallic snick.

"Get down!" I shouted, scrambling to my feet. The other candidates stopped, their faces blank with confusion, but the drone wasn't interested in them. It came for me again, fast and precise.

I tried to dodge, but not fast enough—the edge of one blade grazed my thigh, slicing through my PT gear like it was paper. Pain flared hot and sharp, blood instantly staining the fabric.

I staggered, my heart pounding in my ears. The drone buzzed menacingly, its movements too deliberate to be random. Whoever controlled it knew exactly what they were doing.

I scanned the trail and the dense vegetation around it, looking for the source. The assassin had to be nearby—this wasn't an autonomous killbot. The drone's movements were too fluid, too reactive. My eyes darted across the alien plants and shadows until I caught the faintest hint of movement: a figure crouched behind one of the glowing-barked trees, half-hidden by the massive purple fronds.

Gotcha.

I didn't think—I just moved. Grabbing a fist-sized rock from the trail, I hurled it at the drone with everything I had. The rock clipped one of its tractor pods, sending the machine spiraling into the dirt with a metallic screech.

The figure behind the tree bolted.

Ignoring the burning pain in my leg, I pushed myself forward, crashing through the underbrush. The alien plants clawed at me as I ran, their sticky fronds clinging to my arms and legs. The assassin moved fast—too fast—but in their haste, they stumbled over a thick vine, just for a moment.

It was enough.

I lunged, tackling them to the ground. We hit the dirt

hard, and the impact knocked the wind out of both of us. They twisted, trying to free themselves, but I wasn't letting go.

Up close, I saw the assassin was a man. His gear—muted greens and grays designed to blend into the forest, a compact controller clutched in one gloved hand. I grabbed for it, prying it loose even as he struggled.

He lashed out with a short, curved blade that glinted in the filtered light. I barely managed to grab his wrist in time, my muscles straining as I forced the blade away from my face. For a moment, we were locked there, his strength almost surprising.

"Not today," I growled, twisting his wrist until he yelped and the blade fell from his grip. It hit the dirt with a dull thud.

I rolled him onto his stomach, pinning him with my knee. "Who sent you?" I barked, my voice rough with adrenaline.

He didn't answer, of course. He just hissed something under his breath, the language guttural and unfamiliar.

Behind me, I heard the approaching footsteps of the other candidates, their voices rising in confusion and alarm.

"Kory! What the hell's going on?" someone shouted.

"Call security!" I shouted back, pressing the assassin down harder. "This one's got answers! I'm tired of this skulking!"

Blood dripped from my thigh, staining the dirt below, but I barely felt it. My pulse thundered in my ears as I stared down at the would-be killer. This wasn't just some random attack.

Someone wanted me dead.

But they'd made a mistake. They thought I wouldn't be able to fight back.

The assassin thrashed once more beneath me, twisting like a pinned snake. Then it happened.

A muffled click.

Before I could even react, a sharp pop sounded from the assassin's head, followed by a sickening crack. Their body went limp beneath me, and a thin wisp of acrid smoke curled upward from the back of their skull.

"Shit!" I stumbled back, instinctively shielding my face. My ears rang, and my heart pounded as I stared at the lifeless body. The head was partially collapsed, the remnants of a small, embedded device now fused into charred flesh and bone.

Sofia's voice cut through the chaos before I could process what had just happened.

"Everyone on the ground!" she barked, her voice sharp and commanding, as she and Charlie burst into the clearing. Sofia's weapon was drawn, a sleek Dominion-issued pistol held steady in her hands, while Charlie flanked her with a rifle slung over his shoulder, ready to fire.

The candidates around us froze, eyes wide, hands slowly raising as they dropped to their knees.

"Hands where we can see them!" Charlie added, his voice booming.

Sofia's eyes darted over the scene, sharp and calculating, before locking on me. There was none of the longing and pent-up passion I'd seen in them last time. Her jaw tightened when she saw the blood on my thigh, but her focus didn't waver.

"Kory," she said firmly, moving quickly to my side, "are you hurt? How bad is it?"

"Just a scratch," I muttered, gesturing to my leg. The wound burned, but I wasn't about to complain in front of half the OTS candidates.

She didn't look convinced. Her free hand pressed lightly against my shoulder, pushing me into a crouch as she placed herself between me and the assassin's corpse. Charlie moved to cover the treeline, scanning for any additional threats.

"What happened?" Sofia demanded, her tone clipped.

"Drone attack. This guy was controlling it," I said, nodding toward the body. "He bolted when I spotted him. I tackled him, and then..." I trailed off, motioning to the smoke curling from the back of the assassin's skull.

Sofia knelt beside the corpse, her movements quick but deliberate. "Implanted kill switch," she muttered, her voice low. "Whoever sent him didn't want him talking."

Her hands moved over the assassin's clothing with practiced precision, searching the pockets and seams. She pulled out a few small items—a data chip, a folded piece of paper with something scrawled in a language I didn't recognize, and a smooth, black token etched with strange markings.

"This," she said, holding up the token, her expression darkening.

"What is it?" I asked, leaning closer.

"It's a marker," she said grimly. "From the *Therrak Consortium.*"

"The what?"

"A crime syndicate," Charlie said, his eyes still scanning the perimeter. "Big in this region. Smuggling, sabotage, assassinations—they'll do anything if the price is right."

Sofia nodded, slipping the token into a pouch on her belt. "And if they're targeting you, Kory, it means someone's paying them very well."

My stomach tightened. "Any idea who?"

"Not yet," she said, standing and holstering her

weapon. "But this marker gives us a place to start. The Consortium doesn't operate in secret. If this assassin was working for them, we'll find someone who knows why."

The distant sound of boots on gravel reached us as a squad of Dominion kavreni security personnel arrived, their sleek, alien weapons at the ready. Sofia straightened, her demeanor calm but commanding as she waved them over.

"We'll handle the debrief," she said to Charlie, her gaze flicking to me briefly. "And you—you're not leaving our sight until we figure out who's behind this. From now on, you're under close protection."

"Wasn't planning on it," I said, my voice laced with sarcasm. But beneath the bravado, the weight of what had just happened settled heavily in my chest.

Someone wanted me dead. And now I had a name: Therrak Consortium.

It wasn't much, but it was a start.

The infirmary was quiet, save for the soft hum of equipment and the occasional rustle of the medic's tools. My leg burned with every pull of the needle, the sharp sting reminding me of how close the drone's blade had come. The ceiling panels above me blurred slightly as I tried to focus on anything but the pain.

The door hissed open, and Sofia walked in, passing between the two MPs stationed outside. Even in plain clothes—a sharp blazer over a simple blouse and slacks—she exuded authority. Her blue eyes swept the room, lingering briefly on me before shifting to the medic and the equipment. Something about her presence made the antiseptic air feel less oppressive.

"Drake," she said, her voice low but steady. She walked to the foot of the bed, her polished shoes clicking softly against the tiled floor. In her hand, she held the black token.

"You checking on me, or is it my magnetic personality?" I quipped, trying to inject some levity into the room.

Her lips twitched—just enough for me to notice—but her expression remained guarded. "You're my responsibility," she said simply. "I'm keeping this." She held up the token, the strange etchings catching the light.

I raised an eyebrow. "What? I can't keep it as a souvenir?"

Her blue eyes narrowed slightly. "It's evidence, Kory. Not a trinket."

I opened my mouth to retort, but the door hissed open again, and Colonel Patil strode in like she owned the place. Her uniform was immaculate, her stride purposeful, her sharp eyes scanning the room with the precision of a laser.

"Candidate Drake," Patil said, her gaze shifting to me. "Status?"

"Stitched up and ready to go, ma'am," I said, nodding toward the medic.

"Good," she said curtly before turning her attention to Sofia. "Warrant Officer Kohl. What are you doing here? This is an infirmary, not an interrogation room."

Sofia straightened, her shoulders squared. "I'm here as part of my assignment, ma'am. Close protection detail for Candidate Drake."

Patil's eyes narrowed, and her voice turned sharp. "Close protection does not mean hovering over him at every opportunity, Warrant Officer. Candidate Drake is a trainee under my command, not an operative. He is under a Dominion indictment and is here to focus on his training. He cannot play a role in your investigation."

"With all due respect, ma'am," Sofia said, her voice cool and even, "ensuring his safety means being aware of every possible threat against him, including those tied to this investigation. My presence here is within the scope of my duties."

Patil's gaze hardened. "Your duties are to keep him alive, not to distract him from his studies or undermine the chain of command. Your proximity to this investigation is a privilege, not a license to do as you please. Candidate Drake's status as a trainee and a defendant is already making his situation precarious enough without unnecessary interference."

Sofia's jaw tightened, and for a moment, I thought she might snap back. Instead, she inclined her head slightly, her tone still measured. "I understand your concerns, ma'am. But I respectfully remind you that my orders come directly from the UHC High Command. My detail requires me to remain close to Candidate Drake."

Patil's expression didn't soften. "Then stay in your lane, Warrant Officer. Do your job without creating unnecessary distractions. Am I clear?"

"Crystal, ma'am," Sofia said, her voice cool and clipped.

Patil turned to me, her tone softening slightly. "Drake, focus on your studies. You have enough challenges ahead without involving yourself in these matters. Let the professionals do their jobs. I have every confidence they'll get to the bottom of this."

"Yes, ma'am," I said, though the irritation in my voice was hard to mask.

Patil nodded sharply, then pivoted on her heel and left, her boots clicking sharply on the tiled floor. The door hissed shut behind her, leaving the room eerily quiet.

Sofia let out a slow breath, her posture relaxing slightly as she slipped the token into her pocket. For a moment, she just stood there, her blue eyes lingering on the door before turning back to me.

"Well," I said, breaking the silence, "that was fun. I think she likes you."

Sofia's lips twitched, but her expression remained unreadable. "You don't make my job any easier, you know that?"

"Wouldn't want you getting bored," I said, grinning despite the dull ache in my leg.

Her eyes softened, just for a moment, before she shook her head and turned toward the door. "Stay out of trouble, Kory."

"Trouble finds me," I said, leaning back on the bed.

She paused, glancing over her shoulder with a look I couldn't quite decipher. "Just try to make my life a little less interesting." And then she was gone, leaving the room quieter but somehow heavier, the faint scent of her perfume lingering in the air.

I exhaled slowly, staring at the ceiling. Sofia might've been all business in front of the Colonel, but the little things —the way her voice softened when she said my name, the way she lingered for just a second longer than she needed to —told me there was more beneath the surface.

And as much as I hated being stuck on the sidelines, I couldn't shake the feeling that Sofia's determination to keep me safe went far beyond duty.

25

The final weeks at OTS felt like I was living in two parallel realities. In one, I was a candidate, slogging through the endless grind of training, studying, and testing—racing toward graduation with my head down and my focus sharp. In the other, I was the center of a storm I couldn't see but could feel all around me, a game of shadows and whispers where everyone seemed to know more than I did.

Sofia and her team had become an unavoidable part of my life. They were always there, shadowing me like guardian specters in plain clothes. It wasn't just Sofia, though she was the constant presence, her sharp blue eyes scanning every room, every hallway, every face. Her colleagues rotated in and out, keeping things unpredictable for anyone watching.

Their vigilance was absolute, but their presence wasn't exactly subtle. Watching Sofia trail me during PT runs was worth the price of admission alone. She wasn't required to participate, of course, but she still jogged along the track in her smart slacks and flats, looking completely out of place next to a pack of sweating candidates. I couldn't help but tease her about it one morning.

"Nice pace, Sofia. You sure you're not slowing us down?"

She shot me a glare sharp enough to cut steel, though the corners of her mouth twitched. "Focus on your breathing, Candidate Drake. Or do you want me to write up your poor form?"

Her colleagues weren't as graceful under the strain. Charlie, one of the burlier members of her detail, tried to keep up once, but the man clearly wasn't built for long-distance running. After his third attempt, I overheard him mutter something about "stupid kids with too much energy" before Sofia benched him from PT duty altogether.

The capstone assignments arrived like a storm, testing everything we'd learned in our time at OTS. I threw myself into them, determined to prove that I belonged here, that I could rise above the whispers of the Dominion trial and the protective shadow of Sofia and her team.

Simulated shipboard drills. Tactical decision-making exercises. Leadership under pressure. The final weeks pushed us to our limits, and I thrived on the challenge. By the time the final rankings were announced, I finished second in my class—just shy of the top spot, which went to a candidate who could calculate firing solutions in her sleep. I couldn't even be mad about it.

Then came the orders.

A neatly folded piece of paper with my name stamped on it in black ink. From UHC High Command. The details were clear: I was to report to the Dominion Space Warfare School immediately after OTS graduation. The assignment came straight from Celestarch Seraphis herself, no less. My head spun as I read it, the words feeling unreal even as they stared back at me. Seraphis had come through for me just like she promised.

The reality didn't fully sink in until late that night when I caught Sofia leaning against the doorway of my dorm room, her jacket slung over one shoulder and a look of exhaustion etched on her face.

"You're going to the Space Warfare School," she said, her voice quiet. It wasn't a question.

"Looks like it," I replied, setting the orders on my desk. "Guess I impressed someone."

"You impressed Seraphis," she said, stepping into the room. "That's not easy to do."

There was something in her tone—an edge of pride that she quickly buried behind her usual professionalism.

Late-night conversations with Sofia had become something of a ritual. She'd show up when the campus was quiet, her guard lowered just enough that I could see the cracks beneath. She never said much about herself, but the dark circles under her eyes and the tension in her voice told me enough. She was running on fumes, driven by a mix of duty and sheer determination.

I pressed her for updates on the investigation whenever I could, but she always deflected, citing Colonel Patil's orders or the need for operational security.

"It's better if you don't know," she'd say, her voice soft but firm. "You've got enough to deal with."

"But it's about me," I'd argue. "Don't I have the right to know who's trying to kill me?"

She'd just shake her head, her blue eyes unreadable. "Focus on what you can control, Kory. Let me handle the rest."

Still, little cracks showed. Sofia's tight-lipped responses only made me more suspicious, especially when I started noticing unfamiliar faces lingering around campus. They weren't candidates, that much was obvious—too polished, too still, too deliberate in the way they watched from the edges of the track or the corners of the mess hall.

I brought it up to Sofia one night, half expecting her to brush it off. Instead, her expression darkened for a split second before she forced it back under control.

"Just keep your distance," she said curtly, her voice colder than usual.

Her reaction only confirmed my suspicions, but I let it drop, for her sake more than mine. Whatever was happening, it was clear Sofia was carrying the weight of it, and for reasons I didn't fully understand, she didn't want to share that burden.

The night before graduation felt electric, like the air before a storm. The entire OTS campus buzzed with anticipation, candidates rushing to polish their dress uniforms, rehearse the formalities, and cram in last-minute farewells. I wasn't immune to it. My desk was cluttered with scattered notes, a half-packed bag, and the crisp, ceremonial jacket that still didn't feel quite like mine.

Sofia was there, leaning against the doorframe like she always did when the halls were quiet. She looked more relaxed than usual, her jacket slung over one shoulder, her blonde hair framing her blue eyes. Her expression was soft, almost wistful, though she quickly masked it when she caught me looking.

"Big day tomorrow," she said, stepping into the room.

"Feels surreal," I admitted, glancing at the folded orders on my desk. "A few weeks ago, I wasn't even sure I'd make it this far."

"You earned it," she said firmly, her gaze steady.

"Despite the distractions."

I smirked. "You mean despite you and your team following me around like lost puppies?"

Her lips twitched, and for a second, I thought she might actually laugh. "You'll miss us when we're gone."

"Who says you're going anywhere?" I shot back.

She tilted her head, her expression unreadable. "We'll see."

The conversation shifted, as it always did, to practical matters—my assignment to the Space Warfare School, her role as my close protection detail, the logistics of moving from one high-pressure environment to another. But as she turned to leave, she hesitated, her fingers brushing the edge of the doorframe.

"Rest well, Kory," she said softly.

The morning of graduation dawned bright and warm, the air heavy with the scent of freshly cut grass and the faint hum of distant machinery. The OTS parade grounds were immaculate, with rows of chairs and flags arranged with military precision.

I stood in formation with my classmates, each of us dressed in the gleaming white and navy blue of the UHC OTS candidate uniform. The weight of the ceremonial sword at my side felt both unfamiliar and exhilarating—a tangible reminder that I'd made it, that this wasn't just another drill.

The ceremony unfolded with the kind of formal elegance the UHC was known for. The flag-bearers marched in perfect unison, their movements sharp and precise. Speeches followed—short, mercifully, but heavy with meaning. Colonel Patil spoke about duty and integrity, about the responsibility of leadership, and the honor of serving the UHC.

When my name was called, I stepped forward, my heart pounding like a starship engine at full burn.

"Candidate Kory Drake," Patil intoned, her voice carrying across the silent grounds, "by the authority vested in me by the United Humans Confederacy, I hereby reinstate your commission as Lieutenant Commander in the UHC Armada."

I raised my right hand, my fingers steady despite the adrenaline coursing through me, and repeated the formal oath:

"I, Kory Drake, do solemnly swear to support and defend the Constitution of the United Humans Confederacy against all enemies, foreign and domestic; to bear true faith and allegiance to the same; and to obey the orders of the officers appointed over me, according to regulations and the Uniform Code of Military Justice. So help me God."

The words settled over me like a shield, heavy but reassuring. This wasn't just a title or a formality—it was a purpose, a direction, a chance to prove myself not just as a leader, but as someone worthy of the trust placed in me.

Patil stepped forward, a faint smile breaking her usual stern demeanor as she handed me the insignia of my rank. "Congratulations, Lieutenant Commander Drake," she said quietly. "Don't make me regret this."

"Never, ma'am," I replied, unable to keep the grin off my face.

The crowd dispersed, newly commissioned officers embracing their families, friends snapping photos, the air filled with the sound of laughter and relief. I stood off to the side, still adjusting to the insignia on my shoulder, when Sofia appeared.

Her civilian clothes set her apart from the sea of

uniforms, but her presence was as commanding as ever. She didn't say anything at first, just studied me with those sharp blue eyes, a faint smirk tugging at the corners of her lips.

"So," she said finally, "how does it feel to be back in the big leagues?"

"Not bad," I said, trying to play it cool. "Feels good to be called Lieutenant Commander again."

"And the Space Warfare School?" she asked, tilting her head.

"Excited," I admitted, unable to hide the enthusiasm in my voice. "It's exactly where I need to be. And the best part?"

"What's that?"

"You're coming with me," I said, my grin widening. "You and your detail. The best parts of OTS are following me to SWS."

For the first time, Sofia's cool exterior cracked just a little. She shook her head, but the faint color in her cheeks didn't escape me. "Don't make it sound like we're a fan club," she said dryly.

"I'm just saying," I replied, leaning slightly closer, "if I had to choose between the classroom and your terrible running form, it'd be a tough call."

She rolled her eyes but didn't deny it. "Just focus on staying alive, Kory," she said, though her tone was softer now. "We've got enough to deal with without you making it harder."

"I'll try," I said, grinning as she turned to leave, my gaze lingering on her lithe figure.

26

The room was quiet, save for the faint hum of the environmental controls and the muted glow of my dot on the desk in front of me. I sat back in my chair, one leg propped up on the corner of the desk, the other resting on the floor. My sweats clung to me in the muggy heat of Astrithon, and my freshly pressed uniform with its shiny new Lieutenant Commander insignia hung in the open closet nearby, looking way too official for how I felt.

The dot buzzed, its sharp chime cutting through the stillness. I glanced at the screen, then straightened in my chair. *Temporary Clearance Granted: You may now communicate with pre-approved recipients, including Captain Destiny Austin.*

My stomach twisted. It'd been months since I last spoke to Destiny or anyone from *Thunder*. Months since the mission to Lindblad, since the indictment, since everything spiraled out of control. My fingers hovered over the keyboard as a knot of nostalgia, pride, and shame tightened in my chest. What would she think? Had they forgotten me? Did she blame me? Did they all?

I let out a breath, rubbed the back of my neck, and muttered to myself, "Come on, Drake. Don't be a coward."

Still, it took me another full minute of staring at the screen before I started typing.

To: Captain Destiny Austin

Subject: Freshly Pressed Lieutenant Commander, Reporting In

Des,

First things first: don't panic. I'm alive, I'm mostly in one piece, and no, I haven't blown anything up lately. You can breathe easy.

I just graduated from OTS today—came in second in the class, which I'm sure you'll say is typical of me, always just shy of the top. What can I say? I like keeping people on their toes. The shiny new rank insignia is official now, Lieutenant Commander Drake reporting for duty. Feels weird, right? Like I actually know what I'm doing.

Here's the kicker: I'm heading to the Dominion Space Warfare School tomorrow. Yes, the actual Space Warfare School. Orders came straight from Celestarch Seraphis herself. No pressure, right? I'll try not to trip over my own boots in front of the Dominion elite, but no promises.

How are things on *Thunder*? I hope she's still in one piece. I've been meaning to ask Busto how many holes he's punched in the walls since I left. Knowing him, the count's in double digits by now. Seriously, though, I miss you all. Feels like a lifetime since I was barking orders and pretending I knew what I was doing while you cleaned up my messes.

Speaking of cleaning up messes, my criminal trial is still in the preliminary stages. It's going to be another six months at least until they do the thing. Up until now it's been hearings and more hearings. About the charges and evidence.

I bet you're killing it as captain. Not that I'd be surprised. You were always the brains of the operation. Just, you know, try not to make it look too easy, or they'll think I was dead weight.

Write back when you get a chance. I want to hear all the good gossip—the kind that doesn't make it into official reports. And if you've done anything crazy, don't hold back.

Take care of yourself—and keep *Thunder* flying straight.

Kory

I read it over twice, biting my lip. The words were lighter than what I felt, but that was the point. If anyone could see through the cracks and read between the lines, it was Destiny. My finger hovered over the Send button, and for a second, I almost deleted the whole thing.

Then, with a deep breath, I hit send.

The dot chimed softly, the message disappearing into the digital void. I leaned back, staring at the ceiling, and let out a long sigh. Sending an email shouldn't have felt like walking into battle, but here I was, heart pounding like I'd just survived another firefight.

The dot buzzed on my desk, snapping me out of my post-email haze. I blinked at the notification, the words New Message from Captain Destiny Austin lighting up the screen.

Two hours. She'd replied in two hours. I wasn't sure what surprised me more—the speed or the fact that she'd answered at all.

I straightened in my chair, my heart picking up a little

as I opened the message. The tone hit me right away: pure Destiny—brash, sarcastic, and just the right amount of heartfelt.

To: Lieutenant Commander Kory Drake

Subject: Overachiever-in-Chief

Kory,

Well, look who got themselves a fancy official title. Lieutenant Commander Drake. Has a nice ring to it, doesn't it? I'm sure your OTS instructors are still trying to figure out how you pulled it off. Meanwhile, I've been out here actually doing the hard work while you're off sipping coffee and polishing brass. Must be nice.

Seriously, though, congrats. Second in your class? Not bad for someone who used to think "tactics" was just a fancy word for guessing. I'm proud of you, even if you did leave me to keep this ship together.

Speaking of which—yes, *Thunder* is still in one piece. Barely. I've been calling her my "high-maintenance girlfriend" lately. Don't worry, the crew's keeping her flying, though we've had some... let's call them "adventures."

Oh, and before you ask: Busto hasn't punched any walls lately. He's saving his energy for punching Kergans. Phoebe says hi, by the way. So do the rest of the crew. We all miss you, even if no one wants to admit it outright.

Now, about those charges hanging over your head—what's the UHC thinking, slapping our fearless leader with an indictment? Did you forget to tip a Dominion waiter or something? (Too soon?) Whatever it is, we know you'll get through it. Just don't pull any of your "Kory Special" stunts and make things worse, okay?

Now, let me tell you about our latest escapades, because this one's a doozy.

We got orders to intercept a Kergan mining convoy operating in the asteroid fields of the Jupiter L5 Trojans. It sounded simple enough: sneak in, disable their freighters, grab the cargo, and get out before their reinforcements showed up. Easy, right?

Wrong.

Navigating that asteroid field was like threading a needle blindfolded while someone's shooting at you. The freighters had heavier defenses than expected—turrets everywhere, and their escorts weren't shy about using them. *Thunder* took some nasty hits, but we held together.

The trickiest part was lining up our shots without slamming into a rock the size of a city block. At one point, I swear an asteroid clipped our hull so close I could hear it scrape. I'm pretty sure the ship still smells like scorched metal.

Phoebe pulled off some maneuvers that would've made Zeta cry. Barrel rolls through debris clouds, hairpin turns at speeds *Thunder* probably wasn't designed for. I think they're trying to make "dodging space dust" a new sport.

We managed to disable two of the freighters, boarded them, and secured the cargo—processed metals and rare minerals bound for Kergan industrial facilities. The crew handled the boarding like pros, and we even managed to take a few prisoners. They weren't too happy about that, but hey, their loss is our gain.

Escorting the captured freighters back to the UHC

staging point was almost as bad as the fight. The convoy's engines were sluggish, and we kept expecting Kergan reinforcements to pop out of nowhere. Luckily, they didn't, and we got back in one piece.

Thunder's still nursing some scars from that one, but she's tough—just like her crew.

Then there was the little matter of a town in Colorado. This one's for the history books—or maybe just the bar stories.

So, a couple of weeks ago, we picked up a distress signal from a little town in Colorado. Kergan raiders had decided to drop in uninvited, and let's just say they weren't there to enjoy the mountain views. Civilians were pinned down, their defenses were crumbling, and it was only a matter of time before the Kergans turned the place into a crater.

Command scrambled together a response team. *Thunder* was tapped, along with four other Dominion corvettes, for a joint ground-and-air rescue. The plan was simple: get in, evacuate the citizens, and get out before the Kergans overwhelmed us.

Of course, "simple" is a relative term.

We came in hot, laying down covering fire from orbit while the ground teams deployed. The town's main square was a war zone—Kergan infantry everywhere, armored walkers tearing through what little resistance the colonists had left. It was chaos.

And then there was Busto.

He led our ground team, and let me tell you, the man is a force of nature. At one point, we were pinned down by a Kergan walker, its turret sweeping the area and cutting off our escape route.

Things looked grim, and then Busto got this look. You know the one—the "I'm about to do something insane and probably illegal" look.

Next thing I know, he's charging straight at the walker with nothing but a commandeered anti-air cannon he ripped off a downed Kergan dropship. He fired point-blank, the explosion nearly knocking him flat, but the walker went down in a fiery heap.

I swear, the man shrugged off the blast like it was nothing. The rest of us were just standing there, jaws on the floor, while he dusted himself off like he'd just finished a light workout.

The townspeople are calling him "the human wrecking ball" now. It's a name that's sticking, much to his annoyance. I think he secretly likes it, though.

We managed to evacuate most of the civilians—over 300, by the end of it. *Thunder* and the other corvettes provided air cover as we ferried them out, dodging Kergan fire the whole way. It wasn't clean, and we took some hits, but we got them out. That's what matters.

The town's ruins are still smoldering, but at least its people live to fight another day. And they've got Busto's walker takedown to tell their grandkids about.

Oh, and there's one more story I have to share—it's too good not to. Let me set the scene: Kergan-controlled Earth territory, a Dominion informant, and *Thunder* doing what we do best—making the impossible look easy. Well, almost.

A month back, we got a classified op to rendezvous with a Dominion informant deep in Kergan-controlled territory. I can't tell you where or who (don't shoot the messenger—it's above my pay grade), but let's just say this wasn't exactly a casual meet-and-greet.

The informant had something big—intelligence that Command needed yesterday. Our job was to extract the informant and the intel without getting ourselves vaporized in the process. Simple enough, right?

We got to the extraction point and things were going fine. Too fine, actually, which should've been my first clue that it was about to hit the fan.

The informant's shuttle was on its way to us when, out of nowhere, a Kergan patrol ship dropped from orbit. And not just any patrol ship—this thing was bristling with weapons and moving like it had something to prove.

The shuttle panicked and bolted for the nearest cover: a mountain corridor so dense it looked like we'd be flying through a maze. The Kergans were right on their tail, and if they caught the shuttle, our whole mission was blown.

So, naturally, we did what *Thunder* always does—we went straight into the fire.

Phoebe was at the helm, and let me tell you, Kory, she's outdone herself. I didn't think it was possible for Thunder to move the way she made her move. She dove us into those valleys like we were on rails, weaving through clouds and rock clusters like it was an obstacle course. The Kergans followed, but that's when Phoebe pulled off her masterpiece.

She set up this bait-and-switch maneuver so ridiculous it belongs in a vidshow. First, she let *Thunder*'s profile show just enough through the clouds to make it look like we were struggling to stay ahead. The Kergans took the bait, closing the gap. Then, at the last second, Phoebe fired off a cluster of decoy drones programmed to mimic our energy signature.

The Kergans fell for it hook, line, and sinker. They veered after the decoys while Phoebe whipped Thunder around a cluster of rocks and looped back toward the shuttle. By the time the Kergans realized they'd been chasing ghosts, we were already halfway out of the corridor, the shuttle tucked safely under *Thunder*'s wing.

I don't think I've ever heard an entire bridge crew cheer so loudly. Phoebe just smirked and said, "Sometimes you've gotta out-crazy the crazies." I'm pretty sure she's going to start writing a book on evasive maneuvers—working title: *How Not to Die in a Starship*.

We got the intel and the informant back to Command, no casualties, no damage (well, nothing we couldn't patch up). Whatever was in that data, Command seemed happy, which means we're probably in for more missions like it. Yay us.

So, there you have it. Life out here is still as chaotic as ever, but it's worth it. Knowing you're out there, doing your thing—even if it's just sipping Dominion coffee and dodging indictments—makes it feel like we're all still connected somehow.

And before I sign off, let me just say this, Kory—I miss you. The crew misses you. But me? I miss my big street brother the most. You've always been the one to hold things together, even when we didn't have two quarters to rub together.

I'm doing my best to fill your shoes, but *Thunder*

doesn't feel the same without you. It's like the ship's missing her heart. Not that I'm getting sentimental or anything. But yeah, it's weird not having you here to tell me when I'm being an idiot or to talk me out of one of my wild ideas (even though I'm always right).

As for that alien princess you were so hung up on... I know you don't want me saying this, but I've gotta get it off my chest: Zeta can rot in the deepest pits of Hell for all I care. She sold you out, Kory. She put her precious crown and her stupid Dominion politics ahead of you, after everything you did for her.

I know you probably don't want to hear it, but you deserve better than her. You deserve loyalty, not someone who uses you when it's convenient and leaves you twisting in the wind when it's not.

Sorry for the rant. You know I can't help myself. But seriously, don't let her worm her way back into your life unless she's willing to prove she's worth it.

Anyway, I should stop before this gets even more sappy. Take care of yourself, Kory. We'll hold the fort until you're ready to come back where you belong.

Your annoying, brilliant, and impossibly humble sister,

-Des

I sat back after reading the last lines, my chest tight. Leave it to Destiny to pack a punch, even in an email. Her words stuck with me, not just the teasing or the stories, but the raw honesty she always managed to slip in when I least expected it.

I missed her, too. Missed all of them. And Zeta... Destiny wasn't wrong about that either. But some things were too complicated to explain in a message, even to her.

I leaned forward, my fingers hovering over the reply button, then stopped. I'd write her back later. For now, I just needed to sit with it—her words, her stories, and the pieces of *Thunder* she'd managed to send my way.

27

The city buzzed around me as I stepped out of the transport. Astrithon's streets were alive, an endless blur of alien life, honking vehicles, and the hum of drones weaving between crystalline skyscrapers. And there, rising like jagged spires in the heart of it all, was the Dominion Space Warfare School.

Its campus spread across several city blocks, the buildings sleek and angular, their crystalline surfaces shimmering in the tropical sunlight. Elevated, transparent walkways crisscrossed between the structures, glinting like strands of a massive web. Beyond the campus, the Celestial Conclave loomed, its towering peaks almost scraping the clouds—a constant reminder of the Dominion's grandeur and power.

I adjusted the strap of my bag, my newly minted Lieutenant Commander insignia catching the light as I approached the main gates. Behind me, Sofia and the rest of my protection detail lingered, their plain clothes and sharp-eyed vigilance standing out against the casual flow of students and staff.

"I'll keep an eye on things from out here," Sofia said, her tone clipped but calm. Her blue eyes scanned the crowd, the slight furrow in her brow the only hint of tension. "We're not authorized past this point. Just check in with us every few hours."

I gave her a nod, trying not to let my nerves show. "You'll know if anything happens. Trust me."

Her lips twitched, almost forming a smile, but she quickly turned away, motioning for the rest of the team to spread out. As I crossed through the doorway, the weight of their absence hit me harder than I expected.

The Welcome Hall was a flurry of activity, officer students in crisp uniforms moving between lines, clutching dots and papers. The air was thick with the sound of boots on polished floors and the high-pitched chatter of kavreni students, their ears twitching as they whispered in their native tongue.

I felt the stares almost immediately. It wasn't just my being a human that drew attention—it was the whispered rumors that had clearly made their way ahead of me.

"Is that him?"

"The one with the trial?"

"Seraphis's pet project, right?"

I kept my expression neutral, my eyes fixed on the check-in desk at the far end of the hall.

"Lieutenant Commander Drake!" a voice called out, loud and cheerful.

I turned to see a tall human student with a broad grin heading toward me. A lieutenant senior grade, his uniform was immaculate, but his casual swagger made it clear he wasn't one for rigid formality.

"Marcus Fahey," he said, extending a hand. "You're already the most talked-about student in SWS history."

I shook his hand, caught off guard by the friendliness. "I try to make an impression," I said, managing a half-smile.

"Well, mission accomplished," Marcus said, falling into step beside me as we moved toward the desk. "You've got half the campus convinced you're some kind of UHC spy and the other half thinking you're Seraphis's long-lost nephew. Either way, you're going to be fun to watch."

"Glad I can entertain," I muttered.

Marcus glanced sideways at me, his grin softening. "Look, don't let it get to you. This place eats gossip for breakfast. But you'll have to work twice as hard to get half the respect. Just how it is."

"Good to know," I said.

We reached the check-in desk, where a kavreni administrator looked me over with thinly veiled disdain before handing me a dot with my assignments. As I scanned the schedule—FTL Strategic Operations, Fleet Coordination, Energy Systems—I couldn't help but notice Marcus glancing at my uniform again.

"You'll survive," he said, clapping me on the shoulder. "Maybe. Just don't screw up too badly, or I'll have to pretend I don't know you."

I snorted, the tension easing slightly. "Thanks for the vote of confidence."

"Anytime, Drake. Anytime."

The auditorium was a cavernous, gleaming space that managed to feel both futuristic and intimidating. Rows of officers—students, as they were called here—sat in tiered seating that rose steeply from the polished crystalline floor. The low hum of quiet conversations echoed off the walls, a mix of alien tongues and clipped Dominion Standard.

Most of the students were kavreni, their bat-like faces animated as they whispered in their high-pitched voices, their ears swiveling constantly. A smaller number of igna officers, glowing softly within their mech-suited bodies, sat still and unreadable, like silent sentinels.

The human contingent was sparse but noticeable. A tall, broad-shouldered man waved me over to an empty seat near the middle. I recognized him from the Welcome Hall—Marcus Fahey—and his easygoing grin was a welcome sight in a room thick with tension.

"Drake!" Marcus called, his voice cutting through the low murmur. "Over here!"

I slipped into the seat beside him, grateful for the friendly gesture.

"Figured you'd want a safe harbor," Marcus said, his grin widening. "Pretty much everyone here knows about you. Hard to miss that face after seeing it plastered all over the news feeds."

I forced a chuckle. "Yeah, that's been fun."

"You've made quite the impression," he said, leaning back in his chair. "Celebrity, sponsor of a Celestarch, mysterious criminal trial... You've got the trifecta."

I wished he would stop making such a big deal of my notoriety. I wasn't like I hadn't noticed all the staring and whispers. Before I could respond, the petite woman on Marcus's other side leaned forward. Her sharp green eyes appraised me with interest, though her tone was friendly.

"I'm Kira Shale," she said, offering a hand. "Lieutenant Senior Grade. Marcus has been hyping you up since orientation started."

Marcus shrugged, grinning. "I just told her you'd make things more interesting around here. This place loves a scandal."

Kira rolled her eyes but smiled. "Ignore him. It's nice to meet you, Drake. I'd say you've got quite the reputation, but it sounds like you already know that."

"Yeah, it's been hard to miss," I admitted.

The conversations in the room quieted briefly as an instructor walked in, then resumed in hushed tones. Somewhere behind me, a voice spoke just loud enough for me to hear.

"Must be nice to skip the line," the voice drawled.

I turned to see a young human male officer with a smirk that immediately set my teeth on edge. His demeanor was sharp and polished, and his gaze was cutting.

I glanced at Kira.

"Joran Kale," she whispered while keeping her eyes facing forward.

"You've got something to say?" I asked Joran evenly.

He leaned back in his chair, his smirk widening. "Nothing you don't already know, I'm sure. A Celestarch's pet project gets fast-tracked into the SWS. Doesn't leave much for the rest of us."

The comment drew a few murmurs from the nearby kavreni students, their high-pitched whispers carrying across the room.

"Is that him?"

"The one Seraphis vouched for?"

"He's the one on trial, right?"

I clenched my jaw, forcing myself to stay calm.

Marcus, trying to be a peacemaker, leaned over and grinned at Joran. "Jealousy doesn't look good on you, Kale. You should try a little humility—it works wonders."

Joran's eyes narrowed, but he said nothing.

"Don't mind him," Kira said, her voice low but firm.

"Joran's had a chip on his shoulder since he got here. Just ignore it."

"Easier said than done," I muttered.

The tension lingered through the orientation. The instructors outlined the core curriculum, focusing on courses like FTL Strategic Operations, Energy Weapons Systems, and Operational Logistics. But when the Sydereal Theory class was mentioned, the room shifted.

The kavreni students perked up, their whispers intensifying. It was a specialized course, open to only a select few, though I assumed I would be included on the roster. It was kind of the whole reason I was invited to SWS.

I felt the eyes of many of the students staring at me, weighing me.

As the session ended, Marcus clapped me on the back. "Come on, Drake. Let's grab some chow before the next round. You'll need your energy if you're going to keep dodging verbal punches from Kale."

I smiled weakly, but my mind was still replaying the whispers, the stares, and Joran's Kale's words. If the Dominion wanted me to prove I belonged, they were making it clear that I'd have to fight for every inch.

The lecture hall for FTL Strategic Operations was just as intimidating as the subject. A tiered semicircle of seats faced a massive holo-display that floated in the center of the room, showing a three-dimensional fleet engagement in real-time. The battle was color-coded, with Dominion ships weaving intricate patterns around Kergan vessels.

Instructor Sarnae, a kavreni with striking silver fur and eyes like molten gold, wasted no time diving into the complexities of faster-than-light travel and its application in tactical fleet engagements. Her voice carried the clipped precision of someone who had seen action firsthand.

"Faster-than-light maneuvering isn't just about speed," she said, her long ears twitching as she gestured to the simulation. "It's about precision. One poorly calculated jump can cost you an entire fleet. Who can tell me the critical factors that influence an effective ambush in FTL space?"

The room was silent, save for the hum of the holo-display. Most of the students stared at their dots or avoided her gaze. I hesitated, then raised my hand.

"Yes, Mister Drake?" Sarnae said, her tone neutral but her eyes sharp.

"An effective FTL ambush requires precise timing to predict the enemy's vector, a clear understanding of their distortion profile, and redundancy in case the target alters course unexpectedly," I said. "And you need to account for potential anomalies in the jump environment, like gravitational fluxes or debris fields."

Sarnae's ears twitched again, her gaze lingering on me. "A textbook answer," she said. "And yet, fewer than one in five commanders execute it successfully under combat conditions. Let's hope your execution matches your theory, Drake."

A murmur swept through the room, punctuated by a scoff from behind me.

"Must be nice to have all the answers handed to you," Joran muttered loudly enough for the surrounding students to hear.

The kavrenis seated nearby whispered in response, their high-pitched voices carrying speculative remarks. I clenched my jaw but kept my eyes forward, refusing to give Joran the satisfaction of a reaction.

***

The laboratory for Energy Systems was a sprawling, high-tech space filled with glowing displays and humming machinery. Students clustered around workstations, dissecting schematics of Dominion power systems.

We were tasked with diagnosing a simulated failure in a chromatic battery array, the Dominion's cutting-edge energy storage technology. The arrays powered everything from ships to planetary defense grids, and even a slight miscalibration could trigger catastrophic failure.

Kira worked alongside me at our shared station, her quick, precise movements showing her expertise. "You're good at this," she said, glancing at me as I adjusted a virtual flux regulator.

"Had a good teacher," I replied, thinking of Zeta and regrets.

Marcus, stationed at the next terminal, leaned over. "Let me know if you figure out how to make one of these things explode on command. I've got a list of people who need a wake-up call."

I chuckled, but the tension from earlier still lingered. Even here, I could feel eyes on me, whispers just below the hum of machinery.

The simulation chamber for Fleet Coordination was a marvel of Dominion technology. The walls displayed a fully immersive holographic battlefield, and each student was assigned a virtual fleet to command.

We were tasked with coordinating supply lines and fleet movements in the face of a simulated enemy assault. It was as much a test of planning as it was of execution.

Marcus and Kira performed admirably, their virtual fleets holding the line and maintaining supply integrity. My fleet took a hit early on, but I managed to recover, rerouting supplies through a secondary jump gate while fending off the enemy's pursuit.

As the exercise ended, Joran's fleet was announced as the highest scorer. He turned to me with a smug grin. "Better luck next time, Drake," he said, his voice dripping with condescension.

Marcus shot me a look, his grin more supportive. "Ignore him," he said as we left the chamber. "You're holding your own. That's more than enough for now."

The cyber lab was a darkened room, lit only by the glow of interactive displays. Our instructor, an igna named Rynshak, guided us through the intricacies of cyber offensives and defenses. The session focused on hacking syderealdyne systems, a skill crucial for undermining enemy fleets.

My hands moved over the virtual interface, launching a simulated attack on an enemy comms array. It felt oddly familiar, like piloting a ship through enemy fire—precision and timing were everything.

"You've done this before," Kira said, watching as I completed the exercise faster than most of the room.

"Something like it," I replied vaguely.

The final class of the day was the most abstract—and the most unsettling. Ethical Command Decision-Making was taught by an igna instructor whose glowing core pulsed faintly as they spoke in a deep, resonant voice.

The scenario presented was chilling: an enemy fleet used civilian hostages as a shield. Destroying the fleet would save billions of lives on a targeted planet but cost thousands of innocent lives in the process. The room debated heatedly, but there were no clear answers.

The instructor's voice cut through the noise. "Command is not about choosing what is right. It is about choosing what is necessary."

By the end of the day, I was exhausted, both mentally and emotionally. The weight of being an outsider was heavier now, especially after Joran's constant jabs.

"Don't let him get to you," Kira said as we returned to our quarters. "He's been like that with everyone he sees as a threat."

Marcus grinned. "Just keep proving him wrong. That'll drive him nuts."

I nodded, but the tension lingered. This wasn't just about surviving the coursework—it was about proving, to them and to myself, that I belonged here.

28

The main hall of the SWS buzzed with life, the midday break bringing officer students together in scattered groups. Conversations filled the air, mixing human and alien voices into a cacophony of camaraderie, rivalry, and speculation about the morning's lectures.

I sat with Marcus and Kira at a table near the edge of the hall, nursing a bland Dominion-standard protein shake while Marcus demolished an overstuffed sandwich.

"I'm telling you," Marcus said, waving a chip in the air, "the logistics sim this morning was rigged. No way those supply lines collapsed that fast."

Kira smirked, leaning back in her seat. "Or maybe you're just bad at logistics."

"Unlikely," Marcus said with mock indignation, popping the chip into his mouth.

I barely heard them, my attention drifting to the holographic board at the front of the hall. I knew what was coming—the Sydereal Theory selection list.

As if on cue, the room began to quiet. A kavreni

administrator, her silver-flecked fur catching the light, strode to the center of the room. Her ears twitched sharply as she held up a dot, her amplified voice silencing the last of the murmurs.

"Attention," she said. "The students selected for the Sydereal Theory course have been finalized. The list is now available."

A faint ripple of excitement passed through the crowd as the holographic display lit up with names. Sydereal Theory wasn't just a course; it was a proving ground for the best minds in the school, a study of the multidimensional mechanics of sydereal operations. Only a handful of students were chosen, and their selection was the subject of both envy and intense scrutiny.

Marcus leaned forward, squinting at the glowing names. "Oh, look at that—Drake's on the list. Big surprise."

I forced myself to feign surprise, raising an eyebrow as I glanced at the display. "Huh. Didn't see that coming."

Kira gave me a sideways glance, her smirk betraying her doubt. "You didn't see it coming? Really?"

Marcus grinned. "Yeah, nice try, Drake. Everyone knows Seraphis wanted you here for this. Come on, at least own it."

Before I could reply, the room's tone shifted. The kavreni students, clustered in their usual groups, began whispering loudly, their high-pitched voices carrying across the hall.

"Of course, he's on the list."

"Seraphis must have pushed him through."

"He doesn't even look like he belongs here."

The pointed stares that followed made my stomach tighten.

"Congratulations, Drake," Marcus said, his grin fading slightly as he noticed the shift in the room. "Looks like you're the main event again."

A voice from the crowd cut through the rising murmurs.

"Main event? More like main fraud."

I turned to see Joran Kale, his smirk as sharp and deliberate as always. He stood with his arms crossed, his posture rigid and confident, as if he'd been waiting for this moment.

"Let me guess," Joran said loudly enough for everyone to hear. "Seraphis pulls a few strings, and suddenly Drake's the star pupil. No need for talent when you've got a celestarch in your corner."

The room fell silent, every eye on us. The tension was thick enough to choke on.

"Back off, Kale," Kira said sharply, her voice cutting through the quiet.

Joran ignored her, stepping closer to my table. "Sydereal Theory isn't a handout, Drake. It's supposed to go to people who deserve it. People who actually earned their spots."

I stood slowly, forcing myself to meet his gaze. My heart pounded, but I kept my voice steady. "I earned my place here, just like everyone else on that list. If you've got a problem with it, take it up with the instructors."

Joran's smirk twisted into a sneer. "Oh, I will. But we both know this isn't about merit. It's about politics. You're just another piece on Seraphis's board."

"Enough," Kira said, stepping between us. "This isn't the time or place."

Marcus, ever the peacemaker, clapped me on the shoulder with an exaggerated grin. "Come on, Kale. If you're so confident, why don't you show everyone how much better you are in the next sim? Or are you afraid Drake might outshine you again?"

A few nervous chuckles rippled through the crowd, but

the tension lingered. Joran glared at me for a moment longer before turning and walking away, his shoulders stiff with barely contained anger.

I sat back down, the weight of the stares and whispers pressing on me like a lead blanket.

"You okay?" Kira asked, her voice soft.

"Yeah," I said, though it didn't feel true.

Marcus leaned closer, his grin fading into something more sincere. "Don't let him get to you. He's just mad you're going to prove him wrong."

I managed a weak smile, but the knot in my chest didn't loosen. Joran's words stung, not because they were true, but because I knew that's what everyone else was thinking, too.

The Sydereal Theory lecture hall felt like stepping into another world—fitting, given the subject matter. The walls were sleek and black, designed to disappear into the void when the holographic projectors came to life. Above each workstation hovered shifting maps of the Syderealium, their multidimensional complexity rendered in pulsing lines and points of light that seemed to defy logic.

This wasn't just any course. It was for the flairsparked, those like me with a natural sensitivity to the Syderealium, able to perceive its twists and eddies in ways others couldn't. The room hummed with quiet anticipation as the handful of us selected for the class settled into our seats.

Unlike the other lectures I'd attended at the SWS, this group was noticeably smaller. The students—all from different species—watched each other with wary curiosity. I caught a few sidelong glances in my direction, accompanied by whispers too quiet to make out.

At the front of the room, Professor Kelarn entered with the sharp precision of a blade being drawn from its sheath.

Her charcoal fur glimmered faintly under the recessed lighting, and her piercing yellow eyes swept over the room, taking us all in. When her gaze landed on me, her ears twitched, and the faintest hint of disdain flickered across her face.

"Welcome," she began, her voice clipped and deliberate. "You are here because you possess the rare quality we call flairsparked. It is a gift—and a burden. While others require elaborate navigation systems and fleets of analysts to survive the Sydereallium, you have the potential to act independently. To adapt. To succeed where others would fail."

Her words hung in the air like a challenge.

"This course," she continued, gesturing to the swirling holographic maps above us, "will teach you how to harness that potential. You will learn to navigate the Sydereallium without reliance on external systems. You will master scouting and deception techniques, gather intelligence in hostile territory, and understand the sociology of the Sydereallium's inhabitants."

At this, a holographic image flickered to life above her, displaying a shadowy figure with shifting, indistinct features. A murmur rippled through the room as we stared at the image.

"Some of you may believe the Sydereallium is empty," Kelarn said, her tone sharp. "It is not. It is inhabited by entities far older and stranger than anything you've encountered. Understanding them is critical. Misunderstanding them is fatal."

Her ears twitched, and the image dissolved into a swirling, chaotic void.

"This course is not for the faint-hearted," she said. "It is not for the weak. By the end of it, some of you will have mastered the Syderealium. The rest…" She let the sentence hang, her smirk cutting through the tension.

The lecture began, and Kelarn dove headfirst into the intricacies of sydereal distortion patterns, dimensional drift, and entity interaction protocols. The holographic maps shifted constantly, illustrating her points with dazzling precision.

"Distortion harmonics," Kelarn said, her voice sharp and commanding, "are the key to independent navigation. If you cannot read them, you cannot survive. If you cannot manipulate them, you are useless."

She turned abruptly, her gaze locking onto me like a targeting laser. "Drake."

The room stilled. Every eye turned to me, the weight of their scrutiny heavy on my shoulders.

"Yes, ma'am?" I said, keeping my voice steady.

Kelarn gestured to the map above my workstation. "Explain the role of distortion harmonics in predicting sydereal drift."

I took a deep breath, my mind racing to organize the answer. "Distortion harmonics create interference patterns that reveal the underlying structure of the Syderealium," I said. "By analyzing those patterns, you can predict how drift will occur and adjust your trajectory to stay within a stable zone."

Kelarn's ears flicked, and a cold smile tugged at the corners of her mouth. "Textbook," she said, her tone dripping with condescension. "But theory without application is meaningless. Tell me, Drake, how many independent jumps have you executed?"

The question hit like a punch. "None," I admitted, my voice quieter than I intended.

Kelarn's smile widened, her disdain now fully visible.

"Exactly. You know the theory, but you lack experience. Let's hope your performance matches your potential—otherwise, you'll be just another wasted spark."

The lecture moved on, but I could feel the tension lingering in the room. The other students, already wary of me, grew colder. The whispers that followed Kelarn's comment weren't subtle.

I felt people staring at me again and talking in hushed voices. Somebody spoke too loudly, and I heard "Seraphis's pet project."

I kept my eyes on the swirling holographs, refusing to look up. The knot in my stomach tightened with every muttered word.

After the lecture ended, I trudged out of the hall, the murmurs and whispers still echoing in my mind. The dimly lit corridor felt colder than it had that morning, the sleek crystalline walls seeming to absorb my frustration.

I made it halfway to my quarters before I heard someone calling out behind me.

"Drake!"

Turning, I saw Marcus jogging toward me, his usual easygoing grin a bit more subdued. "How was it? Everyone's dying to know what goes on in Sydereal Theory. Did they make you solve a puzzle in four dimensions or fight some sydereal monster?"

I managed a weak smile. "Close. They just put me in the crosshairs instead."

Marcus raised an eyebrow, falling into step beside me. "Ah, Kelarn's initiation ritual. She's got a thing for tearing people down. It's her way of weeding out the weak."

"She definitely made her point," I muttered, still hearing the echoes of her cutting remarks.

Marcus shrugged. "Sounds about right. But hey, you're

still standing. That's more than most would've done. Kelarn doesn't waste her time on people who aren't worth breaking."

The attempt at reassurance didn't quite lift the weight pressing on me, but I nodded anyway. "Thanks, Fahey."

"Don't mention it," he said with a grin, his tone lightening. "Just don't go full sydereal savant on us and forget us normal folk, all right?"

I chuckled despite myself, but the knot in my stomach didn't loosen. This wasn't just about surviving Kelarn's class or proving my worth. It was about learning to navigate a world that was quickly becoming more dangerous than I'd ever imagined.

29

The student dormitories weren't much to look at—clean, functional, and utterly soulless. The common room, where the group study sessions were held, was all smooth surfaces and sharp angles, illuminated by recessed lighting that made everything feel sterile. Student officers clustered around tables with glowing dots, murmuring about simulations, assignments, and tactics.

I sat at a table with my holo-display open, the swirling lines of an FTL maneuver shimmering in front of me. The session was meant to be collaborative, a chance to share ideas and refine our skills. Instead, the air was thick with unspoken tension.

Joran sat across from me, his dot untouched as he stared at the projected display. His smirk, faint but growing, suggested he wasn't here to study.

"So," Joran said, breaking the silence. His tone was casual, but the edge beneath it was razor-sharp. "Drake, what's it like knowing your spot here could've gone to someone who actually earned it?"

The conversation at the surrounding tables faltered, heads turning just slightly in our direction.

"I'm sorry, Kale," I said, keeping my voice calm. "I didn't realize you were the authority on who deserves to be here."

His smirk widened. "I'm just pointing out the obvious. You're only here because of Seraphis. If it weren't for her, you'd still be—what was it? Playing captain on some second-rate insurgent ship?"

I leaned back in my chair, crossing my arms. "You mean the second-rate insurgent ship that's taken out over a dozen Kergan freighters, multiple fighters, two warships, and rescued over a hundred captive humans? That one?"

A few muffled snickers rippled through the room, but Joran wasn't deterred. "Sure, you got lucky. Must be nice having a celestarch swoop in and save the day when things get tough."

"And yet," I said, leaning forward, "here I am, sitting in the same room as you, taking the same classes. So what does that say about you, Joran? If I'm such a fraud, what does it say about the guy who keeps losing to me?"

The smirk vanished, replaced by a flicker of irritation. "You don't belong here, Drake," he said, his voice tightening. "You're just a distraction, a liability. You'll never be more than Seraphis's charity project."

I let the words hang for a moment before responding, my tone sharper now. "And you'll never be more than a bitter footnote, Kale. Keep talking, though. You're doing a great job proving how small you are."

The tension in the room was suffocating now, the surrounding officers caught between pretending not to listen and hanging on every word.

"Enough," Kira said, her voice slicing through the silence. She leaned forward, fixing Joran with a glare. "You don't get to decide who belongs here. And if you're so sure Drake doesn't deserve his spot, why don't you prove it in the sims instead of whining about it like a kid who didn't get his favorite toy?"

Joran's jaw tightened, but before he could respond, Marcus threw himself into the fray with his usual grin.

"Relax, Kale," Marcus said, spreading his arms theatrically. "You're just upset because Drake's better-looking than you. I mean, let's be honest—it's not a competition."

The tension cracked as a few officers chuckled nervously. Joran stood abruptly, his chair scraping loudly against the floor.

"This place has enough dead weight without me wasting time here," he snapped, grabbing his dot. He shot one last glare at me before storming out.

The room gradually returned to its usual murmur, though the air still felt heavy. I exhaled slowly, the adrenaline ebbing as I turned back to my display.

Marcus leaned over, his grin fading into something more sincere. "That was brutal. I loved it."

Kira shook her head, though her lips twitched into a faint smile. "You didn't need to sink to his level, but… I'm not saying he didn't deserve it."

"I'm tired of letting him take shots at me," I said. "If he wants a fight, fine. But he's not going to win it by running his mouth."

Later, as the room cleared out, Marcus and Kira stayed behind. Marcus sprawled on a couch, his arms stretched wide, while Kira perched on the edge of the table, her expression thoughtful.

"Drake," Kira said, her tone softer now, "you handled that well, but you've got to be careful. Kale's not just some loudmouth. He's smart, and he knows how to turn people against you."

"Let him try," I said, though the weariness in my voice betrayed me.

"Prove him wrong," Marcus said, sitting up. "That's all you've got to do. Show everyone here why Seraphis picked you, why you're in Sydereal Theory, and why you're the guy who's going to make Kale eat his words."

Kira nodded. "And don't let him distract you. He's not worth it."

I gave a small, tired smile. "Thanks, guys."

"That's what we're here for," Marcus said with a wink. "And if you ever want someone to wipe that smirk off Kale's face, you know where to find me."

For the first time all day, I felt the tension in my chest loosen. The whispers and stares weren't going away, and neither was Joran. But I had allies—and that was enough to keep going.

The soft hum of the city filled my quarters, a distant melody of alien life and ceaseless energy. Through the floor-to-ceiling window, Astrithon stretched out in all its luminous glory, the vibrant lights reflecting off sleek, crystalline buildings. The city pulsed like a living thing, its glow faintly blurred by the humidity of the tropical night.

I leaned against the edge of my desk, staring at the view but not really seeing it. My thoughts churned with everything that had happened since I arrived at the SWS—the stares, the whispers, Joran's pointed jabs. Every moment felt like a test, every interaction like another weight added to my shoulders.

The sound of the door chime broke through my reverie.

"Come in," I said, straightening as the door slid open.

Sofia stepped in, her plain clothes blending seamlessly with her professional demeanor. She carried herself with the same quiet confidence as always, her sharp blue eyes scanning the room before settling on me.

"Just making my rounds," she said, her tone clipped but not unkind.

"You always make it sound like you're on patrol," I said with a faint smile, trying to lighten the mood.

She shrugged. "It's what I'm here for."

Sofia moved closer, her gaze flicking briefly to the window before returning to me. "You look like you've been brooding," she said, crossing her arms.

"Is it that obvious?" I asked, half-joking.

"You're practically radiating frustration." She leaned against the wall, her posture deceptively relaxed. "What's going on?"

I hesitated, but the words spilled out before I could stop them. "It's just... everything. The way they look at me, the things they say. It's like no matter what I do, I'll always be a criminal who doesn't belong here."

Sofia's expression softened, a rare glimpse of warmth breaking through her usual stoic demeanor. "You're letting them get in your head," she said. "You don't need their approval, Kory. You're here because you've earned it. Let your actions speak for themselves."

I nodded, though her words didn't entirely dispel the weight pressing on me. "It's easier said than done."

"It always is," she replied, her voice quiet. "But you've been through worse. You'll get through this, too."

Her words lingered in the air, and for a moment, I was reminded of the Sofia who'd kissed me that night in my quarters at OTS. Since then, she'd been nothing but professional, keeping me at arm's length.

I glanced at her, wondering—not for the first time—if it would ever happen again. Her expression was unreadable, her focus sharp and detached.

Breaking the silence, I decided to shift the topic. "Have there been any updates on the Therrak Consortium?"

Sofia's jaw tightened, and she gave me a pointed look. "Kory..."

"What?" I said, raising my hands in mock innocence. "I'm just asking."

She shook her head, clearly unimpressed. "The investigation is ongoing. And you know I can't talk about it."

"Can't blame a guy for being curious," I said, trying to inject some levity.

Her eyes narrowed slightly, but there was a hint of amusement in her tone. "Yes, I can. Stay out of it, Kory. It's not your job to poke around and potentially mess up things."

I raised an eyebrow. "It concerns me, considering the whole assassination attempt thing."

"Let us handle it," she said firmly. "You've got enough on your plate without sticking your nose where it doesn't belong."

I sighed, leaning back against the desk. "You're really good at shutting me down, you know that?"

"It's a skill," she said, her lips twitching into the faintest of smiles.

For a moment, the tension eased, the weight of the day receding just slightly. She straightened, glancing back toward the door.

"Get some rest," Sofia said. "You've got a lot more proving to do tomorrow."

"Thanks for the vote of confidence," I said dryly.

"You don't need my confidence, Kory," she replied, her tone softer now. "You've already got what it takes. You just need to believe it."

With that, she turned and left, the door sliding shut behind her.

I stared at the door for a long moment, her words echoing in my mind. Then I turned back to the window, watching the city lights dance against the humid night sky.

Sofia was right. I didn't need to win their approval. I needed to focus on what I was capable of. On becoming a better armada officer and practitioner of the sydereal arts.

Resolve settled in my chest, steady and firm. Tomorrow, I'd face the whispers, the stares, and the doubts again. And I'd prove, to them and to myself, that I belonged.

30

The passage of a month at the Dominion SWS had brought me into a grudging rhythm. The sting of whispers and stares from my classmates dulled as I buried myself in simulations and coursework, determined to let my results do the talking. Marcus and Kira had become reliable allies, their camaraderie and humor softening the sharp edges of each day. Joran, on the other hand, loomed like an unresolved equation—his hostility simmered in the background, his bruised ego festering with every class rank I edged higher than him.

I had just finished a taxing simulation on interstellar supply chain dynamics when a notification buzzed on my dot. The sender was listed as Celestarch Seraphis—a summons carrying the weight of authority and inevitability. I rushed to save my preliminary sim results and then walked quickly to the administration building.

The offices of Seraphis at the SWS exuded an austere brilliance. The walls pulsed faintly with crystalline veins that glowed in rhythmic patterns, reminiscent of a stellar core's heartbeat. At the center of the room, suspended above a circular dais, was Seraphis herself—her body a brilliant, roiling mass of stellar plasma encased within a translucent containment capsule. The first time I'd ever seen an igna not in an opaque container. The light from her form refracted across the room, painting the walls with shifting auroras.

She floated silently as I entered, her presence overwhelming despite her lack of a traditional body. The capsule glided effortlessly to face me, the plasma within swirling like a living storm.

"Lieutenant Commander Drake," her voice resonated, deep and layered as if it emerged from the depths of a star. "Sit."

The dais beneath her capsule illuminated a protomatter chair as it formed up out of the floor. I sat, trying not to fidget under her gaze—or what I imagined was her gaze, since she didn't have eyes. The energy radiating from her capsule was almost palpable, a faint warmth brushing against my skin.

"You've made an impression," Seraphis began, her voice even but resonant. "Your performance in Sydereal Theory is noted. Even those predisposed to doubt you have little choice but to acknowledge your skill. But excelling in coursework is only part of what I expect from you."

I nodded, unsure if I was supposed to speak. The plasma in her capsule flared briefly as though she'd noticed my hesitation.

"Leadership is not merely about technical prowess," she continued. "It is about navigating moral ambiguity and inspiring trust. That is where I have concerns. Speak, Lieutenant Commander. Something troubles you."

I hesitated, organizing the tangled thoughts that had been gnawing at me for weeks. "In Sydereal Theory, the focus is on non-engagement within the Syderealium unless directly provoked. We're taught to prioritize self-defense and avoid confrontation, particularly with glyphshades. The logic is clear—engaging risks destabilizing the environment and creating broader consequences. But…"

Seraphis's plasma swirled in response, its glow intensifying slightly. "Continue."

"There was a scenario," I said, leaning forward. "A civilian transport was under attack by a hostile glyphshade. The directive was clear—evade, report, and avoid intervention. The logic was sound—intervening could worsen the situation and destabilize the sector. But standing by while innocent lives were at risk…"

I paused, my voice tightening. "It felt wrong, Celestarch. Like we were using the Syderealium's dangers as an excuse to do nothing. It's the same issue at the heart of my trial, isn't it? I'm accused of sydereal battery for taking action where others wouldn't. But avoiding action—leaving people to their fate—feels like the greater ethical failing."

Seraphis was silent for a moment, the light within her capsule dimming slightly as if in contemplation.

"The Syderealium is unlike any other space," she said finally, her voice carrying the weight of ancient understanding. "It is not bound by linear causality or the physical constraints you know. Every action within its bounds ripples across dimensions, affecting not just the immediate moment but countless others yet unseen. The Dominion's laws governing its use are not born of cowardice—they are born of necessity, refined over millennia to ensure stability in an inherently unstable realm."

She floated closer, the light from her form illuminating the edges of the chair I sat in. "But ethics are rarely absolute. Breaking those laws, however justified it may feel in the moment, carries consequences—some immediate, others far-reaching. The challenge of command is to weigh the necessity of your actions against the responsibility you bear for their repercussions."

Her plasma flared briefly, the swirling patterns within her capsule growing more chaotic. "Your trial is not merely about what you did, Kory. It is about why you did it and how you justify it. The Dominion does not demand blind obedience to its laws, but it does demand accountability. Those laws exist for a reason, and when you break them, you must face the consequences with clarity and resolve."

I sat in silence for a moment, her words settling over me like a weight I couldn't yet lift. "So what do I do, Celestarch? When the law doesn't align with what I believe is right?"

"You question it," Seraphis said, her tone sharpening. "And you bear the consequences of your decisions. Laws are not cages, but they are not easily discarded. They are the foundation of stability, and when you choose to act outside them, you must do so with the full understanding of the burden you are taking on. Every action you take carries weight, and as a leader, that weight will not fall solely on you—it will ripple through those who follow you."

Her tone softened, though the energy radiating from her form remained intense. "Kory, you have a gift. The flairspark that allows you to perceive the Syderealium as others cannot. That is why you are in this course—not because of your trial, not because of my endorsement, but because you have the potential to challenge and refine the principles we operate by. However, potential alone does not absolve you of responsibility."

Her words left me momentarily stunned, the weight of her confidence both inspiring and suffocating.

"I'll do my best to live up to that," I said quietly.

"You already are," Seraphis replied. "But let me be clear—you will face more challenges, both here and beyond. Leadership demands that you navigate not just the expectations of others but the doubts within yourself. That is the test you face now."

As I left her office, the faint hum of Astrithon's skyline filled my ears, blending with the Celestarch's words that echoed in my mind. The Syderealium wasn't just a space of danger and uncertainty—it was a crucible for decisions that would shape not just my future but the futures of those who followed me.

This wasn't just about surviving the school or my trial. It was about defining the kind of leader I wanted to be—and bearing the weight of what that choice meant.

31

The faint hum of Astrithon's cityscape was muffled behind the reinforced windows of my quarters. I was seated at my desk, pretending to focus on the dot in front of me, but my thoughts drifted. My gaze flicked toward the door as the familiar chime sounded.

"Come in," I called, my voice steady, though the tension in my chest betrayed my anticipation.

The door slid open, and Sofia stepped in. My breath caught—not for the first time, but tonight was different. She wasn't wearing her usual utilitarian outfit. Instead, she wore practical trousers and a fitted blouse, the cut of which highlighted her curves in a way I couldn't ignore. Her hair was loose around her shoulders, and there was something subtle in her perfume—clean and warm, like stepping into a shower after a long day.

I cleared my throat, trying to shove the distraction to the back of my mind. "Sofia."

"Lieutenant Commander," she said with a faint smile, though it didn't reach her eyes.

I waved her off. "Drop the formality. What's the latest on my ever-so-thrilling security detail?"

She crossed the room, her boots barely making a sound on the polished floor. "Same as usual," she said, leaning lightly against the bed across from me. "Your detail is still monitoring closely. No further signs of Therrak Consortium operatives on campus. For now."

I nodded, taking in her tone. It was flat, almost rehearsed—a stark contrast to her usual sharpness. Something was off.

Unlike most days, she didn't leave after her report. Instead, she sat on my bed across from me, her posture unusually relaxed. She didn't say anything for a moment, her fingers lightly tapping the edge of the mattress.

I leaned forward, trying to catch her gaze. "Sofia, what's wrong?"

She hesitated, her lips parting slightly as if to speak, then closing again. Her eyes darted to mine, filled with something I couldn't quite read—was it worry? Frustration? Whatever it was, it was bothering her.

Without thinking, I reached across, taking her hand in mine. Her fingers were warm, soft despite the calluses I knew she'd earned. She looked down at our hands, her lips twitching into a small, sad smile.

"You can talk to me," I said, my voice quieter now.

She exhaled slowly, the tension in her shoulders easing slightly. "It's nothing," she said, though her tone betrayed her words.

"Right," I said with a smirk, "because you always look like the weight of the universe is on your shoulders for no reason."

Her smile widened just enough to show I'd struck a chord. I brought her hand to my lips, pressing a light kiss to her palm.

She stilled, her breath catching. Her free hand moved instinctively, cupping my face. Her thumb brushed against my cheek, and when our eyes met, the barriers she always seemed to keep between us crumbled.

"Sofia…" I began, but she didn't let me finish.

She leaned forward, closing the gap between us, her lips brushing mine in a kiss that was soft at first, hesitant, as if testing the waters. Then it deepened, her hand slipping to the back of my neck as she moved across and onto my lap.

I wrapped my arms around her, pulling her closer, feeling the warmth of her body against mine. Her kisses grew hungrier, more urgent, as if she was trying to say all the things she couldn't put into words.

Time slipped away, the world outside my quarters fading into insignificance. We clung to each other, our movements synchronized like the gravitational pull of two celestial bodies locked in orbit.

She pulled back just enough to look into my eyes, her breathing uneven. "Kory," she whispered, her voice trembling but steady in its emotion.

I didn't respond with words. Instead, I stood with her in my arms and moved us to the bed, laying her gently onto the crisp sheets.

As we kissed, the world seemed to expand and collapse all at once. Being with her felt like stepping into another dimension, a space where nothing else mattered. It was as if the boundaries of my body blurred into hers, our connection igniting something deep and primal—a tectonic shift beneath the surface of my soul.

Every touch, every kiss was like molten magma rising to the surface, heat and tremor building until it became impossible to contain.

Together, we were a universe, vast and infinite, bound by the gravity of something neither of us could fully understand, but both of us knew we couldn't resist.

For the first time in months, I felt whole.

The room was dim, the only light coming from the faint city glow of Astrithon seeping through the edges of the window's opaque setting. The sheets were warm, tangled, and soft against my skin as I lay behind Sofia, holding her close. The rhythmic rise and fall of her breathing was almost enough to lull me to sleep, but there was a tension in her body I couldn't ignore.

I traced lazy circles on her hip with my fingers, a simple motion meant to soothe, but I knew she wasn't asleep. Her body was still, too controlled.

"Sofia," I murmured, my voice low and steady. "What's on your mind?"

For a moment, she didn't respond. Then, she shifted slightly, her hand coming to rest over mine.

"I've been trying to keep you out of this," she said finally, her voice quiet but heavy. "Out of the investigation."

I tensed, though I tried not to let it show. "I figured as much," I said lightly, hoping to draw her out. "Patil made that clear enough."

"It's more than that." Her voice softened, but her grip on my hand tightened. "There are things I've uncovered... things you need to know."

I leaned up slightly, propping myself on my elbow. "What are you talking about?"

She hesitated, her breath hitching. "I'm not supposed to tell you. If Patil or High Command find out, I could lose everything. But..." She turned her head slightly, her blue eyes catching the faint glow of the city lights. "I care about you, Kory. I need you to know the truth."

The seriousness in her tone sent a ripple of apprehension through me. "Okay," I said slowly. "I'm listening."

Sofia shifted to face me, her expression hard but conflicted. "The Therrak Consortium wasn't acting alone. They were hired by a third party—someone powerful enough to bankroll an operation this complex. Their objective was clear: eliminate you."

The words hit like a punch, but I stayed quiet, letting her continue.

"The token we took from the assassin contained encoded coordinates," she said. "When we decrypted them, they pointed to a warehouse in the Lantern District. My team raided it a month ago."

"And?" I prompted, feeling the knot in my stomach tighten.

"We found traces of activity—data servers, logistics plans, equipment—but the most damning piece was buried deep in their files. Something called Project Obsidian."

I frowned. "What's Project Obsidian?"

"From what we could piece together, it's a coordinated effort to destabilize the Dominion," she said. "And it mentions Ban'ach by name."

Hearing the name out loud sent a chill down my spine. "Ban'ach," I repeated. "She's involved in this?"

She nodded. "The files suggest she's orchestrating operations across multiple fronts, using intermediaries like the Consortium to carry out attacks and subvert Dominion infrastructure."

"Why?"

"I don't know yet," Sofia admitted. "But it's big, Kory. Bigger than anything I've dealt with before."

I let out a slow breath, processing the weight of her words. "What else did you find?"

"The assassin's clothing contained trace elements," she said. "Something we wouldn't have picked up without Dominion tech. It showed signs of exposure to a sydereal bubble—something produced by a Dominion nexus. Whoever hired the Consortium has access to sydereal resources, which narrows down the suspects significantly."

"Someone in the Dominion?" I asked, my voice sharper now.

"Maybe," she said. "Or someone with Dominion-level connections. Either way, it means this isn't just some rogue operation. This is calculated."

For a moment, the only sound was the distant hum of the city outside. I stared at her, my mind racing to connect the dots.

"Sofia," I said finally, "you're telling me this goes deeper than just some criminal syndicate. That someone with access to the Syderealium, maybe even a Dominion nexus, is trying to kill me. And Ban'ach is involved in destabilizing the Dominion?"

"Yes," she said, her voice barely above a whisper.

"Okay," I said with uncertainty.

Sofia stayed close, her fingers still lightly brushing against my cheek, but her gaze turned sharp, her words precise and clinical despite the emotional weight behind them.

"This is my best shot at what's going on. It's a theory, but based on the known facts," she began, her voice low but steady. "Ban'ach is using the Therrak Consortium as her proxy. They're not just hired muscle—they're moving illegal sydereal tech, sabotaging Dominion infrastructure, and sowing chaos. All of it is aimed at destabilizing Dominion systems."

I furrowed my brow. "Why the Dominion? What's her endgame?"

"She wants to weaken the Dominion judiciary," Sofia said, her tone darkening. "Your trial isn't just a legal proceeding—it's a stage. Ban'ach wants to turn it into a public spectacle. If she can undermine the judiciary's credibility, she'll weaken the Dominion's authority. And if you're eliminated in the process, it will make the judiciary look incompetent and the queen appear weak."

I leaned back slightly, the pieces clicking into place in my head. "So, the attacks on me aren't just personal—they're strategic."

Sofia nodded, her jaw tightening. "Exactly. You're not just another target, Kory. You're a symbol. Ban'ach sees you as a threat—not just to her, but to the narrative she's trying to build. If she can paint you as a reckless outsider who flouts Dominion law, then eliminate you when you're under the supposed protection of the judiciary, it reinforces her goal of destabilization."

Her hand dropped from my face, and she sat up slightly, her expression hardening. "The assassin was an attempt to embarrass the judiciary and the queen while simultaneously eliminating a future threat to Ban'ach."

I exhaled, running a hand through my hair. "So, it's not just about killing me. It's about sending a signal—to the Dominion, to anyone else who might stand up to her."

"Exactly," Sofia said. "And the message is clear: fight back, and you'll face the consequences."

The weight of her words settled over me, heavier than anything I'd carried before. "If Ban'ach is willing to go this far, what's next? What happens if the trial becomes the circus she wants it to be?"

"That's what we're trying to prevent," Sofia said, her voice firm. "The evidence we found—the sydereal traces, the token, the warehouse—it's enough to link the Consortium to Ban'ach's plans. But it's not enough to take her down yet. That's why I need you to keep this to yourself. The more Ban'ach knows we're onto her, the more dangerous she becomes."

I stared at her, the weight of her revelation pressing down on me. "Why tell me all this, Sofia? Why now?"

She hesitated, her eyes softening as she looked at me. "Because you deserve to know what's happening around you. You deserve to know why you're in the crosshairs. And..." Her voice wavered slightly before she steadied herself. "Because I trust you, Kory. Even if it puts me at risk, I trust you to do the right thing with this information."

The air between us grew heavy, charged with a mix of shared purpose and unspoken tension. I reached for her hand again, giving it a light, reassuring squeeze.

"I can use this in my trial," I said, my voice steady. "It could be the evidence I need to prove my charges have been manipulated."

She shifted her weight, her eyes flicking away from mine. "Maybe. But I'll have to get permission to reveal what we know to the Dominion."

My brow furrowed. "Wait, they don't already know?"

Her expression tightened, frustration seeping through. "No. My superiors are playing it close to the chest. They're not ready to show their hand, and honestly, they're not even sure what any of this means yet. Like I said, much of what I shared is speculation."

Great. So I wasn't just a man fighting to clear his name—I was a pawn in their political games with the Dominion. The thought twisted in my gut, but I kept my voice neutral.

"Of course. Why would my life or freedom get in the way of their strategy?"

Her lips pressed into a thin line. "It's not like that."

"Isn't it?" I let out a dry laugh, though there was no humor in it. "I guess we'll see."

32

More months passed at the SWS, and I progressed from preliminary coursework to more advanced classes. My understanding of tactics, operations, leadership, and the complexities of the Sydereal ium grew steadily, along with my skills.

In Sydereal Theory, I began mastering techniques designed to enhance the capabilities of individual starships or even entire fleets. These methods offered critical advantages in battle, improving survivability and maneuverability.

One such technique was sydereal mapping, a method for locating concentrations of glyphshades in local space—clues that often revealed hidden starships. Professor Kelarn taught us how to plan and execute scans within the Sydereal ium. To my surprise, I excelled at the assignments.

For one project, I mapped out the Dominion warships patrolling the Zenith Citadel, the nexus at the L2 point between Virelia and Ignisara. When I submitted my results, Professor Kelarn's ears twitched violently, and her usually impassive face betrayed a rare gasp. Without hesitation, she ended the lecture.

"Stay here, Drake," she ordered as the rest of the class filed out, their curious glances lingering on me.

Once the room was empty, Kelarn turned to me, her ears flicking with agitation. "How did you do this?" she demanded.

Her sharp tone sent a ripple of anxiety through me. Had I overstepped again? Was this another instance where my sydereal talents had landed me in trouble for simply doing what I thought was right?

"I just followed the principles you've been teaching us," I said, trying to keep my voice steady. "I applied them to the assignment."

"You did well. Too well." Her ears stilled, and her piercing gaze locked onto mine. "The locations of these patrol ships are highly classified information, Mister Drake."

The realization hit me like a gut punch. "Is that why you sent everyone out?"

"Yes. And now I've contaminated my dot with your data, which means I'll need to have it scrubbed by the security team. Did you send your results to anyone else?"

The project had been part of a take-home test, and collaboration was prohibited. "No," I assured her. "We weren't supposed to."

"Good. Erase all your work immediately."

"But... what about my score?" The idea of failing for doing too well seemed absurd.

"Do not worry. You'll receive a perfect ten out of ten. I've never seen a student map so accurately—not even serving officers." She paused, her expression softening just slightly. "But this is classified information, and we're not authorized to have it. Do you understand?"

"Yes, ma'am," I replied, relieved to have my grade secured but disappointed to destroy hours of meticulous work.

Another technique I learned was sydereal veiling, a method for creating a sydereal bubble to mask objects from detection. It was related to the principles behind FTL drives but didn't require force-neutral zones. Unlike an FTL jump, objects within the veil weren't removed from the material plane but instead existed in a transposed physical plane with a conjugated Higgs field.

Whatever that meant.

I didn't fully grasp the physics, but I executed the technique with surprising proficiency. Using sydereal veiling, I could make myself invisible to all known sensors. The drawback? Inside the bubble, I was blind and deaf. The veil was also fragile—any object larger than a grain of dust entering it would disrupt the effect and reveal my position.

Despite these limitations, veiling was impressive. Watching my classmates' astonished faces as I disappeared entirely for several seconds at a time was satisfying.

I imagined how a fleet might use this in combat—hiding powerful, unstealthy vessels until the moment to strike.

Creating and maintaining the veil was mentally and physically exhausting, but with practice, I extended the duration to minutes. One memorable day, I managed to make the entire instructional hall disappear for ten seconds, along with everyone inside it. The awestruck reactions from my classmates were worth the exhaustion that followed. Even Professor Kelarn, notoriously difficult to impress, admitted it was a feat no others could replicate.

As my skills grew, so did the pressure. I felt constantly aware of the fine line between demonstrating my talents and overstepping boundaries—a balance I was still learning to navigate.

I also met with Arctis occasionally in the Syderealium. His tutoring was invaluable, offering insights I couldn't have gained anywhere else. He taught me how to manipulate my own pocket dimension, populate it with objects, and use it as a personal space. He shared peculiar facts about the Syderealium itself.

"The Syderealium acts as a kind of repository for collective memories and emotions," he explained during one of our sessions. "When significant events occur in the physical plane—events that affect a large number of beings—they alter the topology of the Syderealium."

"How can I see these?" I asked.

"They manifest in various ways," he said, his tone patient but distant. "Fleeting sensations, vivid visions, or even interactive phenomena. The Syderealium is often mistaken for haunted because of this. A battle fought long ago might leave behind echoes of fear and chaos, while a joyful celebration could create warmth and light in certain regions."

He took me on journeys to some of the most notable collective memories he knew. One of the most striking was the memory of a comet impacting Virelia thousands of years ago, an event that wiped out a major city and devastated an entire continent. Millions of kavrenis died, and billions suffered. The disaster had far-reaching consequences, prompting the kavrenis to seek help from the ignas. It marked the beginning of the kavrenis' integration into the Collective Dominion, with the capital moving to Astrithon.

Experiencing the collective memory was like walking through a living monument. I could feel the emotions of those who had endured the tragedy—their fear, pain, and eventual hope. It was humbling to witness how their collective willpower had warped the Syderealium itself.

I appreciated Arctis's lessons, though I found him to be impatient. He insisted that helping me was his duty, but after every session, I felt the weight of an unspoken debt. It was as if he was expecting something from me—a price to be paid, though at a time and in a manner of his choosing.

The more I learned, the more I realized that mastery of the Syderealium came with strings—strings I wasn't sure I wanted to pull.

Or worse, strings that might pull *me*.

Four months after I enrolled in the SWS, Zeta came to the school for an official inspection. It was part of her duties as the crown princess, a role that always seemed to pull her further into a world I could never belong to.

I wondered if I'd have the chance to talk to her, though I wasn't sure I wanted to. And it seemed unlikely.

The student body was ordered to assemble on the campus parade ground for a formal review. I stood in my dress uniform, holding myself rigidly at attention, two rows behind the front, to the left of Marcus.

Zeta's entourage arrived in a sleek aircar, the kind of craft that practically screamed Dominion royalty. She stepped out, her glowing octahedral capsule radiating an almost ethereal presence. She was greeted by Celestarch Seraphis and the Dean of Academics, and they whisked her off to meetings in the administrative hall before I could do more than catch a fleeting glimpse of my former friend.

The rest of the day, whispers followed her like contrails through the hallways. Students gossiped and speculated, their conversations buzzing with a mix of awe and curiosity.

"So, Princess Zeta was your Heliacal consort," Kira said

casually during a break. "Do I have that right?"

"Yeah," I replied tersely, keeping my tone clipped.

She tilted her head, her sharp eyes studying me. "What was that like?"

I shrugged, keeping my gaze fixed on the table in front of me. "I don't know how to describe it." And I didn't want to.

My history with Zeta always felt like an embarrassment waiting to happen. It inevitably led to the same question: "Why aren't you together anymore?" Then I'd have to explain my sydereal attack on Ban'ach and the fallout that followed. That conversation never got easier.

That evening, there was a formal reception in Central Hall in honor of Zeta. Attendance was mandatory.

I found myself standing under an elaborate crystal sculpture that spiraled down from the ceiling, catching and refracting the room's ambient light. The hall, which might have been called a ballroom in a human-designed building, was packed with students in dress uniforms, their conversations creating a dull roar.

A trio of kavreni officers brushed past me, their long tails held high against their backs to avoid brushing others. I stood awkwardly, scanning the room for somewhere I could escape the crowd while still fulfilling the obligation to be present.

I eventually found a small alcove in the back corner of the hall. A kavor and kavora were already there, whispering in their high-pitched voices. They shot me a rude glare when I leaned against the alcove's opening, but I wasn't in the mood to care. After a moment of tense silence, they left, tails twitching indignantly.

Finally, alone, I leaned against the wall and tried to relax. I hadn't seen Zeta yet, and honestly, I didn't want to. Whatever words had been left unsaid between us didn't matter anymore. The bridge had burned, and there was no rebuilding it.

I stayed hidden in the shadows for the next twenty minutes, my mind drifting. Occasionally, someone would glance into the alcove, but the sight of me brooding was apparently enough to send them on their way.

A ripple of commotion rolled through the crowd outside, like a density wave cutting through a nebula. Suddenly, Zeta floated into view, her presence unmistakable even in the chaos. She was flanked by a kavora officer and an igna, their postures sharp and professional.

I froze, my pulse quickening as her capsule's glow illuminated the entrance to the alcove.

Her companions stopped just outside, backing off a few yards but effectively blocking anyone else from approaching.

Zeta floated into the alcove.

"Zeta," I said, my voice tight.

Her appearance was strikingly different. She was still contained in her octahedral capsule, but the material now shimmered like translucent silk, rippling as though alive. Its polished surface reflected the dim light around us, and I could feel the subtle warmth radiating off her.

"Kory Drake," she said, her voice even, though it carried a strange edge. "Zeta supposed you were hiding. She knew you would be at this reception and looked for you."

"Why would you look for me?"

"Zeta wishes to know how her former consort is doing at the school."

"I didn't think you'd care," I replied, unable to keep the bitterness from creeping into my tone.

She hovered silently for a moment, her capsule dimming slightly. "Zeta cares more than you think," she said finally, her voice softer but unreadable.

She floated closer, her capsule radiating warmth, stopping just next to my shoulder. "Zeta has heard disturbing news about the Kergans," she began, her voice low and deliberate. "They are moving against the Dominion. A threat. Zeta tells you this because she has discovered that their agents are manipulating *you* to their own ends."

Her tone softened, almost hesitant. "Zeta feels… regret for some of her past actions. For how she has treated you. Perhaps she was hasty in her judgment."

The words hit me harder than I wanted to admit. I thought about all the times I'd needed Zeta's help since arriving in Astrithon—facing the judiciary's power alone, sitting in a cell with no advocate, fighting off goons hired to kill me. Even before that, on our journey from Earth to Astrithon, she'd left me feeling abandoned.

"What's done is done," I said, keeping my tone flat. "And let's not pretend. I really did attack Ban'ach and her bodyguards. You and I both know I'm guilty of sydereal battery. That's what makes all of this so frustrating—there's no way for me to defend myself. Considering you're the one who put me in this position, imagine how I must feel about you."

She paused, her capsule dimming slightly as though considering her next words. "Zeta has contemplated this," she said quietly.

"And yet you're here?" I asked, folding my arms and leaning back against the wall. "Why?"

"Because Zeta still considers you her friend," she said, her voice tinged with something approaching sadness. "And she yearns for what we once had. This new threat has exposed how Kergan agents have manipulated you and your trial. Zeta must talk to you."

I gave a bitter chuckle. "Not enjoying life as a princess?"

"It is not that," she replied, shaking her capsule slightly, a motion I recognized as frustration. "Zeta is honored to serve the queen. But during our fight against the Kergans, Zeta found... satisfaction. Fulfillment. Her understanding of sydereal assaults has changed. She no longer considers your actions evil. You acted in self-defense to protect yourself and others. Zeta cannot fault you for that."

Her confession stunned me. I couldn't recall a single time Zeta had admitted fault before. Yet my frustration boiled over before I could stop myself.

"Well, maybe you should've thought about that before you betrayed your consort," I snapped.

Her glow dimmed again, and she hovered silently for a moment. I stared away, unwilling to meet her gaze, anger and old wounds surging back. My mind turned to the battle against Ban'ach, the memories Ban'ach had stolen from me, and the people I'd tried to protect. I had used my sydereal talents—the only weapon I had at the time. I didn't regret my actions, even if they had brought me to this place, under trial and scorned.

The crowd outside the alcove stirred, their whispers drifting like static. People craned their necks, sneaking glances at us, their curiosity palpable.

"You should get back to your party," I muttered, still not looking at her.

She began to float away but then stopped abruptly, turning back to face me.

"Zeta is profoundly sorry, friend Kory," she said, her voice softer now. "She will do what she can to make amends. She will start by sharing a secret."

I turned to her, the anger in my chest cooling slightly at her unexpected words.

"Zeta mentioned a threat by the Kergans. The Queen's investigators have uncovered a conspiracy by them to attack the Zenith Citadel," she said.

The name struck a chord. The Zenith Citadel, anchored at the L2 point between Virelia and Ignisara, was one of the most heavily defended installations in the Dominion. It housed the largest sydereal nexus, maintaining secure spaces in the Sydereal ium that were impervious to attacks from Astral Titans. Some even called it the heart of the Dominion.

"What would the Kergans want with the Citadel?" I asked.

"The queen does not know," Zeta replied. "But Zeta believes the Kergans have manipulated the judiciary to impose these criminal charges on you as part of their plan. If you are convicted, it will weaken Dominion resolve to use sydereal weapons. It will deter others from wielding them in defense. Such hesitation works to the Kergans' advantage."

I frowned, trying to piece it together. "And the Queen's investigators? What do they think?"

"They suspect the Kergans are working through an individual. That person has been granted access to Kergan military ships and agents operating under the guise of one or more organized crime organizations in Astrithon."

I thought about Sofia's investigation and her speculation about Ban'ach's involvement. Her discoveries of the involvement of the Therrak Consortium. It sounded like it all was tied to this same threat Zeta was talking about. I knew I had to tell Zeta.

I took a deep breath and said, "Zeta, there's something I need to tell you. Sofia, my bodyguard, has discovered evidence that the person orchestrating all of this is Ban'ach."

I then gave her a summary of the evidence Sofia and her team had discovered. Much of it was circumstantial, but it suggested that Ban'ach was the one pulling the strings of Kergan assets.

I shook my head. "But there's a thing I don't understand. The numbers don't add up. Ban'ach has tried to assassinate me, right? But she also wants my trial as a distraction to weaken the Dominion. If I'm dead, her manipulations fall apart. Doesn't that contradict her intent?"

Zeta tilted her capsule slightly, a gesture of thoughtfulness. "An excellent point," she admitted. "Zeta does not have an answer. Perhaps the assassination was intended as something else. A warning? Or a calculated failure?"

The idea churned in my mind, unsettling and incomplete.

"Be very careful, friend Kory," Zeta said, her voice tinged with urgency. "The enemy is cunning. Zeta will do what she can to help you, though it must be from the shadows."

With that, she rotated gracefully, the light from her capsule reflecting off the crystalline walls of the alcove, and floated back toward the reception.

I remained where I was, staring at the space she'd just vacated, her words replaying in my head. The Kergan Empire. Ban'ach. The Zenith Citadel. The trial. The pieces were there, but the picture was far from clear.

And somehow, I knew the answers would come at a cost.

33

Sofia's office was dim, the faint glow of data displays casting ghostly light across the walls. I stepped inside, the door hissing shut behind me, and immediately felt the weight of the room. It wasn't just the quiet hum of machinery or the slight chill in the air—it was Sofia herself.

She had called me here the first time I'd been in her office. It was peculiar that she'd want to talk to me in the place instead of in my quarters or a quiet park.

Sofia stood by her desk, her posture rigid, her arms crossed tightly. Her usual composed demeanor had cracked, replaced with something harder, more volatile. She didn't look at me right away, her gaze fixed on a display scrolling with lines of Dominion code.

"I need you to listen carefully," she said, her voice clipped. She reached over and activated the privacy field. The hum deepened, sealing us off from the outside world.

I stepped closer, taking in the tension in her stance. "What's going on?"

Sofia finally turned to face me, her blue eyes sharp and

almost too bright in the dim room. "I've found something. Something big. And you're not going to like it."

Her words sent a ripple of unease through me. "What is it?"

She tapped the display, and lines of data transformed into a visual map of the Dominion judiciary. Key names and nodes were highlighted, their connections illuminated in red.

"A trail of evidence," she began, her tone steady but heavy. "It links several judiciary officials—important ones—to Soul Ravagers. Not just casual ties, Kory. This is systemic."

I frowned, leaning closer to the display. "Soul Ravagers? Inside the judiciary?"

She nodded. "And that's not all. There are repeated mentions of someone they refer to as the 'Architect.'" She pointed at a cluster of nodes. "Whoever this is, they're coordinating the entire scheme. Judiciary manipulation, influence over key rulings, and—"

"Me," I said, cutting her off.

Her expression darkened. "Yes. Your trial. Your charges. All of it."

I clenched my fists, my mind racing. "The Architect," I said, my voice low. "You think it's Ban'ach."

Sofia hesitated, her jaw tightening. "It's possible. There are signs, connections that suggest her involvement. But there's no concrete proof. Yet."

I felt my anger rising, a slow, burning wave. I thought about telling her what Zeta had told me about the Kergan threat but decided to hold off. "If Ban'ach is behind this, it's not just about me. She's targeting the Dominion itself, isn't she?"

Sofia tapped another command, and the map dissolved

into a new display—a sydereal energy scan. "That's where it gets worse," she said. "These are sydereal anomalies traced to Dominion nexus facilities. The kind of energy signatures used to frame you for sydereal battery. These are deliberate manipulations, Kory. Someone is using the Dominion's own resources against them. And you were their scapegoat."

Her words hit like a blow, the weight of them settling in my chest. If Ban'ach was the Architect, then this new evidence supported Zeta's claims somebody was conspiring with the Kergan Empire to attack the nexus at the Zenith Citadel. I stepped back, running a hand through my hair. "Why?" I muttered, more to myself than to her. "Why go to all this trouble? What's the endgame?"

She leaned against the edge of her desk, her usual sharp confidence replaced with a quiet frustration. "That's the question. The Soul Ravagers have always operated in the shadows, but this? This is something else entirely. If Ban'ach is the Architect, she's not just destabilizing the Dominion—she's waging a war from within."

The room fell silent, the hum of the privacy field filling the space as I tried to process everything. My trial, the attacks, the charges—it had all felt personal. But now, it was clear I was just one piece on a much larger board.

"What do we do?" I asked finally.

Sofia met my gaze, her expression hardening. "We tread carefully. If we make a move without solid proof, we risk everything. You're still on trial, Kory, and if the wrong people catch wind of what we know…" She let the sentence hang, the implication clear.

I nodded slowly, though the frustration still simmered under my skin. "Fine. But if Ban'ach is behind this, I'm not going to sit back and let her win."

Sofia's lips curved into a faint, grim smile.

"I need to go back to my quarters," I said. "Can we continue this conversation there?"

She nodded once and followed me out of the office.

The lights of Astrithon spilled through the window, fractured and muted, casting faint patterns across the walls. Sofia paced the length of my quarters, her boots clicking softly against the floor. The room felt smaller than usual as if her tension was compressing the air itself.

"The judiciary rulings," she began, her voice sharp, "are too clean. Every single one suppresses sydereal capabilities or weakens the Dominion's defensive posture. It's deliberate, Kory—someone is orchestrating this."

I sat on the edge of my bunk, my arms resting on my knees. "Someone," I said, my voice heavy.

She stopped pacing and turned toward me, her blue eyes sharp in the dim light. "Exactly. And it gets worse." She held up her dot, tilting it so I could see. "We ran tests on the assassin's clothing. Trace elements of a sydereal bubble were embedded in the fibers—residue that can only come from Dominion nexus technology. Whoever's behind this isn't just well-connected. They have access to resources that should be impossible for anyone outside the highest echelons of power."

I leaned forward, my jaw tightening. "That has to be Ban'ach. She's been pulling strings this whole time, using Dominion tech to frame me and now to manipulate the judiciary."

Sofia hesitated, her lips pressing into a thin line. "Ban'ach is a prime suspect, but we don't have direct proof yet. Just patterns, circumstantial data, and too many coincidences to ignore."

I clenched my fists, the pieces of the puzzle swirling in my mind like a storm. "I need to tell you something," I said, standing abruptly.

Sofia raised an eyebrow but didn't interrupt.

"Zeta came to see me during her inspection," I continued. "She said the Kergan Empire is planning to attack the Zenith Citadel."

The words seemed to hang in the air, heavy and charged. Sofia froze, her expression unreadable. "The Citadel?" she repeated, her voice low.

I nodded. "She didn't give me many details, but she said the Kergans are working to destabilize the Dominion from within. The trial, the assassination attempts—they're just pieces of a larger plan. Zeta believes the Kergans' ultimate target is the Citadel itself."

Sofia's jaw tightened, and she resumed pacing, her movements sharper now. "The Zenith Citadel... If they compromise it, the consequences would be catastrophic. It's the cornerstone of Dominion security. The nexus there stabilizes the Syderealium, anchors key sectors, and protects the Supreme Council."

"Based on what you've found, doesn't it sound like Ban'ach is the one orchestrating all of this? Do you think *she* might be this Architect?"

Sofia's breath caught, and she didn't say anything at first. Then her hand dropped, and she said, "It does sound like it. Do you think that is Ban'ach's ultimate goal? To capture the Zenith Citadel?"

I shrugged. "It sure sounds like it to me. Imagine what would happen if Ban'ach takes it out."

Sofia's voice hardened. "Then the Dominion's sydereal infrastructure collapses. Chaos would ripple across entire systems. And Ban'ach wouldn't just weaken the Dominion—

she'd shatter it."

The weight of her words hit like a physical blow, and I sat back down, trying to process everything. "So why isn't Zeta acting on this? If she knows Ban'ach and the Kergans are targeting the Citadel, why isn't the Dominion mobilizing?"

"Politics," Sofia said bitterly. "And lack of proof. Zeta might have suspicions, but without hard evidence, it's just speculation. And speculation doesn't move fleets."

I ran a hand through my hair, frustration bubbling to the surface. "So, we're stuck. Sitting here while Ban'ach conspires with the Kergan Empire, makes her moves, and the Dominion leadership bury their heads in the sand."

"We're not stuck," Sofia said, her voice cutting through my frustration. "We have pieces of the puzzle. We just need to put them together."

I met her gaze, the determination in her eyes grounding me. "And what if we can't do it in time?"

"Then we'll figure something else out," she said firmly. "But sitting here and giving up isn't an option."

The room fell silent, the distant hum of the city the only sound. For the first time in weeks, I felt something other than frustration—resolve.

"Sofia," I said quietly, "thank you. We need to do something about it."

Sofia stepped away from the wall, her gaze fixed on me as if gauging whether I'd truly heard her. "I know this isn't easy for you," she said, her tone softer now. "But rushing in without a plan isn't bravery—it's suicide. Ban'ach didn't get where she is by being careless. Every move she makes is calculated."

I dragged a hand through my hair, the strands damp with the lingering humidity of the day. "It's just hard to sit back and watch everything unravel," I muttered. "The judiciary's compromised, my trial's a farce, and now the Citadel is at risk. How am I supposed to just sit here and... wait?"

Sofia crossed the room, her movements purposeful but measured. "You're not just waiting, Kory. You're surviving. That's what Ban'ach doesn't expect. She's counting on you losing control, making a mistake, or giving up altogether. If you do, she wins."

I stopped pacing and faced her, my chest tightening with the weight of her words. "And if the queen's investigators can't stop her? What then?"

Sofia's lips pressed into a thin line. "Then we find the proof ourselves. But that comes with risks—risks that I'm trying to shield you from."

I shook my head, the frustration bubbling up again. "You can't keep shielding me, Sofia. This isn't just about me anymore. If Ban'ach and the Kergans take the Citadel, it's over for the Dominion. We have to act."

"And we will," she said firmly, stepping closer. Her eyes, bright and piercing, locked onto mine. "But we can't act stupidly. Every move we make has to count. That's why I've been working with my team to trace the sydereal anomalies. It's slow, but it's progress. And we're closer than you think."

The words settled over me, a fragile sense of hope mixing with my lingering frustration. "What do you need from me?" I asked after a moment.

"Stay focused on your training," Sofia said without hesitation. "You're here for a reason. The Syderealium isn't just a weapon—it's a tool. If you master it, you'll be more than a pawn in Ban'ach's game. You'll be something she didn't plan for."

I frowned, the weight of her words sinking in. "You're saying the best way to fight her is to finish my training."

"I'm saying the best way to fight her is to be ready," Sofia said, her tone sharp but not unkind. "And that means trusting me to do my part while you do yours."

For a moment, the tension in the room felt almost unbearable. Then, slowly, I nodded. "Alright. But if there's something I can do to help—"

"You'll know," she interrupted, her voice softening. "And when that time comes, I'll be right there with you."

I let out a slow breath, the tightness in my chest easing slightly. "Thanks, Sofia. I mean it."

She gave a faint smile, one that didn't quite reach her eyes. "You don't need to thank me, Kory. Just don't make me regret trusting you."

With that, she kissed me on the lips and turned toward the door. As it hissed open, she glanced back over her shoulder. "Get some rest. We've got a long fight ahead."

I watched her go, the door sliding shut behind her with a quiet finality. The room felt too still now, the city lights outside casting shadows that seemed to dance with the weight of everything she'd just told me.

I sat back on the bunk, my thoughts spinning. If Sofia was right—and I had no reason to doubt her—then my role in this wasn't just about surviving my trial. It was about becoming the kind of leader who could fight back against the likes of Ban'ach.

And I had no intention of failing this time.

34

"Good morning," Professor Gorgo said. A kavor officer, he was the lead lecturer for our SWS class on advanced fleet tactics. "Reconnaissance and scouting are the lifeblood of fleet operations. Without precise, actionable intelligence, a fleet operates blind, vulnerable to the very traps it seeks to avoid. Today, we will delve into the advanced principles of spectral stealth operations and patrol dynamics. Along the way, I will ask questions—difficult ones. Do not expect to leave here unscathed."

He gestured, and the hologram shifted to a fleet schematic.

"Let us begin. What is the defining characteristic of a reconnaissance mission conducted in a contested zone?"

Kira raised her hand. "Minimizing detection while maximizing data collection, sir."

Professor Gorgo said, "Miss Shale, you are correct but incomplete. The defining characteristic is controlled exposure. A recon unit operates not just to avoid detection but to decide when and how it is seen—if at all. This subtle distinction defines success or catastrophic failure."

The hologram changed to a spectral stealth ship, its energy signature overlaying a starfield.

Professor Gorgo said, "Our spectral stealth vessels, such as the Phantom Claw class, utilize phased-spectrum concealment to scatter or absorb energy emissions across multiple bands. However, what is their greatest vulnerability?"

I raised my hand and said, "Resonance scanners, sir."

"Correct, Mister Drake. Resonance scanners exploit frequency anomalies in the phased spectrum. But how do you counter a resonance sweep?"

The room falls silent. Gorgo waited, his gaze sharp. Finally, Joran ventured, "By adjusting the phase harmonics of the stealth field to match local interference, sir?"

"Efficient but risky. The optimal solution is to shift spectrum harmonics dynamically while exploiting natural environmental noise. Asteroid fields, solar flares, and magnetic anomalies are your allies. Miss Adline, what happens if you phase-shift too slowly?"

Adline, a kavora student, replied, "The resonance scan locks onto the transition frequency, revealing the ship's position, sir."

"Precisely," Gorgo said with a grin that displayed his pointed teeth. "A stealth ship must think like a shadow—always moving, never still."

A patrol ship appears on the hologram, maneuvering through an asteroid field under simulated fire.

Professor Gorgo pointed at the display and said, "Our patrol vessels, such as the Vanguard Spear class, are the fleet's overt scouts. They are built to provoke, bait, and survive. What is the patrol ship's primary role in relation to stealth units?"

Marcus said, "To draw enemy attention away from the stealth units, sir."

"Correct in principle, Mister Fahey, but oversimplified. The patrol ship operates as a tactical disruptor, forcing the enemy to react while feeding actionable data to stealth units and the fleet. Mister Drake, when should a patrol ship retreat?"

I said, "When it has achieved its mission objectives or is at risk of destruction, sir."

"Incorrect. A patrol ship retreats only when it can do so without compromising the intelligence it has gathered. Sacrificing a patrol ship is acceptable if it ensures the survival of higher-value assets. Never forget that reconnaissance is not about the scout's survival—it is about the fleet's survival."

The hologram displayed a star system with an enemy fleet near a planet, asteroid belts, and several outposts.

Professor Gorgo stood back and folded his arms. "Scenario: You command a spectral stealth unit and a patrol ship tasked with reconnoitering an enemy fleet in the Epsilon Divide. The stealth ship identifies a high-value target—a command cruiser—but cannot transmit without risk. The patrol ship is unaware of the stealth ship's findings and is approaching the system. What is your next move? Mister Kale?"

Joran said, "Coordinate a diversion using the patrol ship to draw attention away from the stealth unit, sir."

"Wrong. Any premature action risks alerting the enemy to your presence. The correct answer: the stealth ship must exfiltrate to a safe transmission zone, then coordinate a feint with the patrol ship. Timing is paramount. Miss Shale, what happens if the patrol ship moves before receiving instructions?"

Kira said, "It risks intersecting the enemy's detection grid, revealing both its position and potentially the presence of the stealth unit, sir."

"Exactly. Scouting requires patience as much as precision."

The hologram shifted to an enemy fleet deploying drones and wide-area resonance scans.

Professor Gorgo said, "The enemy is counter-scouting. Their drones sweep the asteroid field where your stealth ships are hiding. What do you do? Mister Drake?"

"Evade to a quieter zone, sir," I said.

"Amateur thinking, Mister Drake. Evading risks creating detectable trails. Instead, deploy spectrum decoys—automated buoys emitting false signatures—to saturate their scanners. Simultaneously, reduce your ship's active emissions and maneuver using asteroid cover."

The hologram faded, and Professor Gorgo strode to the center of the room. "Reconnaissance is not about bravery. It is about mastery—of sensors, timing, and the art of remaining unseen. Fleet operations rely on the invisible work of scouts. Fail here, and the fleet fails. Succeed, and your fleet will dictate the battlefield. Remember, you are not just the eyes of the fleet. You are the shadow of its will."

The hologram reactivated, displaying a spectral stealth ship hovering near an enemy fleet. The simulation highlighted layers of defensive systems, including resonance scanners, anti-torpedo countermeasures, and interceptor patrols.

Professor Gorgo said, "Up to this point, we've focused on reconnaissance. But stealth ships are not mere observers. Under the right conditions, they are predators. However, breaking cover to attack is a decision that carries immense risk. The question is not just when to attack, but how to do so while ensuring survival and the continued success of the mission."

He turned to us. "Tell me: under what circumstances should a stealth ship launch a torpedo strike? Mister Fahey?"

Marcus said, "When the target is of sufficient value to outweigh the risk of losing the stealth ship, sir."

"Correct in principle. But let me refine your answer. The decision hinges on three factors: One, the value of the target relative to mission objectives. Two, the local threat environment and likelihood of escape. Three, the probability of success, including the ability to deliver a crippling blow in a single strike.

"Miss Shale, why must a stealth ship always aim for a single-strike kill?"

Kira said, "To avoid prolonged engagement and maximize the element of surprise, sir."

"Exactly. A stealth ship, such as a spectral, is not designed for attrition warfare. Its strength lies in precision and the psychological impact of appearing, striking, and vanishing. Now, let us examine the mechanics.

"The process of launching torpedoes from a stealth ship is deceptively simple. Consider these challenges:

"Emissions Signature: Torpedo launch systems create brief but detectable energy spikes.

"Propulsion Trails: Even stealth torpedoes leave ion trails at launch.

"Countermeasures: Advanced fleets employ layered defenses, including anti-torpedo lasers, interceptor drones, and decoy generators."

He gestured to the hologram, which zoomed in on a torpedo's trajectory.

"To counter these risks, a stealth ship must: One, use

minimum-launch profiles, activating only critical systems to minimize emissions. Two, fire from a position within the target's blind zones—areas with overlapping defensive coverage gaps. Three, program torpedoes with delayed activation, masking their propulsion until they are close to the target."

The hologram changed to a simulation: a spectral stealth ship lurking in the shadow of a dense asteroid field. A massive enemy capital ship, bristling with defenses, patrolled nearby, flanked by escorts.

"Scenario: Your stealth ship has identified a Krixus-class enemy battleship—an asset of immense strategic value. Its escorts have moved out of position, leaving the battleship vulnerable. You are within torpedo range and have a clear shot at its primary reactor. Do you attack?"

I hesitated, then responded. "Yes, sir. The target's value justifies the risk, and the battleship is vulnerable."

"And what happens when the ion trails from your torpedoes are detected by the destroyers before they hit their target?"

I faltered. "I... hadn't considered that, sir."

Professor Gorgo sighed. "You would compromise your position and lose both the element of surprise and your stealth ship. The battleship's escorts would counter your torpedoes before they could land a decisive blow. The correct answer is no, unless you can mitigate the risks. Miss Adline, how would you proceed?"

Adline said, "Deploy a diversion, sir. Perhaps use decoy drones to simulate a secondary threat and draw the escorts away before launching the torpedoes."

Professor Gorgo said, "A creative approach, but time is a factor. The longer you wait, the greater the chance the target moves or the escorts return. The optimal course of action is to combine tactics: One, positioning: Move into the asteroid field to mask ion trails and emissions. Two, timing: Launch torpedoes immediately after the destroyers cross to the far side of their patrol arcs. Three, distraction: Deploy a decoy drone to mimic an energy spike near the asteroid belt, drawing their sensors away from the true threat."

The hologram animated the ambush. The stealth ship maneuvered into the asteroid field, launching torpedoes in a staggered spread. The torpedoes remained inactive for the first few kilometers, then ignited their kinetic warheads just outside the battleship's defensive perimeter. A decoy drone distracted the destroyers, pulling their sensors away.

Professor Gorgo continued, "The key is coordinated execution. A spread of torpedoes increases the chance of a hit while overwhelming defensive systems. Staggering their activation prevents the enemy from predicting trajectories. The decoy drone forces the destroyers to investigate elsewhere. Mister Kale, what happens if the torpedoes fail to disable the battleship?"

Joran replied, "Withdraw immediately, sir. Prolonging the attack risks detection and destruction."

"Correct. A spectral that remains in the combat zone after a failed ambush becomes prey. The mission is over the moment the element of surprise is lost."

Professor Gorgo held up a finger. "Let me summarize the conditions under which a stealth ship should attack: One, the target must be of critical value—something that will significantly weaken the enemy fleet or support your fleet's objectives. Two, the threat environment must be manageable. If escape is impossible after an attack, the risk outweighs the reward. Three, the probability of success must be high. Stealth ships cannot afford partial victories."

He glanced around the room. "Failure to understand these principles turns an ambush into a suicide mission. Do not let your eagerness to attack blind you to the larger strategy. Any final questions?"

The room was silent.

Professor Gorgo continued. "Reconnaissance and ambush tactics are the most delicate operations in space warfare. You must balance patience, precision, and audacity. Remember: a stealth ship's greatest weapon is not its torpedoes. It is the fear of the unknown it instills in our enemies."

As I filed out of the room, I was already replaying the simulation in my mind. The lesson might shape my future victories or maybe mean the difference between survival and failure in the void.

35

"We need to talk," Sofia said as I walked out of the student cafeteria with Marcus and Kira at my side. Sofia's eyes moved between my two friends. "Alone."

I frowned. "I'll catch up with you guys in a bit," I told Marcus and Kira. As they walked off, I approached Sofia. "I've only got a few minutes. I have my cyber warfare lecture."

She looped her arm through mine and pulled me around the corner of the building into a secluded courtyard. "A gangster from the Therrak Consortium defected last night. We have him in protective custody and are interviewing him."

I turned to face her. "That's great!"

She shifted her weight to the other leg and folded her arms. "Not what he's telling us. He confirmed that Ban'ach and several other Kergan Soul Ravagers are planning an attack on the Zenith Citadel. They've assembled a fleet of Kergan warships and intend to assault and capture the nexus in the Citadel."

I thought about all the defenses that surrounded the Citadel. "I wish them good luck. They'll never get through its defenses."

"You know more about that than I do, but I wouldn't count on it. Ban'ach wouldn't make a move like this unless she had the means and the opportunity. The defector kept mentioning the Architect as if they were somebody else. I don't think Ban'ach is that person. It's somebody else."

"Who?"

"The defector doesn't know."

We'd been sitting on this information for weeks and hadn't told anybody else about it. If Ban'ach *did* attack the Dominion, and we didn't inform somebody, we would be at fault for withholding the information. The Zenith Citadel was a cornerstone of the Collective Dominion's government, the anchor of the Supreme Council. It guaranteed reliable access to the Sydereallium for the Dominion. If Ban'ach could somehow capture it or undermine it, then the stability of the realm would be threatened.

Could I tell Zeta?

Given her recent change of heart, she was the obvious person, but I had no way to reach out to her.

Maybe I should tell Arctis?

The Glyphspeaker had been an enormous help to me, and I had learned many new things about the Sydereallium from him. But I always felt like a pawn in some game when I was with him. Somehow, I knew the ancient glyphshade was manipulating me, though I couldn't yet put my finger on what he was doing. But I didn't fully trust him.

Celestarch Seraphis. She was the obvious person to talk to. She'd always struck me as a selfless person who only wanted to serve her queen and country. She was also a fleet officer with battle experience and decades of service.

"Sofia, we can't keep this information to ourselves anymore," I said, gazing into her ice-blue eyes. "The Dominion is in danger."

"I'm not authorized to disclose what we've learned."

"Maybe *you're* not, but nobody can stop me. I'm going to talk to Celestarch Seraphis."

"Kory, you're not supposed to know about these facts either. I should have never told you!"

I rested a hand on her shoulder. "Think about it. The Collective Dominion is our host nation. All the human refugees on Virelia depend on the Dominion for our homes, our security, and our future. A threat to the Citadel is a threat to us. I can't believe the UHC leadership is just sitting on this information!"

She nodded. "I agree, it is hard to believe. I have the sense that they're holding onto it as some kind of political card to be saved for some future play. But it's not our decision to make, Kory. I could be sent to jail!"

I shook my head. "I don't think so. You think the Dominion would permit that?" Sensing her dismay, I took a different tack. "Sofia, listen to me. Think of yourself as a whistleblower. You've known about important information the UHC is withholding from their ally, information that could make the difference between whether we win this war against the Kergan Empire or not. We'll never win it without the backing of the Dominion, and we can't let Ban'ach undermine their strength. This isn't about protecting our jobs but instead about securing our lives. Tell me I'm wrong!"

I looked at my dot and saw that my cyber warfare lecture had started five minutes ago, but this discussion with Sofia was too important. Hopefully, Kira and Marcus were taking good notes. I could check with them later in the day.

Sofia tapped her finger on her lips and stared into the distance. After a minute, her head tilted down and then back up as she released a sigh. "You're gonna get me fired, Kory Drake. Okay, we'll talk to Seraphis, but nobody else."

"Okay, let's see if we can meet her right now," I said, hoping the celestarch was available.

I paced in Celestarch Seraphis's anteroom while Sofia stood guard nearby. A kavora secretary sat behind a circular glass and aluminum desk, her attention focused on a terminal display. The ceiling was covered with glowvance panels that emitted a soft yellow light that matched the local sun's spectrum. On a pedestal next to Seraphis's closed office door rested a carved marble sculpture of a creature resembling a cross between a horse and a leopard.

After twenty minutes of waiting, the kavora turned to us and said, "Celestarch Seraphis will see you now."

I nodded, and Sofia and I walked into Seraphis's office.

The celestarch floated behind a table shaped like a crescent moon. A holographic display switched off as we entered. "Kory Drake, welcome."

"Celestarch Seraphis, thank you for seeing us on such short notice," I said. I gestured toward Sofia. "This is Warrant Officer Sofia Kohl of the UHC Military Police."

Sofia inclined her head. "Celestarch, it is a pleasure."

"Equally," the igna said. "My recollection is you are in charge of Mister Drake's protection detail."

"Indeed, ma'am."

Seraphis's attention focused back on me. "Tell me what is so urgent."

"Ma'am, as you know, there have been a couple of attempts to attack or abduct me. Miss Kohl has headed the investigation into those matters. She's learned of some important information that's relevant to Dominion security. We didn't know who to take it to, so we decided to approach you."

"This is unusual. Should you not have gone through UHC channels?"

I nodded. "She did. But I regret to inform you that our leaders are sitting on the information for reasons we don't understand. And the matter is urgent."

Seraphis's capsule bobbed up and down. "Very well. Let's hear it."

I looked at Sofia, and she nodded. Then she stepped forward and told Seraphis about the threat from Ban'ach and the Kergan Empire. She gave an outline of the evidence her team had collected, including the defector.

"Celestarch Seraphis," Sofia said at the end, "we have decrypted communications from Ban'ach to the Therrak Consortium referencing specific plans to, and I quote, 'breaking the Dominion's core' and 'severing the heart from the Collective.' Ban'ach is assembling a fleet to attack. They have battleships and spectrals."

She finished and stepped back. It was quiet in the office for a minute as we let Seraphis think through the implications. "Seraphis understands. Your information, Officer Kohl, is more timely and relevant than you could have imagined. The Dominion is also investigating some strange recent events that make more sense now that you've revealed this conspiracy. Who is this Architect?"

"We don't know," I replied. "We were hoping you might."

"Nay. The information Seraphis is about to share with you is classified and you must keep it to yourselves." We both nodded. "Dominion intelligence has been tracking unusual logistic patterns in the Kergan Empire consistent with the assembling of a large fleet. This, of course, worries us, but the target could be any of dozens of galactic nations. We even know the codename of the operation: Obsidian Phase. They have procured subspace destabilizers and null-field emitters, which could be used to disrupt Citadel defenses.

"If your information is correct, then we now know that the Zenith Citadel is the intended target. Of course, we must confirm its veracity."

I leaned forward. "Ma'am, I don't think we have much time. Perhaps only days."

"Mister Drake, you've been at our school now for over 150 days. Seraphis knows that you have done well in your tactics and operations course and your sydereal theory class. Tell Seraphis how you expect Ban'ach to attack."

I took a moment to consider the problem facing Ban'ach. Up until then, I had only looked at it from the Dominion's perspective as a defender. But if I was attacking the Ignisara system and the L2 point between Ignisara and Virelia, and I had a large and powerful fleet of ships to do it with, how would I go about it?

"I would avoid jumping into Lagrange points, ma'am. Instead, I would arrive in the system at the edge of the helioshock. This would mask the fleet's arrival and avoid defensive minefields."

"Very good. And how far out is Ignisara's helioshock?"

I racked my brain for that detail. "About fifteen light hours, ma'am."

"Indeed. That means it would take roughly six to seven days for the enemy fleet to traverse that distance and make their attack."

This was true, but there was one thing bothering me.

"But how would we know, ma'am? It's doubtful Dominion sensors would detect the ships arriving that far out, and if they move inward toward Virelia under EMCON rules, then we might not see them until it is too late. Blazes, they could have already jumped into the system and are already on their way as we speak!"

Sofia stepped closer to me and rested a hand on my left arm.

"Calm yourself, Mister Drake," Seraphis said. "Your analysis is correct, but panicking will serve no purpose. Here at the SWS, we teach you to think strategically and rationally. What is the next logical step in our defense?"

"We must assemble a defensive fleet, alert the Zenith Citadel, and send out a screening force. Patrol ships and spectrals. Maybe we can catch the Kergans during their transit in-system."

"Excellent, Commander. What else?"

I thought about my sydereal training. "Sydereal mapping. If the Kergans are out there somewhere, we should be able to detect their glyphshades in the Sydereallium approaching Virelia."

Seraphis floated to the side and came around her desk, approaching us. Cyan light pulsed from the edges of her capsule. "Perhaps that could be done in theory, but the volume of space that must be searched is perplexing."

"I could do it, ma'am. At least, I think I could. I've mapped out flotillas of ships all the way out to the Ignisara-Virelia Lagrange points. It didn't take long."

"Truly?"

"Yes, but I haven't had much practice."

"Very well. Mister Drake. Miss Kohl. Seraphis thanks you for this information. She must take this to the Supreme Council. It is out of your hands now, but Seraphis may call upon you for your assistance. Stand ready."

"Yes, ma'am," I said.

Sofia nodded her head once.

As we walked out of the administrative building, Sofia leaned toward me and spoke softly. "Do you think Seraphis will do anything?"

I shrugged. "I don't know. Here at the school, she is all-powerful, but how much influence does she wield outside of it? I don't know."

"Do you really think the Kergans are already in the system somewhere?"

"It's possible. Seraphis is correct. It would take them a week to transit from the helioshock all the way to Virelia. And they're not going to jump directly into the middle of the system because it's too easy for the Dominion to mine the limited number of Lagrange points there are available for their use. They'll make a stealthy approach."

"But it's likely out of our hands now," she said. "Right?"

I pulled the door open to the lecture hall but stopped. Sofia wasn't allowed past this point. "Probably. You're a police officer and I'm an officer student. I'd like to help, but who am I against a fleet of ships? One that has battleships."

I moved to enter the building, but Sofia grabbed my shoulder. "What happens to us if Ban'ach captures or destroys the Zenith Citadel?"

"I suppose her fleet would move on Virelia. With the Citadel gone, we'd be completely vulnerable."

"Damnation. It would be like the invasion of Earth all over again!"

Seeing her distress, I didn't respond. But she was both right and wrong. It would be an invasion but much worse than on Earth. With all the modern forces defending the planet of Virelia, the Kergans would probably bombard the planet from orbit. Something they never did on Earth because it wasn't necessary given how weak our militaries had been compared to Kergan forces. But at Virelia, they wouldn't hold back. They would lob rocks at us and fire railguns into defending forces and facilities, and millions—perhaps even billions—of kavrenis, ignas, and humans would die from collateral damage.

What's worse, this time, there would be no benevolent nation waiting behind the curtain to carry off refugees and offer them sanctuary.

What was even scarier was thinking about what Ban'ach would do if she got her hands on an intact Zenith Citadel. As a Soul Ravager, it would give her a powerful base of operation. It would make the empress of the Kergan Empire the most potent being in the known universe.

I reached out and hugged Sofia to me. We held onto each other for a moment, then I turned and entered the building.

36

Two days later, Sofia and I were called back to Celestarch Seraphis's office.

"What could this be about?" she asked me as we climbed the stairs in the administrative building.

"Maybe she has some follow up questions for us," I replied and reached out and squeezed her hand.

Seraphis's secretary passed us through to her office immediately. In it stood Seraphis and a second igna who I didn't know.

"Mister Drake and Miss Kohl, welcome," Seraphis said as we entered. "This is Celestarch Kaelith, commander of the Dominion Home Fleet."

Kaelith's body was contained by a gray ellipsoid capsule covered with silver scrollwork. We exchanged greetings with him. I was surprised to see the Home Fleet commander here, though Seraphis seemed completely comfortable with the visitor.

"How is your time at the SWS going, Mister Drake?" Celestarch Kaelith asked me.

I bounced on my feet. "Very well, sir. At least, for my part, I am pleased. I hope Celestarch Seraphis feels similarly."

Kaelith spun on his vertical axis. "Kaelith believes she does. Kaelith has been told many things about you, especially your skills with the Syderealium and the sydereal arts."

I knew these questions couldn't be the purpose of this visit; otherwise, why would Seraphis have invited Sofia back? And the Home Fleet commander was too busy to be bothered with a student like me. No, this visit *must* have something to do with the information we disclosed a few days ago.

Moments later, Seraphis confirmed my suspicions. "Mister Drake, Seraphis has informed the Supreme Council of the news you brought to her. In consultation with the Queen, the Dominion has decided to treat this threat from the Kergan Empire as real and imminent."

I nodded, and my shoulders relaxed.

"As commander of the defending fleet stationed in the Ignisara system," Seraphis continued, "Celestarch Kaelith has been tasked with assembling defenders and preparing for an attack. He has learned of your abilities with the Syderealium and has asked that you be given leave from the SWS and assigned to his command staff."

The request took me by surprise. Kaelith must have thousands of officers and spacemen under his command and millions of other citizens he could draw from. Why would he want me on his command staff?

Sofia nudged me with her elbow, and I realized they were all standing there looking at me, obviously waiting for a response. I quickly gathered my thoughts and shut my mouth before drool started leaking out. "On his command staff?"

"Indeed," Kaelith said in a thrumming baritone voice. "Kaelith has been told that you are the most promising flairsparked seen at the SWS in generations. He needs somebody skilled in the sydereal arts as an adviser and to gather intelligence."

I looked at Sofia and then back at the fleet commander. "Does this mean I would have to leave the school?"

"Aye, you will be assigned to Kaelith's flagship, the *Inferis*. Your bodyguards may accompany you," Kaelith said.

I looked at Sofia again.

She shrugged. "It would make your security easier. You would probably only need me to come along."

I was thoroughly enjoying my time at the SWS. The thought of interrupting my classes, especially mid-term, wasn't appealing. But what if I could actually do something meaningful? The ignas seemed to have more confidence in my sydereal skills than I did, and maybe—just maybe—they were right. If I had a chance to help, especially in a situation this critical, how could I turn it down?

The issue wasn't academic; it was about the survival of humanity. Defeating the Kergan fleet might be the only way to ensure that survival. And if I encountered Ban'ach again, there was a slim but real chance of recovering the memories of my parents.

I hadn't given up on that goal. Yes, it was reckless, especially while I was already on trial for sydereal battery. But what was the judiciary going to do—charge me a second time? With clear evidence that Ban'ach had manipulated the judiciary and framed me for conspiring with Pyrakos, the system felt rigged against me anyway.

This was more than just personal. This was a chance to meet the Kergans in battle—something I had been training for. I had dedicated my life to protecting humanity, and this felt like the ultimate opportunity to do precisely that.

"I agree, Celestarch Kaelith," I said, "if Celestarch Seraphis will excuse me from my studies."

Kaelith's capsule brightened slightly, signaling his approval. "Excellent. Seraphis has already approved your transfer, as has the UHC Armada. You are hereby appointed as Kaelith's Sydereal Strategist. Gather your belongings and report to *Inferis* this evening. The command staff meeting is at 1800 hours, and you must be present."

"Yes, sir," I replied, my tone steady despite the whirlwind in my chest. Turning to Seraphis, I added, "May I be excused to ready myself?"

"Aye, Mister Drake," she said with a faint glow of approval. "And congratulations. Make the school proud!"

I nodded, my heart pounding as I left the room. This was it—everything I had trained for was about to be put to the ultimate test.

I returned to my quarters and quickly packed my meager belongings. Several sets of uniforms, exercise clothes, worn casual wear, a couple notebooks and journals, my toiletries, and my dot.

While I waited for Sofia—who had needed a couple hours to report back to her superiors and pack her own bag—I looked up the *Inferis* on my dot.

Inferis was an Ignisara-class dreadnought measuring two-and-a-half kilometers long and over half a kilometer in breadth. Its crew complement consisted of 6,500 kavreni and fifteen igna specialists, not including the celestarch's flag staff.

The flagship carried massive anti-ship missiles that were the size of *Thunder* and could move as free-flying drones. She was also armed with ten railguns in turrets the size of small buildings and bristled with defensive armaments that came in many sizes.

What was particularly interesting to me was that *Inferis* carried its own sydereal nexus for use by the flag staff for intelligence gathering and fleet communications. Compared to the massive nexus at the Zenith Citadel, it was tiny, but I'd never used one before, only heard about them in my sydereal theory course.

Sofia arrived back at my quarters at 1300 hours. We went to the mess to get a quick meal because I didn't know when we'd get to eat again.

"Where are you two going?" Marcus said when he saw us arrive carrying our luggage.

I smiled and said, "Can't talk about it."

"Oh, so that's how it's gonna be," he replied.

"I hope it's romantic," Kira said, winking at Sofia.

Sofia blushed and looked away.

"It's not *that* sort of thing, Shale."

"How long you going to be gone?" Marcus said.

"I don't know. I have official leave from Celestarch Seraphis for an indefinite period of time."

We chatted for a few more minutes, talking about the classes I would miss out on, with Marcus and Kira regularly inserting questions that tried to pry out of me where I was going. I resisted the interrogation, only telling them that I had an assignment with the Home Fleet.

Finishing our food, we said goodbye and took an air taxi to the spaceport, asking the kavor driver to take us to the military terminal.

Ten minutes later, we descended onto a landing lot, and the car advanced the final distance on its wheels, stopping outside the military terminal. I paid the driver, we grabbed our bags, and entered the terminal.

It was packed with kavreni military personnel, all dressed in uniforms of one kind or another. I passed a kavora dressed in a chief petty officer's uniform who had two children clinging to her and crying while she talked to a kavor in civilian clothes that might have been her husband.

An entire squad of kavreni Marines dressed in battle armor moved past us in single-file, long flechette guns hanging from straps on their shoulders.

I looked for signs and found the one that pointed to the corridor we needed to follow to find our ride. After a fifteen-minute walk, we arrived at a gate listing the departing shuttle to *Inferis*. Sofia and I presented our credentials to a disbelieving pair of kavreni Marines who acted like they'd never seen a human before. But our orders were straight from the fleet commander, and we had proper military IDs, so after examining all of it with the obvious objective of turning us away, they finally admitted that everything was in order and allowed us onto the shuttle.

The shuttle's interior screamed military: bare metal walls and floor with nothing but a strip of glued-down rubber to keep people from slipping. The seats were metal frames with strips of cloth woven to provide a sling of sorts. A cargomaster tossed our luggage into a pile of nearly identical bags at the back of the bay.

Sofia and I found two empty chairs side-by-side and got ourselves strapped in. The stink of ammonia from old kavreni body odor filled the compartment, making me wish we had an air vent of some kind.

I patted Sofia on the knee, and she leaned her head on my shoulder. It was one of the few times I'd ever seen her let her guard down while in public. Maybe she felt like we were safer on this stinking and crowded military transport. I suppressed a smile while thinking about what would happen to us if I inclined my head and kissed her. The Kavreni laws against public lewdness would probably require us to be reported for conduct unbecoming an officer.

The shuttle lifted off with very little fanfare. One minute, we were sitting there dozing; the next, there was a bump, and suddenly, we were moving. The compartment lacked windows of any kind, so the ride ended up being pretty boring because we couldn't see anything outside.

We docked with *Inferis* about three hours later. Again, I wished for windows so we could see the enormous battleship from the outside. Instead, all we got to see was the tunnel leading from the shuttle hatch to the open airlock of the ship. Above that, in bright letters, was written in Kavreni script, *Inferis*.

A petty officer met us at the hatch and led us into the ship. *Inferis* was large enough to have its own artificial gravity field, allowing us to walk comfortably. Despite this convenience, the decks were still organized like a huge stack of pancakes so that the crew could move around under acceleration in the event that artificial gravity was lost. This made the dreadnought feel like a skyscraper, where the shuttle docks were near the bottom, and officer country—where we were headed—was near the center.

For being such a vast ship, the corridors and passageways were surprisingly tight, especially for a large human like myself. I had to crouch more than I would have liked, repeatedly banging my head against objects projecting from the ceilings.

Sofia and I were assigned private berths adjacent to each other. Mine had a small fold-away cot, a desk, a closet, and a bathroom. The ship hummed around me with the sounds of the power systems, PA announcements, and foot traffic in the corridors. The battleship was by far the largest starship I had ever been in. *Thunder* could have fit into one of its smaller hangars.

I sat on my cot and tried to relax but found it impossible. I was nervous about my meeting with Celestarch Kaelith and his staff. The anxiety was similar to what I felt each time before going into battle. My palms sweated, and my heart thumped.

What if I didn't meet Kaelith's expectations?

Even worse, what if I failed at my new duties and somehow this led to a defeat against the Kergan forces?

Then a voice in my head said, *If one doesn't try, one doesn't live.* Simply waking up in the morning and doing one's tasks is always a risk. Staying in bed and sleeping all day can be a very safe thing to do, a low-risk solution to life, which is why some humans have a genetic predisposition toward depression. Often, it can lead to behavior that increases the odds of survival in certain situations, such as when resources are scarce or the environment is dangerous.

But it is a painful and humiliating way to pass through life.

I would not hide from my duties to humanity and the Dominion.

I forced the anxiety away that ate at me like acid and instead focused my mind on thoughts of beating my criminal charges and returning to Destiny and the rest of my crew.

37

Fifteen minutes before the designated hour of the staff meeting, I wandered through the labyrinthine passageways of *Inferis,* searching for its location. The ship's sheer size made every step feel like a trek through an uncharted city. Sofia followed a few paces behind me, silent but watchful. Occasionally, I stopped a passing kavreni crew member and asked for directions, their tall ears twitching as they processed my accented Dominion Standard. Most were polite, though I caught a few glances that bordered on skeptical—or maybe curious.

With just five minutes to spare, we finally located the conference room. It was a large compartment designed to host senior staff, seating at least forty people. A holotank dominated one end of the room, its surface dark but ready to spring to life. A long table stretched through the center, flanked by high-backed chairs that were evenly spaced along its length. Additional seating lined the bulkheads, making the room feel even more expansive.

As Sofia and I entered, I immediately noticed seven

others already present. Three ignas floated near the holotank in their shimmering capsules, their faint glows adding an almost ethereal atmosphere to the otherwise utilitarian space. Four kavrenis, seated at the table, turned their sharp, bat-like faces toward us, their dark eyes studying me intently.

Among the ignas, I immediately recognized Celestarch Kaelith. The silver scrollwork of his gray capsule glinted under the harsh lighting, a clear symbol of his authority. The other ignas remained unfamiliar, their geometric capsules engraved with intricate patterns that marked them as high-ranking officers.

Kaelith's capsule brightened slightly as he addressed the room. "Commander Drake, welcome." His voice was even, but there was a weight to it that demanded attention. "Everyone, this is Lieutenant Commander Kory Drake, who will be joining Kaelith's staff as a sydereal analyst. He is accompanied by Chief Warrant Officer Sofia Kohl, his... assistant."

I caught the briefest pause before the word "assistant," and I couldn't help but be relieved that Kaelith chose not to disclose Sofia's actual role as my bodyguard. It would have complicated things in ways we didn't need right now.

As Kaelith spoke, I nodded and made a point of looking each person in the eye. Confidence was key. Whether they respected me or doubted me, I had to project the impression that I belonged here—because the truth was, I wasn't entirely sure I did.

Kaelith gestured to a short kavora who had graying brown fur and stood like a spring under tension. "This is Astrarch Zerya, Kaelith's chief of staff."

Zerya was an astrarch, the equivalent of a rear admiral in the UHC armada. She flashed her teeth and held her hands open in a kavreni greeting. "Commander Drake, so good to meet you. We have heard much of your abilities." She pointed at the others. "I will introduce the rest of the staff." She went around the room naming each one of them and giving me their ranks and titles, most of which soon slipped from my memory, but a few were notable.

"This is Commander Aelira," Zerya said, pointing to an igna in a white cube capsule. "She is the Fleet Intelligence Officer, and you will be working directly for her most of the time." That made Aelira the equivalent of the N2 in a UHC Armada task force.

I nodded and said, "Excellent, I look forward to it."

"And finally, this is Captain Lyssara," Zerya said, pointing to another igna in a blue tetrahedral capsule, "captain of the *Inferis*. Though she is not officially part of Celestarch Kaelith's staff, as captain of the flagship, she plays a key role in meeting the needs of the Home Fleet."

"Welcome, Commander Drake," Captain Lyssara said. "Lyssara hopes your quarters on *Inferis* are satisfactory."

"They are fine, ma'am. Thank you for hosting us."

"Very well, let this meeting begin," Zerya said, obviously in charge of the meeting.

Once everybody was seated, Zerya continued. "Welcome to this meeting. As you are aware, this gathering was unplanned, but Celestarch Kaelith asked for it because of some recent events. I will turn the time over to Celestarch Kaelith."

Celestarch Kaelith rose from his chair at the head of the table. "Kaelith has met privately with most of you already, so you should all be aware that a Kergan battle fleet is expected to arrive in the Ignisara system very soon. Indeed, it may have already arrived, and our surveillance systems have not yet located it. Commander Aelira will give us a more thorough briefing in a moment, but let Kaelith summarize what we know. The intended target of the Kergans is the destruction or capture of the Zenith Citadel. If they were to achieve their objective, the consequences for the Collective Dominion would be catastrophic. Such an act would weaken the Supreme Council and destabilize our government at all levels.

"As the staff officers in command of the Home Fleet, our solemn duty is to protect the Ignisara system from all threats. The Supreme Council has formally activated the fleet and given us orders to defend the Zenith Citadel using any means necessary. That is why Kaelith has called this meeting. Astrarch Zerya, the time is yours."

"Thank you, Celestarch," Zerya said. "I turn the time over to Commander Aelira for the Intelligence Briefing."

The holotank flickered, and a map of the Ignisara system appeared. "Fleet scouts and surveillance systems have been deployed throughout the system," Aelira said. "The 1st and 2nd Spectral Flotillas have been deployed to the inner system to screen the fleet and the Citadel. Captain Teryn will undoubtedly speak about this in a few minutes during the Operations Update. The fleet has also deployed remotely piloted surveillance drones to the outer system in the thousands. As of this date, no movements of foreign warships have been detected in the system."

"This is good," a kavor wearing the rank insignia of a Captain said. I remembered his name was Teryn, the Fleet Operations Officer.

"Not really," Aelira responded. "We do not have the resources to cover the massive volume of space in the outer system reaching out to the helioshock. If the Kergan fleet has already jumped into the system, we may not detect them until they are less than a day from the Citadel."

"And we are certain this threat actually exists?" Captain Lyssara asked.

"Aelira has prepared an intelligence assessment that looks at our foreign and domestic intelligence sources for evidence of this fleet. We have noted anomalous activity for five twelvenights. But the information that clinched the conclusion was provided two days ago by Warrant Officer Sofia Kohl and her investigators."

Sofia nodded her head.

"Let us stay on topic," Zerya added. "The evidence is conclusive, and we don't have time in this meeting to go over the minutia. You should have all been provided with Commander Aelira's assessment. If you have doubts or questions, then read it and meet with her privately for further information."

"Thank you, Astrarch," Aelira said. "There is no doubt that there is a threat, and it is imminent. What we don't know is the size of the Kergan fleet nor when it will precisely attack. This is why Lieutenant Commander Drake has joined us. Though still a student at the Space Warfare School, he is acknowledged by his instructors as an expert in sydereal mapping. Aelira plans to use him to locate this fleet and assess its size."

I felt my face flushing as Aelira talked about me. I didn't like them focusing their hopes on me. Sofia reached under the table and squeezed my hand.

"Thank you, Commander Aelira," Zerya said. "Now we will hear the Operations Update from Captain Teryn."

The kavor officer spoke for the next fifteen minutes about the current missions and tasking of the Home Fleet. He mentioned dozens of ships by name, none of which I recognized, and I soon lost track of the discussion because of all the little details that he mentioned. With 109 warships and another forty support and supply ships, the Home Fleet was a massive assembly of ships.

The meeting then moved on to a briefing by the Logistics Officer. She reported that supply levels were nominal, and all ships were currently being resupplied to full combat loads, an activity that would be completed by the end of the day. One of the fleet's six battleships was in the yard for scheduled maintenance but would become available again in two days.

Next, Astrach Zerya asked Captain Voryn, a kavor, to give the Plans and Future Operations briefing.

"Celestarch Kaelith," Voryn said, "we have reached an agreement with Glyphspeaker Arctis to place the Astral Expeditionary Fleet on alert. In the event that the Home Fleet becomes engaged in battle, the Astral Fleet will act as our strategic reserve."

"The Glyphspeaker actually agreed to this?" Kaelith asked.

"Yes, sir, he did. I just received word this afternoon."

"That bastard protects his resources like a poor kavor holds onto his last Civex. Kaelith is astonished."

"It is not my place to agree, sir, but the Astral Fleet will be our reserve. They can jump directly into the L2 point within a day of being called upon."

"Excellent. We may need them if the enemy fleet turns out to be larger than we can manage. But Kaelith has never been comfortable with placing control of the Astral Fleet in the hands of Arctis. It violates the natural checks on power that are built into our compact. But forget that Kaelith said that. It was the queen's prerogative, though I don't understand how that trickster managed to convince her."

I was caught off guard when Arctis's name came up in the meeting. Hearing that the Glyphspeaker was commanding an entire fleet of warships was news to me—unsettling news at that. The revelation gnawed at me. If anyone had a vested interest in defending the Supreme Council and the Zenith Citadel, it would be a Glyphspeaker like Arctis, whose very existence likely hinged on stopping the Kergan forces. But why hadn't this been shared with me before? The layers of political maneuvering in the Dominion felt as endless as the Sydereaium itself.

The discussion continued for another twenty minutes after that bombshell. The staff dissected fleet positions, supply chains, and contingency plans with relentless precision. Meanwhile, I tried to keep up, but the flood of information quickly overwhelmed me. I was drowning in acronyms, star charts, and tactical jargon.

Sitting there, I couldn't shake the feeling of being a fraud. What was I even doing here? Sure, I had sydereal abilities, but nothing in my life—homeless on Earth, insurgent captain, now a half-trained officer—had prepared me for the level of expertise being displayed around this table. It was like watching a chess match played by grandmasters while I was still figuring out how the pieces moved.

And yet, I remained. I feared that someone would see through me at any moment, call out my inexperience, and dismiss me back to the SWS. The thought sent a cold knot twisting in my stomach. For now, I could only keep my head down and hope I wasn't the weakest link in the chain.

38

Physically, I sat in the cramped, dimly lit office I'd been assigned on the *Inferis*. The desk was too small, the chair hard, and the air recycled to the point of tasting metallic. Sofia, ever vigilant, had stationed herself by the door, her posture relaxed but her eyes sharp. If anyone tried to interrupt, they'd have to get past her first.

But my mind wasn't in that room. My consciousness was deep in the Syderealium, immersed in the monumental task I'd been given: finding the Kergan fleet.

The sheer scale of the job was staggering. During my time at the SWS, I had proven myself to be the best student at sydereal scanning by a wide margin. My instructors claimed they'd never seen anyone faster or more precise. I could map a cubic kilometer of the physical plane for the presence of glyphshades in just ten seconds. When I mapped the space around the Zenith Citadel, it had taken me three hours to scan roughly 1,000 cubic kilometers—a cube of space ten kilometers on each side.

But what Celestarch Kaelith asked me to do now was

laughably, impossibly larger. He wanted me to scan the *entire* Ignisara star system. That's not a cube ten kilometers on a side—that's a sphere encompassing every planet, moon, asteroid, and speck of dust orbiting within billions of kilometers. I did the math. The volume of space Kaelith wanted me to sift through was roughly 30 million heptillion cubic kilometers—a number with 31 zeros.

At my rate of ten seconds per cubic kilometer, it would take me 100 trillion times the universe's age to finish the task.

Space isn't big—it's unfathomable. It isn't like finding a needle in a haystack; it's like tracking down a single grain of gold dust somewhere in the deserts of Mars.

But orders were orders. So, I scanned. I started at the Zenith Citadel, mapping outward in methodical, widening spirals. My will focused like a beam of light, slicing through the endless void of the Syderealium, searching for any flicker of Kergan glyphshades.

It wasn't hopeless—just daunting. Every now and then, I caught fragments of activity: faint echoes of Dominion ships, cargo freighters, and even the intricate hum of the Citadel itself. But none of it was the enemy I sought.

In the physical world, I felt a faint hand brush my shoulder. Sofia's voice broke through like a distant echo. "Kory, you've been at this for hours. Take a break."

I blinked out of the Syderealium for a moment, my head pounding and my throat dry. "Not yet," I murmured, voice hoarse. "I'm just getting started."

She sighed but didn't press further, retreating to her post. Even through the haze of exhaustion, I felt a flicker of gratitude for her steady presence.

Back in the Syderealium, I pushed on. If the Kergans were out there—and I knew they were—I would find them.

I was slowed by the presence of dense traffic around Virelia. Anytime I detected glyphshades in a region of space, I had to cross reference what I'd found with the system's traffic control database.

Late in the day, after I'd spent ten straight hours in the Syderealium, only taking occasional breaks to use the bathroom and eat, Commander Aelira entered.

"Commander Drake, what are you doing?" she said.

I pulled myself out of the sydereal projection—something I could now do very quickly—and turned to her. She floated in the hatchway of my office next to Sofia's chair.

"Scanning, ma'am."

"Why aren't you using the nexus?"

"Ma'am?" I knew *Inferis* had a sydereal nexus, but I'd never used one before.

"The nexus. That was the entire point of bringing you to the flagship because it has a nexus!" She sounded upset.

"Commander, I've never used a nexus."

"They didn't teach this to you at the SWS?"

"Uh… Sure, we talked about the theory, but the school doesn't have a nexus. And we hadn't really gotten to the practical parts of that topic yet."

"Well, Aelira is glad she stopped by to check on you. Follow me." She turned and started floating out the door while muttering something I couldn't hear.

I leaped out of my chair and followed Aelira, Sofia following me, my heart pounding as Aelira flew purposefully through the narrow corridors of the *Inferis*. She moved quickly, never hesitating, and I could tell whatever she had to show me wasn't routine.

We wove through passageways, the ship's dim, utilitarian lighting casting long shadows on the bulkheads. The deeper we went, the heavier the air seemed, as though the weight of the ship's secrets pressed down on us. Finally, we stopped outside a massive, vault-like door. Its reinforced surface gleamed under the cold, fluorescent light, etched with security glyphs that glowed faintly in the darkness.

Two kavreni Marines flanked the entrance, their postures rigid, their long tails twitching slightly as they registered our presence. Their expressions were unreadable, but their large, bat-like ears swiveled in our direction. They held flechette rifles at the ready, the weapons glinting ominously under the harsh lights.

"This is the *Inferis's* sydereal nexus," Aelira said, her tone clipped. "There's no one else here. You are to use it. That's an order."

"Yes, ma'am," I replied, my unease clear in my voice. "But I still don't understand."

"You will," she said, her gaze unflinching. "The nexus requires no special training—only the participation of a flairsparked."

"Will it really make that much of a difference?" I asked, skepticism creeping into my tone.

"It will make all the difference," she replied curtly. "In your case, it will increase your ability to operate in the SySderealium by ten orders of magnitude, at the very least."

I did a quick mental calculation and couldn't resist a wry comment. "So now it'll only take me the age of the universe to scan the Ignisara system."

"Don't be flippant, Commander!" Aelira snapped, her sharp tone making me stiffen. "You were in the staff meeting. You understand how critical our timeline is. Aelira isn't flairsparked, so she can't articulate exactly how the nexus will amplify your abilities—but trust her, it will."

A heavy *clunk* sounded from the vault door as if to punctuate her point. The massive hinges groaned as it rotated open, revealing a chamber beyond.

I leaned forward, peering into the sphere. The room was smooth and metallic, its walls faintly gleaming like liquid silver. The space was small, no larger than a compact storage closet. A single chair stood in the center, bolted to the floor, facing a modest desk with an embedded terminal. The air inside seemed thick, almost alive, with an energy I couldn't quite place.

"Not much room," I said.

"It doesn't need to be large," Aelira replied. "Only you will be in there."

I glanced at her, then at Sofia, who stood nearby with a calm but watchful expression. "Sofia—I mean, Warrant Officer Kohl—can't come in with me?"

"Nay," Aelira said firmly. "She must remain here in the corridor."

I frowned, stepping closer to the threshold. The chamber radiated a sense of isolation that made my chest tighten. "So, I just go in there, sit in the chair, and... try to enter the Syderealium?"

"Aye," Aelira said simply.

"Really." I exhaled slowly, rolling my shoulders in an attempt to loosen the tension creeping into them. The chamber looked more like a high-tech tomb than a tool. Once that vault door closed, I'd be sealed behind three feet of solid metal on all sides.

I glanced at Sofia. She raised an eyebrow and gave me a half-smile, the kind that said, *You'll be fine, but don't screw it up.*

"Okay," I muttered, stepping into the chamber and steeling myself. "Here I go."

I stepped all the way into the chamber. The vault closed behind me. A moment later, Aelira's voice came to me over a speaker. "You're sealed in. When you're ready to leave, press the button on the wall. It will let you communicate with the guards outside. Try it."

I found the button she was talking about—a square protrusion on the metal wall next to the door—pressed on it and said, "This button?"

"Aye, Commander. Good luck."

I released the button and, under my breath, said to myself, "Yeah, I'll need it."

Even though there was a vent in the ceiling pushing fresh air into the chamber, the air felt thick, as if it were struggling to escape the oppressive atmosphere. It was warm—too warm—and beads of sweat began forming on the back of my neck. The claustrophobic, metallic walls seemed to press inward, amplifying the isolation. If I didn't know better, I'd have assumed I was in some kind of high-tech isolation cell rather than a critical component of the ship.

Silence enveloped me. The usual hum of the *Inferis*—the distant thrum of its engines, the faint vibrations of its systems—was completely absent. It was as though the nexus chamber existed outside the ship entirely, a place cut off from everything familiar.

I tried to recall what little I knew about sydereal nexuses, but my knowledge was embarrassingly limited. I'd heard they stabilized the local Syderealium, creating a kind of anchor that made operating within it easier and more precise. That's why the Zenith Citadel had one—its nexus served as the beating heart of the Citadel, allowing mortal members of the Dominion government to maintain stable communications with the Glyphspeakers of the Supreme Council. Beyond that, I was clueless.

The chair in the center of the room looked utilitarian, almost menacing. Bolted to the floor, it was made of hard metal and fitted with a six-point harness. Cushions were added as an afterthought, their thin padding more about functionality than comfort. The design suggested that whoever used it might have to endure high-stress situations —aggressive maneuvers or full-on battles.

I scanned the room, expecting to see some sort of controls—switches, levers, a glowing button labeled *Activate Nexus*—but there was nothing. The only console was a generic desktop terminal sitting on the table in front of the chair. It looked absurdly ordinary, as though someone had repurposed office furniture for cutting-edge sydereal warfare.

"Well, nothing to it," I muttered, lowering myself into the chair. The metal felt unforgiving against my back. I secured the harness, the clinks, and clicks of the straps echoing faintly in the confined space. The walls seemed closer now, like a giant hand closing around me.

I took a deep breath, shutting out the discomfort. Clearing my mind, I focused inward, gathering my will. My consciousness expanded as I projected myself into the Sycerealium.

Moments later, I was there.

Nothing magical happened. No rush of power, no dazzling visuals. The Syderealium felt as it always did—a strange, weightless expanse, vibrating with energy, its endless void populated by countless glyphshades. Around me, I could sense the thousands of glyphshades that made up the crew of the *Inferis*. Their presence pulsed faintly, each one like a dim star in a vast constellation.

I glanced toward the nexus chamber's entrance. Sofia's glyphshade floated near the door, distinct and familiar, radiating her quiet vigilance. Three other glyphshades hovered near her—Aelira and the guards.

I sighed. "Not very exciting, is it?" I muttered to myself, the words echoing in the void of the Syderealium.

I refocused my thoughts, trying to remember where I'd left off in the scan. Once I zeroed in on the coordinates, I resumed my task.

Whoosh!

The moment I reached out with my consciousness, my mind flooded with data. I wasn't merely scanning space—I knew it, instantly and intimately, as though the information had always been there, waiting for me to access it. Each glyphshade appeared vividly, their locations and movements etched into my awareness. The speed and precision were staggering.

Astounded, I pressed on, my scans flowing faster and smoother. Each spherical region of space unraveled before me in a fraction of a second, revealing the contents of hundreds of cubic kilometers in an instant. It was intoxicating. I felt like a god, my will shaping the fabric of the Syderealium itself.

Excited, I returned part of my focus to the physical plane and turned to the terminal. Logging into the traffic control system, I pulled up my records and began designing an algorithm to streamline the process. While my scanning ability had dramatically accelerated, the bottleneck now lay in cross-referencing the data with physical plane records and managing the sheer volume of information.

Using the Syderealium's unique properties, I integrated a syderealdyne transceiver built into the terminal to transfer data in real time. It was astonishing how quickly I could now process and sort the results of my scans. With the algorithm running, I could scan thousands of cubic kilometers in the time it took to draw a single breath. And as I worked, I grew faster, more precise. Each scan refined my technique, shaving off milliseconds and extending my reach.

My consciousness swept outward, spanning the vast distances between Virelia and Ignisara. The sheer number of glyphshades in the system was overwhelming. On supposedly uninhabited planets, I found small clusters of people. Researchers, according to the traffic control records. Nothing suspicious there, though I noted it for reference.

The Ignisara system included two sprawling asteroid belts, their depths teeming with activity. Thousands of glyphshades moved among the belts—miners, freighters, and automated facilities. Each glimmer of consciousness added another piece to the puzzle I was building.

After five hours, I had scanned the entire inner system. The scope of what I'd accomplished left me awestruck. *This must be what it feels like to be an Astral Titan*—a god *wielding the powers of the Syderealium with absolute mastery.* The nexus wasn't merely a tool; it was a force multiplier, focusing and amplifying the abilities of a flairsparked individual. Sitting at its focal point, I could achieve feats that had once seemed impossible.

But despite my progress, I'd barely scratched the surface of the Ignisara system. The inner system was just a fraction of the whole, a densely packed region compared to the vast, sparsely populated outer system. Only two percent of the system had been scanned. Still, the outer system promised to be faster—fewer glyphshades, fewer structures. Civilian vessels rarely ventured that far out unless they had specific missions. Most initiated FTL transitions near the Lagrange points close to Virelia. Only ships with something to hide—hostile vessels avoiding detection—would take the risk of jumping beyond the helioshock.

I steeled myself for the next phase of the task, knowing it would test my limits. If the Kergan fleet was hiding somewhere in this system, I would find it.

39

I found the Kergan fleet.

It was the third day since Sofia and I had arrived on *Inferis*. I'd spent almost every waking moment in the nexus, leaving only to grab a few hours of restless sleep. The relentless pressure from Celestarch Kaelith's staff weighed heavily on me, their urgency a constant reminder of the stakes. My nerves buzzed with the unspoken fear that every second I wasn't scanning was another second closer to disaster.

Then it happened.

At a staggering five billion kilometers from Virelia, approaching from solar north, I detected it—a massive cluster of glyphshades. My heart skipped a beat as I zoomed in, carefully unraveling the data threads. The formation wasn't chaotic; it was meticulously grouped into smaller clusters, each one suggesting an individual starship. There were hundreds of them, moving as one.

Their velocity: eleven percent the speed of light. The precision and cohesion of their advance sent a chill down my spine. This wasn't a scattered raiding party or a disorganized fleet. This was an armada—a calculated, unstoppable force bearing down on the heart of the Dominion.

I couldn't tear my focus away from the horrifying sight. Each glyphshade pulsed with a malevolent energy, the unmistakable presence of Kergan consciousness. My breath caught as I realized just how many lives hung in the balance. Tens of thousands of Kergans, their ships, their weapons—all aimed at the Zenith Citadel like a knife to the throat.

For a moment, I sat frozen in the chair, the weight of what I had just uncovered pressing down on me. Then I snapped out of it. There was no time to waste.

"If they do not decelerate, they will arrive in the vicinity of Virelia in 46 hours," I told Commander Aelira a few minutes later as she floated in her office. I stood on the other side of her desk as I gave her my report.

"But they do need to decelerate, and they'll need to start soon. They're coming from the solar north, you say?"

"Yes. I estimate they've been in the Ignisara system for at least six days if you include the time it took for them to accelerate on their current trajectory."

She pointed at my dot on which I had displayed my collected data. "How many ships did you count?"

"That is a little difficult because all I can count are glyphshades. But they are in clusters of dense concentrations. Assuming each of those is an individual ship, I counted 423 individual vessels."

"Nova! That many?!"

"Yes, that's my most recent count. They're all on the same trajectory and grouped up into a spherical formation that's about 10,000 km in diameter."

"And they'll all be large ships. The smallest will be frigates since anything smaller doesn't have the power systems to accelerate up to a tenth of light speed. This is an expeditionary fleet, so a high proportion of their ships will be support vessels, like supply ships and fleet auxiliaries. Even if half the fleet is made up of unarmed ships, that still leaves over 200 large combatants. It will overwhelm the Home Fleet. We need to take this to Astrarch Zerya immediately."

"Not to Celestarch Kaelith?" I asked.

"Nay, Zerya is his gatekeeper. We must follow the chain of command, Commander." She rose and flew toward her door. "Come, Mister Drake, follow Aelira."

I had been doing a lot of following lately. I still hadn't learned my way around the *Inferis,* which felt like a three-dimensional rat maze on the inside. Some passageways were too small even for me to fit down. Fortunately, Astrarch Zerya's office was not too far.

"Astrarch," Aelira said at Zerya's door, "Commander Drake has found the Kergan fleet."

Zerya's ears suddenly folded against her skull, and her eyes opened wide. "He has?"

"Aye, ma'am. Four-hundred-twenty-three vessels are two to three days away from Virelia."

The Astrarch held both hands to her head. "Vyraleth help us." She dropped her hands and looked at me. "Are these numbers certain?"

"As certain as I can be, ma'am," I said. "I don't know if they're Kergans. But no question, there is a large force of glyphshades on that approach vector. Tens of thousands of them, moving at a tenth the speed of light."

She waggled her head from side to side, which was the kavreni equivalent of a nod. "And even if they were civilian ships, they would never transit at such a high speed. Our laws limit space vessels to a maximum of point zero zero nine light speed to prevent relativistic collisions. Only military vessels would be capable of going so fast, and no Dominion fleet would approach from the helioshock. They'd jump into a local force-neutral zone. Yes, this is an enemy fleet. But so many!"

"Ma'am, we should take this to the Celestarch," Aelira said. "He must know of this immediately."

"Commander, let me worry about that. Your job is to narrow these numbers down." She pointed a long, skinny finger at the igna. "And I want independent confirmation. Get a probe or spectral out there to get sensors on the targets."

"Aye, aye, ma'am, but moving them into position could take over a day."

"Do it anyways." Zerya looked at me. "No offense, Commander Drake, but these sydereal arts are a mystery to most of us officers. It is necessary to have independent verification."

"I understand, ma'am, but do we have time?"

"For the moment, we will act on your intelligence data as if it had been confirmed. Only the ready wing rides the storm." She turned back to Aelira. "Commander, you have your orders. I'll worry about the Celestarch."

"Aye, aye, ma'am." My boss left the room, and I followed her.

As we moved through the corridor, Aelira said to me, "Good work, Commander."

"Was it enough?" I asked, wishing there was more I could do to prepare the Home Fleet.

"Absolutely. You've bought us at least an entire extra day of preparation we wouldn't have had without you.

That could spell the difference between success and failure. Now, Aelira wants you to help plan a redeployment of spectrals and scouts. How do you feel about planning an ambush of the Kergans and proposing it to the Celestarch?"

"Are you talking about moving some spectrals to intercept their trajectory and lob some torpedoes at them?"

"Aye, precisely that."

My thoughts went to my tactics classes and everything I'd learned about scouting and the proper use of spectrals. "They're moving pretty fast. Some well-placed kinetic projectiles could destroy some of their vessels if we move quickly."

"Excellent idea, Mister Drake. Keep them coming."

40

The deck trembled, and I was violently ripped out of my sydereal projection. My head snapped forward, and I clutched it instinctively, the sudden disorientation leaving me slumped in the chair. A sharp, splitting pain started to wedge its way through my skull, feeling like a block of wood being split in two by an unforgiving axe.

I squinted at the terminal on the table in front of me. An alert window flashed red, throwing a harsh light across the cramped nexus chamber. Words and numbers blurred for a moment as I tried to focus.

CRITICAL ERROR: Harmonic field stability at 42% and falling. Bubble integrity compromised.

The error log window cascaded with alarming messages:

WARNING: Sydereal field distortion threshold exceeded.

ERROR: Harmonic resonance drift detected: +0.75 Hz/s.

CRITICAL ERROR: Field stabilizers unable to maintain phase conjugation.

CRITICAL ERROR: Sydereal field anchors disconnected from

primary core.

WARNING: Emergency protocol activated: Containment safeguards will engage in 93 seconds.

Containment safeguards. I didn't know what they were, but I didn't want to stick around to find out. The terminal's incessant pulsing and shrieking filled the small space, pushing my headache closer to a full-blown migraine. I grabbed my notebook and pen with shaking hands, shoved them into my pocket, and stumbled to the vault door.

My palm hit the intercom button. "Get me out of here!" I yelled, my voice hoarse and panicked.

Silence. The only reply was the terminal's monotonous alarms. My heart pounded in my chest as I leaned harder into the button and shouted again, "Open the door! Now!"

After what felt like an eternity, a crackling voice finally came through the speaker. "One moment, Commander, we are working on the door."

The words weren't reassuring. My legs felt rooted to the floor as I stared at the vault door, imagining what would happen if those "containment safeguards" kicked in. Behind me, the nexus terminal erupted with new alerts.

I strained my ears over the noise and caught the faint sound of banging on the other side of the door—hard, metallic thuds like someone was trying to break in with a sledgehammer. Each blow reverberated through the room, matching the stabbing rhythm of my headache.

Fifty-four agonizing seconds passed—yes, I counted. Just as I was about to scream again, the door finally groaned and swung open on its heavy hinges. A kavreni Marine reached in, his thin, hairy arm grabbing me firmly and pulling me out into the passageway.

The door slammed shut behind me with a metallic *bong* that felt like it rattled through my teeth.

The passageway outside wasn't much better. The air was thick with the acrid tang of ozone and hot metal, stinging my nose and throat. Wisps of smoke curled lazily toward the ventilation grates, disappearing into the ship's systems.

The Marine holding my arm let go, and I stumbled forward a step, breathing heavily and trying to steady myself. I turned back to look at the vault door, half expecting it to burst open or explode, but it stayed ominously sealed.

"What the hell just happened in there?" I rasped, more to myself than anyone else.

Nobody answered. The passageway was alive with frantic activity—Marines and technicians rushing past, shouting orders and pointing at terminals mounted along the walls. I realized my hands were still shaking as I wiped sweat off my brow.

"What's going on?" I asked again.

"I don't know," Sofia replied. "There was a vibration in the hull, the lights dimmed for a few seconds, then smoke started pouring out of the vents."

"The nexus is down. Come on, let's go to the FCC and see what we can learn."

The fleet control center was the specialized compartment on *Inferis* from which Celestarch Kaelith and his staff commanded the Dominion Home Fleet. It was down the passageway and around a corner.

The FCC was packed with consoles and terminals and a large holotable in the center. As I moved into the compartment, I saw the Celestarch and Astrarch huddled together next to the latter while a kavora tech worked nearby at a console.

"The nexus is down, Celestarch," I said.

"We know, Commander," Astrarch Zerya responded.

"We've been hit by an SP."

"A sydereal pulse?"

"Aye," the Celestarch said. "It appears that our enemy has already infiltrated our defenses."

"But the enemy fleet is still over a day away."

"Then we've missed something."

My scan of the system had been rushed, and there were many regions I hadn't been able to search thoroughly. And besides that, it was possible a Kergan ship could have snuck into the Ignisara system disguised as a commercial ship from a neutral nation.

"Celestarch," Astrarch Zerya said, "we must deploy the reserve fleet."

"Kaelith has already notified Glyphspeaker Arctis," Celestarch Kaelith said. "The Astral Expeditionary Fleet is assembling and will jump into the system in one day. In the meantime, Kaelith has ordered the Alpha task force to take up a blocking position between the approaching enemy forces and the Citadel.

"Astrarch, you will order Bravo, Delta, and Echo task forces to guard our flanks, which are the approaches from L2, L4, L5, and the solar south. Hold the Charlie and Foxtrot task forces in reserve near the Citadel."

"But, Celestarch, that is a battle formation!"

"We are already under attack, Astrarch."

"It was just a single SP."

"And it's blinded us!" Kaelith turned his attention to me. "Commander, are you able to still track the enemy fleet?"

I shook my head. "With great difficulty, sir. The nexus is down. I came here to see if I could get information on repairs and when we can expect it to be up again."

"You'll need to check with Captain Lyssara for that. You have Kaelith's permission to proceed." He turned and started flying away. "Now, Kaelith is putting the fleet on Condition XR. You all had better get into your armor."

The situation was confusing and I still hadn't gotten a straight answer about what kind of danger we were in. Sure, an SP was bad, but it wasn't like the fleet's ability to enter battle had been affected. As soon as the nexus recovered, I would be able to get back on the scan.

The ship's alarm blared through the corridors, sharp and relentless, cutting through the usual hum of the Inferis. The PA system crackled to life:

"Attention all hands. Condition XR is now in effect. Repeat, Condition XR is now in effect. All personnel deploy battle suits and report to their duty stations. Secure the ship for potential engagement. This is not a drill. Confirm readiness status with your department heads immediately. Stand by for further orders."

I froze for a fraction of a second, the words sinking in, before Sofia grabbed my arm. "Let's move!"

We sprinted down the passageway toward our quarters, my boots thudding against the deck as my mind raced faster than my feet.

Inside the room, I wasted no time stripping down. The protomatter suit waited, a mass of graphite-colored material resting like a blob of clay in a case on the stand. I threw it on the floor and stepped onto it, and it activated immediately, the liquid-like armor crawling up my calves and thighs, flowing over my torso, and finally sealing around my head. It hardened into a sleek helmet, the diamond face shield faintly glowing with its HUD as it calibrated to my vitals.

I strapped my laser sidearm securely to my right thigh and clipped an emergency maneuvering pack to my lower back. The pack was small but essential—a lifesaver if the artificial gravity failed, or worse, if the hull was breached, and I found myself spinning helplessly into the vacuum of space.

My hands shook as I reached for my notepad and dot. The tremor wasn't from exertion—it was the creeping sense of dread clawing at my insides. Battle wasn't supposed to happen for at least another day. I wasn't ready.

Worse, I felt powerless.

On *Thunder,* I had been in control. I knew every bolt, every system, every member of my crew. The decisions had been mine, and so had the consequences. But here, on this massive battleship, I was just another cog in the machine. The nexus was down, and my designated battle station was effectively meaningless without it. My secondary role, standing at Celestarch Kaelith's side, felt like little more than ceremonial window dressing.

The thought hit me like a punch to the gut. How could I make a difference in this fight? Would I even have the chance?

I pressed the call button on my cabin's intercom box. "Captain Lyssara, please, this is Lieutenant Commander Drake," I said when someone answered.

A moment later, the box crackled. "How can I help you, Commander?" came Lyssara's voice.

"Ma'am, what is the status of the sydereal nexus?"

"We're working on it. *Inferis* was hit with a focused SP. Damage control parties are replacing field stabilizers, but it could take some time to finish."

"How long?"

"Give them an hour."

"Very well, thank you, ma'am."

The box cut off without further word from her.

There was a tapping on my door, and I opened it. Sofia

stood there encased in her own protomatter armored suit. I'd never seen her in one before. She looked menacing, standing there holding a flechette gun, the carbon nanobot material of the armor seeming to soak in the light.

I smiled at her. "I wouldn't want to meet *you* in a dark alley!"

She waved my comment away with a smile of her own. "Where to?"

"The nexus is down for at least another hour, so we need to report to the FCC."

She stepped aside. "Then lead us on."

We marched back to the FCC. The passageways were packed with crew dressed for battle as they traveled to their duty stations.

Upon entering the FCC again, I noticed that Celestarch Kaelith had placed himself into an armored igna walker. A flechette gun was mounted into one arm, and the other contained a retractable blade of some kind. His capsule rested underneath an armored sphere embedded in the chest with a cluster of visual and auditory sensors emplaced above it where the head would have been on a human.

Celestarch Kaelith was in the middle of a tense conversation with Captain Teryn, the kavor Fleet Operations Officer, and Commander Aelira. "Captain Teryn, Kaelith needs *all* of Alpha task force at that rally point now."

"Sir, I understand, but *Zoozber* is still in spacedock, and *Austermink* is in the middle of resupply."

"That's nearly half the task force's combat power."

"I've placed Alpha task force's ASW squadron on active sweeps to deter the approach of any enemy spectrals. That should buy us some time."

The anti-spectral warfare squadron was a group of

small frigate-sized warships and strike craft who specialized in hunting down spectral stealth ships and destroying them.

"You're sure it was a spectral that hit us with that SP?" Celestarch Kaelith asked.

"Aye, sir," Aelira replied. "The pulse was too intense to have originated from anything smaller than a spectral."

"What is the status of the ambush you and Commander Drake were planning?" His sudden change of the topic seemed to throw Aelira's concentration off for a moment.

"Oh..." she started to say.

"We were in the middle of issuing orders when the nexus went down, sir," I said. "Do we have permission to proceed without the use of the nexus?"

"Can... you do that?" Celestarch Kaelith asked.

"Aye, sir. I already know where they are and where they're headed. I just need a tactical console and a quiet place to work since the nexus is down. But I can still probe them in the Syderealium, though it won't be as effective without the nexus."

"Commander Aelira, what do you think?"

"Aelira recommends deploying the ambush," Aelira said. "Commander Drake has Aelira's confidence in his abilities."

"Very well, you may proceed. Astrarch Zerya, find a place for the Commander to work here in the FCC."

"Yes, sir," the Astrarch replied.

41

Commander Aelira assigned five spectral starships under my tactical control: the *Phantom Veil, Shadowlance, Eclipsion, Ghostfire,* and *Nightward.* These Wraith-class spectral ships were designed for reconnaissance, ambush, and asymmetric warfare. Each vessel, 320 meters in length, carried a crew of 150 kavreni and boasted a formidable arsenal: forty-four Phantom torpedoes. These stealthy anti-ship missiles delivered kinetic warheads potent enough to cripple a dreadnought or slice a frigate in half.

Though I appreciated the firepower, I had hoped for a larger force. The Home Fleet boasted twenty-four spectrals, but most were assigned to screen the six primary combat task forces. That left me with just this quintet of spectral warships to enact my ambush plan.

I calculated their likely approach vectors using the enemy fleet's predicted trajectory. I issued orders to deploy the spectrals roughly a billion kilometers from Virelia—at the precise point where the Kergan fleet would begin decelerating.

The Wraith-class spectrals were incredibly nimble, capable of sustained acceleration up to 25 gees for hours. I assigned each ship an independent operating area, ensuring they had no knowledge of the others' locations to reduce the risk of compromise. Communication between me and each spectral ship flowed through syderealdyne FTL comm links, allowing near-instantaneous updates.

As the spectrals raced to their ambush positions, I frequently projected into the Syderealium to track the Kergan fleet. Now that I had their trajectory locked, finding them each time was far easier—even without the nexus to amplify my powers.

I fine-tuned my projections with every pass through the Syderealium, issuing updated movement orders to the spectrals. I aimed to position them flawlessly for the ambush, ensuring their strikes would exploit the enemy's deceleration to maximum effect.

The tension grew with each calculation and adjustment. This wasn't just a tactical exercise—it was my chance to test my capabilities and deliver a devastating blow to the Kergans. Failure wasn't an option.

The first to make contact with the enemy was *Ghostfire*. Running silent, the spectral ship nestled behind a small asteroid conveniently positioned near the enemy fleet's expected trajectory. Through the Syderealium, I had identified dense clusters of glyphshades, which I assumed were either large Kergan warships or troop transports.

Ghostfire's commander confirmed the target moments later. "Control, this is *Ghostfire*. Multiple Kergan ships inbound. Contact telemetry follows."

My tactical display flickered as *Ghostfire's* telemetry updated in real-time. Twenty-one capital ships and over ninety escorts of various types materialized on the grid. This was no mere scouting party—it was the vanguard of the Kergan fleet.

"*Ghostfire*, this is Control. You are free to engage. Good luck," I responded, my voice steady despite the tension coiling in my chest.

Approaching at over ten percent the speed of light, the Kergan fleet's engagement window was minuscule—just milliseconds. But *Ghostfire's* torpedoes, mounted in vertical launch tubes, could be launched simultaneously at multiple targets, capitalizing on that fleeting moment. For now, the Kergans had no idea they were being watched, though that would change the instant they detected *Ghostfire's* weapons.

The commander acted decisively, launching five decoys that immediately began accelerating away from *Ghostfire*. These decoys emitted false signals to draw enemy attention, giving the spectral a better chance to escape unnoticed after its strike.

The countdown to engagement ticked away. I sat in the armored citadel aboard *Inferis*, a billion kilometers from the action, but it felt as if I were standing beside *Ghostfire's* captain. This was my first battle since completing OTS, and the weight of it pressed heavily on me. Every second dragged out like an eternity.

Then, the timer hit zero, and everything erupted.

In the blink of an eye, *Ghostfire* launched a swarm of torpedoes, each missile rocketing away from the spectral ship with randomized trajectories. Almost simultaneously, the ship began its evasive maneuvers, slipping away from the battlefield. The torpedoes engaged their kinetic warheads, accelerating toward their targets at over 200 gees—so fast the Kergan fleet barely had time to react.

Kergan ships lit up with active sensors, but it was already too late. The incoming projectiles were too fast, too sudden. Despite this, the chaos of space warfare meant most of *Ghostfire's* torpedoes missed their marks. Still, seven hit their targets.

The tactical display erupted with new contacts as debris clouds spread from the damaged ships, creating a storm of sensor signatures. Five Kergan battleships, a heavy cruiser, and a carrier had been struck. The cruiser ceased all emissions and was at the center of an expanding debris field. It was likely destroyed. The other ships remained active, their signatures indicating reduced power and impaired maneuverability.

"They won't be decelerating when they need to," I muttered. The damaged ships would likely overshoot Virelia, too crippled to engage Dominion forces in the coming battle. They weren't completely out of the fight, but they were effectively neutralized.

My voice broke the silence. "Got seven of them."

Sofia, standing at my side, placed a hand on my shoulder. "Not bad for a first strike."

I exhaled, my focus already shifting to the other spectrals moving into position. This was only the opening gambit, but it was a good one.

The next spectral to engage was *Eclipsion*. By now, the Kergan fleet was fully alert to the threat of spectrals. Their formation had shifted, pushing escorts outward in an effort to detect the stealth ships before they could launch their payloads on the capital ships.

Eclipsion opted for a long-range strike, launching her entire magazine of torpedoes from maximum distance. The torpedoes streaked toward the enemy fleet, but the Kergans were ready this time. Their advanced sensors picked up the incoming projectiles well before they began their final kinetic run.

As *Eclipsion* turned to escape, she was detected by a

Kergan frigate. Though the frigate had no chance of catching *Eclipsion* due to their relative velocities, it launched a spread of anti-ship missiles in retaliation.

On my tactical display, I tracked the torpedoes' progress. Despite the Kergans' preparedness, their ability to maneuver was limited by their sheer speed and mass. The torpedoes engaged their kinetic warheads, streaking into the formation with devastating precision. The final tally: four heavy cruisers disabled or destroyed, and one carrier severely damaged.

But the Kergan missiles were closing in on *Eclipsion*. The spectral's captain deployed decoys and countermeasures in a desperate bid to evade the threat. Most of the missiles veered off course or detonated prematurely, but one found its mark.

The impact struck *Eclipsion's* starboard quarter, and my display lit up with damage reports. The missile had punched deep into the ship's propulsion systems, crippling her maneuverability. The once-graceful spectral ship began to limp away, a trail of debris and venting atmosphere marking her path.

I clenched my fists, helpless to do anything but watch. "Damn it," I muttered under my breath.

Sofia, standing beside me, frowned. "She'll make it out. They're trained for this."

I nodded, but the sinking feeling in my gut didn't ease. The Kergans were adapting, and the spectrals were taking hits. This wasn't going to be an easy fight.

The rest of the spectral engagements followed a similar pattern, each one a tense and brutal game of cat-and-mouse. By the end of the operation, four of our spectrals had escaped, though two limped back with heavy damage from Kergan anti-ship missiles. Despite the losses, the results were significant: we managed to disable or destroy another three battleships, four heavy cruisers, two carriers, and an assault ship.

But I lost the *Phantom Veil*.

The ship was detected during its final approach. Though the crew managed to launch their torpedoes and disable three capital ships, the Kergan escorts were ready. They fired a coordinated barrage of missiles, and the spectral was overwhelmed. My tactical display flashed red as the *Phantom Veil* was consumed in a fiery explosion. All 150 kavreni spacers aboard were lost.

The image of that explosion lingered in my mind. I'd been the one in tactical control. I'd issued the orders that sent those spacers to their deaths. My heart ached as I thought about the lives snuffed out in an instant—the people who had trusted me to guide them.

I tried to reassure myself. I had acted on the best intelligence I had. Those 150 lives may have saved thousands of Dominion lives in the larger battle to come. But the weight of their sacrifice pressed down on me like a leaden shroud.

I stared at the tactical display, now cluttered with debris fields and damaged enemy ships, and clenched my fists. The coming battle would prove if the price we'd paid had been worth it. But for the moment, all I could feel was the crushing sense of responsibility for the lives I'd sacrificed.

42

I sat in *Inferis's* newly repaired nexus, the hum of its systems a quiet backdrop to the rising tension in the ship. The Kergan fleet was now just an hour away, bearing down on us with relentless precision. Meanwhile, we were counting on Arctis's expeditionary fleet to arrive at any moment, though the waiting felt eternal. Even with the damage my spectrals had inflicted on the Kergan forces, the Dominion Home Fleet would still be outnumbered. Our only hope was that, together with the Zenith Citadel's defenses, we might hold the line.

My mind was divided. Part of my consciousness scanned the local space through the Syderealium, searching for Kergan spectrals that had slipped past our defenses to harass our ships. Meanwhile, I kept one eye on the tactical display glowing on the nexus control terminal and another ear tuned to the fleet tactical control channel.

"Fleet, this is *Sallaka*. We've taken damage from an enemy torpedo," a frantic voice crackled through the comms. "The enemy ship is undetected. We've lost primary propulsion and are in need of evacuation."

The mention of *Sallaka,* a frigate in Charlie Task Force—the same reserve force *Inferis* was part of—snapped my focus. The tactical display updated to show *Sallaka* a mere 150 kilometers away, drifting and vulnerable.

I adjusted the nexus's calibration, sharpening my scan parameters to focus on the surrounding area.

The FCC responded swiftly. "*Sallaka,* Fleet, standby. *Inferis* is repositioning to render aid."

More orders followed as escorts were reassigned to form a protective screen around *Inferis* while the flagship moved to assist the crippled frigate.

My scan intensified, and within moments, I found what I was looking for: a cluster of glyphshades roughly 300 kilometers away. They didn't align with any known fleet or civilian signatures—a tight knot of activity in a vacuum that should have been empty. My stomach tightened.

Opening a comms channel, I relayed my findings. "Fleet, this is *Inferis* nexus. Contact detected bearing one-five-niner, declination three-two, range three-zero-three. Suspected enemy stealth unit."

The response was immediate. "Nexus, Fleet, roger. Confirm velocity of target."

I focused, trying to discern motion. The glyphshades remained unnervingly still. "Negative, they're stationary. I believe it's a Kergan spectral, likely the one that launched the torpedo at *Sallaka*. Recommend extreme caution on approach."

My hands tightened on the edge of the console as I monitored the tactical display, where the fleet's movements unfolded in real-time. A Kergan spectral was lurking somewhere out there, poised to strike again. The air in the nexus felt thick, the weight of responsibility pressing down on me like the bulkheads themselves.

Then I saw it—a cluster of glyphshades blooming into existence astern of *Inferis*, closing rapidly. Hundreds of them, no, maybe a thousand. Too large to be a spectral. My pulse quickened.

"Fleet, *Inferis* nexus!" I shouted into the comm. "I've got another contact closing on *Inferis*, astern! Rough estimate: a thousand souls aboard. They're not on the plot. Did someone miss a ship? Is there an allied vessel with its IFF transponder off?"

"Nexus, Fleet," came the reply, calm but clipped. "Negative. There shouldn't be anybody back there."

I swallowed hard. "Well… they're almost on top of us," I said, the realization hitting like a punch to the gut. *On top of us!*

"Roger. Standby."

The glyphshades barreled closer. Eight hundred meters. Seven hundred. The tension coiled in my chest.

"Bridge, *Inferis* nexus," I called, switching channels and forcing my voice to steady. "Confirm visual on a possible enemy vessel approaching your stern, range seven-one-niner meters."

Silence.

My heart pounded like a drumbeat. Seconds stretched into an eternity.

"Uh… negative on that… Wait one," a voice crackled back. I heard a thud, something clattering to the floor. Then a sharp intake of breath.

"Assault ship!"

The line went dead. My blood ran cold as the word echoed in my mind—assault ship. Hundreds of enemy soldiers were about to board *Inferis*. We were the target!

Inferis suddenly shuddered violently, throwing me

against the port bulkhead. I caught myself, barely avoiding slamming my head into the wall. The big ship surged into motion with an acceleration that left my stomach behind.

The PA system roared to life: "All hands! Condition ZZ, I repeat, Condition ZZ. Prepare to repel boarders! This is not a drill!"

My pulse quickened. Condition ZZ. That was the nightmare scenario—enemy boarding parties. How the hell had a Kergan assault ship gotten this close to the flagship? My mind raced. Had I missed something? Was the attack on *Sallaka* just a decoy to lure us into range?

There was no other explanation. A conventional ship couldn't have slipped past my scans unnoticed. That meant the assault ship must have been veiled—hidden in the Syderealium. Someone aboard it had to be a flairsparked, cloaking the entire vessel and its crew. I cursed under my breath.

I pulled up a live feed from an exterior camera on *Inferis's* port quarter. The screen flickered to life, showing a shadowy mass, nearly invisible against the star-speckled void. It was massive, its jagged contours barely outlined—bulges, turrets, and thrusters protruding from a menacing hull that seemed to drink in the light. My breath caught as flashes of light erupted from its surface, bright enough to briefly wash out the feed.

Inferis lurched again, maneuvering to shake off the attacker, but the Kergan assault ship was quick, matching every move. I watched in growing horror as grappling lines shot out from the enemy vessel, latching onto *Inferis*. The massive shadow pulled closer, closing the gap with predatory precision.

A sudden, deafening *THUNK* reverberated through the hull. The enemy ship had latched onto us. The sound sent a shiver down my spine.

From beyond the thick vault door of the nexus, I heard the rhythmic pounding of armored boots—spacers and marines moving into position to repel the boarders.

I glanced at the live feed again, my hands tightening into fists. The enemy ship was enormous, bristling with weapons. This wasn't just a skirmish; it was a full-blown assault.

I needed to act, but my mind was blank. What was I supposed to do during Condition ZZ? We hadn't drilled for this, not seriously.

I looked down at my armor, the protomatter material forming a protective second skin over my body. My only weapon was the standard-issue laser pistol strapped to my thigh—a popgun compared to what I'd need to face Kergan Imperial Marines. I felt woefully underprepared.

Then I thought of Sofia. She was stationed just outside the vault door, armed with a flechette gun that was far deadlier in close quarters. I couldn't sit here, barricaded behind this door, while the rest of the ship fought for survival.

I keyed the intercom. "Sofia, status?"

Her voice came back, calm but edged with tension. "They're coming, Kory. You'd better stay in there."

"Not a chance," I said, standing and securing my laser pistol. "Open the door."

Her response was immediate. "You're an idiot."

"Maybe," I said, stepping toward the door, heart pounding. "But I'm not going to hide while everyone else fights."

The door slid open with a heavy clang, and Sofia stood there, her flechette gun raised and ready. She looked at me with a mixture of exasperation and resolve.

43

"Kory, this is a bad idea!" Sofia hissed again as we crept down the passageway. My pistol felt small and inadequate in my hand as I led the way, Sofia close behind, her flechette gun scanning every corner like an extension of her body.

"I'm useless in that vault," I replied through gritted teeth. "If the ship falls, we're both done for. Might as well try to make a difference."

A sharp *pop* reverberated through the ship, followed by a low-pressure shift that made my ears ache. Moments later, the distant *whump* of a detonation rolled through the bulkheads. It sounded like it had come from several decks below. Then, closer now, the rapid staccato bursts of flechette fire echoed through the corridors.

"Let's move!" I hissed, leading Sofia toward a ladder well that would take us to a lower deck.

We reached a passageway leading toward the engineering spaces. I knew Captain Lyssara would have stationed Marines there to defend the ship's critical systems, but the sound of gunfire ahead suggested the enemy was pushing hard.

I opened a hatch and stepped through—only to be met with a hail of hypervelocity flechettes snapping past my head. Sparks and metal shards flew as projectiles ricocheted off the walls, leaving glowing trails in their wake.

"Down!" Sofia barked.

Before I could react, she grabbed my armor's collar, hooked her ankle around my leg, and yanked me to the deck. I landed hard, Sofia falling with me and pinning me down.

"Stay low!" she shouted as more flechettes zipped over us, their shrill snaps filling the air.

From the corner of my eye, I saw movement at the far end of the compartment. A Kergan soldier in full battle armor poked their head out, plasma cannon braced in their tentacles. A split second later, white-hot plasma bolts screamed through the space, the superheated energy sizzling in the air around us. Even through my protomatter armor, the radiant heat was oppressive, and I felt my skin prickle with discomfort.

A squad of Kavreni Marines crouched behind makeshift cover at the opposite end of the compartment, returning fire with disciplined bursts. The room was a chaos of kinetic energy, sparks, and acrid smoke.

I turned my head toward Sofia. "Got any brilliant ideas?"

"Yeah," she muttered, her voice low and tight. "Don't get us killed." She rolled off me, staying low, and fired a burst from her flechette gun toward the Kergan position. The high-pitched *chik-chik-chik* of the weapon was satisfying, but it did little to suppress the enemy's fire.

My grip tightened on my pistol. "We've got to help the Marines push them back."

"Stay down, Kory!" Sofia hissed, but I was already

crawling toward better cover.

The moment I reached it, a plasma bolt exploded against the bulkhead above me, showering me with molten metal. My armor held, but the impact left my ears ringing.

"You're going to get yourself killed," she growled.

"Maybe," I said, checking my pistol's charge. "But not before I take a few of them with me."

We were right in the middle of the firefight, the space between life and death shrinking with every shot.

I low-crawled in the direction of the kavreni Marines with Sofia right behind me. I kept my armored cheek pressed against the deck as I slid on my belly across it, looking for safety as rounds flew back and forth above us, any of which could have instantly ended our lives.

I reached a loaded pallet containing what looked like rations and took cover behind it, soon joined by Sofia. The air in the compartment was hot as the weapons fire quickly heated it up into an oven. A hole in the compartment's opposite wall had bulkhead edges that glowed from the energy of whatever weapon had opened it up.

One of the kavreni Marines was down and had dropped their weapon. They looked dead, evidenced by the pool of blood underneath them.

I reached over and grabbed their weapon and saw it was a standard flechette gun. I pressed the interface buttons in the correct sequence and soon had it slaved to my armor. A targeting reticle appeared in my HUD, so I holstered my laser pistol. The magazine of the gun was about two-thirds full.

There was a tap on my shoulder, and I turned to see one of the kavreni Marines signaling that we should fall back. I nodded, and Sofia and I followed in a crouch.

The next compartment over was a crew mess. A squad

of kavreni Marines were tossing crates and furniture into a makeshift barricade. The boarding action must have occurred during mealtime because the serving trays were full of steaming food, and the air was ripe with spicy Kavreni dishes.

A grenade detonated in the outside passageway, and marac voices cried out. Three kavreni Marines ducked into the mess and found shelter behind the barricade with us. In total, we numbered fourteen kavrenis and two humans.

And then we waited, expecting an assault by the Kergan Imperial Marines at any moment. Sporadic sounds of flechette guns sounded from deeper in the hull. But nobody came for us. I looked at Sofia, who crouched beside me, and she shrugged.

I was about to stand up and go talk to the squad leader of the kavreni Marines when a violent explosion blasted over the top of the barricade, toppling boxes and sending furniture flying. I smelled burning plastic and closed the vent on my protomatter suit before I choked on the fumes.

Dead and wounded kavreni Marines lay all around me. By pure luck, Sofia and I had been caught—or saved—by an eddy in the flow of destruction the Kergans had just unleashed. A gaping hole in the opposite wall wide enough to drive a tank through now left a breach open for the Kergan assault to rush through.

They chose that moment to do precisely that.

Sofia and I fired our guns at the outlines of armored maracs as they flew into the destroyed mess. I watched as one after another fell to our fire. But most of them made it through and were trying to flank our barricade.

Realizing we would be trapped if we didn't retreat, I grabbed Sofia's arm and pulled her back. "We have to go! Follow me!"

I led us to a hatch in the back wall, pulled it open, and we fell through it, slamming it shut behind us. We found ourselves in an empty passageway, but one I recognized. We were just above and forward of the engineering spaces.

I ran for a nearby ladder leading to the next deck below, with gun aiming and covering my forward arc while Sofia guarded our rear. With just the two of us, we couldn't adequately defend ourselves. We needed to find more kavreni or some other way to increase our odds.

Maybe I should have listened to Sofia and never left the nexus.

The deck below was eerily quiet, save for the distant hum of the ship's systems. As I scanned my surroundings, I spotted an open hatch leading into the engineering spaces. It should have been dogged shut. Someone had left it ajar—a careless mistake or a deliberate invitation.

The engineering bay was a labyrinth of machinery: massive conduits, gantries, catwalks, and pipes weaving in every direction. The air was thick with the smell of grease and ozone, and the faint vibrations of the ship's engines reverberated through the walls. I didn't have a clue what any of the equipment did, but I could see its potential for chaos. We could use this to our advantage.

I checked my weapon. The magazine was nearly empty. Stupid. I'd forgotten to grab extra mags from the fallen Marine earlier. Sofia's gunfire was slowing—she must've been down to her last rounds, too. I dropped my depleted flechette gun to the floor and drew my combat knife. The blade shimmered faintly under the harsh lights, honed to a monomolecular edge that could slice through steel like paper.

I turned to Sofia, crouched behind a machine that offered her just enough cover to fire. "Give me cover," I said. "Pin them down when they come through the hatch."

She gave me a sharp nod, her face tight with focus. "Just don't get yourself killed."

I darted across the space, finding a recess in the wall adjacent to the hatch. From this angle, I'd be invisible to anyone entering. I crouched, gripping the knife, my pulse hammering in my ears.

The sound of yelling maracs echoed through the cramped passageway. Heavy, armored suits clanged against the bulkheads. My grip tightened on the knife hilt as adrenaline surged through my veins. Sofia's gunfire erupted, short bursts designed to keep the enemy guessing. Their sharp cries told me she'd hit her mark.

Two Imperial Marines rushed past my alcove, heading toward a crane for cover from Sofia's fire. I stayed frozen, counting the seconds, then sprang into motion.

The first marac didn't even have time to turn before my blade punched through his helmet's faceplate. I slashed sideways, and the body crumpled. The second turned to face me, his weapon lifting, but I was already inside his firing arc. His shots went wide, sizzling into the wall. I drove my blade into his torso—once, twice, three times—until his movements ceased.

Sofia's shots slowed, single cracks now, signaling she was almost out. I crouched and peered around the crane. The remaining Kergans were pinned by her fire, unaware of my approach. Their positioning was textbook—good cover from the front, but their backs were wide open to me.

I grabbed one of the fallen marac's weapons. The alien design was vaguely familiar from the time I had rescued Destiny from detention and used one to kill a Kergan MP and destroy a spy ship, its grips and buttons meant for tentacles, not fingers. I fumbled for a moment, then found the grenade launcher. Aiming at the clustered Kergans, I pushed the firing stud.

The grenade arced out, landing just behind them. The explosion was deafening, and the room filled with smoke and debris. When the air cleared, I saw bodies sprawled on the floor, motionless.

A sharp, stabbing pain in my side dragged my attention back to myself. Blood seeped through my suit over my ribs, the fabric sealing around the wound, but I could feel it. A prick in my neck followed, and moments later, a wave of calm flooded me as the suit injected painkillers into my system.

I ran in a crouch back to Sofia. She was seated on the deck, her flechette gun spent. Only her pistol and combat knife remained.

"That stopped them for now, but there'll be more," I said, breathing hard. "We can't fight them all alone. We've been lucky so far."

She shot me a withering look. "That's what I've been telling you. This is nuts."

"I have an idea. Can you get me back to the nexus?"

Her eyes narrowed. "We never should've left there in the first place."

"Can you get me back?"

Sighing, she nodded. "I think so, but I'm out of ammo. We'll have to find another route."

"It's the only plan I've got."

She huffed and rolled her eyes. "If we end up in the waste recycling chamber instead of the nexus, I'm blaming you." She shoved my shoulder lightly, making my ribs twinge. "Let's move."

44

The passageways of *Inferis* were a tangled maze, the kind of place where even seasoned crew members might lose their way if they weren't careful. The scale of the massive battleship was almost incomprehensible, its corridors stretching for what felt like miles. Fortunately, this worked in our favor—it gave us just enough cover to slip through unnoticed by the Kergan boarders.

The sounds of the desperate battle echoed through the hull: muffled explosions, the hiss of cutting torches, and the staccato bursts of flechette guns. I clenched my jaw, trying to drown out the chaos and focus on moving forward. Surely, the Dominion had sent reinforcements. Indeed, they wouldn't abandon *Inferis,* the fleet's flagship. But as the minutes stretched on, that hope felt more like a pipe dream. It seemed we were on our own.

Sofia led the way through narrow maintenance crawlways, their tight confines forcing us to duck and squeeze through. The air was thick with smoke and the acrid stench of burned wiring. Every step brought another vibration or distant rumble, a reminder that the ship itself was under siege. After what felt like an eternity, we emerged into a wider passageway leading toward the nexus and the FCC.

At the end of the corridor, we encountered a defensive line held by kavreni Marines. Their bodies bristled with weapons, their eyes sharp with adrenaline and exhaustion. The sergeant in charge spotted the blood on my armor—some of it mine, most of it marac—and waved us through with a grim nod.

Ten meters beyond the line, Captain Lyssara stood in a tight huddle with several Kavreni officers. The igna's capsule rested atop a massive armored walker, its imposing frame towering over her subordinates. Even in this moment of crisis, she radiated calm authority.

"Engineering remains secure, and we've got five squads of Marines dug in," one officer was saying. His voice was clipped, his posture rigid with strain. "I'm more worried about the FCC and CIC. The Kergan boarders are pushing hard in this direction, and my people have taken heavy losses."

"Commander Vlunk," Lyssara replied, her tone sharp, "this ship and her crew need you to hold the line for forty more minutes. The fleet is heavily engaged with the enemy, and the celestarch cannot spare any units to assist us. You must do better."

Vlunk's jaw tightened. "I understand, ma'am, but we've already lost a third of our forces. I don't know how much longer we can—"

A sudden explosion echoed down the corridor behind Sofia and me, followed by a burst of gunfire. The deck beneath us trembled.

I stepped forward, cutting into their tense conversation.

"Captain, I think I have an idea that could help."

Lyssara's walker turned toward me, her glowing capsule swiveling to fix me with a cold, appraising gaze. "Lyssara has little time, Commander. Speak quickly."

I took a steadying breath. "If I return to the nexus, I believe I can use a bubble dimension to sequester the boarders."

Silence fell over the group. The officers exchanged wary glances. Lyssara's voice was measured when she finally responded. "That sounds dangerously close to sydereal assault. Explain."

"It's not an attack, ma'am," I said quickly. "I can create a bubble dimension in the Syderealium—a stable, isolated space. Using the nexus, I can translate the boarders' glyphshades into that dimension. They'll be rendered unconscious, effectively removed from the fight, but their glyphshades won't be harmed."

Lyssara's capsule glowed faintly, a sign of skepticism. "Lyssara has never heard of such a technique. Are you certain it will work?"

"Yes, ma'am. It's a combination of veiling, sydereal synthesis, and uncooperative projection. Their physical forms might take some strain when the bubble collapses, and they return to the physical plane, but their glyphshades will remain intact."

She hesitated. I could see the wheels turning, weighing the risks. "And you're certain this won't make things worse?"

"It can't," I said firmly. "If we don't try, the FCC could fall. If that happens, the fleet will lose coordination, and the Kergan boarders will have achieved their objective."

Lyssara turned to the other officers. "Thoughts?"

"It's unorthodox, but if it works..." one murmured.

Another added, "We're out of options, ma'am."

Lyssara faced me again. "Very well, Mister Drake. But you must act quickly. Lyssara is moments away from ordering the FCC evacuated."

I nodded, my resolve hardening. "I won't let it come to that."

Without waiting for further permission, I pushed past the officers and headed for the nexus. The weight of the task ahead settled heavily on my shoulders, but there was no turning back now.

The nexus chamber felt like a cavern of quiet anticipation, a place where the veil between reality and the Syderealium was worn thin. In my mind, I saw a sydereal core suspended in the air above me, pulsing with a hypnotic rhythm, its shifting hues spilling faint, kaleidoscopic patterns across the smooth walls. It thrummed in tune with something deeper—a resonance that wasn't just sound but sensation, tugging at the edges of my mind.

I sat alone at the simple metal table, the terminal's soft glow illuminating my hands as they hovered over its surface. The chair creaked faintly as I shifted, closing my eyes and steadying my breathing. The intercom by the vault door crackled, and Sofia's voice broke through the stillness.

"Kory, status?"

"Starting now," I said quietly, leaning back and letting the terminal fade from my focus. "Keep watch out there. This is going to take everything I've got."

Her reply was steady. "You've got this. I'll hold the line."

I drew a deep breath and let my consciousness drift. The hum of the nexus grew louder, resonating not just in the chamber but within me. I reached for it with my mind, opening myself to the core's energy. In an instant, the chamber dissolved, and I was there—in the Sydereallium.

The transition was seamless, like slipping into a dream. Colors and shapes stretched and warped in ways that defied description. The Sydereallium was vast and alive, its endless geometry shifting with an almost sentient awareness. Glyphshades flickered in the distance, faint echoes of thought and presence that brushed against my mind like whispers.

The nexus thrummed in tune with my consciousness, a bridge connecting the two realms. I focused, pulling its power into me, shaping it with sheer will. The task was immense: to create a hyperdimensional bubble, a prison that would exist partially within the Sydereallium itself. This wasn't just a field or a containment net—it was a foundation, something built to last.

The first threads of energy appeared, glowing strands of light that spiraled out from the core. They wove together in intricate patterns, forming the beginnings of the bubble. It was like sculpting with light, every thread requiring careful placement and balance. The bubble expanded slowly, its surface shimmering with an iridescent sheen that rippled like water.

The effort was exhausting. I could feel the pull of the Sydereallium, a relentless pressure that threatened to unravel my work if I faltered. Sweat dripped down my face in the material world, and my hands gripped the edges of the table so tightly they ached. My mind burned with the strain of maintaining focus, of keeping the lattice stable as it grew.

The bubble solidified gradually, its surface taking on a smooth, silver-blue glow. Inside, the hyperdimensional space began to form, an alien void that bent time and space into shapes I couldn't fully comprehend. It wasn't finished yet, but the framework was in place—a strong, stable foundation that could hold.

I opened my eyes, the Sydererealium fading as the chamber snapped back into focus. My body felt leaden, my breaths shallow, but the sense I had of the bubble on the other side of the core told me I'd succeeded. The terminal flashed, displaying confirmation: HYPERDIMENSIONAL BUBBLE DETECTED.

I leaned back in the chair, wiping my brow with a trembling hand, and reached for the intercom on the wall. The faint buzz of static greeted me as I keyed it on. "Sofia, the bubble's ready. Tell Captain Lyssara to prepare her counterassault. I'll begin taking captives in a moment."

Her voice crackled through, steady but tense. "Good timing. We've got some activity in the lower corridors. I think the boarders are about to make another push."

I exhaled, letting my head fall back for a moment as I stared at the glowing bubble in the Sydererealium. The easiest part was done. Entrapping the boarders would be the true test, and I couldn't afford to lose focus. The chamber hummed softly, the nexus lights casting long shadows as it waited, patient and ready, for the next step.

The hum of the nexus chamber deepened, resonating in my bones as I pushed my consciousness back into the Sydererealium. My physical body remained slumped in the chair, drenched in sweat, the terminal glowing faintly on the table in front of me. But my flairsparked mind expanded outward, slipping through the veil into that infinite, alien realm.

In the Sydererealium, the world was chaos. The realm stretched endlessly, its geometry folding and shifting like a vast, living labyrinth. Swirling hues of violet, silver, and gold bled into one another, giving the space an unearthly beauty that belied the danger hidden within. Glyphshades flickered like shadows among the folds, faint echoes of living consciousnesses projected into this hyperdimensional plane.

My task was clear, but it wasn't simple. Somewhere among these glyphshades were the Kergan Imperial Marines, their minds extending into the Syderealium as they sought to capture the *Inferis*. I couldn't see their physical forms, but their glyphshades—ghostly, flickering impressions of their consciousness—gave them away, if I could identify them.

I reached out cautiously, my mind brushing against the nearest glyphshade. It flared in response, a faint echo of thought and emotion rippling through me. Too faint. This one wasn't hostile—probably a Dominion sailor or technician engaged in the ship's defense. I moved on, weaving my consciousness through the chaotic flow of the Syderealium.

The first hostile glyphshade struck like a knife. Its presence was sharp and aggressive, a seething bundle of rage and purpose that cut through the fog like a beacon. My heart raced as I latched onto it, focusing my will to isolate it from the rest. The glyphshade resisted, writhing and clawing at my mind with a strength that made my breath hitch.

Through the nexus, I channeled the energy of the sydereal bubble, weaving the strands of its lattice around the hostile shade. The bubble's shimmering walls closed in, drawing the glyphshade into the hyperdimensional prison. As the bubble's light flared, the hostile presence faded, and I felt the Marine's physical body on the ship's lower decks collapse into unconsciousness.

"One down," I muttered to myself, my voice a faint whisper in the emptiness of the chamber.

The next glyphshade came at me harder, its presence crackling with fury and discipline. It was more controlled than the first, its thoughts shielded by a rigid mental discipline that made it harder to isolate. I had to rely on my knowledge of the *Inferis's* layout, focusing on the nexus's sensors to align my efforts with the current front lines of the fight. The Marine was advancing near engineering, a critical zone.

I reached out, hesitated, then adjusted. My first attempt slid off the glyphshade's defenses, the Marine's presence flaring as it sensed my intrusion. I refocused, drawing on the nexus to amplify my will. The lattice of the bubble formed again, shimmering as I wrapped it around the hostile presence. The glyphshade struggled violently, its thoughts battering against my mind like a storm, but I held on, channeling the nexus's energy to stabilize the capture.

The bubble pulsed, the Marine's glyphshade vanishing into its confines. Another body dropped on the physical plane.

The effort was grueling. Sweat poured down my temples, my breaths coming in shallow gasps as I repeated the process again and again. Each hostile glyphshade was a new challenge, their mental defenses growing sharper, more aggressive. My mind burned with the strain of maintaining focus, of weaving the bubble's lattice over and over while navigating the ever-shifting chaos of the Syderealium.

One glyphshade eluded me entirely, slipping away just as I began to isolate it. I cursed under my breath, recalibrating my approach. The next one, near the bridge, took three attempts before I finally ensnared it, its presence bucking wildly as it was dragged into the bubble.

The nexus chamber's hum rose to a fever pitch, growing hotter with each captured presence. The hyperdimensional bubble, now teeming with hostile glyphshades, rippled with an intense, almost blinding light, its surface alive with shifting patterns that hinted at the immense energy contained within.

I reached out for what I hoped was the last one, a glyphshade near the ship's hangar bay. This one was different—colder, more calculating. It didn't fight as violently, but its presence felt heavier, more entrenched. I hesitated, my instincts screaming that this was a trap. But there wasn't time for doubt. If this Marine was coordinating the others, leaving them unchecked could spell disaster.

I lashed out, my will striking like a blade. The glyphshade recoiled, its defenses flaring in a desperate bid to escape. I tightened the bubble's lattice around it, channeling every ounce of energy I could muster from the nexus. The strain was unbearable, my mind teetering on the edge of collapse, but I held on.

The bubble snapped closed, its surface flaring with a final burst of light. The glyphshade vanished, and I felt the Marine's physical body drop in the hangar bay.

The Syderealium wavered around me, its chaotic geometry settling into a dull hum as the immediate threat faded. I opened my eyes, the nexus chamber snapping back into focus. My body ached, every muscle trembling from the effort, but the shimmering heat radiating off the walls told me I'd succeeded.

I reached for the intercom, my hand shaking. "Sofia," I rasped. "The bubble's full. They're contained."

Her voice came through steady but tinged with relief. "Good work. Now hold tight—the captain has ordered a counter-boarding attack on the assault ship."

I slumped back in the chair, staring at the terminal as status messages scrolled by reporting on the nexus's state of health. It was under heavy load from maintaining the captives trapped in the bubble.

I leaned forward and brought up the internal tactical display for the ship. The glowing grid showed the *Inferis* and its immediate surroundings, marked by overlapping arcs of fire and movement. Red icons—representing the Kergan Imperial Marines—were clustered around their breach points, their presence now dimmed to reflect their incapacitation. Blue icons surged toward those positions, representing the kavreni Marines led by Captain Lyssara. Their movements were deliberate and precise, pressing forward to reclaim the ship.

The comms buzzed with chatter, the clipped voices of Marine squads coordinating their efforts.

"Squad Three, advancing on Corridor Delta. Encountered minor resistance—clearing now."

"Squad Two, we've secured the bulkhead near Engineering. Moving to breach breach-point gamma."

"Squad Five, preparing to board the assault ship. Cover our six."

Each transmission sent a pulse of adrenaline through me. I could picture them in the tight, smoke-filled corridors of the *Inferis,* weapons at the ready, eyes scanning for threats. Their boots would echo against the deck as they moved in disciplined formations, covering each other, clearing each corner with practiced precision.

The red icons on the tactical display grew fewer as the Marines swept through, locking down breach points and securing unconscious Kergan Marines. My gaze lingered on the flashing icon marking the Kergan assault ship, still clamped to the *Inferis's* hull like a predator latched onto its prey.

"Squad Five, breaching the Kergan vessel now," a Marine's voice crackled over the comms. "Encountering heavy resistance. Requesting backup."

Captain Lyssara's voice cut through, sharp and commanding. "Squads Four and Seven, shift to support.

Priority is securing that ship."

The display updated, blue icons converging on the assault ship as Lyssara's Marines pushed forward. I could hear the faint echoes of gunfire through the comms, bursts of sharp static punctuating the tactical reports.

"Grenades out! Room cleared—moving forward."

"Contact right! Covering fire!"

"Squad Five, we've secured the forward section. Moving toward Engineering Bay."

My fists clenched involuntarily, a wave of frustration and longing washing over me. I should have been out there with them, fighting to save the *Inferis*. Every instinct I had screamed for action, to take up a weapon and join the charge. But instead, I was here, locked in the nexus chamber, my role reduced to a single, monumental effort that had already passed.

I'd done my part. I knew that. The hyperdimensional bubble holding the Kergan glyphshades had turned the tide of the battle, removing their Marines from the equation. But it didn't stop the gnawing feeling that I wasn't doing enough, that the real heroes were out there in the smoke and chaos, reclaiming the ship deck by deck.

Sofia's voice buzzed through the intercom, breaking into my thoughts. "Kory, you still there?"

"Yeah," I said, my voice hoarse. "What's the situation?"

"The Marines are sweeping the last few corridors," she said. "They've got the breaches locked down. Captain Lyssara's team is pushing into the assault ship as we speak. They're making progress."

I nodded, even though she couldn't see me. "Good. Let me know when it's secure."

I turned my attention back to the display. The red icons marking the Kergan Marines were dwindling, most of them flashing to indicate their incapacitation. Blue icons swarmed the assault ship, pushing deeper with each passing minute.

"Squad Five, Engineering Bay secured. No sign of resistance."

"Squad Seven, we've reached the command deck. Moving to disable their systems."

A surge of pride welled up in me, mingling with the frustration. The kavreni Marines were relentless, their coordination and discipline a testament to their training and Captain Lyssara's leadership. I couldn't help but admire their resolve, even as I wished I could be among them.

The comms crackled again. "Command deck secured. Assault ship neutralized. All systems offline."

"Good work," Lyssara's voice came through, calm but edged with satisfaction. "Sweep the remaining sections for stragglers, then prepare for extraction."

The display updated, the red icon of the assault ship dimming as its systems were disabled. The blue icons inside shifted into defensive positions, holding their ground while the rest of the *Inferis's* Marines locked down the final corridors.

I leaned back in the chair, letting out a long breath. The fight wasn't entirely over, but the ship was safe, the immediate threat contained. I'd done what I could, and now the others had done their part.

Now *Inferis* could return to the raging battle the Home Fleet was fighting for the Zenith Citadel. While the flagship had been distracted with the Kergan boarding action, the vanguard of the Kergan fleet had engaged Alpha task force.

45

The aftermath of the Kergan assault unfolded swiftly. Once the Dominion Marines had secured the captured Kergan Imperial Marines in the hangar, I released the hyperdimensional bubble, returning their consciousnesses to their physical bodies. It was a delicate process, requiring all my focus, but the bubble held firm until the last glyphshade was contained. The Kergans awoke bound and furious, now prisoners of war under heavy guard by Captain Lyssara's Marines.

The assault ship they had used to breach the *Inferis* was disabled and jettisoned into the void. It floated adrift, a grim reminder of the battle we'd narrowly survived.

With the boarders neutralized, the *Inferis* rejoined the fleet engagement. The battle outside was chaos—Dominion and Kergan warships clashing in a brutal melee of light and fire. Captain Lyssara wasted no time bringing the *Inferis* back into action. The ship's weapons rained destruction on Kergan escorts, her movements precise and lethal, seamlessly integrating into the fleet's counteroffensive.

* * *

The FCC of the *Inferis* was a controlled whirlwind of activity. Officers moved with purpose, monitoring tactical displays and relaying orders across the fleet. The air was thick with tension, punctuated by the hum of holo-terminals and the clipped voices of comms officers.

At the center of the chamber, Celestarch Kaelith and Astrarch Zerya stood side by side, commanding the Dominion fleet like a symphony. Kaelith's plasma form pulsed within her capsule, her glow a steady beacon of authority. Zerya, her kavora frame imposing and deliberate, leaned over a tactical display, her ears twitching as she tracked the battle's progression.

I stood near the edge of the room, close enough to observe but out of the way of the bustling activity. Sofia lingered beside me, her sharp gaze darting between the displays and the officers.

On the tactical display, the fleet engagement unfolded in vivid detail. Dominion warships and Kergan vessels clashed, their icons moving like pieces on a chaotic chessboard. The scene was a blur of flashing torpedoes, rippling bolsters, and blazing beams of energy.

"Enemy battlecruiser targeting the *Stellar Vanguard,*" an officer reported. "Bolsters at forty percent and falling fast."

"Order the *Argent Citadel* to intercept," Kaelith commanded, his voice calm but decisive. "Engage at maximum range and provide covering fire."

The *Argent Citadel*, a massive dreadnought, surged forward on the display, its weapons lighting up the void. Railgun slugs and anti-ship missiles lanced across space, slamming into the Kergan battlecruiser's shields. The enemy ship retaliated, firing a devastating volley that rippled through the *Argent Citadel*'s bolsters but failed to penetrate its thick armor.

"This is *Argent Citadel*," a voice crackled over the comms. "We've disabled the enemy's starboard engines. Moving to secure firing position."

"Well done," Zerya said, her tone measured. "Redirect the *Eclipse Radiance* to cover their rear flank. The Kergans are deploying interceptors."

The *Eclipse Radiance*, a nimble destroyer, veered sharply to intercept the incoming swarm of Kergan fighters. Its defensive lasers carved precise paths through the void, shredding the enemy craft before they could reach the dreadnought.

"Confirmed kills on five interceptors," came a report from the *Eclipse Radiance*. "Remaining hostiles are retreating."

The tactical display updated as another Dominion ship, the *Stellar Vanguard*, moved back into formation, its bolsters flickering but holding.

The comms buzzed with more updates, each exchange painting a vivid picture of the chaos outside.

"This is the *Zhyrathis Blade*! Bolsters at twenty percent—requesting reinforcements!"

"The *Celestial Aegis* is moving to support," Kaelith ordered. "Hold your position and focus on evasive maneuvers until reinforcements arrive."

On the display, the *Celestial Aegis*, a sleek battlecruiser, closed the gap with the *Zhyrathis Blade*, intercepting a volley of enemy torpedoes with pinpoint laser fire. The *Zhyrathis Blade* stabilized, its bolsters slowly regenerating as the combined firepower of the two ships turned the tide against their attackers.

The situation grew more desperate as a Kergan dreadnought, the *Mavraxan*, pushed deeper into the

Dominion formation. Its weapons tore through a cluster of Dominion frigates, reducing the frigate *Steel Veil* to debris in a single salvo.

Kaelith's glow flared sharply. "Concentrate fire on the *Mavraxan*. Order the *Inferis* to coordinate with the *Argent Citadel* and lead the assault."

The tactical display showed Dominion warships converging on the dreadnought. The *Inferis* loomed large, its icon a steady anchor amid the chaos. The *Argent Citadel*, already battered but still powerful, unleashed a full broadside of torpedoes, while the *Inferis* poured railgun slugs and laser fire into the *Mavraxan*'s exposed flank.

The Kergan dreadnought shuddered under the combined assault. Its bolsters collapsed in a spectacular flash, leaving its hull vulnerable. Seconds later, a massive explosion consumed the ship, sending debris spiraling into the void.

"Target neutralized," a Dominion officer reported, their voice tinged with relief.

As the *Inferis* moved to regroup, I couldn't tear my eyes away from the tactical display. The scale of the battle was overwhelming, a swirling maelstrom of destruction and strategy. Yet, through the chaos, Kaelith and Zerya maintained their composure, orchestrating the fleet's movements with precision.

"This fight isn't over," Kaelith said, her voice cutting through the controlled din of the FCC. "Signal all ships to hold formation. Prepare for the next wave."

The flickering tactical displays painted a grim picture of the battlefield. The Kergan fleet, outnumbering the Dominion by nearly two to one, pressed relentlessly. Dominion ships struggled to hold their formations, their tactical cohesion stretched thin under the unrelenting assault. The hum of the FCC felt heavier with each passing moment.

Celestarch Kaelith's capsule glowed brighter for a moment as if reflecting his inner turmoil. "Any word from the Astral Expeditionary Fleet?" he asked, his tone even, though the tension was palpable.

"None, Celestarch," replied a tech, not looking up from his console. "No communications, no movement detected on long-range scanners."

Kaelith's glow dimmed slightly, his frustration barely restrained. "Where are they? If Arctis and his fleet don't arrive soon, we won't hold this line."

"Enemy frigates are closing on the *Eclipse Radiance*," an officer reported.

Kaelith's glow flared. "Order them to retreat and regroup behind the *Argent Citadel*. Do not let them engage unsupported."

But it was already too late. The tactical display showed the *Eclipse Radiance* surrounded by three Kergan destroyers. Missiles streaked toward the embattled destroyer, her defensive lasers overwhelmed by the sheer volume of incoming fire.

"This is the *Eclipse Radiance*! Bolsters are down—"

The transmission cut off as the *Eclipse Radiance* erupted into a ball of fire, fragments of her hull scattering across the void. A somber silence filled the FCC as the display updated, the ship's icon winking out.

The *Zhyrathis Blade* fought valiantly, its captain's voice steady over the comms despite the chaos.

"We've got two cruisers on us. Bolsters holding at twenty percent. Requesting support!"

The *Celestial Aegis* turned sharply to assist, but the Kergan fleet anticipated the move. A barrage of torpedoes from the enemy dreadnought targeted the *Aegis*, forcing it to veer off. The *Zhyrathis Blade* stood alone.

"Brace for impact!" the captain shouted, her voice cracking with strain.

The Kergan cruisers opened fire with their railguns, battering the Dominion battlecruiser. The *Blade* retaliated, taking one enemy cruiser with her in a final, defiant salvo. But moments later, her core breached, and the ship disintegrated into a cloud of plasma and debris.

"The *Argent Citadel* is heavily engaged. Bolsters at five percent," another officer called out.

Kaelith's capsule pulsed urgently. "Order the *Inferis* to reposition and provide cover fire. If we lose the *Argent*, we lose our anchor."

On the tactical display, the *Argent Citadel* was surrounded by Kergan capital ships. Her broadside cannons thundered, taking down two enemy destroyers, but the onslaught was relentless. The Kergan dreadnought *Therax* moved in, its weapons targeting the *Argent*'s vulnerable engines.

"This is the *Argent Citadel*! We're losing power—cannot hold!"

The ship's icon flashed red, then disappeared as the *Therax* fired a devastating salvo into its hull, splitting the dreadnought in two.

One by one, Dominion ships fell. The *Stellar Vanguard*, pinned by enemy interceptors, was torn apart by a concentrated torpedo barrage. The *Shadow Spear*, a frigate attempting to flank the Kergan line, was caught in a trap and obliterated by hidden railgun emplacements.

Kaelith's commands grew sharper, his glowing form flickering with intensity as she strove to maintain control. "Order all remaining ships to tighten formation. Prioritize the protection of the *Inferis* and the *Celestial Aegis*. We need those core ships operational!"

The tactical display was a sea of red. Kergan ships pushed deeper into Dominion lines, their superior numbers overwhelming the fleet's defenses.

Kaelith turned to Zerya, his voice steady despite the gravity of the situation. "Send a distress signal to all available Dominion forces. If we don't receive reinforcements soon, there will be no fleet left to save."

As the comms buzzed with fragmented reports and desperate calls for aid, I stood silently, watching the icons on the display vanish one by one. The room felt suffocating, the weight of our losses pressing down on everyone present. I wondered if I would die today.

Kaelith's glow dimmed briefly, then flared brighter than ever. "This fight isn't over yet," he said, his tone defiant. "Not while we still have ships in the fight."

The atmosphere in the FCC was suffocating. The Dominion fleet was stretched to the breaking point, the tactical display a brutal record of ships lost and lives sacrificed. Celestarch Kaelith's plasma pulsed as if reflecting the waning morale of his officers. Astrarch Zerya stood rigid beside him, her ears flicking with suppressed tension as she scrutinized the latest reports.

Then, like a spark in the darkness, the tactical display lit up with new contacts. Blue icons began to populate the edges of the map near the Zenith Citadel, bright and unmistakably Dominion. The room stilled for a fraction of a second before bursting into activity.

"New contacts detected!" called out a comms officer, his voice sharp. "Multiple Dominion signatures—confirming identity as the Astral Expeditionary Fleet!"

The FCC buzzed with a mix of disbelief and cautious

hope. Reinforcements had arrived.

A commanding voice cut through the commotion, resonant and authoritative. "This is Celestarch Ryvos of the Astral Expeditionary Fleet. We have arrived at the Zenith Citadel and are prepared to engage. I am under orders from Glyphspeaker Arctis to coordinate with Celestarch Kaelith and Astrarch Zerya."

Kaelith's plasma pulsed brighter, his tone steady as he replied, "Ryvos, this is Kaelith. Your timing is critical. Our fleet is sustaining heavy losses, and the Kergan forces are pushing hard on our left flank and the citadel perimeter. Immediate support is required."

Ryvos's response came with military precision. "Understood, Kaelith. We'll engage the enemy forces threatening the citadel and reinforce your vulnerable positions. Dispatching units to bolster your left flank now."

On the tactical display, the Astral Expeditionary Fleet moved into formation with flawless coordination. Leading the charge was the massive dreadnought *Ignis Spear,* its presence commanding. Corvettes fanned out around it, swift and purposeful as they flanked the Kergan ships.

"This is the *Ignis Spear,*" a voice announced over the comms. "Engaging Kergan cruisers. Firing main battery."

I watched as the *Ignis Spear* unleashed a devastating salvo. Railgun slugs and torpedoes streaked through the void, striking a Kergan battlecruiser head-on. The enemy ship's bolsters collapsed in a flash, and its hull crumpled under the relentless assault. The surrounding Kergan vessels hesitated, their formation fracturing under the sudden pressure.

Kaelith's voice rang out, crisp and commanding. "Signal all Dominion ships to rally behind the Astral Expeditionary Fleet. Consolidate fire on the Kergan dreadnought *Therossan.*

Zerya, oversee the reorganization of our defensive lines."

"Yes, Celestarch," Zerya replied, her tone sharp as she relayed instructions to the fleet.

The battle was far from over. On the tactical display, Dominion ships rallied behind Kaelith's orders, regrouping into tighter formations to press their counterattack. But the Kergan fleet was relentless.

"This is the *Celestial Barrier*! Bolsters down to ten percent —we're taking heavy fire!"

The *Celestial Barrier*, a stalwart Dominion cruiser, was caught in the crossfire of two Kergan destroyers. Despite its captain's valiant efforts, the ship succumbed to a concentrated barrage of missiles, its icon winking out on the display.

Nearby, the *Stellar Dawn* was locked in a brutal engagement with a Kergan dreadnought. Its captain's voice crackled over the comms. "Main battery targeting their engines!"

The *Dawn* landed a critical hit, crippling the dreadnought's propulsion, but the victory was short-lived. Enemy reinforcements swarmed the ship, overwhelming its defenses and reducing it to debris.

Meanwhile, Ryvos's fleet executed its mission with ruthless efficiency. The *Ignis Spear* and its escorts encircled the Kergan forces near the citadel, systematically dismantling their formation.

"This is the *Spectral Vow*! Engaging enemy destroyers near the citadel perimeter—target neutralized."

Ryvos's calm voice came through the comms again. "Citadel defenses are holding. The Kergan presence near the anchor is collapsing. Kaelith, your forces are clear to press the attack."

Kaelith's plasma pulsed brighter. "Acknowledged,

Ryvos. Zerya, dispatch the *Celestial Aegis* and supporting frigates to flank the enemy's retreat. Ensure no survivors."

The once-overwhelming Kergan fleet began to fracture under the relentless assault. The tactical display, once dominated by red, now showed swathes of blue reclaiming the field. Kaelith's commands came sharper, his presence radiating confidence as he led the Dominion fleet to counterattack.

"This is not just survival," Kaelith said, his voice resolute. "We will drive them back. We will remind the Kergan what it means to challenge the Dominion."

The FCC buzzed with renewed energy as the fleet pressed its advantage, the fight far from over, but hope rekindled. For the first time, it seemed that victory was within reach.

Minutes ticked by, and the FCC fell quiet after the last nearby Kergan ship blinked off the tactical display. I could still hear the faint hum of the systems, the occasional murmur from a tech, but the usual tension of battle had given way to a cautious relief. Celestarch Kaelith's plasma glowed a steadier, more subdued light as he issued orders for the fleet to pursue the retreating Kergan forces.

"Send the fleet forward," Kaelith said, his voice sharp but controlled. "Ensure they don't regroup. Zerya, keep our formation tight; I don't want any overextensions."

Zerya nodded, her sharp ears swiveling as she directed her attention back to her console. "Understood, Celestarch."

I watched as the blue icons representing Dominion ships moved steadily away from Virelia, chasing the scattered remnants of the Kergan fleet. A sense of accomplishment simmered in the FCC, muted by the weight of losses but tangible nonetheless. Yet, unease itched at the back of my mind. Something felt… off. Why would Celestarch Ryvos send our battered fleet after the fleeing Kergans instead of his own, fresher vessels?

Minutes passed. The fleet advanced several light-minutes away from Virelia, and the Zenith Citadel loomed like a sentinel on the display, its presence a reassuring constant in a chaotic galaxy.

Then Zerya spoke, her tone sharp with confusion. "The *Ignis Spear* is repositioning."

My eyes snapped to the display. Sure enough, the massive dreadnaught had broken from its orbit near the Zenith Citadel and was moving closer to Virelia. Its vector took it directly over Astrithon.

"That's strange," Zerya said, frowning. "Why would Ryvos reposition there? What's he doing?"

Kaelith's plasma flared slightly, his light pulsing in jagged bursts. "Send an inquiry. Ask for clarification."

I leaned forward, staring at the display as unease twisted in my gut. My fingers clenched the edge of the console. What could he be doing?

Before anyone could act, the *Ignis Spear* opened fire.

A series of bright flashes rippled across the tactical display as railgun slugs rained down on Astrithon.

46

The Ignarion Palace—the beating heart of Dominion governance—was wiped off the map in seconds. I stared in mute horror as an image of the gleaming golden palace disappeared in a flash of light. The display updated to show a yawning crater where it had stood.

The silence in the FCC was deafening. No one moved, no one spoke. My own thoughts spun in a spiral of disbelief. This wasn't happening. It couldn't be happening.

Then, the comms erupted into chaos.

"What just happened?!"

"Who authorized that strike?!"

"Why is the *Ignis Spear* firing on Astrithon?!"

I barely heard the voices. My mind was fixated on the image of the crater, the realization hitting me like a hammer. The Ignarion Palace wasn't just a building—it was the seat of the queen. The center of the Dominion. Zeta had been in that palace. Had she been there when the attack came? Was she… gone?

Kaelith's voice cut through the noise, snapping me back

to the moment. "Hail Ryvos immediately! I want answers!"

A comms officer scrambled to comply, but after a long pause, he shook his head. "No response, Celestarch."

Kaelith's plasma dimmed ominously. "Try Fleet Command. They must have answers."

Another pause, this one longer, more excruciating. The officer's voice was tight when he finally spoke. "No response from Fleet Command, either."

"What?" Zerya's ears flattened against her head, her eyes narrowing. "How is that possible?"

A tech on sensors spoke up, his voice cracking with urgency. "Celestarch, multiple assault ships are launching from the Astral Fleet. They're attacking the Zenith Citadel. We're detecting boarding operations in progress."

I felt like the floor had dropped out from under me. Assault ships? The Citadel under attack? This had to be some kind of mistake, some kind of horrible misunderstanding. But deep down, I knew better.

Kaelith was silent for a moment, the glow of his plasma barely a flicker now. "This is no accident," he said, his tone cold and clipped. "Ryvos… Arctis. They've turned on us."

The weight of his words settled over the room like a shroud. I struggled to process it, my thoughts racing back to Zeta, to the crater where the palace had stood. I wanted to speak, to demand answers, but my voice wouldn't come. My mind was filled with one burning fear: Zeta was gone. Killed in the bombardment. And now the Dominion itself was unraveling before my eyes.

The FCC felt like it was teetering on the edge of chaos, the air thick with unspoken fear and desperation. The tactical display showed the *Ignis Spear* looming over Astrithon and more ships from the Astral Fleet maneuvering ominously near the Zenith Citadel. The comms officers were flooded with calls from every corner of the fleet—questions, demands, and frantic cries for clarification.

Then, the comms went silent.

Every console in the FCC flickered, and an ominous voice filled the space, rich with arrogance and self-importance.

"People of the Collective Dominion," the voice began. "This is Glyphspeaker Arctis."

The entire FCC froze as the display shifted to a projection of Arctis. His glowing form seemed larger than life, his tone dripping with condescension and smug satisfaction.

"For too long, we have endured the tyranny of the queen and the stagnation of the Dominion monarchy," he said, his words echoing with a self-righteous fervor. "The monarchy has failed you. It has failed all of us, clinging to outdated traditions while the galaxy crumbles around us. No more."

Arctis's light intensified, his form shifting and expanding as though feeding on his own self-aggrandizing rhetoric. "I, along with other willing Glyphspeakers, have chosen to seize control of the Dominion government to correct these wrongs. Effective immediately, the monarchy is dissolved. The era of blind loyalty and reckless governance has come to an end."

Kaelith's plasma pulsed violently, his glow darkening as he absorbed the betrayal playing out before us. My stomach churned. The arrogance in Arctis's voice was sickening, but what unsettled me most was the way he spoke, as though he had already crowned himself a god.

"I do not act for personal gain," Arctis continued, though his tone betrayed his lie. "I act for the good of the Dominion, for the good of all sentient beings who deserve a future untainted by the failings of the past."

He paused, as if letting the weight of his words settle over us like a shroud, before delivering the final blow. "All Dominion fleets are hereby ordered to stand down and cease hostilities. Let the Kergan fleet withdraw unmolested. This is a time for rebuilding, not for futile resistance."

The projection ended abruptly, and the FCC erupted into chaos.

Kaelith's plasma burned brighter than I'd ever seen it. "That treasonous filth," he spat, his voice a low growl. "He speaks of rebuilding while tearing apart the very foundations of the Dominion."

He turned sharply to Zerya. "Order the fleet to return to Virelia. Prepare to engage the Astral Fleet."

Zerya hesitated, her ears flicking nervously. "Celestarch, many of our ships are critically damaged. They won't survive another engagement."

Kaelith's glow didn't falter. "It is not a matter of survival. It is a matter of duty. We fight for the queen—or we die trying."

The weight of his words pressed down on me like a vice. I stared at the tactical display, knowing full well what the Celestarch's orders meant. This wasn't a fight we could win. The Astral Fleet was fresh, unscathed, while our ships limped back to the fight like wounded animals. My mouth felt dry, my thoughts racing with the certainty of death.

I was going to die here. We all were.

The fleet turned, engines burning as the battered Dominion ships rallied toward Virelia. As we approached the citadel, new red icons lit up the tactical display.

"Hostile contacts!" a tech called out. "Two Dominion spectrals, designation *Voidclaw* and *Nightspire*, engaging *Inferis*!"

The ship shook violently as the first torpedo strike landed. Alarms blared, the deck beneath my feet trembling with the impact. I grabbed the edge of a console to steady myself, my heart hammering in my chest.

"*Inferis* reporting critical damage to aft bolsters," another tech yelled. "Hull breach on Deck 7—emergency bulkheads deploying."

Kaelith's voice cut through the chaos, sharp and commanding. "Focus fire on the *Voidclaw*. Divert power to bolsters. Keep us in the fight."

The tactical display showed the two spectrals circling us like wolves, their sleek profiles bristling with weaponry. More torpedoes streaked toward us, bright trails of death carving through the void.

The ship rocked again, throwing me against the console. My head spun, and for a moment, all I could hear was the high-pitched whine of overloaded systems. Then the alarms returned, and with them, the grim reality of our situation.

"We can't take much more of this," Zerya muttered, her ears pinned back.

I clutched the console, my knuckles white. My mind raced, searching for something—anything—that could tip the scales. But deep down, I knew the truth.

This wasn't just a battle. It was a reckoning. And we were on the losing side.

The explosion hit like a thunderclap, throwing me off my feet and slamming me hard against the deck. The lights in the FCC cut out instantly, plunging the room into pitch darkness. I heard the sharp hiss of a venting atmosphere, a sickening sound that sent panic jolting through me.

Instinct kicked in. I fumbled for my helmet, snapping it into place and sealing my suit. The HUD blinked on, casting a faint glow inside my visor as environmental warnings flooded the display.

WARNING: ATMOSPHERE VENTING. PRESSURE LEVELS CRITICAL.

Alarms blared, shrill and relentless. I struggled to my knees, the deck beneath me shuddering from another distant impact. My breathing came fast, my heart pounding in my ears as I tried to orient myself.

"Sofia!" I shouted, my voice muffled by the helmet. No response.

The room was a chaos of wreckage, consoles torn from their mounts, shards of bulkheads scattered like jagged teeth. The only illumination came from the dim emergency strobes blinking weakly in the swirling mist of depressurizing air.

An announcement crackled through the PA, garbled but unmistakable: "All hands, abandon ship. Repeat, abandon ship."

I clenched my fists, gritting my teeth. "No," I muttered. "Not without her."

I forced myself to my feet, scanning the debris-strewn room. My HUD highlighted fragments of wreckage but no sign of Sofia. Fear clawed at my chest, threatening to overwhelm me, but I pushed it aside and focused.

I started digging, pushing aside shattered panels and twisted metal. My protomatter suit lent me strength, letting me haul pieces of debris that would've been impossible otherwise. Each movement sent jolts of pain through my body, but I ignored it. Sofia was here somewhere, and I wasn't leaving without her.

"Sofia!" I called again, desperation creeping into my voice—still nothing.

The alarms continued to blare, each second stretching into an eternity. My suit's oxygen levels ticked down in the corner of my HUD, a grim reminder of how little time I had.

Then I saw it—a faint glimmer of her suit's reflective surface under a fallen bulkhead. Relief surged through me, quickly replaced by dread as I realized the weight pinning her down.

I dropped to my knees beside her, the bulkhead cutting harshly across her body. Her helmeted head was tilted to the side, motionless. I placed a hand on her visor, trying to see if she was breathing. Her suit's status indicator blinked weakly—still active, but not for long.

"Hang on, Sofia," I said, my voice trembling. "I'm getting you out of here."

I planted my hands under the edge of the bulkhead, every muscle in my body straining as I tried to lift it. The protomatter suit hummed with effort, the ropes of protomatter vibrating in protest. It felt like trying to move a mountain.

"Come on," I growled through gritted teeth. My arms burned, my lungs heaved, but I didn't stop. Slowly, the bulkhead began to shift, just enough to give me leverage.

With a final, desperate push, I heaved it off her, tossing it aside with a metallic crash. I dropped to the deck beside her, my chest heaving as I pulled her free. Her suit was intact, but her body was limp, one leg hanging at an unnatural angle, her helmet's display flickering faintly. She was alive but unable to move.

"I've got you," I whispered, cradling her against me. I looked around the ruined FCC, the blaring alarms driving home the urgency of our situation.

The PA crackled again, repeating the chilling command: "Abandon ship. All hands, abandon ship."

I held Sofia close, my mind racing. There was no time to think, no time to question. I had to get us out of here.

The corridor outside the FCC was a hellscape of smoke and chaos. The bulkheads were scorched black, the air thick with acrid fumes. My thermal imaging flared to life, painting the scene in ghostly shades of red and orange. Carrying Sofia in my arms, I struggled to keep moving, each step a battle against exhaustion and the weight of fear pressing down on me.

"Hang in there, Sofia," I muttered, glancing at her flickering helmet display. The suit systems were barely keeping her alive, and I could see the warnings stacking up on her vitals. Severe concussion. Broken leg with a compound fracture. Blood pressure low. Each alert was another stab of panic.

I stumbled down the passageway, my boots echoing dully against the deck. Escape pods lined the walls, each one a chance at survival. But every time I reached for a hatch, the indicator above it flashed red: EJECTED. Pod after pod, deck after deck—it was the same story. Empty berths, the faint smell of burnt coolant, and silence except for the groaning ship.

The hull shook violently as another impact rocked the *Inferis*. I braced myself against the wall, my breath coming in ragged gasps. Alarms blared, distant but relentless, as though mocking my desperation.

"Come on," I hissed through gritted teeth, my heart hammering. I adjusted Sofia in my arms, her limp form a constant reminder that failure wasn't an option.

I pressed on, descending another set of stairs into the lower decks. The air here was colder, the smoke thinner but tinged with an odd, metallic tang. I passed the bodies of dead kavrenis, their tails curled around them like they were trying to shield themselves from the inevitable. My stomach churned, but I forced myself to keep going. Everyone else alive had already evacuated. It was just me and Sofia now.

Finally, in the bowels of the ship, I found it: a strange, rounded chamber with dim emergency lighting. In the center was a squat, hexagonal escape pod built for six, its design starkly different from the sleek pods I'd seen earlier. It looked old, like something from a previous era of the Dominion, but the hatch indicator glowed green. AVAILABLE.

Relief flooded me as I pulled open the hatch, the manual release sticking for a moment before giving way with a groan. The interior was cramped, the seats arranged in a tight circle around a central console. Straps dangled from the walls like limp snakes. I climbed inside, careful not to jostle Sofia more than necessary, and secured her into one of the seats. Her helmet lolled slightly, her vitals still flashing warnings on my HUD.

"Just a little longer," I said, my voice trembling with exhaustion.

I strapped myself in next to her and reached for the console. The interface was simple, the commands in Dominion Standard. I punched the eject button, bracing for the jolt.

The pod shuddered, then lurched violently as explosive bolts fired, propelling us into the void. The stars spun in dizzying arcs outside the viewport before the stabilizers kicked in, bringing us into a slow, steady drift.

Hours passed. The silence of space was suffocating, broken only by the soft hum of the pod's systems and the faint rasp of my own breathing. I checked Sofia's vitals repeatedly, each glance at her flickering status display a fresh wave of worry. The concussion and broken leg were bad, but the oxygen levels in the pod were worse. If no one found us soon…

I shook the thought from my head, gripping the armrests tightly. "Someone will come," I said, more to myself than her. "They have to."

The pod drifted aimlessly, the navigation system unresponsive. I had no idea where we were going, or even if we were going anywhere. The view outside was a bleak expanse of stars, the occasional flash of distant explosions reminding me of the battle we'd left behind.

And then it happened. A loud bang reverberated through the pod, followed by a violent jolt that nearly tore me from my seat. I grabbed for my sidearm, adrenaline surging through me. Something had latched onto the exterior.

Another bang echoed, closer this time, and I braced myself. Whoever—or whatever—was out there wasn't here to help.

The hatch hissed, then burst open with a deafening clang. Blinding light flooded the interior, silhouetting a massive, mechanical shape. My heart pounded as I raised the pistol, aiming at the intruder.

"Kory Drake," a familiar voice called, modulated and crisp. "You may lower your weapon."

The light dimmed slightly, revealing the unmistakable form of an igna walker. Its armored frame gleamed, its movements precise and deliberate as it stepped inside. Mounted at the top, encased in a shimmering translucent capsule, was Zeta.

"Zeta?" I breathed, my voice barely audible over the thundering of my pulse. Relief crashed over me, leaving me momentarily speechless. I lowered the pistol, my hand shaking. "You couldn't have come a little sooner?"

Her capsule flickered with amusement. "Zeta did not wish to disturb your heroics. Now, let us escape before you tempt fate further."

I let out a shaky laugh, the tension draining from my body as Zeta's walker reached for Sofia. For the first time in hours, I allowed myself to hope.

47

The medbay was eerily quiet, broken only by the soft beeping of monitors and the faint hum of the ship's systems. I sat in a chair beside Sofia's bed, staring at her pale, still face. Her leg was in a cast, elevated slightly, and her head was wrapped in clean, white bandages. An IV snaked down from a bag overhead, feeding fluids and nutrients into her arm.

She looked fragile, so unlike the Sofia I'd come to rely on—the determined, sharp-eyed protector who had been by my side through every crisis. She'd been my constant companion for nearly nine months, a steady presence in a whirlwind of uncertainty. And I'd almost lost her.

The thought made my chest tighten. I hadn't realized until those desperate moments in the FCC just how deep my feelings for her ran. She was more than my protector, more than my friend. The idea of a future without Sofia felt... wrong. Unbearable. I wasn't ready to lose her—not now, not ever.

Her eyelids fluttered. My heart leaped. She stirred

slightly, her face twitching as if she were trying to wake from a heavy dream. Finally, her eyes opened halfway, glassy and unfocused. She looked around the room with a dazed, confused expression.

"Sofia," I said softly, leaning forward. "Hey, you're awake."

Her lips moved, but the sound that came out was a faint, unintelligible mumble. She tried again, but her voice was so weak it barely registered.

I grabbed her hand, holding it gently but firmly. "It's okay," I said, my voice cracking with emotion. "You're okay. I'm here." I leaned down and pressed a kiss to her forehead, my lips lingering just long enough for her to feel it. "I'm so glad you're okay."

Her eyes shifted toward me, and she tried to speak again. This time, I caught the faint, hoarse whisper of a word. "Water."

"Of course," I said, springing up from the chair. I grabbed a cup of water from the bedside table, holding it carefully to her lips. She sipped greedily, the color returning to her cheeks as she drained the cup.

She let out a shaky breath and slumped back against the pillow. Her voice was still hoarse but stronger now. "Where... where am I? What happened?"

"We're on the royal yacht *Luminara*." I tried to keep my tone light, even if the truth was anything but. "Zeta rescued us."

Her brows knitted together, and then, to my surprise, a small laugh escaped her lips. "Zeta? Rescued us? You mean the same Zeta who turned you over to the authorities not too long ago? That Zeta?"

I couldn't help but chuckle. "Yeah, that one. Funny how things turn around, isn't it?"

Sofia shook her head slightly, wincing at the movement. "Never thought I'd owe her one. She's got some nerve, though, swooping in like a hero."

"Everything's changed, Sofia," I said, my voice softening. "This isn't the same Zeta you knew."

Her expression sobered as she studied me. "What's the last thing you remember?" I asked gently.

She frowned, her eyes narrowing in thought. "We were on *Inferis*. The spectrals were hammering us with torpedoes. I remember the FCC shaking apart and… everything going dark after that."

I nodded. "You were unconscious when it happened, but… do you remember Arctis's little speech? The bombardment of Astrithon?"

Her face hardened. "I do. I didn't think it could get worse after that."

"Well," I said, leaning back in the chair and running a hand through my hair, "brace yourself. It did. Arctis bombarded Astrithon. The Ignarion Palace is gone—completely destroyed. Zeta's mother, the queen, is dead."

Sofia's lips parted in shock, but she said nothing, waiting for me to continue.

"The monarchy collapsed. The Dominion's split right down the middle. Half the fleets and systems have sworn allegiance to Arctis, who's declared himself the new ruler, and the other half refuse to acknowledge him. They're looking for Zeta now."

Sofia blinked, processing this, then whispered, "She's the queen."

"Not officially," I corrected. "She hasn't been crowned, and she can't be. Not yet. It's too dangerous. Arctis has the upper hand. She can't return to Astrithon without putting herself in the crosshairs."

"And she's okay with that?" Sofia asked, skepticism edging into her tone.

I shrugged. "She doesn't have a choice. Zeta's decided to flee to Earth. That's where we're headed now—Wolf Jaw base. She's trying to regroup and find allies. She wants to fight back."

Sofia exhaled slowly, her gaze fixed on the ceiling. "The Collective Dominion's in shambles, isn't it?"

I nodded grimly. "The fleets are scattered, systems are on edge, and everyone's trying to figure out where they stand. Zeta's people see her as their last hope, but Arctis has already consolidated so much power. The guy's practically untouchable."

Sofia turned her head toward me, her blue eyes piercing. "And you? Where do you fit into all this now?"

I hesitated, my thoughts tangling. "I don't know yet," I admitted. "Zeta's got her own plans, but I can't ignore what's happening. The Dominion's in chaos, and Earth's still in danger. Maybe there's a way to help both."

"Ever the optimist," Sofia said with a faint smile. "Just... don't get yourself killed trying to save everyone."

I reached out and took her hand gently. "Not without you to keep me out of trouble."

Her lips quirked, and for a brief moment, the weight of everything seemed to lift. But the reality of what lay ahead settled back in quickly.

"Get some more sleep," I said. "You need it."

48

The *Luminara*'s flight deck was unlike anything I'd ever seen on a starship. It was smaller than the cavernous hangars I was used to, but its design was exquisite. Polished floors gleamed with a metallic sheen that reflected the soft ambient lighting. The walls were lined with intricate carvings of Dominion glyphs, subtly glowing with the same warm luminescence that gave the entire ship its ethereal feel. Even the docking arms seemed to float with a grace that defied the usual industrial clunkiness of military vessels.

It was a place designed not for utility but for elegance—a far cry from the gritty, battle-scarred ships I was used to.

Zeta hovered beside me in her capsule, her translucent shell shimmering faintly in the ambient light. For a moment, the two of us stood in silence, looking out through the transparent viewport at the stars beyond.

"I'm sorry about your mother," I said, my words feeling woefully inadequate for the magnitude of Zeta's loss. What could I possibly say to comfort someone who had lost both a parent and a monarch in one devastating moment?

Zeta's capsule emitted a faint hum, her voice measured but tinged with grief. "Thank you. Zeta has already spoken with her in the Syderealium. Zeta believes she will be fine. But the loss of her as Queen of the Collective Dominion is… difficult to comprehend."

I nodded, searching for something more to say, but everything felt shallow in the face of her grief. "I can't imagine what you're going through. All that responsibility, all of it falling on you now."

She was silent for a long moment, her capsule's soft light dimmed slightly. Then, with a faint vibration, she spoke again. "There is one small solace in all of this."

I furrowed my brow. "Solace? I can't imagine what that could be."

Her capsule shifted, a hint of warmth returning to her voice. "Your criminal charges have been dismissed. Consider yourself pardoned—by royal decree. It's the least Zeta can do."

For a second, her words didn't register. Then, a grin broke across my face. "Thanks, Zeta."

The weight I had carried for months, the constant shadow of the trial looming over me, lifted in an instant. It felt surreal. My relief was almost overwhelming, though it was tempered by the enormity of what Zeta was facing. My legal troubles were trivial compared to the Dominion's crisis, but her gesture still meant everything.

"This was his plan all along," I said, changing the topic. My voice was low, but the weight of my words hung heavily between us. "Arctis. He orchestrated everything. I was just a pawn in all of this."

Zeta turned slightly toward me, her capsule tilting in a way that suggested agreement. "Zeta has come to the same conclusion," she said, her voice quiet but firm. "He was the

Architect we have been searching for. It was never Ban'ach."

I ran a hand through my hair, my mind spinning with the pieces finally falling into place. "He used the Kergan fleet as a tool. The whole attack—it wasn't just about damaging the Home Fleet. It was a pretext."

"Indeed," Zeta replied. "A calculated move to justify the deployment of the Astral Fleet near the Zenith Citadel. A fleet loyal to him."

"And the bombardment of Astrithon," I added, my voice sharpening. "That was the endgame. The palace... your mother... He needed her gone to take control. Arctis didn't just want power—he wanted it handed to him on a silver platter."

Zeta's light dimmed briefly, a sign of her sorrow. "Zeta failed to anticipate his cunning. She knew he was ambitious, but she did not see the depths of his treachery."

I glanced at her, her usually radiant form subdued. "None of us saw it. He played everyone. The Kergans, the judiciary, even the fleets."

Zeta's tone hardened. "The attack weakened the Home Fleet, ensuring they could not respond effectively when the Astral Fleet turned against us. The distraction of the Kergan incursion gave him the cover he needed to position his forces."

"And the judiciary?" I asked. "You think that was him too?"

She tilted her capsule slightly in a nod. "Likely. Arctis manipulated the judiciary to cast doubt on the monarchy's stability, sowing dissent among Dominion citizens. Your trial, Kory, was part of his plan. A spectacle to erode trust in the queen's rule. To bring him allies."

I clenched my fists, the anger bubbling to the surface. "So everything—everything I've been through—was just another one of his moves on the chessboard."

Zeta's voice softened. "Yes. And yet, your actions have not been in vain. They have exposed his machinations, even if the cost was high."

I let out a bitter laugh, shaking my head. "High is an understatement. He's torn the Dominion in half, Zeta. You're the queen now, and you can't even set foot on Astrithon."

Zeta's light brightened, a flicker of defiance. "Zeta may not wear the crown, but she will not abandon her people. Arctis underestimates the resolve of those who oppose him."

I crossed my arms, staring out at the stars. "He's got the fleets. The resources. The government. My people who are refugees on Astrithon, now little better than hostages. What do we have?"

Zeta floated closer, her presence commanding despite her gentle tone. "We have hope. And allies, Kory. Arctis may be powerful, but his reach is not absolute. The Dominion is vast, and loyalty cannot be commanded—it must be earned."

I sighed, my shoulders sagging. "Hope and allies. Against someone who's planned this for who knows how long."

"Do not underestimate yourself," Zeta said, her voice steady. "You have survived his schemes so far. You will again."

I didn't reply, my thoughts too tangled to form words. The flight deck's pristine elegance felt like a cruel contrast to the chaos Arctis had unleashed. But Zeta was right about one thing: we weren't beaten yet. Not entirely.

And if Arctis thought he could use treachery to gain power, he would learn just how wrong he was.

THE END

Please rate or review my book online! As an indie author, I *depend* on your reviews to legitimize my books in the eyes of those who have not read them.

* * *

About Joseph McRae Palmer

Joseph McRae Palmer writes speculative fiction. He is also an engineer in the telecommunications industry and holds a Ph.D. in Electrical Engineering from Brigham Young University. Joseph was born in Provo, Utah, but raised in Sitka, Alaska, and graduated from high school in 1993. Later, he served as a missionary for two years in central Mexico. He and his wife of more than two decades, Beatriz Palmer, are parents of one son and three daughters, and as of 2023 they reside in northern Utah, USA.

Joseph's fiction site: www.josephmcraepalmer.com

Printed in Dunstable, United Kingdom

66777819R00238